ANDROMEDA ⚡ KLEIN

ALSO BY FRANK PORTMAN

King Dork

Andromeda  Klein

Frank Portman

DELACORTE PRESS

Copyright © 2009 by Frank Portman

All rights reserved. Published in the United States by Delacorte Press, an imprint of Random House Children's Books, a division of Random House, Inc., New York.

Delacorte Press is a registered trademark and the colophon is a trademark of Random House, Inc.

Visit us on the Web! or www.randomhouse.com/teens

Educators and librarians, for a variety of teaching tools, visit us at www.randomhouse.com/teachers

Library of Congress Cataloging-in-Publication Data
Portman, Frank.
Andromeda Klein / Frank Portman. – 1st ed.
p. cm.
Summary: High school sophomore Andromeda, an outcast because she studies the occult and has a hearing impairment and other disabilities, overcomes grief over terrible losses by enlisting others' help in her plan to save library books–and finds a kindred spirit along the way.
ISBN 978-0-385-73525-4 (hc)–ISBN 978-0-385-90512-1 (glb)
ISBN 978-0-375-89095-6 (e-book) [1. Occultism–Fiction. 2. Tarot–Fiction.
3. Hearing impaired–Fiction. 4. People with disabilities–Fiction. 5. Books and reading–Fiction. 6. Libraries–Fiction. 7. Family life–California–Fiction.
8. California–Fiction.] I. Title.
PZ7.P8373And 2009
[Fic]–dc22
2009015879

The text of this book is set in 11.5-point Caslon Book BE Regular.

Book design by Angela Carlino

Printed in the United States of America

10 9 8 7 6 5 4 3 2 1

First Edition

To the memory of Erika Hynes

0.

The Universe is huge. The Universe is complex. Everything in it is connected to everything else. And it knows who you are and sometimes wants to show you things.

Andromeda Klein's front wheel sliced through a shallow puddle, spattering yet more mud on her boot ankle, glazing the grassy embankment on the left side of the bike path.

"Trismegistus," she said under her breath, invoking the Egyptian god Thoth, lord of language and magic, and, if the theories of Mrs. John King van Rensselaer were to be believed, the god upon whose ancient temple at Hermopolis the book now known as the tarot was based. This oath, an expression of frustration, had nothing to do with the puddle or the boots: muddy boots are nothing but bad-ass. It was rather an offhand, grumpy plea for insight, for clarity. And the answer came almost immediately into view: a discarded half-crushed Styrofoam take-out box floating in a flooded storm drain had two plastic knives lying crossed on top of it.

"Okay, I get it," she muttered. The Two of Swords. She had drawn it from her tarot deck in the girls' bathroom before leaving school that day, and here it was again floating in the gutter. And with a box, to boot. Sometimes the Universe was subtle; other times it hit you over the head like it thought you were stupid.

One dream, one card, an otherworldly instant message, and dozens of synchs involving swords, boxes, and the vexing case of Twice Holy Soror Daisy Wasserstrom: it had been an unusually weedgie week. She rose from the seat to pedal up the hill.

The Universe, continued the silent lecture in her head, chooses to show itself in tiny flashes, revealing connections amongst its diverse elements at odd moments. *Coincidence!* say the unobservant or the spiritually obtuse, when they notice them at all. And such they are: points where aspects of reality coincide, or overlap, from this or that perspective. But educated people, adepts and scholars, seers and magicians— the weedgie people—know them as synchs, since the common understanding of *coincidence* implies something accidental, and there are no accidents.

"So what do you think would happen, Dave," Andromeda continued, out loud now, practicing a well-rehearsed portion of her tarot lecture, "to an adept armed with a perfect model of the Universe?" Dave Klein was Andromeda's cat, upon whom she often practiced her orations, and to whom she tended to address them without regard to his physical presence. He was a tough audience, either way. And his steely stare would, she imagined, prepare her for the hostile response of many of her students, when, far in the future, she would deliver her notorious series of lectures on magic theory and practice in a hidden underground hall in the secret labyrinth beneath the Warburg Institute in London.

The answer, was, of course, that such a model of the Universe in the hands of the skilled adept became a laboratory for generating and observing synchs at several times their naturally occurring rate. In the ancient Temple of Thoth Hermes Trismegistus–itself a compact model of the Universe–magicians cast rods or arrows on the central altar and noted the results, which temple symbols they pointed to and in what number, teasing out the significant synchs and interpreting them. The modern tarot pack was in a sense a portable temple. Shuffling and laying out the cards invited such synchs, grand and trivial, though interpreting them was never a straightforward matter.

That was Andromeda Klein's best, simplest answer for why and how the tarot "worked," aware though she was that her views on the matter were controversial. The tarot was a collapsible temple, a laboratory, a synch factory. If anyone ever bothered to ask, she would be ready. And this answer would figure prominently in her Warburg lectures, to be published in volumes III through IV of her soon-to-be-celebrated, as-yet-unwritten work of magical history, theory, and practice, *Liber K.*

The main road in front of the school parking lot had no bike lane. This period immediately after school let out was perilous. It was impossible to know for certain which after-school clusters of students would be overtly hostile, but it was wise to avoid them all, just in case. This required a zigzag pattern, crossing from one side of the street to the other as necessary. They could throw rocks at you or even thrust a stick through your spokes to knock you off your bike, and then ... well, it had never happened to her, but she'd seen it happen to others, and she didn't want to find out what they would do next. A few kids yelled at her un-intelligibly at she zipped past, or at least, she was pretty sure she was the one they were yelling at. Some unpleasant varia-tion on her name, perhaps, or the perennial favorite "No-Ass." It was nice of them to take the time to bring it to her attention, but Andromeda Klein, as it happened, needed no reminder of that particular deficiency. She was well aware.

Andromeda Klein sliced through yet another shallow puddle and whisper-shouted "A.E.!" It is probable that she was the only student at Clearview High School, and perhaps the only person in Clearview itself, who had a favorite nineteenth-century occultist; and of those anywhere in the world to whom it might have occurred to make such a list, it is doubtful that many would have put A.E. first. But A. E. Waite, the gentle, sad-eyed, reluctant magician, was one of Andromeda Klein's heroes. In his own way, he was as mis-understood as the very misunderstood Mr. Crowley, who owed quite a lot to A.E.'s direction and influence, yet who had, as a theorist, magician, and writer, overshadowed and outpaced him in every way. And who had, incidentally, despised and ridiculed him. Andromeda's heart went out to people who were overshadowed and outpaced and ridiculed and despised. She even fake-believed the dubious notion that such people might be destined to have the last laugh in the end. So she said "A.E." on occasion, as a kind of casual invocation. In high-spirited moments, she and Twice Holy Daisy Wasserstrom used to giggle-shriek it, confusing the masses and emphasizing the exclusivity of their Society of Two.

Andromeda could imagine other magicians of note, long since dead, looking down from their star thrones and snorting derisively at A.E.'s finicky writing and innovations on the customary design of the "small cards," the minor arcana. (An exception was Dame Frances Yates, who appeared, like Andromeda, to have a bit of a crush on him.) Mr. Crowley's deck might have been more theoretically sound, but A.E.'s was the deck Andromeda had learned on and still used, so the image on the card of the day was his design, painted per his instructions by Pamela "Pixie" Colman Smith in 1909 e.v.

The Two of Swords, reversed, in the tenth position, which in the Celtic Cross layout described in Waite's *Pictorial Key to the Tarot* was meant to depict "the outcome." There hadn't been time to do a full spread, so she had quickly counted off cards in the girls' bathroom just before leaving school, saving the first nine for later and noting the tenth: the Two of Swords, reversed. A blindfolded girl kneels, arms crossed, with a sword in each hand, on guard, perhaps, against unseen foes. Andromeda closed her eyes, trying to visualize the card's image and its Qabalistic correspondences, but she had to open them again because blind bike-riding is no more practical than blind swordplay and she nearly ran her bike into a hedge.

The Dominion of Air, the Hebrew letter *vau*, Yetzirah, the world of Formation, Chokmah, Wisdom . . . No matter how hard she studied she could never hold the attributions in her head. She wasn't sensitive or intuitive as Daisy had been. She needed the books, with their charts and diagrams, spread out. The feeling evoked by the image of the kneeling girl strobed in her imagination between dread and peace, but that was an emotional rather than an informed response.

Several of the figures depicted on Pixie's cards, some of them in pretty bad shape, had appeared in her dream the previous night, though the Two of Swords girl had not been among them. Now she appeared as "the outcome," yet, somehow, much obscurity remained.

Anyone observing Andromeda Klein from a distance at that moment would simply have seen a slender teenaged girl on a bicycle splashing through puddles; any who happened to glimpse the face looking out of the black zip sweatshirt's hood might have noted a tense, rather worried expression. But anyone reading her mind would no doubt have been taken aback by the confused riot of arcane images to be found within. A limitless host of glyphs, sigils, images, and mathematical processes unfolded from the Two of Swords and flashed around the edges of her awareness; yet each receded and faded when she tried to examine it directly. With enough time and study, and enough discipline, these connections could be specified and mapped; then would come a stage of knowledge when the model of reality inside her head would correspond to that upon which it was modeled so closely as to be indistinguishable from it. At that point the world could be shaped and changed as easily as one might move a token on a game board.

Andromeda Klein had a long way to go in that regard. So instead, she set the elusive symbols aside, looking ahead to a stage yet further beyond, to the book she would write one day, the comprehensive, multivolume treatment of the history and theory of magic that would supersede all others: the subscription edition limited to eleven numbered, signed copies would be bound in full goatskin with gilt-edged pages, false raised cords, and marbled endpapers, and embossed in silver with her personal sigil beneath the backward, mirror-image title, *Liber K.* (This title, an abbreviation of *Liber Klein,* was the sort of sly joke for which she intended to become known, since the literal meaning "little book" would be belied by its massive content: twenty-two volumes of exactly thirty-two chapters each, not including the two-volume index.) A satisfying achievement indeed for her future self.

By the time Andromeda Klein emerged from the eucalyptus grove that bordered the school's southern edge, her thoughts had turned from the Two of Swords and *Liber Klein* to the Golden Dawn, Pixie Colman Smith, and A. E. Waite's enormous mustache.

The Hermetic Order of the Golden Dawn was the most influential magical society to have emerged in the last several hundred years, its comprehensive magical system charting the course of Western occultism to the present day. A.E. had been a member, and Pixie had joined one of the splinter groups led by him after the order's demise. Among the male adepts of the order, there had been no shortage of elaborate and often quite crazy-looking facial hair, and A.E. was no exception. Andromeda pictured Pixie Colman Smith: small, round, smiling like a cherub, and draped in brightly colored silks, strings of beads around her neck, her head wrapped in a bandana or turban, circumambulating the altar with an enormous sword held aloft under the eyes of a circle of somber, heavily mustachioed men in hoods. Had Pixie found these human whiskers "dashing" or "distinguished," as women were supposed to consider such mustaches in those days? The young A.E., in Andromeda's favorite picture of him, dating from c. 1880 e.v., had looked rather nice, though by the time he met Pixie he was, by Andromeda's calculations, already beginning to resemble another A.E., the elderly Albert Einstein, who was not nearly as appealing. A.E. (Waite, not Einstein) always had the same melancholy eyes, however, in every picture. Had Pixie been thinking of those sad eyes while painting her tarot images? The King of Pentacles, though clean-shaven, had A.E.'s eyes. Had A.E. noted or appreciated her respect and devotion? Even if so, he had mispelled her name in his autobiography. . . .

Thoughts of A.E. and the King of Pentacles and indifference in the face of devotion inevitably led to thoughts of St. Steve. While the mustaches of yesteryear were allegedly dashing, most contemporary ones just looked sleazy. St. Steve's was somewhere in between. Andromeda had recoiled at first, but her feelings on the matter had evolved; St. Steve and A. E. Waite were linked by a mustache.

Andromeda Klein glided through Clearview Park via the recently paved bike path. It had been raining off and on all day. Pools and puddles were everywhere, just like in Pixie's drawings of Swords cards, displaying muddy reflections of the sky.

Andromeda preferred rain to sun, even though most of her intellectual heroes, from Giordano Bruno straight through to Mr. Crowley, were Sun Worship revivalists. All people– including magicians–were supposed to love being in the sun. Andromeda did not. It was yet another way she was "wired up wrong," as the mom, in her characteristically off-kilter "Australian" phrasing, had put it so many times.

So Andromeda had felt fine, almost glad to be alive, this morning when she woke up to drizzle and muted light and to the smell of ozone and damp eucalyptus. Nevertheless, the previous night's dream, with its instant message from be-yond and its astral journey through a deformed Pixiescape, was weighing on her mind.

The hood of her zip sweatshirt–she refused to call it a hoodie–was blown half on, half off, then all the way off. The wind was certainly a relief after the oppressive Clearview High School heat. Those in charge at the school always cranked the heat as high as it would go at the first hint of cloud cover. But the wind made it hard to keep the hood in place while riding. Andromeda Krystal Klein was not a fan of her own hair, which she felt tended to look better hooded; that is, veiled.

Thousands of wet eucalyptus leaves rattled against each other in the wind; no matter how many times she heard the sound, she was always taken aback by how loud it was, even through her defective ears. As little girls, she and Twice Holy Daisy Wasserstrom had imagined they could detect patterns in this sound, that it was the chatter of tree spirits or witches, aliens or Lemurians. At the strange little school where Daisy and Andromeda had attended kindergarten, they had been encouraged to ask the gnomes for permission to enter these woods on their daily nature walks, which might have been where the idea originated. (Also, incidentally, it was why Andromeda and Daisy used to say that they had been gnomeschooled.) Lemurians, the ancient, lost race of hermaphroditic, egg-laying giant humanoids described in Madame Blavatsky's *Stanzas of Dzyan*, were far more interesting than imaginary hippie-school gnomes.

Imagining that she was herself blindfolded and frozen in time with a sword in each hand, she ran through the moment's uncertainties in her mind, under the heading *not sure.* Not sure if counting off cards quickly and secretively in a girls' bathroom stall and noting the tenth was the most respectful or effective way to invoke a god and attempt to examine a map of the Universe. Not sure to which of the several anxieties vibrating through her head and beneath her skin the Two of Swords reversed might refer. The previous night's disturbingly lucid dream; St. Steve's inexplicable, and now continuing, silence; Twice Holy Soror Daisy Wasserstrom's sudden refusal to remain silent, as the dead are supposed to. Her own clumsiness. Her social discomfort. Her twice-failed driving test. Her skin (oily), her hair (flat), her body (aerodynamic and featureless). Her unreliable, unfathomable emotional weather system, continually bounding between extremes. Her accursed bones.

A distant voice barely perceptible amidst the clattering of the eucalpytus leaves reminded her: St. Steve's silence was not all that inexplicable. His absence made far more sense than his presence ever had. It is not in the nature of life for human beings to get what they want the most. Almost nobody gets that.

She had to dismount to walk her bike through the Safeway parking lot, feeling overheated and *action-populated*. The term had entered her vocabulary years ago when she had misheard something that might have been "discombobulated." It meant "bubbling over with concerns."

Mishearing was Andromeda's life; if she had grown up hearing properly, the resulting girl would have been very different. Her body's collagen, she had been told back in the days when her family still went to doctors, was "disorganized," so her bones had formed improperly and tended to be fragile. According to the books, a violent sneeze or simply rolling over in bed could be enough to break a bone, though that had never happened to her. Her case was "mild," and she was "very lucky," though her mother still spoke and acted as though Andromeda were liable to shatter spontaneously at any time. "Brittle bones!" the mom would cry out when she suspected her daughter of harboring the intention to do something dangerous, like stand up or sit down or simply do anything the mom wished she wouldn't, or fail to do something the mom wished she would. Sometimes Andromeda did imagine herself shattering, her jagged pieces then to be vacuumed or swept up by an angry mother or other type of demon or unearthly creature. The more common image, though, was that of cooked chicken bones inside

her body: dry, brittle, pulverized, apt to splinter and dangerous to any cat or other predator that might try to eat her. It
was the most pathetic of defense mechanisms. An Andromeda Klein would prove to be, if eaten, a thoroughly unsatis-
factory meal.

Other times, as she wrote in the essay she turned in with
slight modifications for most school writing assignments, she
felt as though her bony inner core had been mysteriously
cursed. *Osteogenesis imperfecta,* the condition was called, and
so Imperfecta, meaning "incomplete" and implying a universe of deficiencies, was her chosen, exceedingly apt magical name. Hence her formal name in the Ninety-threes,
otherwise known as the New New Temple of Thoth Hermes
Trismegistus: Soror Cancellaria Imperfecta Stella Matutina
Adepta ("Sister Female Chancellor Incomplete Morning
Star, Adept").

It had been years since her core had broken or fractured.
But, as most people fail to realize, you hear with your bones.
A bone malleus, which is a hammer, hits a bone anvil, which
jostles a bone stirrup and transmits sound vibrations to the
ear's inner sanctum. The tiny ossified cartilage instruments
in her ears didn't seem to vibrate quite as well as the instruments in the ears of the well-organized-collagen people.
There was, she had read, an extremely painful operation you
could have to replace the bad cartilage with steel parts,
which might be something to consider in the future, assuming she was to win the lottery or somehow acquire the steel
parts and a manual explaining how one might conduct the
surgery upon oneself, which was not too likely.

There had been a good illustration of the Soror Imperfecta Disorganized-Collagen Effect in its classic form earlier

that day, at the end of sixth-period Language Arts, when a girl she didn't really know but who was also in her Keyboarding class had asked Andromeda Klein if she was into wicker. Her name was Amy something.

Wicker? Andromeda's first thought was of the rattan patio set the Kleins used to have back in the days when they lived in a much larger, much nicer detached home in the Hillmont hills and actually had a reason to own patio furniture—that is, a patio. Now all they had was a narrow deck and a driveway, and a semi-enclosed carport.

So Andromeda's response to Amy Something was: "Yes, I celebrate all furniture of the world." Or rather, Alternative Universe Andromeda Klein said that. Actual Plain Old Universe Andromeda just muttered the word *furniture* and looked confused, then reflexively pulled her hair back from her good ear and murmured "What?" Amy Something rolled her eyes, said "Freak" or "Weak," or possibly "Geek." As usual, even as her mouth was forming the "What?" Andromeda had worked it out: "wicca," witchcraft, she meant.

There was more to Andromeda than her *ouijanesse* (the Daisy-Andromeda term describing their own spooky, occult experiments—pronounced "weedgie-ness"). She hated being looked at and analyzed, and she did her best to keep what was secret hidden. People with mildly disorganized collagen, the books said, could be "visually difficult to distinguish in the general population," and the same went for the weedgie, if they didn't advertise their *ouijanesse*. Most in the General Population saw Andromeda Klein as quiet, shy, too small, too skinny, nondescript, in her own world, even "stuck-up" because of her frequent insecure silences—a weak freak or geek, maybe, but not necessarily a weedgie one.

Nevertheless, the Amy girl must have noticed something: Daisy's ankh ring on her first finger or her tarot deck in her backpack when she was putting away her Language Arts journal, which Mr. Barnes had just returned with a *See me* note. Perhaps this girl was herself "into wicker" and had wanted to make friends, compare wicker notes? To gather information for some future program of harassment? Either way, the moment had passed. Making enemies was astonishingly easy. All you had to do was stand there.

No, not "wicca," certainly not. Andromeda and Daisy had had their witch phase, which they had called "doing spells." This was their own Hellfire Club, one of many two-girl organizations they had dreamt up and dropped over the years till Daisy's death put a stop to the process. The Stealers, the Dirties, Girls in the Mist, the Ninety-threes, the Ladies Spiritual, and many more—all harmless, except perhaps for the Murderers, which had overlapped with the witchcraft club in its herbalist phase, and also with Daisy's murder-mystery kick and her idea to found a kind of Reverse Detective Agency, dedicated to plotting the Perfect Murder. That one hadn't turned out so well. Poor old Mrs. Finn. Her illness, in fact, had had nothing to do with the belladonna, still less with any spell, Andromeda was sure of that. But they had shredded and burned their workbooks, of course, and never mentioned the project again. It would have been hard to explain.

The Stealers, a two-girl shoplifting ring, had also ceased to be when Daisy had been caught and issued a warning and had been banned from entering any Mervyn's for life, a ban that had now expired.

All that wicker now embarrassed Andromeda faintly. Her views had changed a bit since those days, when she had always instinctively deferred to Daisy's confident, yet uninformed, will. Real magick, Andromeda had come to believe, was a complex science that required far more training and study than most people could manage in a single lifetime. It was presumptuous to fake it, maybe even dangerous if you annoyed the wrong Intelligences with your yammering and blundering, or manifested and let slip Things you couldn't control. Daisy had had no such qualms. She just charged in as though she knew everything, and the spells she "did" were a mishmash of poorly researched nonsense, culled from a variety of suspect sources. It was no wonder nothing had ever quite "worked." Yet Daisy had had gifts, or at least luck; quite often her uninformed impulses had turned out to reflect real insight upon further study.

It had always been maddening that Daisy put in such little effort yet did so well, while Andromeda slaved away tirelessly with little result. But reality had to be faced: it had been Daisy's role to act and Andromeda's to study and interpret, in magic as in much else.

Daisy had used the words *witchcraft* and *magick* interchangeably, a common enough habit. *Wicker* isn't a bad term, Andromeda concluded: a naïve, cuddly-wuddly, immature, reckless, faintly embarrassing, rather low form of shallow, new age, mock-religious garden furniture, constructed by techniques supposedly stretching back to remote prehistory but actually fabricated and plagiarized in the 1940s e.v. by a sad old English guy named Gerald and of no use whatsoever in the real world of narrow decks and driveways. Real magick wouldn't be wicker: it would be a golden throne radiating astral light. Or perhaps merely a tree stump.

"You are a good student, Andi," Baby Talk Barnes had said after Amy the Wicker Girl had left them alone in room C-12. "But if you don't put more effort into your journal, you will fail this class." As though anyone with perfect attendance ever got less than a B in any subject at Clearview High School. Andromeda Klein's Language Arts journal had had only two entries for the week. Five would have been an A, twenty points each. You could write almost anything in there and get a nineteen or twenty. Her entry about how giraffes have long necks had earned a twenty-five, because it had been almost a whole page. "Here are some other things that are long: roads, time, spoons, knives, poles, string, rope, swimming pools, sighs . . ." (*Sighs* had earned a red exclamation point.) Wide margins and large handwriting were the key. But Andromeda tended to have other things on her mind, and coming up with entries that were numerous enough to satisfy Mr. Barnes yet bland enough that he wouldn't be inspired to turn her in for psychological reprogramming was more than she could manage sometimes.

"There's no wool against shaking things up, if you don't like kisses," said Mr. Barnes.

By "kisses," he meant "essays." "Wool" was how he said *rule*. Disorganized collagen was not to blame for that one: he had trouble with his *R*s, as well as a slight lisp, which was why everyone called him Baby Talk.

"How about a poem? Or dwaw a pick-thaw? Multimedia it up!" The expression on his face was evidently meant to be sly, or devil-may-care, or something.

Despite the speech impediment, Mr. Barnes thought of

16

himself as the Cool Teacher type, which was quite an impressive demonstration of the power of self-esteem. He had a leather jacket and wore cowboy boots, and tended to do things like trying to turn *multimedia* into a verb. "You owe me thwee," he said with what might have been intended as a wink, "pwuff two fwom waft week and . . ." She didn't catch the last part. She would have to come up with at least ten entries for next time, just to stay even.

Andromeda Klein, now pedaling past the Community Bible Center Church on Broadway, envisioned a journal entry that went *Thingv I am bad at: dwawing, witing poemv, multimedia-ing . . . making eye contact . . .* Her thoughts strayed to less amusing avenues.

Her red mom-phone vibrated in her backpack and she had to stop in front of the post office to dig it out.

"Dromeda, honey, have you left school yet?" asked the mom.

"Yes," said Andromeda, hanging up, hating her name.

"Bone to pick with you," said the mom after vibrating in again, meaning she was ready to recite today's list of instructions, schedules, and complaints. Andromeda hung up and pressed Reject when the phone vibrated again. Seven messages had been left since the morning switch-off. The mom had advice on everything: how to pour coffee, how not to drink water, how to pet the cat, how to read the newspaper, how not to shut the front door, the right way to stand or sit, the way you should and should not breathe, on and on. Complaints were generally texted in truncated form during the day and later elaborated into a full lecture. The day a person's mother discovers text messaging is a dark day indeed. Delete All.

"I am at work," she texted back, and switched the red phone off and returned it to its usual place in her makeup bag.

She panicked slightly when she couldn't feel her blue phone–her "real" one–in her bag, but there it was in the outside pocket. No new messages, one saved, which was St. Steve's deeply disappointing final text, now rather ancient:

"Hi there just checking in hope ur well, miss me?"

Hi there. There were no words for how much that "hi there" had hurt, and he'd had to have known it, too. It was still hard to look at. Before, it might have been "hey gooey" or "hi authe." ("Authe" was a predictive text typo for "cutie"; "gooey" was "honey" though it could also be "goofy.") She had texted back "toy away," which meant "thinking of you and wild about you." Wild was right. She had been wild, panic-stricken, as action-populated as she had ever been. There had been no response. That was when everything had finally begun to go wrong, as it had been intending to from the beginning. Then Daisy had died and the final spark had gone out of Andromeda's life.

As always, something prevented her from deleting the message. She stared at it, dwelling on the pain. Or maybe, to be honest, the name for this version of the "hi there" distress wasn't really *hurt,* since at this late stage it was different from the frantic, desperate madness it had once evoked. A cold, mature despair, it might be called–a growing thing, becoming ever more complex as it aged. Bitter wine.

Despite her best efforts to remain distant and neutral, thinking of Daisy and the "hi there" had its usual effect: Andromeda felt hot tears blown across her cheeks by the wind, sliding back into her ears, and prickling a little as they dried.

You weren't supposed to read the pictures on the cards

literally, they were symbols, and Pixie's pictures had little basis in the mainstream of traditional tarot anyway. But Andromeda Klein couldn't help seeing something of herself in the Two of Swords girl. She made a quiet explosion sound against the roof of her mouth and imagined herself bursting into flames as she rolled down Glen Crest Boulevard. She was also thinking about her box, and about another sort of box as well.

Here's the reason for the sound effect, and how it tied into the Two of Swords, reversed, and why she was also thinking about a couple of boxes. At moments of minor stress, ever since she was small, Andromeda Klein had found relief and comfort in thoughts and images that most people would find repellent. They were not the sorts of things you said aloud, nor would anyone write them in a Language Arts journal. One was to imagine her own head being blown apart, either from outside as from a bullet or in the form of some pressure-relieving explosion from within. For a second everything disappeared, but not really. She knew a head explosion shouldn't be a comforting thought, but it was, and she had given up trying to stop thinking about it. No one else knew about it, so nobody would have been impressed by her sacrifice if she had been able to prevent the thought from arising.

Andromeda's thoughts about head explosions and boxes were interrupted by a text message from Rosalie van Genuchten:

"you will be very very VERY sorry if you miss AT today . . ."

"AT" stood for Afternoon Tea, a semiregular after-school gathering where Rosalie and the other *dime soda* friends

Andromeda had inherited from Daisy would congregate and attempt to drink the contents of this or that parent's liquor cabinet.

Andromeda was the same age but a junior, because she had been held back in elementary school in a vain effort to increase her size relative to her classmates. She had never been sure she and Afternoon Tea were cut out for each other, an attitude that had earned her the nickname Stick or Sticky, short for "walking around with stick up butt" (though it also could refer to her slender, featureless body, which everyone seemed to feel was fair game for ridicule–Anorexia Klein was another one, and so was Fence Post. Sometimes it was Stucky). Andromeda was always technically welcome to Afternoon Tea, but was formally invited like this, she suspected, only to bump up the numbers when it was feared there might be poor attendance. This had begun to happen more and more frequently as the girls in the group got real boyfriends, jobs, a life, etc. (*Dime soda* was AK lexicon for "kindasorta.")

Andromeda one-thumb-texted a polite, regretful RSVP as her front wheel cut through another puddle and she sped past what they used to call the Dog Area. There were no dogs out in the rain today, though she thought she could smell them and the smell of wet dogs always reminded her of St. Steve's car.

And with that, her thoughts returned to the exploding head meditation and then to the Andromeda Box. Thinking about the Box could put her in a kind of trance. She would picture herself tightly bound up like a mummy in raw silk, unable to move at all, in a box with an oval hole that just fitted her face. Her eyes were either bound shut, or they were covered with a gauzy fabric that revealed only shadows. Sometimes, a mask of heavy iron, with a small breathing hole, would be placed over her face and bolted to the box. A dark, silent figure would occasionally come to remove her mask, to give her food and water, and to ensure she was still alive. The binding and the box held her together when she felt she was falling apart, yet it also kept the world out. Symbols inscribed on her lid warned intruders of a terrible fate for their transgressions. The Andromeda Box meditation made her feel safe when nothing else could.

She wasn't quite certain why the Two of Swords, reversed, made her think of her box, but it did, and it soothed. It was a cheap and shaky sort of peace, but it was all her world had to offer at the moment, and she was happy to take it.

Perhaps the association was due to another box, the one she had painted black and decorated with sigils and given to T.˙. H.˙. Daisy W.˙. to house her tarot deck in its Eye of Horus bag, from within which last night's dream had seemed to unfold.

Rosalie was on the phone, but Andromeda rejected the call. Andromeda was a girl with a mission, and she had one stop to make before the library. Despite the weather, she was pretty sure he'd be there, by the grove of elms on the border of the middle school's lower fields, his group's after-school spot. And she was right. There he was with his friends: Twice Holy Daisy Wasserstrom's younger brother Den. Andromeda was not welcome in what had been Daisy's house, so Den was her only way in.

i.

Andromeda Klein paused for a moment by the middle-school drinking fountains to regain composure and clean herself up. Her eyeliner was supposed to be smear-proof, but the eyeliner people obviously hadn't tested it on weeping teenaged girls riding through drizzle-wind. Her Egyptian eyes were mere smudges. She swung her bike up the asphalt lane and stopped about ten yards from the boys. They scrambled to hide their cigarettes and whatnot when they noticed her. They were bear cubs, sparring, grappling, tumbling. Their loose-laced puffy sneakers were giant kitten feet. Their clothes . . . when, historically, had the males of the world lost the ability to dress themselves? Somewhere along the line someone had decided it was desirable to look like you had lost control of your faculties.

One of the boys called out something that sounded like "pelican heater moosh mosh."

"I'd hit that," said another, preposterously, "four times."

Den punched them goodbye and stumbled over to Andromeda. She thought she smelled pot.

"Umba," she said, in that "I'm gonna tell on you" way. But he knew she was kidding.

"Ninety-three," said Den. He had overheard Daisy and Andromeda greet each other like this. He had no idea what it meant—how could he?—and so it was in fact rather inappropriate, but it was a small way of invoking Daisy's memory, a thing they could share. She always smiled at least a little when she heard it coming from him.

"Ninety-three," said Andromeda, feeling a little silly. Then she haltingly added "Ninety-three/ninety-three," feeling even sillier. She wasn't sure whether you were technically even supposed to say that part aloud. People on message boards had jumped all over her for using this abbreviation of the formal Thelemic greeting. That ended her participation in the message boards, though not her interest in the 93 current. "Any time people form groups," the dad would often say, "they begin to worship dead things and to persecute heretics." He was talking about the government and religion, and how his record store and label had been kicked out of the anarcho-libertarian collective. But it was as true of magick as of anything else. Magical nostalgia had little to do with the scientific evaluation and exploration of a live magical current. She was on her own, a solitary theoretician-practitioner, by design and default. (*By Design and Default* was to be the subtitle of volume X of *Liber K,* the only one bound in red, and meant to be shelved upside down.)

Den was looking at her with a goofy half-smile.

She asked, just in case, if his house had burned down last night, and he said it hadn't.

"That's good. Because I need you to get something from Daisy's room." Then she added, "That's not the only reason it's good, obviously."

Den tilted his face and gave her a puzzled-dog look.

"I mean, I'm very glad your house didn't burn down."

Dog look.

"Seriously."

He continued to stare till she realized he was kidding.

Daisy's bedroom had been kept more or less intact since she died. Den had let Andromeda in a few times, while his mother was still working a regular schedule. On one visit Andromeda had spent an entire hour kneeling by Daisy's bed with closed eyes, smelling, remembering, missing her. She had also attempted to do some scrying, with Den assisting as scribe, in the cramped walk-in closet that had once been an altar site of the New New Temple of T.·.H.·.Tris, as well as the Barbie Hospital and Star Chamber of the Ladies Spiritual. (The scrying had been unsuccessful, as always. Andromeda Klein, like Dr. Dee, had scant talent as a medium, just as Den was useless as a scribe: his transcription page had in the end shown little more than doodles of a marijuana leaf and a guitar shaped like a machine gun. She had tried him out as a scryer, too–this as a scientific experiment to test whether Twice Holy Daisy Wasserstrom's scrying ability might have had a hereditary aspect–and the results were clearly negative. Dennis Wasserstrom was no Edward Kelley. "I see a wine bottle," he had said. "I see a candle behind the wine bottle. The bottle is on a card table in a closet. There is a girl named Millie staring at me with kissable lips. . . ." Millie was one of Andromeda's names, derived from the fact that according to Agrippa's system of gematria for Latin characters, her full name added up to an even thousand; that is, M or *mille*. That was the name she had given St. Steve when he had asked about her *M* pendant, so he had called her Millie, when he didn't call her goofy or gooey.)

At any rate, now that Daisy and Den's mother no longer had a predictable schedule, such visits were out of the question. There was no telling what would have happened if she'd caught Andromeda there. Andromeda had once dreamt that Mrs. Wasserstrom had stabbed her through her sleeping bag, and Daisy had claimed that her mother used to threaten her with knives when she was little. Since then, Den had managed to retrieve some books and clothes, the ankh ring, and a few other items for Andromeda. Daisy's mom was no longer Mrs. Wasserstrom, though; she had gone back to her maiden name, MacKenzie, and now called herself Ms. like some sad teacher. Andromeda and Den had called her Miz MacKenzie, or Mizmac, sarcastically, ever since the change.

Andromeda wore the ankh ring on her first finger, of

course, in the manner of the classical Renaissance mage. When the ring was on the right finger, she was supposed to manifest a Jovial, vibrant, warm, and open-hearted temperament; when it was on the left, she was supposed to switch her mood to a Saturnine, brooding, inspired melancholia. The personas were supposed to have opposite tastes and opinions, which was meant to loosen the bonds of the ego and teach tolerance by showing the arbitrariness of opinion. (This was something she had adapted from Mr. Crowley, who had imposed the exercise on his students.) Andromeda constantly found herself slipping back into Saturn regardless of which Ring Day it was. Realizing she had failed again, she switched the ring from right to left and bit the back of her hand as a punishment, but breathed an inward sigh of relief because Saturn was so much more comfortable.

"What's my percentage?" Den was saying, meaning, what would he get in return for his services. They had been trading things for favors since they were both kids.

"What do you need?" Not drugs, she promised herself, I won't get him drugs. The ankh ring had been exchanged for candy, but since then his tastes had . . .

"Feel you up?" he said.

. . . matured, she had been thinking.

"Gross," she said. "How old are you?"

"Old enough."

He looked so hurt at how hard she snorted at this that she actually made a sincere attempt to straighten out her face.

"That?" she said. "Is not going to happen." He was twelve. She wasn't a *complete* degenerate. "Anyway, there's nothing to write home about on me. I wouldn't want to cheat you."

"Bagel worm agony," he said.

"What?" Andromeda pulled hair and hood back from her right ear. "Wait: did you just say 'Naked girl magazine'?"

He nodded, a very serious expression on his face that almost made her giggle again. Hadn't computers solved the boys' dirty-magazine problem forever? Perhaps he wanted something he could take to the elms to share with the other cubs. Well, it wasn't as bad as drugs. She'd try to keep it as clean as she could. "I'll see what I can do."

She described where he would find Daisy's tarot deck, in a yellow and purple Eye of Horus bag inside a black box with a silver glitter eight-rayed star of Ishtar on the underside of the lid, and on the outside, a heptangle glyph–a simplified version of Dr. Dee's Sigillum Dei Aemeth painted on it in true gold leaf. The bag and the box had been Saturnalia gifts from Andromeda to Daisy a couple of years back; Andromeda had painted the sigils herself, after carefully outlining them with a compass and straightedge.

"She'd have hidden the box somewhere, away from the light and where your mom couldn't find it, probably. A big pack of cards about this big." She held out her hands. She took out her Moleskine notebook and drew a clumsy star of Ishtar, a squiggly version of Dee's heptangle, and finally an Eye of Horus. "See? An eyeball. Growing from a . . . stalk. And a, kind of, curly branch. And an ear. And, a nose. And . . . an eyebrow!" She tore off the page and handed it to him. "Ta-da."

If only it were so easy to talk to everyone. This is how

privileged socially secure people get to be all the time: comfortable, unconcerned, in charge of the situation. It was hard to draw geometric sigils without a compass and straightedge, but she was very comfortable drawing Eyes of Horus freehand, partly because the more off-kilter they were, the better they looked. If there were a way to do it professionally she'd have it made.

She and Den had always gotten along. They both missed Daisy. They were both scared of Ms. MacKenzie. If only the rest of the world missed Daisy and were frightened of Mizmac to the same degree, the entire social landscape would be transformed in her favor. . . . Comfortable, unconcerned, in charge of the situation. The feeling passed.

The drizzle began to turn into actual rain. The bear cubs were gathering their stuff and trip-waddling down the field. Den kissed a peace sign and ran after them, holding his pants up with one hand and stumbling over his shoes. Why do they all want to show the world their underwear? "Because," replied Alternative Universe Andromeda, "they don't let you have belts in prison," which actually did seem like a good point.

"See you Thursday," he called out.

"Word," she said quietly. Daisy and the texted "hi there" and the Two of Swords reversed were still hovering, darkening the world. Then she mouthed an expression that had been Daisy's: "Oh, life." She zipped up and pushed off down the path. She would be soaked by the time she reached the library.

"Trismegistus," she said, looking toward where she supposed the sun might be if it weren't for the iron-gray clouds.

"Jesus, Andi," said Marlyne, one of the library assistants. "You look terrible."

"What?" said Andromeda Klein, even as she caught up to what had been said. Then: "I try." People who knew her well had learned not to answer every "What?" right away.

"Could you watch the desk for like ten minutes while I go get my lady on?" Marlyne meant fix her makeup. The chances of anyone coming to the front desk in the next ten minutes were close to zero. As always, the library was almost completely deserted, except for staff and a few elderly, half-alive patrons. It was the quietest place Andromeda knew, like a church or a museum, or something abandoned. The main building had a big, steep, pointed roof in front. It almost looked like it might have once been a church of some kind; though it could just as plausibly have been an International House of Pancakes. Whatever it had once been, it was now the most underutilized branch of the system. Most people went to Central, which was bigger, better located, and allegedly nicer, though Andromeda preferred the shabby, crumbling stillness of the International House of Bookcakes. The recently remodeled and modernized Central Library looked like a place in a futuristic movie where people take their kids to get their brains replaced so they can be controlled by robots.

She stared at the clock and thought about swords and blindfolds and boxes and robots in order to avoid glancing at any shiny surfaces: she didn't even want to see what she looked like after that ride. Andromeda checked her blue phone. "Get your bony non driving ass over here jk," said another charming text from Rosalie van Genuchten.

"I can't think why you come here on your day off," said Marlyne, when she returned looking marginally more sparkling. Then she added something else that sounded a bit like "Large bundle of Arthur eggs."

"Mm," said Andromeda. Sometimes it wasn't worth even trying to figure them out, and *mm* was the thing to say. It meant "How interesting, and exciting."

Andromeda only worked two weekday evenings during the school year, but she had somehow managed to leave the impression on the mom that she worked quite a bit more. At this point, though, she didn't have anything to do on her fake work nights. Daisy had officially left this world, or most of her had. And St. Steve would not be calling up to offer to take her to the Old Folks Home. Rosalie and Siiri and Co. meant well, but they could be their own special flavor of nightmare unless you were in the mood for them—the International House of Bookcakes was the least unpleasant thing on an unsavory menu. It was quiet, and expected little of her, and it was free.

"You should let me do your makeup for you sometime," said Marlyne. Translation: You look like shit, Andromeda.

A visit to the bathroom confirmed it, to no great surprise. Her "look" was one big ball of terrible. She had started the day with decent, straight hair and a subtle hint of Egyptian eyes, but both had rapidly degenerated in the wind and drizzle and heat and anxiety. She did what she could. Hair up was slightly better, even if it meant people could see her ears and more of her neck, which she felt was far too long and narrow. As at school, the heat in the library was deathly. She visited the thermostat on the way back from the bathroom and turned it down from the maximum (which was so high it didn't even register on the gauge), though she knew it would get turned right back up again as soon as an elderly patron complained that the heat was "blowing cold air."

"The new you," said Marlyne. "How'd you get here, on your bike? You need to get your license."

Andromeda was aware.

"Or a boyfriend to drive you around."

"Mm," said Andromeda Klein. Marlyne was wearing a sweater. How could she stand it? Even in her light, cotton button-down men's dress shirt from Savers, Andromeda felt like melting cheese. Marlyne never broke a sweat, somehow. The crisscross pattern of her sweater evoked, once again, the Two of Swords, yet another minor synch.

Andromeda retrieved a couple of cartomancy volumes from the 133s and took them to a table in the deserted Children's Annex, one of four trailerlike structures joined to the main building by covered paths they called breezeways. If, in your head, you divided the main building into three sections (for Reference, Periodicals, and General Fiction upstairs), the library complex as a whole could be viewed as an astrological temple in the classic Renaissance Hermetic style, with a room for each of the seven traditional Ptolemaic planets. This Andromeda had arranged by discreetly consecrating each room or section to the appropriate planetary demon and placing charged sigils—in colors drawn from Agrippa's gemological-planetary correspondences—in hidden spots at each location. She made a point of visualizing astral diagrams of the appropriate planets when she entered each room, in order to strengthen the links. Thus had the Clearview Park Public Library become the Bibliotheca Templi Hermetici, known and seen only by Andromeda Klein and whatever spirits might happen to notice. The Children's Annex had small tables and chairs and was a little uncomfortable, but it had been consecrated to Mercury—so it was the appropriate area for drawing down influences of use in studying and interpreting the Book of Thoth, she reasoned.

No one was near, so she risked a very quick, very low-key Lesser Banishing Ritual of the Pentagram and followed it with a truncated Invocation of Thoth. The Sign of Harpocrates, a finger or thumb over the lips, looked perfectly normal in a library, but once, she had been caught doing the Sign of Horus in the Temple of the Moon and an elderly lady had complained that there was a "crazy person loose upstairs."

She carefully laid out the Two of Swords and the nine cards she had drawn before it earlier that day in the girls' bathroom, working backward from position ten at the top of the column at the right, to the circle of future, past, crowning, and grounding, ending with "this crosses you" and "this covers you." This procedure always gave her an odd sense of going back in time. She gasped slightly because card number one, the "covers you" card, denoting the general situation, was in fact the Magician, who appeared to have played such a prominent role in the Daisy dream. Major synch, if only to indicate that Andromeda was on the spread's wavelength and vice versa.

There was no law against it, but she always felt just a bit

furtive and nervous about spreading the cards–especially in public like this, though there was no one there to observe.

Traditional tarot readings often begin with a significator, a card chosen to represent the querent or questioner, over which the other cards are laid. Daisy's method had been haphazard and unpredictable, but she had tended to use the Lovers to signify Andromeda in readings, because the Golden Dawn attributions specifically associated this card with the Andromeda legend in Greek mythology. This was, obviously, a terrible idea, since it removed a very important card from the divinatory possibilities at the outset. Because of this, many authorities question whether a significator should be used at all; most tend to reject the traditional method of selecting a significator from the court cards on the basis of hair and eye color. The significator should be chosen, if at all, on some basis with more depth: psychology, astrology, level of magical attainment. That was Andromeda's view. However, it occurred to her that, rightly or wrongly, she had begun to think of the Two of Swords as a kind of significator, a symbolic picture of Andromeda Krystal Klein. Perhaps that was the sense in which it was "the outcome." She was being shown her own, rather counterintuitive significator.

It was because of this train of thought that Andromeda snickered out loud in spite of herself when, just to see, she drew a card at random to serve as her significator, and it turned out to be the Page of Cups–the traditional card for females with light brown hair and eyes like hers. That was a big, and fairly weedgie, synch because the figure Pixie had depicted as the Page of Cups had played a role in the weedgie Daisy dream. Also, it was, perhaps, the Universe telling her not to dismiss traditional customs and practices so lightly.

The other cards in the spread were mostly small cards, bristling with swords, though the King of Pentacles in the "hopes and fears" space might allude to–had always seemed to allude to–St. Steve, who was certainly a hope and a regret, if not exactly a fear. There he was, staring at her with A.E.'s sad eyes as Pixie had drawn them. It was hard to decide how to relate A.E.'s court cards to the Golden Dawn's *Book T* attributions, but if A.E.'s Kings corresponded to the Golden Dawn's Princes rather than to the Knights, then he was also, apparently, Emperor of the Gnomes.

Swords are spiritual, creative, but couldn't they also be dangerous? They could slice you up. All depends on who holds them. In position seven was the Eight of Swords, another "hoodwinked" girl (in A.E.'s phrasing), this one tied to a post amongst a garden of eight swords: conflict, crisis, betrayal. It had never struck her just how many blindfolded girls there were in this deck. Besides the Magician, there was only one other major arcana card in the spread, in the second "crossing" position, the High Priestess, who has a crescent moon under her foot. She represents not only the moon, but also the Egyptian goddess Isis, as well as the priestess of the Temple of Thoth, according to Mrs. John King van Rensselaer, whose book lay open before Andromeda.

As for the Two of Swords, the Shemhamphorash attributions assigned to it the angels Ieiazel and Mebahel; and also, of course, by implication, the Goetic demons Sallos and Orobas.

"Mmm, Orobas," Andromeda said, nodding, as though

that explained a lot. Andromeda's cards were covered with her own careful notes, fit into the margins and around Pixie's figures: Hebrew and Greek characters, Qabalistic attributions, planetary symbols, page references to Agrippa's *Three Books of Occult Philosophy* and other important works. But she hadn't thought to note the small cards' Goetic demons and the Shemhamphorash angels till now. She wrote the names in the upper and lower margins of the card, the angels' names on top and its demons' names upside down on the bottom; then she carefully drew their seals lightly in pencil, so that they could be traced over in ink when she got home. She would have to find the time to inscribe the names and sigils on the rest of the cards as well, for the sake of completeness. "And for the sake," said Altiverse Andromeda K, "of providing evidence, should you ever be put on trial for a crime you did not commit, that you are not guilty by reason of insanity." Andromeda's mind formed silent words to the effect of "Shut your trap," though AAK did not actually have a trap.

Aside from the Magician and the Page of Cups, none of the figures depicted on the cards in the girls' bathroom spread had appeared in her dream, that she could recall, though she had seen the High Priestess's pillars, minus the High Priestess herself, flanking an empty chair. They had looked like a large number eleven–the number of magick.

She took a breath. Numbers are living things, the key to understanding "euery thing hable to be knowen," as Dr. Dee had rendered Pico della Mirandola's famous thesis in his introduction to the English edition of Euclid. They are their own worlds, every one of them infinite, and each a gateway to the others. The spread vibrated with Two-iness, Six-iness, Airiness, and a kind of Mooniness, too. For a fraction of a tick it was a vision of deep, dramatic beauty, of numbers and planes and spheres and things inside and beyond themselves, of abstractions and embodiments and their emblems pulsing beneath the mercurial sector of the heavens represented by the astral symbols on the annex ceiling. Such moments were priceless and felt like falling. But she failed to hold the flash in her mind, and it faded to darkness and confusion almost at once, as though someone had suddenly extinguished a lamp and kicked everything over in the shadows. That was how it always was.

She noted the spread in her tarot diary and gathered up the cards. The tarot diary was a list of dates with strings of Roman and Arabic numerals, Hebrew and Latin letters, a record of readings she had done with herself as the subject. It looked like a crazy person's math homework. A wiser or more learned person, a Master Therion or a Giordano Bruno or a Pythagoras, or a god, could have made sense of the numbers and letters, might have translated them into a map of Andromeda Klein and the bit of her that overlapped with the Universe, but Andromeda Klein herself was lost.

THE HIGH PRIESTESS

ii.

Why did Andromeda Klein want Den to retrieve Daisy's tarot deck all of a sudden? It was because Daisy was coming back to life and had instant-messaged her in a dream.

Daisy's death from leukemia the year before had been sudden. Andromeda certainly hadn't expected it. She had returned from the deeply regretted family trip to Mount Shasta, full of St. Steve anxiety, only to discover that Daisy was gone forever. Remission is only remission until it's not, and what they had celebrated as a cure had turned out not to be in the end. The week before the Shasta trip, just as St. Steve had abandoned her with his horrible "hi there," Daisy had also broken up with her, as she did from time to time. This meant a total cutoff of communication, and the cold shoulder at school, followed by a subsequent reconciliation, if Andromeda tried hard enough and gave Daisy presents.

One of the mom's many accusations against Andromeda was that she lacked the capacity to feel guilt. There might have been some truth in that, despite the trivial nature of the mom's complaints. Was it possible for anyone to feel truly guilty about using the wrong cup or walking down stairs on the wrong side or failing to hold toast the right way? Guilt of any kind was usually little more than regret plus embarrassment, with a bit of showing off added. Yet with Daisy, Andromeda had felt something close to guilt, not only because of the trip (which had left Daisy to do a planned Operation of Magick alone) but also because St. Steve had been a strain on their friendship right to the end. Andromeda had kept him as secret as she could, as she'd promised, though Daisy had suspected and had tried everything—from threats to pleading to trickery—to uncover the details. Andromeda had let a few things slip, and Daisy had been able to guess a few more; but Andromeda, usually a pushover, had never given in. In time, it might have blown over, as things do, but of course there had been no time. Daisy had died resentful and abandoned, and now there was no remedy.

It should have been easy to predict: everything about Shasta had portended doom. Andromeda had felt like a dead thing, and the landscape had mirrored her mood. Lemurian remnants were reputed to live in tunnels under Mount Shasta, were said to pay for provisions in local shops with mysterious gold nuggets and to conduct rituals and experiments that caused the strange light sometimes seen crowning the Northern Californian mountains. It was, ironically, the main reason she had consented to go to Lake Shasta in the first place, hoping to bring back the results of her Lemurian investigations as a peace offering to the sullen, silent Daisy. She thought she might have seen one, too, and had returned eager to tell Daisy all about the tall, misshapen shadow man she had glimpsed briefly in a headlight flash, and about the other sheets of blue fire she believed she had seen above trees beyond bends in the road. But the trip had been cursed. There had been an unpleasant, ill atmosphere around the lake. The 'rents had been grim and unbearable. On the tense drive home they had passed an overturned truck on fire. In movies, flaming vehicles always exploded, and Andromeda had braced herself for it, and might even have welcomed a fiery end, but the explosion had never come.

It was as though somehow her family's craziness had been amplified and the landscape was reflecting it. Andromeda had attributed these phenomena to Lemurian experiments, but later it seemed they might be read as the reverberations of Daisy's cataclysmic slide into death. The fiery truck suggested the Tower, the most ominous of the tarot trumps, and the shadowy Lemurian had looked a bit like the Hermit. As a pair, they suggested catastrophe and isolation, a prediction borne out in spades.

Daisy had returned none of Andromeda's messages.

39

Andromeda had assumed it was because Daisy was angry with her over St. Steve. But it had turned out she was not angry but rather dead; or she might have been angry as well as dead. Den eventually told her, in the same breath with which he also informed her that he was no longer allowed to speak to her himself. It had been during the week of St. Steve estrangement that Daisy had reentered the hospital, and in the midst of the Shasta week she had been dying of "respiratory complications." Andromeda considered that she had every right to feel aggrieved that she had been kept out of the picture. Why did Andromeda experience this sense of injustice as self-reproach and guilt and regret for things not done or poorly managed? Such inversions happen when people die in the midst of things, which is the only way they ever die. At least it proved the mom wrong about Andromeda and guilt, if proof about the mom's being wrong were ever needed.

Andromeda had not even been told about the memorial service. "You need to put those females on a leash," Mizmac had screamed into the phone to Andromeda's dad, in response to an e-mail from Andromeda's mother accusing her of denying "closure" to Daisy's best friend in such a difficult time.

Leave it to the mom to get both the etiquette and the facts so wrong. They had loved each other, but Andromeda had hardly been Daisy's best friend. Daisy had had many friends, including but not limited to the ones who were even now watching horror films and guzzling, inhaling, snorting, or doing only the gods knew what at Afternoon Tea. Andromeda had never been in doubt about her place, and it wasn't "best." "Who's the main character and who's the side-kick?" Daisy and Rosalie and the others would sometimes ask when they were trying to flirt with boys who traveled in twos. No one would ever have asked that question about Andromeda and Daisy. Not her best friend: her sidekick, rather; her assistant, her secretary, her ... minion. In the New New Temple of T.∴. H.∴. T.∴. they had been *sorors,* "sisters" in Latin, but Andromeda had been like the kid sister even though they were the same age. In formal temple mode, Andromeda had addressed her as *cara soror,* "dear sister." Daisy usually said merely: "Klein." Which means, and by which she meant, "little."

At any rate, "closure" was scarcely possible. For months, in fact, Andromeda had found it difficult to believe Daisy could really be dead. Daisy had moved to Chicago, Andromeda had told herself, to live with her father; the death had been faked in order to allow her to start off fresh with all new friends, and especially to keep Andromeda's allegedly bad influence away from her. Andromeda had even tried dialing a few Wasserstrom numbers in the Chicago area just to see if Daisy might answer. "Paranoid runs in the family," said the mom, not shy about drawing a comparison to the dad's worries about shadowy supragovernmental conspiracies. In fact, the Chicago calling was an idle ritual, but Daisy's presence was very strong, particularly in those first months. Daisy, Andromeda felt, was still there somehow, somewhere, even if not exactly in Chicago.

Memories of dead people rely on standing still, and for a time Andromeda's mind had been nearly as frozen as Daisy's bedroom. Nevertheless, the Universe continued to expand at its stately pace, violent up close, beautiful and seemingly still at a distance. Each person's tiny, individual world can feel the tremors. This item shifts, that article falls, while yet another breaks apart and crumbles. The new arrangement settles and becomes the norm. That is Death, Key XIII, the aggregate of tiny deaths that make up time, the new worlds that continually replace old or damaged ones. Eventually periods of several days would go by and she would realize with shock that she had hardly thought of Daisy at all. That is how dead people fade and gradually disappear from the present time. Those who survive always try to resist the process, preserving a little house for the *nephesh,* the animal soul, to inhabit and feeding it with attention and inadvertent rituals of remembrance, as Mizmac had clearly done. Eventually, though, this shadow fades to near nothingness, to sentimental memories and vague feelings of loss and guilt amongst loved ones.

That was how it had been with Daisy, until the last couple of weeks, when her *nephesh* had seemed to stop fading. It was as though Daisy's scattered remnants were attempting to reassemble themselves and as though Daisy herself were steadily coming back to life.

The first thing Andromeda had noticed was Daisy's scent. It had manifested without warning during Wellness one day; then she had smelled it again at the library, later on at home, once in the supermarket, and once even while riding in the mom's car, coming through the vents. It was very strong, and instantly recognizable: the citrus shampoo, the candy-flavored lip gloss, the vinyl coat, and a vague hint of cinnamon, perhaps, plus a damp, sour-sweet Daisy element she couldn't quite identify. After so many months of absence, this scent's reappearance had been dramatic. At first she had walked around sniffing, looking, she knew, like a crazy person. Soon, and bit by bit, Andromeda became accustomed to the reality that some rooms would randomly smell like Daisy.

The smell phenomenon was soon followed by visual synchs and manifestations. Daisy, or others who looked a lot like her, would appear in Andromeda's peripheral vision, only to disappear or assume another shape when she tried to look at them directly. Daisy also began to turn up more and more often in dreams, usually as a little girl pretty much as Andromeda remembered her from childhood, or as a corpse. She would appear in tarot spreads in the form of moon cards and Cups and watery images juxtaposed with flowers—*Daisy Wasserstrom* meant "water streaming over a daisy," and she was, or had been, a Cancer with her moon in Aries. Sometimes the indications were tricky and clever, as when Andromeda had happened to find two twenty-dollar bills in her copy of Agrippa's *Three Books of Occult Philosophy.* Andromeda had, of course, absentmindedly left them there and forgotten about them, but as for the significance: two twenties, i.e., 2020, just happened to be the number of the letters in the name Daisy Wasserstrom according to Agrippa's system of Latin gematria. That could hardly be a coincidence.

She soon began to hear, or rather, half hear, Daisy's voice sometimes, speaking unclear syllables, not in her head, but as though Daisy were standing somewhere behind her. Andromeda would respond with her characteristic "What?" and pull her hair back from her ear and turn around, but the voice would go dead and there would be no one there.

What were the powers of an unfading dead person?

Could they make phones ring? Knock you off your bike? Hide your keys? Disrupt your TV reception or lock you out of your house? Bill you for unwanted magazine subscriptions and move your car to the wrong side of the street? Such things seemed to happen quite often at Casa Klein. The mom would usually find a way to blame the dad for such phenomena; the dad would suspect the government; but Andromeda always wondered if it might not be Daisy, coming back to life and trying to attract attention, and no doubt enjoying the chaos. If spirits from beyond knew all, and if Daisy had indeed become such a spirit, the truth about St. Steve would no longer be hidden from her. Indeed, she might know more than Andromeda knew herself. Perhaps she had a message to impart. Or perhaps the malice remained, and Daisy's goal was simply to haunt her.

There was a game Andromeda had played ever since she was small, a game called "What would happen if?" More often than you'd think, the idle propositions had a way of coming out true. What would happen if she got kicked out of the Gnome School? she had once wondered: bang, the Kleins could no longer afford the tuition and Andromeda wound up in public school, though she hadn't been kicked out. What would happen if St. Steve disappeared and no longer cared for her? Bang, "hi there." This could be seen as a kind of perverse magic. She had learned to be very careful about questions silently asked, though some inevitably slipped out.

So when Andromeda had asked herself, in an idle moment, what would happen if spirits or demons could communicate with the here and now using instant messaging, in the same way they sometimes used Ouija boards or appeared in crystals or mirrors like Dr. Dee's angels, the result was: bang, she began to imagine she could see, on occasion, a little instant-message window pop up in the upper left corner just beyond her field of vision, sending her a message that was usually too dim to read. When she tried to follow it with her eyes it would slide off and vanish into her peripheral vision. When it happened in dreams, her eyes were usually bound or her lids glued shut so she couldn't see the window, or the message would be written in a language she didn't understand.

What would happen if Daisy came back and sent her messages? It looked as though Andromeda was going to find out.

In the IM dream of the previous night, the message had read:

Call the police. ☺

The avatar in the dream IM window was the same kitten face Daisy had used in her real-life account, though in the dream it was peeking out from what looked like a seal of Babalon.

Andromeda's dream wrists had been tied to the arms of a dream chair, so she couldn't type to respond. A door appeared to her left, on which shone a golden Sigillum Dei Aemath. When it opened she saw a silver flashing eight-rayed star of Ishtar on the other side, and a purple curtain beyond that, upon which an Eye of Horus in a triangle glittered yellow-gold with blue flecks. Andromeda recognized it instantly: this door appeared to be the lid of Daisy's lost tarot box, and the curtain was the velvet Eye of Horus bag. The curtain fluttered as if in the wind, and Andromeda also recognized the view beyond it, which was the scene of Pixie Colman Smith's painting of the Fool, though the Fool himself was not in it. She managed to slide her chair through the door and curtain and into the painting.

For a moment, all was bright and clear and peaceful. There was an echo, a fading, a trailing-off of a beautiful chord made up of thousands of perfect notes, sounding as though it had been struck just before she had entered the scene. The chord was the sound of the grass growing and of the clouds rolling by and of light flooding in to destroy darkness. Andromeda had now replaced the Fool in the center of the picture. She breathed in and a kind of vibrating elation spread from her lungs to the rest of her body. Daisy's scent suddenly descended in a cloud, so distinct that Dream Andromeda expected Daisy to be standing in front of her when the fog lifted.

Then it all went wrong. The peace was shattered. Pixie's cool blue sky darkened to gray, then to a deepening red. The Fool's little white dog bounded in and attacked Andromeda, sinking its teeth into her leg. She tried to scoot her chair back toward the door and the safety of her room, but the dog was pulling her in the other direction. She teetered and finally tipped over the cliff, dog, chair, and all. She landed on top of the crying man from the Five of Cups, knocking over the two standing cups and scattering the others. The Five of Cups man was still crying and bleeding underneath her and her chair, his blood steadily seeping into the green grass and forming a dark purple, stinking marshland. Mosquitoes buzzed in her ears. Globes of bright fire formed and exploded all around her. She felt scalding drops of rain that tasted of blood. The Fool was lying dead on the grass nearby. Flies poured out of his mouth and open wounds. The dog was still gnawing her leg, which had broken off.

In the distance, the Tower was blazing. A cascade of burning books poured out its windows. And the High Priestess's throne was empty between the two pillars labeled *B* and *J.* Andromeda had a feeling that if she could scoot her chair over between the pillars, she might have the power to tame the world and restore everything to balance; but the blood of the Five of Cups man and her own blood was a rising tide that was pulling them both down, a viscous, warm quicksand. The empty cups floated by.

Then she saw the Hierophant and the Star—who seemed to have lost one of her pitchers—along with the Hermit and the Page of Cups, stumbling blindly along the river. They couldn't see where they were going because their heads were all on fire. The head of the little fish in the Page's cup was also on fire. "Call the police," the fish said in a giggly, watery, Irish-accented voice. Then an enormous hand scooped them all up and deposited them in a gigantic bag and all was dark. Finally, she heard the sound of the door-lid slamming shut. Andromeda's hands and wrists were numb and tingling when she woke up. Daisy's smell, along with the acrid, smoky scent of the Hierophant's burning mitre, remained faintly in her room.

All the people in the dream had been from Pixie's tarot drawings, with one exception: a distant figure in a black hooded Tau robe, who had been on the mountain behind the river, gesturing wildly. Daisy? That part was a mystery. Andromeda hadn't been able to make out the gestures, but they had seemed like a kind of dance.

Upon awakening she had reached for her notebook and written down an account of the dream immediately, before even getting out of bed. She knew full well that the act of reducing the complexity of the dream experience to mere words on a page would change it irreparably, but she believed she had gotten most of the details.

"They are burning down my room," said a distant voice she thought she could just make out behind the sound of the water rushing out of the tap into her bath that morning. This was more common: she often heard indistinct voices underneath rushing or mechanical sounds like running water or the vacuum; the chatter of elementals, she had often speculated, which was just as likely as her father's explanation of such phenomena; that is, governmental telepathic experiments or neighbors talking behind their backs, their voices amplified by an inadvertent alignment of magnetic or atmospheric conditions. But this time it was recognizably Daisy's voice, and it was Daisy's scent blowing in through the window as well. There was another voice too, but it turned out to be the mom yelling "Two and ten o'clock!" which was her way of advising Andromeda not to fill the bathtub up quite so quickly and to use less hot water. She had drawn little arrows and x marks on the tiles by the taps.

Call the police? And tell them what, exactly? "Someone is burning down my dead friend's room." Andromeda listened below the water for the familiar Daisy refrain "Fucking with you, Klein," but if it was there, she could not discern it.

One thing she knew: the deformed cards in the dream recalled a series of paintings that Daisy had done for an art-class exhibition her sophomore (Andromeda's freshman) year; she had painted and pasted over enlarged color copies of the Pixie-Waite cards to include whimsical features from Clearview High School culture and society. Andromeda wished she could consult the paintings but was doubtful they still existed. At any rate, though she was not about to call the police, it was clear she was meant to rescue the tarot deck in the Eye of Horus bag in the blackened cedar box from whatever fate might be awaiting it. She imagined Mizmac cutting the cards into strips with scissors and burning them in the patio fireplace. It had to be prevented.

Now, in the library's Temple of Mercury, as she was closing up the cartomancy books and sniffing the air to determine whether she could smell Daisy mingling with the book smell she loved, she noticed something. Why had she thought the blindfolded girl in the Two of Swords was kneeling? She had looked at the card hundreds of times, and the kneeling image was clear in her mind. But looking at it now, she saw that the girl was not kneeling at all. She was seated on a bench or box of some kind. Strange how Andromeda had never noticed that before. The girl also seemed to be peeking from behind her blindfold, and her hands were . . . not very feminine–they were huge, in fact. What would happen if the Two of Swords girl was actually a boy?

This question strengthened rather than diminished

Andromeda's sense of the card as her significator, as it pointed to one of the recurring anxieties in her action-populated head, one that had resulted in several attempts to charge sigils derived from the statement "This is my wish to become more feminine." Boys tended to lack enthusiasm for aerodynamic bodies like hers, though some girls could make it work. Despite Bryce's claims to be attracted to her during the brief time they had technically been boyfriend-girlfriend, he hadn't seemed too interested in touching her, despite considerable encouragement. And St. Steve: she hated to admit it, but he had been the same way, the main difference being the intensity of her wishes. Bryce was sweet, and Daisy had averred that he was cute, even, but he was not the sort of person to inspire passion in anyone.

The number two–that is, Chokmah–lies on the masculine Pillar of Mercy; perhaps that was what A.E. and Pixie were getting at with their Two of Swords design.

At any rate, when she really looked at the Two of Swords, it was a totally different card. There were no shallow pools as she had thought, like on so many of the other Swords cards; rather, the aerodynamic girl-boy was in the foreground of a lake or sea, with an island in the distance and two rocky formations in the midground. And she wasn't really sitting on the box; it was more like she was floating above it. Or maybe she had just gotten up from kneeling and was now in the act of sitting down on the box. No wonder the Two of Swords made Andromeda think of her own box: there it was, underneath a hovering girl who was not quite feminine enough and who now looked to her a bit like a cemetery angel with swords for wings, the box a marble sarcophagus.

She put the cards back in the box, but then pulled them out again because she thought she had seen, out of the corner of her eye, the Tau-robed figure on the crest of the larger island behind the Two of Swords girl. She was mistaken. There was no one on the hill in the picture on the card. As an afterthought, she wrote down the cards she remembered from the dream, just in case they might have any divinatory or forensic significance: the Fool, the Hierophant, the Page of Cups, the Five of Cups, the Hermit, the High Priestess, and the Tower. That was seven of the ten cards in a Celtic Cross spread, leaving three unknown, unless the dancing Tau-robed one represented a card as well. If so, the Magician was a strong possibility—the figure might have been conducting a rite of some kind, and he might even have been juggling as well as tumbling. The fact that the girls' bathroom spread had placed the Magician in the first "this covers you" position seemed to confirm that supposition. Strangely, Andromeda noted, Pixie's Magician rather resembled the Two of Swords figure, giving the whole spread a curious symmetry.

Her quick, mouthed, surreptitious banishing ritual was interrupted by Darren Hedge, the reference librarian who supervised the pages. He was standing in front of her when she looked up.

"Do you feel like packing up Sylvester Mouse tonight?" he said. "Picking up some extra hours," he meant. "We need to pull these books."

Marlyne was going home "sick" again, and Weird Gordon, another page, was going to fill in for her at the desk. ("Sick" probably meant Marlyne was hanging out with

Tommy the maintenance guy, with whom she was having a not-too-discreet affair.) Darren Hedge handed Andromeda a list that had been printed on the library's ancient machine-type printer, a thick stack of paper accordion-folded along perforated lines, with the strip of holes on either side. Nearly an inch thick, which meant hundreds of books, probably.

"What's it for?" she asked, but he had already disappeared, leaving the list behind.

Weird Gordon walked by on his way to the main desk, quietly singing a little song that went "Filling in for Marlyne, at the front desk, filling in for Marlyne . . . ," and clumsily swaying while he walked. It was perhaps the most annoying habit for a coworker to develop, Gordon's little songs about everything he did. "Time to get out the stapler. Stapler!" "Everybody's taking their break, in the break room, break room. . . ."

"Gordon has a little crush on you," Marlyne had once sung, parodying his singing style. "I'm picking up a vibe." Marlyne was always "picking up vibes" and thought everyone had a crush on everybody else. Andromeda knew that, for her part, she could never come close to feeling attraction for a boy with such poor taste in shoes: today, despite the damp weather, he was wearing his mandals. For the love of Mike, as the dad would say in the Groucho voice when he was doing the corny dad routine, there was no excuse for that. She cracked herself up, though, imagining the song Gordon might sing if they were ever to hook up somehow: "Here we go unbuttoning, here we go unbuttoning, unbuttoning Andromeda, Andromeda's shirt from Savers, kickin' off my mandals, my man sandals, kicking off my mandals. . . ."

Then she saw him smiling back at her and accelerating his clumsy dance, showing off, and she felt bad for encouraging him, so she lowered her eyes and turned her attention back to the book list.

It couldn't be for interlibrary loan. There was no red I.L.L. ticket, and besides, it was just too many books. I.L.L. would be two or three at most, if any at all. The IHOB, that is, the International House of Bookcakes, had books that no other library in the system had, she knew, but people rarely requested them. When they did, and it was a significant title, it made her sick with worry, as it had a year ago when the library's copy of *True and Faithful* had had to travel to Sacramento. This was a facsimile edition, now quite rare, of *A True and Faithful Relation of What Passed for Many Yeers Between Dr. John Dee . . . and Some Spirits* (London, 1659), which she herself had once owned but had donated to the library for the public good and to protect it from the mom's predations. It was the only copy to which she was likely to have access, and it was crucial to her studies. The book was returned safely three weeks later, to her immense relief. The *Blue Equinox* had come back with the seals cut out, by some profoundly small-minded occult dilettante, possibly a "goth" or heavy-metal rock fan, she imagined. Such people were around, a blight on the occult landscape, though fortunately they rarely had a long-enough attention span to do much damage. Frater Achad's *Egyptian Revival* hadn't come back at all, which was a shame because Andromeda wished at present to consult its countertraditional analysis of the tarot trumps that had stumbled through her dream.

She got a cart from the back room and began with the

000s. Generalities and Information. She had never read the first one on the list, but it looked interesting and she made a mental note to look at it when it was returned: *The Egyptian Miracle: An Introduction to the Wisdom of the Temple.* Following were three books by Robert Anton Wilson that she had always meant to check out. Packing up Sylvester Mouse that evening only got her through the 001s, because she spent most of the time standing by the cart in the stacks reading the temple book and thinking about numbers and swords and boxes, and about how a compass and straightedge were the only tools necessary to build the world.

The Sylvester Mouse list was great, consisting almost entirely of books she had read, or had pretended to have read, or felt she ought to have read, or had been meaning to read, or had not known about but which were thoroughly up her alley. She had looked ahead to the selection of 133s, "her" section, Parapsychology and Occultism: it was particularly impressive, including nearly all the good ones and leaving the wicker behind. Here was Mrs. van Rensselaer's rare and quite underestimated *Prophetical, Educational, and Playing Cards;* and there was nearly everything the library had of Waite and Crowley, as well as Agrippa, Bonewits, Mathers's translation of the *Abramelin* text, Eliphas Levi, Dame Frances Yates, Francis Barrett, all the classics . . . *Abramelin the Mage* wouldn't be on the shelves. She knew because it was the library's only copy and she herself had had it and somehow managed to lose track of it sometime during the past year. Currently, she had the Eliphas Levi and one of the

Yates volumes at home–she would have to replace them by the time she got to the 133s, she supposed. She decided to staff-check A.E.'s *Book of Ceremonial Magic*, because she had just been using it to look up the sigils for Sallos and Orobas, and she wanted to note the sigils of the remaining Goetic demons on her cards.

Those who had made the Sylvester Mouse selections, whoever they were and whatever their purpose, really knew their stuff. The 296 section was great as well; it included the classic texts and left behind the dumbed-down self-help mumbo jumbo. It was a kind of showcase of the best the IHOB had to offer, which was considerable, and Andromeda caught herself feeling weirdly proud of it.

Books could get her excited, not just reading them but touching them. She had been known to caress her van Rensselaer or her *Magick Without Tears*. That is, she thought of them as hers, though they belonged, strictly speaking, to the library, which meant the county and ultimately the state. But they were from her section, and she was the only one who cared about them. The library's copy of *Magick Without Tears* was particularly fine, a small quarto, bound (or possibly rebound) in quarter calf and white buckram with gilt edges, a strange, obviously limited edition she had been unable to find on any official bibliography. Such books were themselves talismans, or they could be, powerful as objects. Hands laid on them could absorb their power, and even, some said, their contents. Living with them or around them could influence and transform your world.

There were three of the library's six Crowley books on the list and they were excellent choices: *Magick in Theory and*

Practice, of course, and *Magick Without Tears* because it was a rare special edition, and *The Vision and the Voice,* or *Liber 418,* an underappreciated classic documenting the exploration of the Enochian Aethyrs of Dr. Dee in the Sahara with Frater Omnia Vincam in 1909 e.v. It could also be read in *Gems from the Equinox,* but the stand-alone edition on the list was a far better text. It was odd, though, that *True and Faithful* was not one of the selections, as it was one of the library's most impressive volumes and a text of great importance.

The Sylvester Mouse list had its reasons, evidently.

iii.

Andromeda Klein was thinking of "her" *Magick Without Tears,* the way it felt and the way it smelled, so her ride home was much more high-spirited than her previous ride had been.

But the Klein household killed high spirits with striking regularity and precision. Andromeda made sure the red phone was turned off, in case she got a call or text from the mom on the wrong phone as she was walking in. It was a complicated system, but it was necessary. The mom had gotten her the blue phone, on a shared-minutes plan, a transparent scheme to keep track of whom Andromeda was talking to by means of the bill, which registered both incoming and outgoing calls and texts for all numbers on the account. The mom was not above calling numbers and interrogating whoever answered. The "Why have you been calling a health clinic?" conversation was infuriating and humiliating nearly a year later. And it still amused Andromeda to think about the mom's response to the Old Folks Home ("Dromeda, it's wonderful that you are volunteering, but you shouldn't let it interfere with your schoolwork or work around the house. . . ."). Yet it had been clear that the mom had to be stopped if Andromeda was going to have any privacy.

St. Steve had suggested the solution, an additional prepaid phone, same make and service but red rather than blue so you could tell them apart. Switch the SIM cards and use the blue phone with the pay-as-you-go chip, so the mom would think it was the family-plan phone if she saw it, but the calls made on it wouldn't turn up on the family bill. Keep the red phone with the family-plan chip hidden, and use it only for mom communication and for decoy calls to make it look like the phone was being used often enough to be believable. The decoy calls could even be fun, to the degree that they could elicit questions like "Honey, are you thinking of having something upholstered?" It kept them both busy.

By the time Andromeda had locked up her bike and had gone in and up the stairs, she was already in a bad mood again, thinking about the hoops she had to jump through just to reach everybody else's starting gate.

The building was a Spanish-style duplex in the flats, a part of Clearview that Rosalie van Genuchten regularly referred to as "the ghetto." The Klein family occupied the top half, left entrance. A combination of water damage and poor design and materials had caused the building to warp and settle oddly. From the outside, it looked a little strange, but the effect was really noticeable inside, where the floors slanted enough that smooth objects tended to slide if not secured. It was also quite small, which meant that the three Kleins' agenda of staying in separate rooms whenever possible could require some fancy footwork.

The mom was in the dining room at the computer, which had been moved there from its previous, more convenient location in the kitchen nook on the advice of a television program about Predators. This move had effectively killed the Internet for Andromeda, and at the moment it seemed to be cramping the mom's style too, which was slightly satisfying: she appeared to be IMing furtively with somebody, and even at a distance it was clear from the strobing monitor that she was riding the Hide button, as though worrying about over-the-shoulder spying. She had her earbuds in and her butt was chair-dancing slightly. From one position at the top of the stairs, there was a "split-screen" view of part of the dining room and part of the kitchen, where the dad sat on the floor, dismantling the microwave.

"I can't get on the network," said the mom, half turning in her chair. "I can't get on the network." Then she added: "I can't get on the network."

"Let me guess," said Alternative Universe Andromeda. "She can't get on the network." Then it added, "I guess the ninjas will just have to slay themselves." The mom often had trouble with her virtual reality networking games because of the slow speed of the dial-up connection. Andromeda trudged down the short hallway in a slouching manner intended to reflect her state of mind.

"Oh, not more books!" the mom said.

As at school and the International House of Bookcakes, the atmosphere at Casa Klein was near tropical, overbearingly hot, with moisture heavy in the air. Andromeda deftly nudged the sliding thermostat down with her shoulder as she walked past it.

"Your father is destroying another appliance, so if you want to heat something up you're out of luck." Everything was quite heated up enough as it was, no oven required. Andromeda had already had a plum baby food and some red whips for dinner in the break room with Marlyne earlier anyway.

A barrage of complaints and suggestions followed, once the mom was certain she had communicated her inability to get on whatever network she had been trying to get on. Tonight's lecture might have been entitled: "Vegetarianism as Eating Disorder: The Roots of Adolescent Depression." Goading Andromeda about vegetarianism was the one thing her parents seemed to enjoy doing together, even though the dad claimed to have once been a vegetarian himself, but he was too preoccupied with the microwave to join in this time. In truth, Andromeda was only a vegetarian every other day, on Saturnine Ring Days, but even on Jovial days she shied away from meat because fat was gross and the smell nearly always made her feel ill.

"Just having some tea," said Andromeda, filling the kettle.

The water pressure was low, as it had been for the last several weeks, so she had to stand in the mom's presence for far longer than she would have liked. Nothing ever functioned fully at Casa Klein.

"Tea, that's a nutritious meal," the mom was saying. She went on to complain about the water pressure and to accuse Andromeda of hiding her address book and using her iPod, which had gone missing and finally turned up in the refrigerator. The idea that Andromeda would have any interest at all in the horrible music on the mom's iPod was almost as preposterous as the idea that she would, for some reason, decide to put it in the refrigerator. The mom's checkbook had also disappeared and was still missing; again, it was ridiculous to accuse Andromeda. It was doubtful that the checking account had any money in it. And it was a good bet that the mom had already accused the dad of hiding or losing it before Andromeda had come in.

Refrigeration hadn't seemed to hurt the iPod; there it was, buzzing away through the slightly nasty earbuds now hanging around the mom's neck. Andromeda immediately thought of Daisy and whether it might be possible for her in her current state to dematerialize objects and rematerialize them inside boxes like refrigerators.

"Things are always disappearing around here," the mom repeated, with an accusing look in Andromeda's direction, and another in the direction of the dad.

"Jesus, will you leave the kid alone?" said Andromeda's father. "Hello, cupcake." She wasn't sure how he did it, but he managed to make "cupcake" sound sarcastic and affectionate at the same time. There was no person in this world who resembled a cupcake less than Andromeda Klein. It was nicer than Fence Post and no more inapt than her own name, which meant "Little Crystal Ruler of Men" in a variety of mismatched languages.

"Here's what happened: the earth revolved, the rain fell on the fields, and the Little Crystal Ruler of Men earned thirty dollars before taxes working in the public sector." That was Alternative Universe Andromeda. Regular Universe Andromeda simply left the room. As the mom continued the bone-picking she had mentioned earlier, remaining at the computer and shouting out rapid-fire complaints about insufficient this and excessive that, Andromeda settled down in the living room to study her *Teach Yourself Hebrew* book and tuned her out as best she could. There was a phrase from the most recent Language Arts handout that seemed to sum up the mom's philosophy on parenting and domestic organization. The wizard Merlin has turned the boy King Arthur into an ant, and the sign on the gate of the ant colony reads: EVERYTHING NOT FORBIDDEN IS COMPULSORY. Andromeda was an ant, crushed by a heavy maternal boot of iron. The mom had presumably absorbed these methods in her childhood in Australia under the Nazis.

Downstairs, the Champlain baby was screaming and the Champlains were screaming and it sounded like there was someone on the television screaming too. Andromeda's defective ears tended to screen out important information like syllables while still managing to pick up the irritating background noise. It didn't help that certain low tones from the sound track of whatever the Champlains were watching made the whole building vibrate abrasively. She could feel it in her back teeth. Andromeda's dad insisted that the cable be disconnected and the TV unplugged when not in use, so she had to stoop and reconnect everything before settling back on the couch. She picked up the remote and found the channel they were watching downstairs, not because she wanted to watch TV, which she didn't often like, but just in order to create a slightly less chaotic atmosphere where the sounds all matched. It was a movie in which a puzzle man was drugging people and sewing their mouths shut.

Soon the dad emerged carrying a circuit board and some other bits extracted from the now-destroyed appliance, a "See, what did I tell you?" look on his face.

Andromeda's father suspected the government of spying on American citizens by implanting surveillance devices in electronic products. All the manufacturers and the governments and the corporations that control them were in on it. He had several boxes of extracted circuit boards and other electronic parts, collected over a lifetime, carefully dated and labeled, evidence for the book he claimed he was planning to write on Surveillance and the State; accordingly, the carport in the back was filled with appliances that no longer worked, alongside all the recording and music equipment he collected from yard sales and pawnshops and never seemed to use for anything.

The dad frowned at the TV. It is well known, he often said, that the FBI keeps files on everything you watch, and that the cable could transmit information to them even as it brainwashed, which was a neat trick. It would have been safest to have no television in the house at all, but unfortunately there was no other way to watch sports. Even the supermarkets keep track of all your purchases for use against you later, which is why it was best to vary your patterns and shop at different places, and to buy everything with cash whenever possible, though new bills shouldn't be handled more than necessary because they put toxins in the ink that absorb into the skin and can be used to track you as well.

"You hear them?" he said, shaking his head. "They're talking about us again." He whispered: "Stalkers." He meant the Champlains, or the government, or some other shadowy organization; in his view someone was always stalking, or scheming, or up to no good.

The mom scuttled in. All three Kleins were rarely in the same room at the same time.

"Your tea water, Andromeda!" she said. "You should eat something, not just tea. It's an appetite suppressant." Then: "You shouldn't boil the water so hot, it's not good for the bleeding helmet." Heating element, perhaps? "*What* are you watching? That's terrible. You'll give us all nightmares. . . ."

Andromeda and the dad briefly shared a look of wonder over the concept of boiling water too hot.

"‏איפה השירותים?‏," said the dad, after a pause, which made Andromeda crack up in spite of herself after a moment of thumbing through the glossary at the back of her Hebrew book.

The mom glared with suspicion.

"I think he said 'Where's the bathroom?' " said Andromeda.

"Well, there's a surprise," said the mom, speaking fluent sitcom.

Andromeda had had no idea that the dad knew any Hebrew. It was difficult to learn the language from a book.

64

Many of the letters were so similar, and she was always getting them wrong. She was studying it mainly to help with her understanding of the Holy Qabalah and gematria, the ancient art of rendering words and sentences into numbers and drawing correspondences between them, which was an important part of magick training and practice. But she also imagined a day when, after years of study, she might find herself, like Dame Frances in the Warburg or A.E. in the British Library reading room, in a vast library of ancient, secret texts of occult lore; and what use would such a library be without a working knowledge of Hebrew? She had a lot of catching up to do, as her current education was essentially worthless for her purposes.

"I was a religious fanatic in a previous life," said the dad. "They try to get you while you're young." One of the stickers on the back of his van said BAD RELIGION and had a cross inside a red circle-slash; another said RELIGION IS CHILD ABUSE. That sentiment was presumably why he had opted to raise Andromeda as Nothing. There was also THE STATE IS NOT YOUR FRIEND and a fish with feet that said DARWIN instead of Jesus. The dad wasn't a big fan of the Pledge of Allegiance, either.

The dad was still talking. Part of whatever he said next sounded a bit like "Punch and Judyism" or it might have actually been "Judaism"—the dad and her poor hearing had similar senses of humor sometimes.

"The reality of it is," said the mom, interrupting the brief father-daughter conspiracy of ordinary conversation, "that religion goes through the mother. It's not Judyism at all. She's Spinach U-turn if she's anything."

"What?" Andromeda and the dad said it almost in unison.

"Finnish Lutheran," the mom repeated slowly. "She's Scotch, Irish, French, Italian, Swedish, and Indian, mm, Native American, and, ah, Austrian, from me, plus New Jersey and L.A. and nonpracticing Jew–Jew*ish* from you. But religion goes through the mother, so she's technically U-turn." Indian was familiar, if preposterous, and so was Austrian, or Australian–the mom never seemed quite sure which. But Finnish? Neither of them had ever heard that one before.

"Oy vey," said Andromeda, and the dad laughed as the mom went back to the computer, muttering, and leaving nothing in her wake but a potentially awkward father-daughter moment. It was rare for him to be home at all. He was usually at the studio, and even when he was home he spent much of his time in his van listening to recordings of his sessions or to the radio. He liked the sound system in the van, he said. What he meant, Andromeda knew, was that the mom would complain incessantly whenever he listened to his music in the house.

"Rosalie stopped by earlier," he said, "to drop off something for you." He handed her a little white box tied with a sloppy green ribbon. The first-name-basis-ness of this bothered Andromeda a bit; she would have preferred for him to say "your friend Rosalie" or "that Rosalie" or something more distancing. He hovered, plainly curious as to the contents of the box, but she didn't dare open it in front of him. There was no telling what might be inside. The mom would have simply opened it and peppered her with questions.

"What could it be, he asked knowingly," the dad said, raising and lowering his eyebrows. Then his cell phone blipped. Judging from the violence with which he stabbed the keys with his fingers in response, the text must have come from the mom, whom Andromeda could see in the dining room, still at the computer, earbuds back in and cell out. The 'rents preferred to communicate in text form when possible.

"Your mother," the dad said when he had finished, leaning in and slipping into one of his unidentifiable accents, "is half Irish and half Scottish. Half of her always wants a drink and the other half never wants to pay for it."

Andromeda gave up on the movie after a few more shouted-over maternal complaints about how "terrible" it was. She retreated to her little bedroom with her Soupy Soupy Chang Chang. (The source of this term for Lapsang souchong tea was obscure and long-forgotten, but it remained in the lexicon nonetheless.) The box from Rosalie van Genuchten contained one of Rosalie's deep red lipsticks, used, which would have looked utterly horrible on Andromeda, and a condom (not used, thank goodness). Rosalie had a strange sense of humor. She was always leaving bizarre, random items for Andromeda. "I just stopped by to drop off this" flip-flop, stapler, stick of gum, yardstick, pinecone, etc. "She'll be expecting it." In this way, the blame for the weirdness landed on Andromeda, as usual. It was an inside joke that no one got but Rosalie.

Andromeda Klein had tried as best she could to arrange her room following Marsilio Ficino's advice for decorating the dwellings of Renaissance youths, symbolically representing the heavens on the ceiling–sadly, in this case, not domed–and emphasizing the beneficial influences of Sol, Venus, and Jupiter. In this she had to be nearly as tricky and subtle as she had been in the Hidden Temple within the International House of Bookcakes, because anything too outlandish might attract the attention of the mom, who had been known to ransack and pillage a person's room when the mood struck her. So Andromeda had tacked triangles of green, gold, and blue silk on the ceiling in what she hoped was an unobtrusive arrangement. Mentally, she'd tried to imprint them with Pixie's images of the Empress, the Wheel of Fortune, and the Sun. This technique had failed to deemphasize Saturn enough to make much of an impact on Andromeda's melancholy moods, although the melancholia might well have been even worse without the ceiling. Mercury, the Moon, Mars, and Saturn (that is, the Magician, the High Priestess, the Tower, and the World) she grouped, colorless, near the closet.

When Andromeda finished her tea, she performed a quick and dirty Lesser Banishing Ritual of the Pentagram, for no other reason than to clear the air of confusion and preserve a bit of peace. It was always worth a try. Some authorities recommended vibrating the invocations in a voice like the howling wind, but as in the library, there was no way she could get away with any howling. The mom would charge in and strike, like lightning, or a cobra. Proper invocations would have to wait till she had her own dedicated temple, like that of Dame Frances in her secret underground chamber at the Warburg. So she whispered them instead, imagining how the wind chant might sound as she visualized the four columns of light.

She put on her Guillaume de Machaut CD (a recording

from the library's collection of an unearthly song cycle that helped to put her in a weedgie frame of mind). Practically everything she knew anything about, and possibly everything she cared to know about, resided in the International House of Bookcakes. *Ars nova,* or "new art," the music was called, though it was in fact seven hundred years old. Andromeda was the only person she knew who could stand it.

She seated herself on the floor with her back against the door to read from the temple book and one of the Illuminati books by the light of a single candle. This was the best position to guard against surprise mom invasions, which no banishing ritual known to science could prevent. A couple of years back, the dad had removed all the doorknobs in the house, as the first step of a door-painting project that had never gotten past the planning stages. He had never managed to replace them, meaning no door was lockable and no room was safe, not even the bathroom. As much as the mom complained about the missing doorknobs, it was a convenient domestic espionage arrangement of which she made frequent use.

Andromeda was stroking Dave with her bare feet, the candle on the floor between her knees. "Spinach U-turn, Dave," she said, "what do you think?" Dave responded with a silent meow. He had his own, unknowable cat religion, centered on the concept of unquestioning Dave worship, and like Andromeda on Right Ring Days, he was clearly a monarchist. He had an *M* of deepest black above his eyes. When he scrunched it up, as now, it turned into a *V.* Did Dave's *M* connect him to her own numerological *M,* she wondered, when he was calm, whereas the *V* of consternation shattered the connection? She had never thought of that before. She reached over and flipped through to the table in the twentieth chapter of Agrippa's *Second Book* to add up *Dave Klein:* 794, a number with no significant attribution that she could identify. *David Klein* was 802, which also could reflect 401 x 2, but she had no way to look that up at present. She really needed her own copy of *777;* the library's was missing, and the mom, during one of her manic cleaning episodes, had managed to round up and give Daisy's to the Goodwill, along with Andromeda's own extremely rare copy of *Hecate's Fountain,* which had been a gift from Daisy. She often wondered who had it, what kind of shelf it was on, and what sort of room was absorbing its weird, weird emanations.

Anyway, Dave had never been called David, only Dave.

Dave hated noises, so he got up, stretched, and padded around her to stare up at the missing doorknob when her cell phone began to vibe-ring. She had to lean and slide forward to let him out before settling back again and answering. It was Rosalie van Genuchten, calling to complain about Afternoon Tea. It had only been Rosalie and the Thing with Two Heads—that is, Siiri Fuentes and her current boyfriend, Robbie What's-his-face. No wonder Andromeda had been invited: things with two heads could be indescribably tiresome.

"Next time," said Andromeda, playing with the candle flame, "if you really want me to come, it would help if you mentioned the venue."

"It wasn't at a venue. It was at Siiri's house, duh."

"Well, I didn't know whose house," said Andromeda, deciding against trying to explain how she had meant the word *venue.* She changed tack. "I'm afraid I'm not–"

"Don't be afraid."

"What?"

"You said you were afraid and I said don't be. What could you possibly have to be afraid about?"

"What? I'm not."

"Then why did you say you were?"

"What? No, it's an expression." She was doing it again. This was actually a more coherent conversation than some she had had with Rosalie van Genuchten. "It's like 'I regret to inform you, but . . .' It's like 'I'm sorry, but . . .' "

"Well, you should be sorry. There was a Long Island iced tea with your name on it, Dromedary. It is no more. We had to feed it to the dog." There was a pause, during which Andromeda thought she could hear bong bubbles. "And by the dog, I mean Robbie. I'm just kidding." Another bubble-pause. "Anyway, it'll be my house on Thursday. A small and sensual get-together. My mom has Investment Club, and then she goes straight to Debtors Anonymous." Andromeda was aware: their moms went to the same Debt-Anon group.

"I have something I want to ask you about," continued Rosalie. "A kind of favor. I'll even give you a ride."

"What? No Jesus Truck this time," Andromeda said. "I mean it." And she did mean it. The last time Rosalie had invited her so emphatically to her house, it had been a matchmaking ploy. Rosalie, Daisy, and the rest of their friends had locked Andromeda out of the house and there had been J.T. waiting in the driveway.

"No, it's nothing like that," said Rosalie. "This will be for fun, not self-improvement."

Jesus Truck was Kevin Maloon, a mullet-headed guy from the Thing's community church. His bumper-stickered parent-purchased pickup truck was in every way the antithesis of the dad's rickety anti-everything van. Daisy's friends' low opinion of Andromeda's "dating" potential was clearly expressed in the sorts of guys they tried to push on her, always somebody's boyfriend's lamest or most insipid hanger-on. Andromeda had never seen much more of J.T. than the back of his head from a distance, but she had seen the truck and that was bad enough, even though the GENUINE PRAYER sticker, made to look like an aspirin package, was quite funny. The truck was supposed to be this huge selling point, but it didn't really do anything for her, and the Six Flags over Jesus routine was ninety percent creepy, ten percent hilarious, not quite the dream-guy formula. She wasn't all that crazy about the back of his head, either.

The hand-me-down lipstick had been simple kindness, Rosalie said, because Andromeda's lips were almost the same color as her face and whatever she was doing now, if anything, clearly wasn't working. And the . . . other item?

"What was it? Oh, yes. That's just in case you start looking hot and get yourself into trouble. I'm just kidding." Good one.

Andromeda felt sudden pressure on the door against her back. "Got to go, and I won't die," she said in a rush, and hung up. "Don't die" was Rosalie's usual way of saying goodbye, on the phone or in person.

"Is that someone on the phone?" asked the mom, pushing the door open. Andromeda's butt slid with the door along the floor. She chose her moment and slammed it shut again with her back and shoulders. One of her knees had knocked over the candle, which had gone out and had spattered an arc of tiny red beads across her leg, pinkening as they dried. She was lucky she hadn't gotten any splinters in her legs from the flooring.

"No one, it's okay," she said. She almost added a bitter "Check the bill" but stopped herself. The last thing she wanted was to make the mom think of actually checking. There was no time to arrange a decoy call from Marlyne to match it.

"How can you stand that awful, awful music," said the mom. "You shouldn't sit against dwarves like that. You'll hurt yourself. A person can't walk into their own daughter's room! Are you hiding camels in there?" She meant "lighting candles." A ribbon of smoke hung in the air, the smell quite strong. Andromeda switched off the *ars nova* and braced her back against the door till the warnings about unintended camels burning down sickle family gnomes and how interns won't cover chairlessness and negligees faded out and lost themselves amongst the faint rushing and ringing that was always somewhere in her head. She could hear the echo of Dave's claws on the wood floor as he scampered after the mom in expectation of treats.

"Traitor," she said under her breath.

A few minutes later she heard the dad's van start up and creak and rumble off, ferrying him away from what she imagined could only be Part II of whatever the mom had been lecturing him on before she had heard Andromeda's phone and interrupted herself to come by to investigate. Perhaps he had a late-night recording session–he did have those, sometimes.

Andromeda had meant to put in some time on her

Language Arts journal, but she had forgotten all about it and it was now getting quite late. She skimmed over the photocopied handout. There was, as E. M. Butler's *Myth of the Magus* made clear, a real, quite powerful magician behind the legendary figure portrayed as a kind of cartoon in the handout, and Andromeda was far more interested in this real magician than in the handout magician. In fact, she was slightly offended by how the handout's author had decided to deform this reality in order to teach a trite lesson to "young people." However, that was too complicated to get into. She wrote the following entry:

> *"Everything not forbidden is compulsory."–King Arthur handout*
> *This is from history's greatest handout,* Hi-lites from King Arthur. *It is the police state, much like my mother from Australia, who is very annoying. Most people think Hitler was German, but a little-known fact is that he was actually Australian, which explains a lot.*

It was whimsical, but too short; personally satisfying, if not gradeworthy. There wasn't much more to be said on the subject, however. She had already turned in her essay on how her bones were cursed by God to Baby Talk Barnes this year, so that was out. Being utterly unable to draw pictures that looked like anything was going to make multimedia-ing it up a little tricky. If she had had Daisy's artistic talent, she might have tried drawing a new version of the Two of Swords, the one she still held in her memory, though she realized it was false: a kneeling girl with smaller hands, a more detailed Andromeda Box behind her, and shallow pools everywhere. She could include a bicycle, and the International House of Bookcakes in the background too, perhaps, and the St. Steve–like King of Pentacles or the High Priestess with Daisy's face walking into the frame.

Just to show she'd tried, she began a sketch of what she was now thinking of as the "Two of Swords of the Mind," and what she ended up with was: something that looked like a deformed sheep with antlers and around six or seven legs. She scribbled it out, and tore out the page and crumpled it up, but not before she noticed another difference between the Two of Swords of the Mind and the version of the Two of Swords drawn by Pixie, which was that Pixie's card had a crescent moon in the background, while the moon she remembered had been more like a half-moon.

No, if she wanted to multimedia it up, she would have to cannibalize something else. She had under her bed a rather large collection of interesting found items she and Daisy had collected over the years. It had been one of their hobbies, collecting discarded shopping lists, letters, photos, doodles, and whatnot and using them to try to imagine the lives of those who had discarded them. Though Daisy had kept much of the best stuff for herself, and most of it would be unsuitable for the journal in any case, some of it might be usable. The prime candidate was material from the Emily File, a collection of drawings and other art that had been done by a previous inhabitant of the duplex. (They were unsigned, but Andromeda thought of the artist as Emily because Mr. Champlain downstairs had told her there had been a girl named Emily who had lived in their unit two tenants ago and she surmised that that would have been her.) She had found the large string-closed envelope containing them under a pallet in the carport when they had first moved in. She hadn't looked at them in a long, long time, but she remembered them being pretty good. It might be possible to paste a couple of those in the journal notebook, here or there, to pad it out. She didn't quite have the energy to dig through her underbed at the moment, however. It would wait till another time, if she got really stuck.

Even though she couldn't draw most things, she wasn't too bad at drawing sigils. So she got out A.E.'s *Book of Ceremonial Magic* and turned to the section summarizing the Goetia. She found a couple of sigils she liked from the *Lemegeton*, the Lesser Key of Solomon the Great, and copied them out as large as she could, each on its own page. The Seal of GAAP, and, in honor of the wicker girl, the Seal of AMY, a Being who is described as "a great President" and who comes first as a flame and next as a man. If these passed muster, there were seventy more Goetic Dignitaries to choose from, so if she played it right they could augment the journal pretty well for the rest of the year.

Enough homework for the night, then.

Dave was scratching at the door, so she opened it a crack to let him back in.

The weedgie mood had returned. She got out the Two of Swords again and placed it on the floor in front of her, half expecting the blindfolded girl to have resumed her kneeling position while she had been put away. But there she was again, hovering above the box, with a crescent moon in the background. What did they call it when it was a little more than half a moon? Gibbous. Best word ever. It was possible, or so the Golden Dawn taught, to transfer one's consciousness to an astral image and enter the card as through a gate, rather as she had done in her dream. She stared at the card for some time but did not succeed.

"Time to put this day away forever, Dave, don't you think?"

Dave responded with an unsympathetic stare, but he did lick her ankle.

Andromeda thought of all the tiny blindfolded, bound girls in the deck, imagined them squirming and shifting position on their cards, getting up and sitting down, even wriggling out of their bonds and leaving the frame when she wasn't looking. Or of the Page of Cups or the Hierophant wandering around throughout Pixie's tarot landscape as they had been doing in her dream, perhaps checking the blindfolds, making sure no one was peeking, maybe up to other mischief as well. She imagined the Tau-robed figure from the dream, tumbling and dancing through everybody else's scene, casting spells to control the moon and cause the tides to fall and rise. She enjoyed a brief shiver at the absurdity and the slight *ouijanesse.*

She fell asleep thinking of herself in her box, iron mask bolted in place, a girl or boy with swords in enormous hands sitting or floating on top. No way was she getting out of there.

She was awakened by a knock on the box. The Two of Swords girl had gone, apparently, or had stepped aside to allow the knocker to knock. The box's lid creaked open like a door. The hooded Tau-robed figure from the tarot dream was floating above her, with a silvery book in one hand and a kind of trumpet in the other. He blew the trumpet and sat down in a chair, and two angry men appeared before him and started yelling at each other. Then the robe fell open to reveal the heart beneath, punctured by two crossed blades; then the robed figure stuck another sword through it, down the middle, so that it looked like Pixie's Three of Swords card.

"I am the King of Sacramento," said a voice from within the robe's folds.

It was realizing that she was still asleep that woke Andromeda up.

iv.

Most magical writing is deliberately obscure, designed to hide crucial matters from the uninitiated yet reveal them to those who know how to read the texts properly. Writers of such material often include blinds, deliberate inaccuracies to fool all but those who know enough to spot them. The occult literature concerning the tarot is full of such blinds. A.E. was a master of them. Even his language itself, each sentence, comprises a dense network of interlocking subordinate

clauses and passive constructions that can be read in different ways depending on how you look at the matter. A.E.,
Andromeda believed, had been a kind of genius, but he was
a genius who could be very tiring to read and who never
seemed to mean exactly what he said and who always
seemed to be mad at everyone.

Liber K would be different, Andromeda pledged, sitting
on the toilet and leaning forward with her palms against the
door to hold it closed and prevent any interlopers. It would
betray the influence of A. E. Waite, no doubt, but unlike that
of A.E., Andromeda's prose would be notable for its lucidity.
No blinds. All revealed in language as plain as the difficulty
of the subject allowed. Millennia of error and nonsense corrected for good and all. This would ruffle feathers, naturally,
and would make her a number of dangerous enemies. But
hers would be the way of the future.

At times deftly worded phrases from this opus echoed
through her head. They would come to her in snatches, like
something blown her way by the wind. Or she would hear
their cadence in her head being spoken in an English accent.

Andromeda imagined her future self standing in the center of the octagonal subterranean hall, lecturing for an audience of hooded students on the wisdom of *Liber K*. It would
be a far different sort of world than the one she currently
occupied.

There was only one bathroom in Casa Klein, and like all
the rooms, it had a big round hole where the doorknob
ought to have been, so you could see in, and it didn't lock.
The system was, if anyone started to open the door while
the bathroom was occupied, the person inside was supposed

to call out "I'm in here." Andromeda didn't like to take chances, so she always leaned forward against the door as a precaution, with her palms over the doorknob hole in case anyone tried to look in. She imagined a boy might be able to balance on one foot while holding the door closed with the other stretched out behind him, his back blocking the view; perhaps that was how the dad did it.

Wednesday was "collaboration day" at Clearview High School. The teachers had a planning period in the morning, and first period started forty minutes late. Wednesdays were difficult at Casa Klein, because the mom and Andromeda tended to be getting ready at the same time. It was much easier to wake up early and get out of there beforehand, as Andromeda did sometimes even on Wednesdays. The sound of the mom's shoes clacking reproachfully up and down the hallway, the more distant sound of her blow-dryer cord slapping and clacking reproachfully against the wall, and of course the stream of actual reproaches that echoed through the house regardless of who might be there to hear them—it would shatter anyone's peace of mind. It was best to stay out of the way if you could.

The dad was irrelevant; he never got up before noon.

There had been no dreams or visions of any significance since the King of Sacramento had revealed himself as the figure wearing the Tau robe on Friday night. The weekend's attempts to scry with wine bottle and candle had yielded no results. She had had two shifts in the library, which she had spent catching up on her shelf-reading, working on the Sylvester Mouse list's fiction section (every bit as impressive as the 000s and the 133s), dodging Weird Gordon's sad attentions, and reading up on the Two of Swords. The Lord of Peace Restored, the Golden Dawn called it, though Mr. Crowley in his later writings disputed the "restored" part. In this view, it was best visualized as locked swords, a balance of conflicting forces, and hence a kind of peace, though an impermanent one. There was another theory that the cards in each suit in Waite's deck told a story in reverse order, and that for swords, it was a story of a murdered knight and a sister's unsuccessful attempt at revenge, leading finally to the Two of Swords, a grieving widow with swords at the ready to defend her husband's body. To Andromeda's way of thinking, this was a shallow approach, and a bit of a letdown if all the card was meant to convey was her own grieving. Of course she was grieving, and it didn't take an oracle or the trappings of a secret tradition to point it out.

Her plan for that morning before school had been to attempt to charge a dream-generating sigil, if the mom would ever finally get out of there and leave her in peace.

She looked in the mirror and wished she hadn't. Her hair didn't look too bad right after blow-drying, but the not-too-bad-ness lasted about ten minutes before it all began to degenerate, and the point of no return had been reached during the brief time she had been peeing. "You sure do sweat a lot, for a girl" was one of Rosalie van Genuchten's charming recurring observations, though she often followed it up by saying she was just kidding. It was true, anyway. It was only when Andromeda was overheated or nervous, but she was practically always overheated and nervous, and they don't make antiperspirant for your head, which was where she really needed it. She switched on the hair dryer to try to dry it again but instantly regretted it. At this stage, further styling only made it flatter. She had no time to reshampoo her hair and start over, as she might have done if she hadn't had ceremonial magic to perform. She turned away from the mirror with an exasperated, Davelike growl-sigh and threw her sweatshirt hood over her head, pulling the string taut under her chin.

"You're planning on going out in public like that?" said the mom, materializing in front of her. "Did you hear the fire engines last night? Another one of your Corona Slurpees and bastards. You really should be careful with your gambles, you could kill us all."

"What?" said Andromeda, edging past her. The mom meant "aromatherapy disasters." The police and fire department and the newspaper, like the mom, for reasons known only to themselves, preferred to blame such fires on unattended candles, though it was clear to anyone who paid attention what was really going on.

"They're meth labs, Mom," she said.

"Oh, look at you, then, Miss Meth Lab Expert," said the mom. "My streetwise daughter. Drug labs all over Clearview, is that it? You just watch the camels."

Andromeda headed to her room, deeply regretting that she was the only self she had and wishing she could conjure a better-looking, less sweaty servitor to go to school in her place and represent her in public. Crowley had probably done it all the time, and though he had tastefully refrained from boasting about it, she was sure A.E. had done it as well. How else would he have been able to read everything in the British Library's collection and copy down all the manuscripts, *and* have a wife and family, *and* be a Mason *and* run secret orders *and* indulge in wild, debauched rambles through the countryside *and* write so many books? The real A.E. stayed in the British Library reading room, and the look-alike servitors handled the rest. That had to be how it was done.

Andromeda's powers at the moment were, however, sufficient only to enable her to reach the end of the hallway and enter her bedroom without being able to make out the instructions and complaints the mom was shouting back at her as she clattered down the main stairs and finally slammed the outer door. Being a little deaf had its rewards.

Andromeda Klein waited with her back against the door till she heard the mom's car start, die, then start, die, and then start again and skid off, before she let out her breath. She had no more than an hour of peace ahead of her.

She closed the curtains on the bedroom window and drew the curtain in front of the door. She had sewn them herself out of floor-length black velvet. The room was in nearly complete darkness when they were properly closed. She lit a single white candle, wriggled out of her clothes, and put on her white silk Tau robe, another item she had sewn herself. She hung around her neck on a purple thread a lamen of parchment, depicting the current version of her personal seal in ink, a large *M* in a circle and the word *Imperfecta* spelled out in Theban characters from Agrippa's book running counterclockwise around the outside. She had been thinking of updating the seal to include the Lord of Peace Restored, i.e., the Two of Swords, in some way, if that card continued to resonate and signify her; perhaps the two crossed swords forming the *V* of her *M,* a box below and a pair of veiled eyes in the center of the *M*'s *V,* but that was something she was still working on.

Her card table became a cubic altar once she had draped it with a white silk cloth. She placed the candle and a small piece of banded agate, a type of chalcedony formed by layers of quartz, on the altar in front of her. For a pantacle, she drew out the tarot trump Justice and laid it in the center of the altar. She poured a small cup of wine from Daisy's scrying bottle and placed the bottle directly in front of the candle. At the proper distance the flame of the candle shone red-yellow-black through the bottle and appeared to float in front of it above the table. The ghost light confused the senses, and Andromeda could well imagine that a talented or well-trained scryer or astral traveler might be able to see or pass through the space between the lights, to a plane beyond this. It would be like crossing your eyes and entering the space between the overlapping images, which she was sure could be done.

Daisy had been able to scry quite impressively through the bottle, though Andromeda had never had results. But it did create a magic, weedgie mood, which was as important as anything.

After performing the Lesser Banishing Ritual of the Pentagram and consecrating the hastily constructed temple and altar, she sat down at the table and began to construct a sigil based on the motto THIS IS MY WISH TO DREAM OF THE KING OF SACRAMENTO. In modern sigil magic, the practitioner usually begins with a phrase embodying the Will, reduces it to its essence by crossing out the double letters, and forms a sigil from the remaining, unique letters. Like so much contemporary practice, this technique is merely simplified, personalized, no-frills Agrippa, but one thing in its favor is that conducting it requires no special training or education, and it is supposed to work just as well. One problem is that, because of *my* and *will* or *wish,* *M*s and *W*s are overrepresented in most such sigils, and it requires considerable creativity to distinguish the sigils from each other when you have done a great many of them. Andromeda had done dozens of sigils calling for the affection or the return of St. Steve, and they were all dominated by *V*s and *W*s, because the *S*s, *E*s, and *T*s cancel out and *V*s are rare. You weren't supposed to think about this or correct for it when formulating your phrase, or to think about the sigils or preserve them after charging them, though she retained the designs in her magical diary for future reference if necessary. Nevertheless, she had tattooed some of the good ones in a small spiral around her left leg, just below the unicursal hexagram she had done on her hip. She hadn't done a St. Steve sigil in quite some time. Realizing this made her sad, but she shook it off.

The first, conventional phrase THIS IS MY WISH TO always reduces to MYWISO. The further reduced letters for the full sigil were thus MYWDAHKG. Rearranged to a Carrollian mantra, this yielded *hwkadygm,* which she pronounced "hook-a-dime." This she chanted under her breath as she drew diagram after diagram, slowly refining the letters into a single glyph embodying her wish to encounter the King of Sacramento in a lucid or astral dream or in crystal–that is, as an image in the wine bottle's dark mirror.

She used her dedicated ritual pen and the same consecrated black ink she used for her tattoos to draw the finished sigil on a square of parchment, within a perfect doubled circle drawn with her compass.

The next step was to charge the symbol, focusing on the image and imprinting it in the deep mind. Then you were supposed to destroy the physical talisman and forget all about it, allowing it to do its work on the level of the unconscious. For the King of Sacramento dream sigil, she charged it thus: she tied her wrists together, drank the wine, intoned the mantra, and, while the square of parchment was burning in the incense burner, attached her tied wrists to her chair's lower rung with another piece of cord. Then she held her breath, looking into the wine bottle's deep, dark, multiple mysterious flames and visualizing the burning glyph's lines in flashing, lightning-colored astral hues.

Her vision became patchy and her head throbbed, and a curtain of darkness began to drop over her. Then she felt herself rising quickly and began to see color flashes with spiraling shadows that looked like faces and streaks of white-flecked green light rushing by. There was a deafening cacophony of voices, some screechy and mechanical, some resonant and burbling, till they too began to fade, as though becoming distant, and when she was far enough away from them they began to sound less harsh and threatening and chaotic and more like a kind of music.

She found herself in a sort of dreamworld. The King of Sacramento was nowhere to be seen, but the distant backdrop of yellow-brown hills and towers, of trees and shallow pools, might conceivably have been a scene drawn by Pixie. The sun shone down from between the clouds, and the rays seemed to carry the echo of music, grand and harmonious, the sound of a chorus of countless voices and trumpets, quiet and barely perceptible, reaching earth like a fine mist or a subtle color.

The earth to which it fell was quite concrete and mundane. The scene unfolded like a memory. She was four. It was her first day at the Gnome School, long ago. She had been removed from her regular kindergarten in the middle of the school year, because she had been bad and had gotten her parents in trouble by misbehaving and getting hurt. She was meeting Daisy for the first time, even though they discovered, once they became friendly, that they lived down the street from one another. They were outside the building with Teacher Joycelin, waiting to be picked up by their mothers.

"I'll be your friend if you promise to do everything I say," said Daisy.

"Okay," said the four-year-old Andromeda. She was inside her four-year-old self, seeing through those eyes, but she was also seeing the scene from some other vantage point, as though watching a movie; and she was aware of her motionless, entranced, embodied self lying still on the floor of her bedroom.

Each Gnome School kindergartener had a wispy white doll with a pointed head and no face, referred to as a Little One. Daisy threw her Little One into the parking lot, looked at Andromeda, and said, "Pick it up and give it to me."

Andromeda gave her a puzzled look but hurried to comply once Daisy repeated the command impatiently. Teacher Joycelin snatched Andromeda out of the way as a car narrowly missed her. The teacher was yelling at her, but Andromeda was watching Daisy, who was looking back at her with a blank expression. When Teacher Joycelin was through with cautioning her against running out into traffic, Andromeda rejoined Daisy, who merely shook her head and pointed to the Little One, still lying on the dusty asphalt. Andromeda retrieved it and handed it to her.

"Okay," said Daisy. "You can be my friend." But she was looking at the soiled Little One with a sad expression, so Andromeda said, "Maybe my mommy can clean it." So Daisy and Andromeda exchanged Little Ones. You were supposed to hand-wash them, but Andromeda's mother put hers through the washing machine and it ended up kind of pinkish and misshapen when it came out, and Daisy decided not to have it back. Your Little One was supposed to be like a little you, a little self to whom you told your secrets. Andromeda wondered if Daisy could hear the secrets she whispered, since she had Daisy's Little One instead of her own; but she was certain she couldn't hear any of Daisy's secrets, if indeed Daisy ever whispered any into the nonexistent ear of the faceless Little One that used to be Andromeda's. Even then, Daisy was a mystery to her.

Little Ones didn't come cheap, and Andromeda's mother shouted about it.

"We have a better house than you," Daisy said, when they went to Andromeda's house to play after school that day. She turned on her heel and briskly walked out, never looking back, but clearly confident that Andromeda would follow her. Andromeda liked her own house, but Daisy's was bigger and had more stuff in it. Back in those days Daisy's parents had been married. Her mother smiled at Daisy and Andromeda and gave them cookies, and played a game with them where they made a castle and a king and queen and knights out of wooden blocks and kitchen utensils and aluminum foil. Gnome School families were forbidden to have plastic toys or television or computers in the home. Daisy's house was full of expensive wooden toys and cushions and drapes of gentle, fuzzy rainbow colors. The Wasserstroms had put a lot of effort into the Gnome School environment, which the Kleins had not come close to matching. Mr. Wasserstrom winked at Andromeda and gave her a friendly smile and said, "What a pretty name!" when she was introduced to him when he came home from work. "My best friend in college was a Klein," he said later, walking her home. She hadn't known there were any other Kleins, and thought it might be a joke, so she laughed shyly and hesitantly. He laughed too, a warm laugh with an accompanying smile like sunshine. Her wrist and forearm were killing her on that walk back, but she tried her best to smile and be good.

He was an architect and had brought home rolls of old plans that day for Daisy to draw on, but Mrs. Wasserstrom gave him a look that Andromeda would later understand: drawing was forbidden to Gnome School kindergarteners, who weren't supposed to be exposed to the limits of the line or the color black till they were old enough to handle it. Until a certain stage of Gnomeschooling, which Andromeda never reached, you were supposed to use wet paint on wet paper, to guarantee that vague color blobs rather than representative figures would result. Andromeda was to excel at formless, vague blob art. Daisy, who could actually draw well, even as a little girl, had to do her real drawing in secret, like so much you had to do when you were in the Gnome School. Mrs. W. pulled him into the kitchen so they could have an argument about it. The Gnome School caused many arguments between Andromeda's parents too.

"Get me a drink of water," said Daisy in a haughty royal voice, holding the lemon-juicer queen and moving it from side to side and up and down as though it were speaking. Andromeda was playing the role of the tinfoil knights directed by the queen to fight each other. Andromeda dutifully went to the kitchen to get a glass of water for Queen Daisy and found Daisy's parents kissing, something she had never seen her own parents doing. She was very embarrassed. Mr. and Mrs. Wasserstrom giggled, and Mrs. W. poured out two purple plastic glasses of water from the refrigerator jug, two other things (a jug in the fridge and parental giggling) Andromeda had never seen before. When she returned with the glasses of chilled water, Daisy kept one for herself and poured the other into the fishbowl.

"Harold is thirsty too," she said. Harold was her pet fish, who didn't like the ice water and was to die shortly thereafter.

"Queen!" Daisy's shaking queen had said, meaning "I win."

When the time came for Andromeda to go home, Daisy ran up and threw her arms around her, and said, "You're my favorite favorite." She kissed Andromeda on the cheek, and was looking at her mom while she did it, and Mrs. W. smiled back at her as though she were the loveliest little angel. What her mother didn't know was that all the time, Daisy was twisting Andromeda's wrist in opposite directions behind her back, what Andromeda later learned was called an Indian burn. She was too embarrassed to cry out, plus she knew it wouldn't be appreciated, but the tears slid from her eyes, and Daisy's parents looked at her with a puzzled, pitying look, which she later grew to recognize, as many, many grown-ups would look at her in much the same way.

By nightfall her wrist and arm had swelled to double their normal size. Andromeda had to skip the following day of Gnome School to see the doctor, and when she returned the next day she had a cast, making her temporarily the most popular kindergartener in the school. "Gold star, goofy," said Daisy. "Good girl."

Wait, that wasn't right, it was the older Daisy who said "gold star" and "goofy" instead of "honey," and "good girl," not the kindergarten Daisy . . . or was it St. Steve who used to say that? Did they both used to say it? But that didn't make sense. Text-messaging and predictive-text typos hadn't even been invented yet. The timing was all off. There were two tiny birds with sharp steel beaks pecking at her head, screeching, the alternating pecks so fast they trilled and echoed.

Then the trilling metallic pecking sound was coming from outside her head, beyond thick dark curtains. She pulled them apart and pulled herself through, into her flickering room, where she found herself lying on her back on the floor. Dave had tucked himself together neatly on her chest while she was out, and was purring. The back of her head hurt where she had bumped it. She detached her hands from the chair rung and switched off the kitchen timer, which she had set for thirty minutes. This was recommended for astral travel and séances in which candles were used, just in case you lost your way wherever you were or didn't notice if a fire started. She might really have ended up as one of the mom's "Corona Slurpees and bastards."

She banished the temple, removed her robe, put away the altar, and re-dressed herself in underwear, stockings, jeans, boots, T-shirt, and black hooded sweatshirt.

Magic could be hit or miss. Sometimes it didn't seem to work at all; other times, things certainly happened, but they weren't the particular things you were going for. Still other times, as now, it was hard to say what happened. This experience was more like a memory than a dream, though it had contained details she hadn't been aware of, such as the cause of Harold's death and walking in on Daisy's parents kissing and the fact that the broken wrist, her first official breakage that she remembered very well indeed, had resulted from Daisy's Indian burn.

The dream, or vision or whatever it had been, had zipped back and forth in time, too, even though she had experienced it from within her four-year-old self as though it were happening in real time. And it had gotten all mixed up at the end. Andromeda wasn't certain how closely it squared with her actual memory, and as soon as she asked herself the question, the dream details integrated themselves with it, indistinguishable from whatever her memory had contained before. Had she really time-traveled astrally?

Whether it had been a dream or a kind of memory, the sigil magic had seemed to send her back to the past, even if it hadn't actually conjured the King of Sacramento. Not yet it hadn't, anyway. Sigils of this kind were supposed to work forgotten in the background, after all.

V.

    Anorexic.

    No ass.

    Deaf.

    Retrogressive.

    Old-lady hands.

    Maledicted.

    Evil.

    Demon girl.

    A strange child.

Ambivalent.
Nondescript.
Dire.
Reticent.
Odd duck.
Malformed inner core.
Ectomorph.
Drunkard.
Addicted to love.

Language Arts the previous day had been devoted to poems called acrostics, in which each line was to begin with the first letter of your name, and Andromeda was working on the assignment in her head on her way to school. Clearview High School was very acrostics-focused, she realized, now that she knew the word for it. The school motto, displayed on banners in the quad and recited once a day during the KCHS announcements, was T.E.A.C.H. (Teamwork, Effort, Achievement, Citizenship, Hard work hard work hard work!)

Did they realize, or did they care, that they gave high school students and second graders the same assignments? In high school, of course, the "poems" no longer had to take the shape of an ice cream cone. And they were now organized by theme: the first was supposed to be how the world saw you, and number two was how you saw yourself. Andromeda Klein wasn't so sure there was that much of a difference, nor was she sure she could turn these in, in the end. She didn't want to get dinged for negativity or reported to the authorities for being a sociopath or a noncomformist.

There was no rain today, but the sky had remained a reassuring deep gray all week. You were supposed to greet the sun and perform a brief solar ritual four times a day, as prescribed in *Liber Resh,* but she had let that slide since Daisy's death, and almost always forgot. In the days of the Ninety-threes at their most observant she and Daisy used to keep up with it fairly well, though Daisy usually abbreviated it to her own taste and would often simply grab Andromeda's hand, drag her to an open area, and shout "Resh!" and jump around. Everyone looked at them like they were crazy, which was part of why Daisy did it, the main reason, perhaps. These days Andromeda could summon very little enthusiasm for the sun and its poisonous, accursed rays. This attitude nullified whatever spiritual effect reshing might have had, she was pretty sure, but now that she thought of it, and in honor of Daisy more than for any other reason, she glanced eastward and muttered a desultory "Hail to thee who art Ra in thy rising."

You couldn't miss the burned building from the fire overnight. The top-floor, corner window of a small, two-story apartment building at the end of the block had been blown out. The whole corner was blackened and obviously destroyed inside, but the building still stood and the rest of it seemed relatively unaffected. A pile of half-burned timber and trash was on the street. The sour smell of wet ash and charcoal was overwhelming. Andromeda thought she could smell Daisy underneath it, so she stopped to sniff, but then it was gone.

She noticed, caught in the branches of a tree across the street from the building, a charred paperback book, which appeared to have been blown there through the window by the force of the explosion. Strangely enough, it happened to tip and fall into her bicycle basket as she stood looking up at it, straddling her bike on tiptoe, and the only visible word on what remained of the cover was *Tower*. Nice synch, Universe, thought Andromeda Klein. A bit heavy-handed, wouldn't you say? The Tower is a form of the Hebrew letter *peh*, which means "mouth," and the black, empty window certainly looked like one, gaping and stinking too.

"Call the police ☺." Too late for that. Here was one part of the Daisy dream replicated almost perfectly in real life, a burnt-out upper floor with a burnt book falling out of it. She looked around for other elements but could discern none. Daisy as an antidrug crusader from beyond? That seemed very unlikely. Still, stumbling on a real live Tower was nothing to take lightly. The singed title page of the book revealed it to be *The Black Tower* by P. D. James, a mystery, and the bar code on the back revealed that it was in fact from the International House of Bookcakes collection. How strange to imagine a methamphetamine manufacturer curling up with a cozy P. D. James novel, blown to bits just before the killer's identity was revealed.

She pushed off and pedaled. She had to stop by the ATM on her way to school. Everyone else drove. The school wasn't far from her house, but if she'd had a license and a car like everyone else she'd have driven too. Both of Andromeda's driving tests had ended with her driving into a hedge; the first time had been accidental, because she had been in the dad's jerky van and couldn't quite control the acceleration, while the second had been deliberate, because even though she had been in Rosalie's mom's more reliable car, she had wanted to end the test–the DMV man had been obnoxious and insulting and had tried to look up her skirt, she was sure, even though he had also made malicious observations about how skinny her legs were. She had panicked, and suddenly: a hedge had appeared, a different one this time. "You need a few more lessons," he had said dryly, failing her. "And a thicker skin."

Everyone was always telling her to "lighten up" after hassling her.

The third and final time, so far, that she had driven a car into a hedge had been at the wheel of St. Steve's Plymouth Gold Duster, and that had been because she had been nervous and scared and excited and sad all at the same time and because some force beyond her control had diverted her attention at an inopportune moment and placed a hedge in her way. Clearview was all hedges. It was amazing they didn't cause more accidents.

She got forty dollars out of the ATM. Then she had to turn back halfway up the hill and dig through the trash because she realized that she had thrown the money away and put the receipt in her bag rather than the other way around. Head explosion sound. Had the world ever known a bigger, more comprehensively idiotic idiot?

✳ ✳ ✳

The name "St. Steve" was a classic Andromeda Klein misheard utterance that got stuck in the lexicon.

He was the only person she had ever met who seemed to appreciate the lexicon as much as she did. Most people rolled their eyes or smiled weakly when she tried to involve them, though it was true that several of the lexicon's terms had made it into the Klein family vocabulary after years of repetition. With St. Steve, though, it was effortless. It was amazing how little work she had to do when he was around. By the end of their first evening at the Old Folks Home, they had already acquired several other terms besides "St. Steve." She told him a few preexisting ones; some came up naturally; soon he joined in and created some himself, which was an amazing thing that no one had ever thought of doing before. He'd had her almost completely figured out, she realized later, after a single conversation.

"I need to use the bathroom," she had said.

"What?" he said, pulling his hair behind his ear just as she always did when she said that. "The vacuum?" From then on, just between them (though also in her own mind), any bathroom was a vacuum. Or sometimes it would be an ashram, or a mushroom.

Andromeda had tried to explain it to Daisy without revealing who she was talking about, yet had been unable to conceal her enthusiasm.

"Vacuum," Daisy had said. "Mushroom." Then she stared at Andromeda for a long, long time, expressionless, as though carefully composing her response. Then she tilted her head slightly, and her face softened into a beatific smile.

"That," she said brightly, "has got to be the gayest thing I have ever heard in my life."

They laughed so hard they both fell over.

She never mentioned the St. Steve lexicon to Daisy again, however. And with great difficulty she suppressed the impulse to explain, to boast, about how St. Steve looked like the younger A. E. Waite, and how his initials were actually A.E., and how his baseball cap had had an *I* on it, suggesting the Roman numeral one at the top of the Magician card, and how his true name in Agrippa's Latin gematria added up to 1234.

But Andromeda for once kept her wits about her and the details to herself, and managed to leave the impression that this mysterious stranger with "item" potential happened to be a boy of their own age, from another school, passably good-looking, good at conversation, and kind enough to indulge some of Andromeda's eccentricities, such as the lexicon. She did say his name was Steve, which Daisy lengthened to Steven whenever she mentioned him, conveying a vague sense of derision. "Is *Steven* at least cute?" she had asked.

"He's okay," said Andromeda. "Cute" was not how you'd describe St. Steve. Andromeda might have said "handsome" except that she would have been ridiculed, and she doubted any of the Rosalie girls would have been charmed by the mustache, so she said only "okay." The ridicule took the form of a recurrent joke, begun by Daisy and soon taken up by Rosalie and even, it could be argued, by Andromeda's own mother, that Andromeda had an imaginary boyfriend. This was a convenient way to keep the secret, and Andromeda reinforced the misapprehension at times by making similar jokes herself, even though she didn't much care for the implication that attracting a mate was so obviously beyond plausibility where she was concerned. But Daisy was no fool, and she was certainly not fooled, despite how good she was at *Steven* jokes.

The vacuum lexicon, an important cross-referenced

appendix to the main Andromeda lexicon, expanded over time. At its best it was a spoken code only the two of them could understand. It had developed without premeditation, on its own. In a similar spirit, they would consistently choose the incorrect option, technically known as a typo, when texting. "Of" was always to be read as "me." A "headacid" was a headache. Andromeda hadn't been able to resist telling Daisy about all the puppy jokes, and Daisy had conceded that that was marginally less lame than "mushroom," and was even interested enough to quiz her on other meaningful typos, but Daisy wasn't interested enough to join in when Andromeda tried to typo-text her. That was okay, though. The predictionary was better as just a St. Steve–Andromeda thing.

The only rule was Rule P. *P* was short for *PSDTN,* which was short for "p.s.: destroy this note." She was to delete each message after she read it, no exceptions. Andromeda had more or less obeyed Rule P too, except for that last "hi there" message and one other transgression. There were some messages that meant too much to her to lose forever. These she had dutifully deleted from her phone, but–and this was a transgression even though it didn't technically break Rule P– she had also written some of them in a notebook, disguised as a poem entitled "Preto," beginning with "hex acad" and ending with "loud wa," which was the closest St. Steve had ever come to saying he loved her. She had even included this "poem" in her Language Arts journal earlier in the year, with no one the wiser, not least Baby Talk Barnes, who had given her double points on it and written *More like this, please* in the margin. More like this, please, indeed. And how.

As for "St. Steve"?

"I'm a St. Steve guy," he had said, when the subject of his almost supernatural ability to pick up on her thoughts and moods came up that first night.

"What?" she said, realizing almost immediately that he had meant "sensitive." He was joking, but it was true in a way all the same. He probably would have been a good scryer or tarot reader, a thought that was rather amusing. He was especially good at reading her, knowing her concerns and worries almost before she understood what she was implying when she tried to express them. No one had ever seemed to understand her so well, and certainly no one had ever seemed so interested in giving it a shot. Most people, pretty much everyone, even the few-and-far-between boys who had pursued her for whatever reason from time to time, gave up on that in advance. Somehow, it was always assumed that she was the deficient one who had to shape herself up to meet the other's standards, something she accepted even as she resented it, and at which she was rarely even close to successful.

When she and St. Steve were together, they were, she felt, a functioning system; he was an ally who knew what he was getting into and didn't mind; she felt calm and clear-headed, filled with a sense of purpose and vibrating beneath her skin—all things that had been unfamiliar to her before.

But of course, she hadn't been calm and clear-headed, not in the least. She had been in a desperate panic, in fact, and spent a great deal of her time consumed with fear that she would lose him. From almost the first time she spoke to him, that fear was hovering, and it had in the end proven to be justified; reverse "what would happen if" magic again, perhaps. The calm, clear-eyed Andromeda she remembered was more a potential Andromeda, an ideal, the one she thought of when she imagined some future time when the uncertainty and complications would vanish somehow, leaving only the vibrating happiness and sense of purpose—which had been genuine enough.

In real life, his sensitivity and understanding of her was the worst part. The sudden disappearance, the period of radio silence, and then the strange, almost cruel spate of maddeningly bland messages following the silence that had seemed to offer hope but that had come to nothing—he would have known how much she was suffering, and obviously, he didn't care. "Hi there," for gods' sake.

Andromeda was so caught up in thinking about St. Steve that she rode right past the school. There really should be some kind of law against thinking while biking: it's a public menace.

Empress plus two other girls and two boys were sitting on the bike rack, blocking the empty slots. Candy, sugary drinks, and all junk food were forbidden on Clearview High School's grounds at all times in order to HELP THE STUDENT BODY STAY IN SHAPE, as one of the signs in the main lobby put it. And as the dad was apt to point out in his tirades about the War on (Some) Drugs, as soon as something is forbidden, a black market immediately pops up, creating crime where there once was none, and providing a pretext for state oppression of individuals. "Ban Tinker

Toys," he would say, "and you'll wind up chasing Tinker Toy dealers out of the park and fishing the corpses of Tinker Toy victims out of the bay." Then he would patiently explain what Tinker Toys were–round wooden blocks with holes that you put sticks into, a real Gnome School type of toy. Then he would give another example, like "Ban pizzas, and..." PREVENT FOREST FIRES–REGISTER MATCHES was one of his van's oldest stickers, the one that had gotten him barred from the Gnome School parking area when some other parents complained, not wanting their children exposed to such a message. Plus, the van was ugly. Everybody else's parents had much nicer cars. He had had to park down the road when he picked her up from then on. Another of his van's mottoes was LEGALIZE BREATHING. These people were only proving his point, he was fond of saying.

Most schools with a candy ban have at least one student who fills the gap by selling candy and soft drinks at a slight profit over the 7-Eleven price, and at Clearview High School, Empress was it. Andromeda had nothing against Empress but stayed out of her way because she shied away from large groups and Empress was always at the center of a crowd. Andromeda stood in front of the bike rack, waiting for the girl to Empress's left to move aside for her.

"I need to lock my bike," she said at last, finding herself unable to make eye contact with the big, immovable girl in front of her, though she did try. High school survival skill #1: Learn to avoid eye contact, which may be regarded as provocative, without appearing to be trying to avoid eye contact, which may also be regarded as provocative.

"If you want me to move out of your way," said the girl sitting on the rack in front her, "you can just ask me. You don't have to–" Andromeda didn't catch what she didn't have to do, but the phrase ended with what sounded like ". . . a toe-ass butter-sucking fish . . ."

"What?" said Andromeda instinctively, pulling her hair and hood back from her ear.

The girl grabbed her by the chin and pulled her face up and stared Andromeda in the eye.

"What? What?" she said, mimicking her. "Here's *what,* Concentration Camp. Next time you want something, you can ask for it respectfully like a person and not just stand there like some sucking . . ." Andromeda missed that, too, but it also seemed to involve a fish. The girl released her face. She could still feel the impression of those fingers and their sharp nails. The boys and the other girl were laughing. Andromeda's face was bright red, she could feel it.

Empress came over from where she had been dispensing Bubblicious to a couple of freshmen and said, "Hey now, leave her alone. KK's all right, aren't you, KK?" She was smiling a broad "such commotion is bad for business" smile straight out of a movie about the mob. It took Andromeda a second to realize that "KK" referred to her–"Concentration Camp," apparently a testament to how Empress couldn't spell and a reference to Andromeda's skinny body, which seemed to make everyone so angry or concerned or condescending or hostile, depending on temperament. Was that her new name now? It was even worse than Anorexia Klein. "Come on, Drommie, you're sorry, aren't you?" Drommie. Trismegistus.

Andromeda was not in the least sorry for anything but having bothered to get up that morning.

"Well, I do not accept her apology," said Bike Rack, but she sullenly got off the rack and began to fumble around in her backpack, mumbling something else that Andromeda couldn't catch. All other girls seemed to hate Andromeda. All of them except Empress, who seemed to love everybody. She had a glittery heart on her shirt to prove it too.

"I'll see you later at your spot, KK," said Empress, meaning the area where Andromeda and Rosalie and company ate lunch. Rosalie was one of Empress's favorite customers because she bought large quantities and even tipped sometimes.

"And you might want to find somewhere else to park your bike. Lacey's having a bad day. You still riding that thing? You need to get horizons, or a boyfriend to drive you around. . . ." She meant "your license." Everyone was always saying that. "You should get a tattoo of *that*," said Altiverse AK, "on your nonexistent ass."

Lacey. The most inapt name in history, second only, perhaps, to that of Andromeda Krystal Klein herself.

The bell rang and Empress and Lacey and the others began a lugubrious, slouching march to the school steps.

Maybe she should have taken Empress's advice and parked her bike somewhere else, but the slot was there, now unguarded, so she pushed her front wheel into the groove and snapped and locked the lock.

She went to the girls' vacuum to wash her face and was horrified by what she saw, as usual. Lacey's fingers had left scratches and a bruise on her cheek. Attempting to cover the marks with makeup was so pathetic that she couldn't even bring herself to try. She pulled her hood and hair around her face and hoped for the best.

"A.E.," she said, louder than she intended. "Trismegistus." Then: "Jesus Christ."

A voice from a stall shushed her. One of those godbotherers, as the dad called them. They were everywhere. "That's how you know Clearview is hell," Altiverse AK said to her reflection, not sure whether it was one of the dad's jokes or if she had made it up. "Because there are so many damned Christians in it."

✳ ✳ ✳

Andromeda managed to make it through the whole day up to lunch without crying at all, which was something of a marvel. She was a year behind most of the girls in Rosalie's crowd, and no one in her own classes paid her much heed, thank goodness. But after fourth period she found she just couldn't face Rosalie and Empress, and, gods forbid, Lacey, so she spent lunch period by herself in the coffee place by the Safeway. It was a Right Ring Day, so she was a carnivore. She stared at the sandwiches in the display counter—turkey, chicken salad, tuna, roast beef—but as usual couldn't bring herself to get one. She'd already been through quite a lot, and decided not to make it worse by subjecting herself to the ordeal of choking down a hunk of slimy meat.

Outside food and beverages were not allowed, but she sank into the puffy blue armchair and hunched over her Tupperware container and ate her hummus-filled pita bread and a radish and no one complained.

After eating, she used the Two of Swords as a significator for a tarot spread on the shiny blond wood coffee table in front of her. Once again, the High Priestess, the King of Pentacles, and several other Swords cards were present, and the Magician was in the tenth position, "the outcome"; the Tower was "crossing" her, and Ace of Cups "covered" her, which was about as schizophrenic a juxtaposition as there could be. Her perspective was getting warped by all the synchs: she had to make a real effort not to see the High Priestess as Daisy, the King of Pentacles as St. Steve, and the Magician as the King of Sacramento. The little white booklet wasn't much help. She needed access to the resources in the International House of Bookcakes to interpret it, or anything, properly.

She slunk in late to Language Arts. Baby Talk Barnes said nothing but raised an eyebrow. Most teachers made her sit in front because of her hearing issues, but not Baby Talk, which was a great mercy. Amy the Wicker Girl was standing in front of the class reading one of her acrostic poems; Andromeda was unable to make out most of it, but the *B* in *Bellinger* was "bangin'," which earned a big laugh and some "yow's" from the class, and a look of mock reproach from Mr. Barnes. Andromeda had the sense that she would be called on and was sweating in dread of it, but there were short periods that day, so she was spared the ordeal of having to say "ectomorph" and "no ass" while facing twenty-five pairs of hostile, uncomprehending eyes. Mr. Barnes, she had believed, would accept the self-deprecation and the ironic, resentful spirit in which she intended it, but for the students it would just be giving them more ideas. She had had no idea that recitation was to be part of the assignment; next time, she decided, she would choose random, totally unrelated and neutral words: Anniversary, New Jersey, Door, etc. Some people loved being the center of attention, but it was hard to see why. Just being stared at seemed to raise Andromeda's body temperature several degrees, causing her brain to short-circuit and flattening her already quite flat hair. Thank goodness that threat at least was over.

vi.

Her bike lock cable had been cut and lay on the ground, a dead blue snake with a lock head. The bicycle itself was nowhere to be seen.

"My bike," she said, and that was when she started crying, finally. Empress had warned her and she should have listened.

Andromeda had never felt so action-populated in her life. There was potentially a great deal of power in such a mental state, and she knew that if she were disciplined enough to spark it and control it and direct it, it could be used to manifest powerful magical effects. What would happen if she were to attempt a magical operation in this state? a small part of her mind, distant from the rest of it, wondered.

And something happened.

According to Bonewits, subtle results cannot be expected from the hate spells of a beginner; if you wish to harm someone, say, a girl named Lacey, by magic, you might as well make up your mind to kill her. Lacey. She wouldn't know how to begin, and she had no tools, no ritual materials. By the time she got to a suitable temple location, at home, or at the library, or in the water tower or the bell tower of the closed-down high school, the feeling would have passed. You can't preserve mental states for later use, or at least, Andromeda could not, though theoretically a sigil or talisman might help to achieve such an effect, storing the magical energy like a battery. A skilled magician could deftly slip into an inner plane and construct a temple and tools out of astral matter and take care of it right away. How was she going to get home?

The sun was behind thick clouds, and even what light there was had to travel through the redwood and eucalyptus and oak branches hanging over the footpath. They seemed to grow taller and thicker and denser, and the sky assumed a darker shade. She felt a swirling sensation. She felt a throbbing in her head and legs. She felt a twisting, a rising, with a rushing sound.

The last thing she remembered thinking consciously before she dissolved into it was: So this is it, this is magic.

The spell was happening all on its own. Once again, as she had in the transition from state to state in the sigil trance that morning, Andromeda heard the great clatter of voices jabbering nonsense, shrieks that sounded like metal scraping and nails being ripped from boards, an incredible, ugly, overwhelming cacophony echoing through her head and through the Universe, sounds she could almost feel. They swarmed over her like insects, and did not fade into music as before. She saw a pinpoint of shimmering darkness that widened into a kind of tunnel, dark green and flashing, with a transparent lightning-colored cube at its mouth.

Then her mouth, beyond her control, formed the words she heard in her head:

"Hekas hekas este bebeloi . . ."

The swirling stopped, and the throbbing ebbed and died and the cube and tunnel collapsed and her mind spiraled back to the size of a human girl's brain and with it the expanded world.

She realized she'd had her eyes closed tightly, because they hurt when she suddenly opened them and because the light was so bright; there were people staring at her, so she must have been doing something to attract their attention; and her throat hurt, so she must have been shrieking the incantation amidst all the other shrieking.

There were six or seven people staring, puzzled, seemingly frozen in time, until she spoke.

"Someone took my bike," she said. The frozen people began to move again, as though they were paused on video and someone had pushed Play. No one was the least bit interested in her or her missing bike, now that the spectacle was over. They were whispering, laughing, cackling amongst themselves.

"A.E.," she said dejectedly. "Resh." She was worn out.

When she looked toward the spot where the sun ought to have been, around twenty degrees from the western horizon, she noticed something hanging a bit higher, so she looked up and saw the bike. How had they gotten it up there? It was dangling precariously from its front wheel, which had been lodged in a fork of an oak branch. The rest of it was swaying in the wind. If it fell, it would be wrecked.

A couple of boys from the basketball courts helped her. You could never tell whether people were going to be nice or not, whether they were going to ridicule you or sympathize or just walk by. And boys could be incredibly mean and harsh, especially to people who didn't look like models. But these ones were all smiles, and seemed to enjoy showing off their tree-climbing and bike-rescue talents.

"Someone must really hate you," said the one who had scrambled up the tree. He detached the wheel from the branch and carefully lowered the bike down to the other one, who held it by the back wheel and caught the rest of it when it swiveled down. He presented it to her and bowed, which was cute. It seemed in decent shape, though the front wheel looked slightly out of true. At least they hadn't vandalized it.

The other boy hung from the lower branch and dropped down heavily.

"Like 'em hunky," he said.

"What?" she said. "Oh right, yes, like a monkey."

They were being so nice, she didn't know how to react.

These boys were not her sort, to the degree that she had a sort. They were like aliens.

"Thanks," she finally said, and did her best to smile back at them. The smile wouldn't, it just couldn't, come. Back at home, and with Daisy, appreciation or greeting was sometimes expressed with a Dave salute, the hand held up as a claw and then closed. She instinctively did this in lieu of a smile and realized how stupid it looked only after she had already done it. They were confused but still smiling at her. How could any non-insane people smile that much?

One of them seemed to be staring at her nonexistent chest.

"Teenage Head," said one, "what's that?" Andromeda's sweatshirt zipper was undone and she was wearing one of the dad's old T-shirts that she had rescued when the mom had packed them up to give to Goodwill. Most of them were very old and far too small for him to wear, but he had seemed really sad when he'd noticed them missing. Not least of the reasons she liked wearing them was that it irritated the mom so much. This one said TEENAGE HEAD, which would have to be a band, or a software company, or a restaurant.

"It's my dad's," she said. One of the boys raised an eyebrow at that.

This was perhaps why it was so often said that practical magic of any kind can be dangerous for the neophyte. Not so much because of what you can do or manifest, but because whatever it is, is hard to control when you lack understanding, and because true understanding is so hard to achieve. What had happened by the bike rack under the trees was a kind of magic, if anything was. Now that Andromeda had recovered from her shock and had her bike back, she was certain that, though she would very much enjoy it if Lacey were to feel her wrath in some manner, she did not actually want Lacey dead. And that if she were to discover that her spell actually had killed Lacey somehow, she would be dismayed. Not overwhelmingly dismayed, perhaps; but it would add greatly to her worries, which were already too heavy. All she needed was two angry dead people on her back instead of only one. And she disliked the idea of tainting her magic by association with Lacey. She should attempt, at least, to preserve such magic for higher things. How to do it, though, when everything is so utterly beyond your control? The answer must lie in training and discipline, of course, as all experts said, though till now she had not perhaps fully realized why they said that.

Lacey had left a note wedged in her bicycle basket, which was why the monkey boy had said that someone must really hate her: *fucken bitch constantration camp,* it read. Not good, as the dad might say. "Learn to spell, at least," said Altiverse AK, fortunate at that moment that there was not an Altiverse Lacey around to clobber it or sit on it or something.

The magic appeared to have been set off inadvertently by her agitated mood. Had she been in control, and with the proper protection and weapons, she might have entered the cube and passed through the tunnel, learned what she was meant to learn, and conducted a ceremony or operation astrally while in the alternate plane. Skilled magicians did this all the time, but in the event, she had only caught a brief glimpse of it and moreover had had no idea what sort of world or plane it might have led to.

The *hekas hekas* incantation was not one she usually used, but it was Golden Dawn, she was pretty sure. Why had she intoned it? Or shrieked it, rather. It seemed like she had shrieked it. Her throat still hurt.

Andromeda Klein stopped by the bike shop to get a new lock, one they told her would be very difficult to cut or crack. Ness was a good guy who often fixed her bike for free. If Andromeda had been the kind of girl who could pick and choose which guys to attract, and if she had been in the market for another impossible, unattainable boyfriend, he was one she might have chosen. He was tall and not bad-looking, and dressed reasonably well, and often wore decent rather nice clunky leather shoes even in the shop, in sharp contrast to the slovenly ragamuffin guys who worked for him. There was nothing fiery or deep about him, but he was kind and well groomed, two incredibly rare qualities.

"Your front whale's spit out," said Ness, meaning the wheel in front was a bit out of true, and he offered to fix it when she had more time. He also gave her a great deal on the heavy-duty U-shaped lock.

Despite the day's trouble and the extra stop, Andromeda Klein arrived at the International House of Bookcakes with twenty minutes to spare before her shift began. She locked her bike to one of the breezeway poles and rushed straight past Marlyne to the 133s without pausing to hear today's review of her appearance.

"Her" section was looking a little ragged. It had been

several days since she had tidied it up. There were quite a few empty spaces, familiar colors and shapes missing from the shelves. Of course, the Sylvester Mouse list, that was it. Someone must have pulled more while she was off. *True and Faithful* was still up there on the top shelf with the over-sizeds, but a quick inspection revealed that the library's edition of Dee's *Five Books of Mystical Experience* was now missing. It must have been added to the list—it was certainly unlikely that anyone had checked it out.

She pulled a few books and retreated to a semiprivate table behind Reference to study them. There were several things she wanted to check.

Dr. Regardie confirmed that *hekas hekas este bebeloi* was Golden Dawn, a banishing formula known as the Cry of the Watcher Within, adapted from the Greek Eleusinian Mysteries; it means "away, away, profane spirits," the equivalent of the more familiar *apo pantos kakodaimonos* or the *procol, O procul este profani* of the Star Ruby, for example.

As best she could analyze it, then: the magic by the bike rack had begun, sparked spontaneously by her action-populated state of mind, and a wave of hate had somehow formed itself into a directed force; a gateway to somewhere had opened; she had heard the voices of the entities or agents or spirits from within and beyond the gate. And then, for some reason and by some means, she had uttered the Greek banishing formula, which had in fact banished the voices, the gateway, and the directed magical wave of ill will, leaving everything deflated and inert. So had the magical state itself been caused by profane spirits? If so, what a successful use of banishing, and far simpler than that of an entire formal ritual. Or had it been something inside her, some buried part of her will, that had called the magic into being, had opened the gateway, had constructed a kind of magical bomb, only to deactivate it at the last moment, as though two parts of herself were at war with one another, canceling each other out in the end?

It was confusing. She had never opened a gateway before. It was hard to know what to think.

Crowley, Regardie, Dion Fortune, and Agrippa had nothing to say regarding any King of Sacramento.

She had put away the books and scanned herself in before it struck her that the unintentional magic under the oak tree might well have arisen from, or been instigated by, her sigil magic of that morning. If so, it had been one hell of a powerful sigil, to manifest a dreamworld in the waking world; and if so, the King of Sacramento might well have been involved, though she had not seen him.

He couldn't possibly be the state's governor somehow, could he? That would really make no sense.

✳ ✳ ✳

Gordon was leaving, thank gods. It had been a hard day. She didn't have the strength to smile weakly at him all through the shift. She just didn't.

It occurred to Andromeda that she hadn't thought to turn her phones on since the morning school switch-off. She turned on the red mom phone and saw that there were zero voice mails and seven text messages. Menu-Up-Select-Txts-down-down-down-Select-down-down-Select-Delete-Yes. That was the formula for Delete Unread, and she could do it with her eyes closed and without thinking, which was pretty much how she did it just then. Then she realized what she had done on automatic pilot and undeleted the unread messages to check, just to make sure the house hadn't burned down or anything. No messages from St. Steve (UNAVAILABLE) on the other phone, as usual. She redeleted the mom messages, sighed, and cursed herself for being an idiot.

Gordon was pulling his jacket on as she came back into the back room.

"There you go," he said. "That's not so hard, is it?"

It took Andromeda nearly a second to realize that these condescending, encouraging words were not directed at her to congratulate her on a successful entrance into the break room. He was talking to his sleeve, praising it for its success in going all the way up his arm to his shoulder, leaving the hand exposed at the other end.

He looked up at Andromeda, and the next thing he said was to her, not his own clothing. At least, she was pretty sure it was to her.

"You look nice today."

She smiled weakly. Okay, he's on drugs again, she thought. Maybe he had been talking to his jacket after all. No way on *earth* could she look nice, by any measure. Marlyne said if Andromeda would give him the time of day he'd be over the moon and all over her. It was really a shame he was such an unappealing goofball who wore mandals. Even if he were to clean himself up a little, or a lot, she'd never be able to forget them.

"Where are the Sylvester Mouse carts?" she asked. She was returning the rather rare first issue of *S.S.O.T.B.M.E.;*

Euclid's *Elements,* books one and two; and *Shadows of Life and Thought,* A. E. Waite's memoirs, all of which had been on the list, and had them out of her bag ready to file them amongst the others. For all her admiration for A.E., she had never gotten around to reading *Shadows* all the way through. She had studied only the pages on the tarot, which were difficult and obscure enough. She felt she owed it to his memory to wade through the entire book, and she was sure there were great truths hiding in the convoluted, cranky, scolding language, as there always were; but now it was needed by Sylvester Mouse, for some as-yet-unspecified reason.

Gordon was staring at her, trying to reverse-engineer *Sylvester Mouse* to trace it to its misheard original form. He got them sometimes.

"The whatie whats?" said Gordon, finally.

"The, you know, the carts. We're pulling books from the list?" The three Sylvester Mouse carts were no longer tucked along the wall in the break room with DO NOT SHELVE signs taped to them.

"Well, the carts are over there," said Gordon, breaking into a song, "but the books are gone. The carts are over there, but the books are gone. . . ." He stopped the chant when he noticed Andromeda's mouth beginning to form itself into one exceedingly thin line. "They packed them up this morning, I think. But there's still more list to go. Lots more." He pointed and she saw it, a new chunk of list in her mail slot with her time sheet. So that was what she'd be doing tonight. She was looking forward to it. It sure beat shelf reading.

"So they packed up the books," she said. And then, before

he could burst into song again, she quickly added: "Lots of good books there. What are they for, do you know? No one seems to know." Some important Foundation or other wanted them for a class on the World's Great Works of Esoterica, maybe, or there was going to be a display at Central of Wonderful and Unusual Featured Finds from the County Collection—something like that.

"They're for reading," said Gordon.

"What?" she said. "Oh." Humorous.

"Damned witty," said Altiverse AK.

"Yeah, of course they're for reading. . . ." Andromeda paused. Then it dawned on her what he had meant to say. A tiny droplet of disquiet opened into a limitlessly wide and deep ocean of pain. "Weeding? *Weeding?*" she said. "Weeding?"

"Yes," said Gordon, more befuddled even than usual. "Weeding. What did you think it was? Don't you read your e-mails?"

"Weeding?" she whimpered.

In fact, Andromeda rarely read any of her e-mail, figuring what was the point now that Daisy and St. Steve were gone. She had deleted most of her accounts and all of her Web sites, too, when she had realized there was a strong chance that her mother had been reading them. There was a library account, and a library staff Web site you were supposed to check, but it wasn't something Andromeda was in the habit of doing and she hadn't, she now realized, done it for some time.

She stood motionless in front of Gordon with a look of horror on her face as he explained.

"They're weeding the collection to make room for more multimedia," he said. "It's never been done at this branch."

"Yes," she said, and Altiverse AK added: "Of course it hasn't. That's why it's such a good collection!"

There was a lump in her throat, which was the only thing that prevented her from shouting those words. "Don't melt down," said Altiverse AK quietly, "just don't." She was trying not to. At this rate, there would be a gateway opening any moment, she could feel it.

It was a small building, Gordon went on, quoting the e-mail from memory, and an underutilized branch. The system regarded it as superfluous, and there had been talk of closing it down entirely, but the current plan was to "modernize" the collection and refocus on more popular titles and items like DVDs and magazines and workstations for accessing the Internet and digital files.

The resulting plan, explained in the staff newsletter and sent to everyone's mailbox: Every book that hadn't been checked out in the last eighteen months was to be pulled, discarded, and sold by the Friends of the Library. They were updating their usual sales methods by holding an online auction instead of the usual rummage sale for the more valuable titles.

"Friends!" was all she could say, thinking of three carts full of excellent, hard-to-come-by titles that had already gone, never to return, and the sinister "Friends" of the Library who were collaborating in the book purge. Many of the books already pulled were quite rare, and some nearly unique, and would fetch high, high prices–the real reason, certainly, that the "Friends" of the Library were so eager to sell them. *Magick Without Tears!* It was priceless. She would never be able to afford many of them, and perhaps not any, if it came to that. Obviously, staff-checking didn't count as a checkout in the eighteen months; otherwise, a great many of the books would have been spared, as she'd staff-checked them many times.

She allowed herself a rueful snort. She had been so impressed by the list. What a wonderful choice of titles! Well, of course they were great titles: they were the ones no one ever checked out! The popular dreck, the wicker, the self-help, the sleazy novels were there to stay, of course. On that basis, the collection weeded itself. If they left it up to the patrons of this branch, all they'd have left would be romance novels and Civil War alternative histories and self-help and large-type and books on tape. Wasn't the library supposed to be better than that, better than the lowest and most geriatric common denominator?

It was Altiverse AK who said that, but Andromeda herself asked a form of this final question aloud in a kind of despairing hiss, and Gordon finally seemed to realize that she was not pleased with the situation, though he appeared to have no idea why.

"Are you okay?" he was saying, but she had already snatched the list from her mailbox and zombied out of the room to find Darren Hedge.

✳ ✳ ✳

"It's beyond our control," said Darren Hedge wearily. "No need to get hysterical." He had the look of a man who devoutly wished someone else had his shift that day.

"Take your break," he told her, when it became clear that hysteria, there and then in front of the reference desk, might well materialize.

He met her out in the breezeway.

"Don't you read your e-mail? I thought you were taking this too well."

"It's not the books' fault nobody uses this library."

"That's the problem," said Darren Hedge. "We're actually lucky. The family who donated this building to the city stipulated that it had to be preserved intact and used only as a public library, or else it would revert to the estate. Otherwise, they'd probably just close it and move everything to Central." It was a valuable property, and they wanted to hang on to it, he added, but the board still felt they couldn't justify the expense of running and staffing the branch in its current state.

"But look at this list," said Andromeda, reading off titles from General Fiction. *Don Quixote.* Saki. Novels by Hemingway. Books by Lovecraft and Algernon Blackwood and Arthur Machen. *The Marble Faun. Uncle Silas.* Jane Austen, for gods' sake. Didn't even old people read that? Andromeda hadn't read most of those herself, but she certainly had been planning to at some point in her life.

"So they want to turn the library into an airport bookshop," she said.

A small branch library, explained Darren Hedge, needed to cater to the needs of its patrons, and the mostly elderly patrons of Clearview Park just weren't interested in reading any of that stuff.

"They're not going to discard anything that isn't already in a collection in the state. And if a patron wants something, there's always interlibrary loan."

"Fuck interlibrary loan," said Altiverse AK, but Andromeda didn't say it, because Darren Hedge was her boss and she disliked being vulgar anyway. She didn't believe for one moment that they would hang on to every one of the unique titles, not if they could sell them for big money.

"But look," she pleaded once again. *"Zanoni! The Golden Bough!"* She paged through the list. "Oh my gods. Look at this one: *Babylonian Liver Omens!"*

Darren Hedge scrunched up his face.

"Do we really have that?" he said, and shook his head when she pointed to it on the printout. "How did we ever get that one? Can you imagine anyone at any time coming into this library and asking where they could find more information on"–he checked the list again–"Babylonian liver omens?"

He was trying to get her to laugh along with him, and was even arranging his face into a rueful expression as though to say "I share your distress, but you have to admit it's kind of funny." But she wasn't going along with it. A world where the elderly were interested in Babylonian liver omens would be far superior to one where they were not, and it wasn't the fault of *Babylonian Liver Omens* that the inferior world was the one the International House of Bookcakes happened to be stuck with. It was an important book. And quite hard to come by. And if the few elderly patrons who wandered into the library from time to time because they forgot where they lived didn't realize it, it was their loss.

There was so much more to say, but not to Darren Hedge. Darren Hedge wasn't in charge, and it was pointless to argue with him. The "Friends" of the Library were the culprits, the real enemy.

If a wave of hate magic had somehow arisen and formed

itself into a corrosive cone of caustic black energy, and had smitten and destroyed Darren Hedge, the board of supervisors, and every single "Friend" of the Library simultaneously, she would not have minded all that much. But it was not to be. She was spent, deflated, defeated, incapable of summoning any type of cone.

Pulling the Sylvester Mouse books that night was the saddest, most dreary of tasks. *The Greater Trumps. Empire of the Sun. Five Children and It. The Castle of Otranto. Flatland.* It took her a long, long time because she had to pause to kiss and say goodbye to every one.

vii.

No single magical text, perhaps, has had more impact on modern magic than *The Book of the Sacred Magic of Abramelin the Mage*. A corrupt late French manuscript version of this mid-fifteenth-century grimoire was translated into English by Golden Dawn founder Samuel Liddle MacGregor Mathers. Then, the most influential magician of the twentieth century, Aleister Crowley, interpreted its ideas for use in modern times and used the Abramelin Operation as the basis of his own system, changing the face of practical occultism from that point forward. The text describes a lengthy magical operation intended to allow the practitioner to achieve "knowledge and conversation of" his Holy Guardian Angel. Once summoned, the Holy Guardian Angel, or HGA, as the entity is often known, instructs the practitioner and guides his further magical development.

Daisy had, from time to time, announced her intention to perform the Abramelin Operation. That was an absurdity. The Operation requires a strenuous period of magical retirement, of isolation from society, for a period of at least six, and possibly even as long as eighteen, months. Andromeda couldn't see how anyone could manage it. You'd have to be rich, and have tons of time on your hands; and most of all, it would be best if the practitioner happened not to have a mother who was liable to burst into the temple at any moment to accuse the magician of putting her iPod in the refrigerator. In any case, it was not something to be taken lightly: Mathers, by the mere act of translating the text and transcribing the magic squares, so it was said, inadvertently conjured a horde of demons, who then pursued and hounded him to his doom.

Still, it was an important text. The International House of Bookcakes's copy of *The Book of the Sacred Magic of Abramelin the Mage* had been on the Sylvester Mouse list but had been missing for some time. That is, Andromeda had staff-checked it long ago and somehow managed to lose track of it. It was still, technically, checked out to her. The sinister nature of the Sylvester Mouse Project was such a shock that she hadn't stopped to consider till much later that night what might happen to her if she couldn't replace it. She'd be charged for the book, perhaps. But worse, Darren Hedge would certainly suspect her of stealing it, given her well-known interests and her outburst that day.

She needed a Sylvester Mouse strategy. She simply couldn't function without the library's collection, especially the 133s and 296s. She needed it for her work, not to mention to help her get to the bottom of the Daisy and King of Sacramento problems, and she had been counting on its continued existence and availability to any future self of hers that might have need of it. This was why she had donated *True and Faithful* and *Nightside of Eden,* thinking there was nowhere as safe as a public, little-used facility. Surely she should at least be able to get those back?

Many of the most important 133s were already gone, packed up and sent to the "Friends." Unless she could acquire a great deal of cash to buy them back herself when they came up for auction, they would soon be gone forever. So it was Andromeda Klein against the world, or more accurately, Andromeda Klein against the "Friends" of the Library.

She hadn't been able to bring herself to put *S.S.O.T.B.M.E.* and *Shadows of Life and Thought* back on the cart in the end, and she had returned them to her bag once Gordon had left. She wasn't sure what she was going to do with them, or regarding anything. And there was the Lacey problem. The Daisy problem. The St. Steve problem. The Language Arts journal problem. No wonder she had trouble sleeping. Action-population late at night always caused insomnia, so the King of Sacramento was unable to make an appearance, despite the sigil.

And yet, the *Abramelin* problem, at least, had managed

to resolve itself by the time of Rosalie van Genuchten's "small and sensual get-together" the following afternoon. That is, when Andromeda Klein finally found herself standing at Rosalie van Genuchten's door, she would be wearing a blond wig, a vinyl coat, and a studded belt with a skull buckle, and she would have *The Book of the Sacred Magic of Abramelin the Mage* in her bag.

The dad was in the living room quietly playing his guitar with his eyes closed when she got home from work. He was at a low ebb, having recently switched to new meds, because the clinic had run out of free samples of what he had been on previously. The transitions were always difficult. Family and friends were supposed to watch carefully and note behavior changes when medication was initiated or changed, because the person taking it couldn't always see themselves clearly. Andromeda had had lots of practice with the dad, and so had taken careful notes of Daisy's behavior when Daisy had gone on Paxil. There had been no change, however; Daisy's behavior had remained just as inconsistent and erratic, and had defied understanding right up to the end, though she had said she had much, much more vivid dreams after the Paxil kicked in.

"Cupcake," the dad said mournfully. He tried to smile at her, and it didn't work out too well. She knew where he was coming from with that. She Dave-claw-saluted him, and unlike the basketball boys, he returned the salute.

"Bad night?" she said.

"The baddest," he replied.

"Me too," she said, and she told him, a bit, about the

"Friends" of the Library and *Babylonian Liver Omens*. She didn't mention Lacey and "constantration camp." It would have been too much for him in his current state.

The dad made a sympathetic face.

"The first step to controlling the people is preventing the free exchange of information," he said, brightening slightly, warming to his favorite subject. "They burn the books, then they take the guns away. Soon everything is a crime, your neighbors turn you in, and the state confiscates your worldly goods. And the entire population is either in prison, on trial, or on parole or being investigated. Sound familiar? It's an old, old story." It was a good try, but his heart wasn't really in it, she could tell.

They both winced as the mom suddenly slammed something in the kitchen, then winced again as she slammed the kitchen door and sat down at the computer. It was a wonder the door was still on its hinges and that the keyboard didn't break under the violent assault of her fingers.

"Home sweet home," said Andromeda cheerily.

"Rim shot," the dad said in his Groucho Marx voice. He slapped the top of the guitar, which was lying faceup on his lap, with his two hands and then knocked it with his elbow, in a *ba-da smack* rhythm. He often did this rim-shot impression on tables, but on the guitar it made a hollow echo and sounded all the strings faintly. "It's been a hard day's night," he sang under his breath, and let his voice trail off. . . . "You don't know 'Hard Day's Night,' " he said. "People think the open strings sound like that first chord, so . . ." He sighed. "No wonder no one gets my jokes around here."

Andromeda had no idea what he was talking about.

Guillaume de Machaut was about as modern as her taste could handle, and he was mid–fourteenth century. She didn't get it. The music her friends listened to, their boyfriends' rock groups, and popular hits, it was all unnerving, chaotic, anxiety-inducing. She preferred her ancient and medieval music, the *ars nova* or *ars subtilior*, or, in a pinch, classical, orderly music, which made the world seem more sane while it was playing. The Goldberg Variations. That was what she needed at the moment. Something to organize her mind.

"I do sometimes," she said, however. "Get your jokes. Go on, try me. Play something jokey."

He picked up the guitar again and began to play and sing to a familiar tune:

"Joy to the world
The teacher's dead
We cut off her head . . ."

The mom stomped up the hallway and glared at them before heading into the bedroom and slamming the door.

"Not a great review," said Altiverse AK. The song was so ridiculous it was kind of funny, and Andromeda found herself kind of smiling.

"But wait," said the dad. "There's more." He continued.

"What happened to the body?
We flushed it down the potty.
And round and round she goes,
And round and round she goes,
And rou-ow-ow-ow-ow and round she goes . . ."

He looked at her seriously and raised his eyebrows. She returned the look. Then they raised and lowered their eyebrows together, hers going down as his went up, till they lost the rhythm.

"What the hell is that?" said Andromeda. "It's so"–she paused with a mock-serious expression, as if searching for the right word, then continued–"stupid!" He was such a goofball.

"It is a well-known teacher song. Don't you have any of those?"

She didn't. Andromeda couldn't imagine how it must have been, when teachers were important enough in kids' lives that they took the trouble to make up songs to popular tunes to ridicule them. She could think of no teacher she had ever had who had ever been much more than a feeble-minded irrelevancy. In her head she tried it out, but "Joy to the world, the 'Friends' of the Clearview Park Library are dead" wouldn't fit into the song; she did better with Lacey.

"Hey, Dad," said Andromeda, before she left him to his strumming. "How do you know Clearview is hell?"

He was blank for a bit, then he said: "I don't know, Mrs. Teasdale, how *do* you know Clearview is hell?" Mrs. Teasdale was Margaret Dumont's character in *Duck Soup,* and Andromeda was sure she was the only person in the whole town other than the dad who knew that.

She supplied her punchline about damned Christians, and was rewarded by a real smile and a genuine laugh.

"That's a hot one!" he said. "A-plus. So there are still a lot of steak antlers down at your school?" He meant "snake handlers," another of his terms for religious people, roughly equivalent to *godbotherers.*

134

"You know it," she said, pleased with herself for managing to cheer at least one person up, and allowing herself to enjoy "steak antlers."

Dave was scratching on the vacuum door when she walked past. He had probably been hiding–he hated noise, and the guitar most of all–and the mom had closed the door on him without realizing he was in there. He bounded out with a yowl.

Andromeda had a vague idea that if she was ever going to read *Shadows of Life and Thought* this might be her only chance, so she banished the room and lit her single candle and opened up the book. But she was too action-populated to concentrate on anything as difficult as A.E.'s meandering, convoluted language, and she kept losing the thread. It was also a bit depressing, because A.E. seemed resigned, wistful, despairing, rather than his usual feisty, cantankerous self in this book, so she closed it up. "A.E.," she said. "Poor little A.E."

She had yet to make another entry in her Language Arts journal, which had to be turned in on Friday. She dug around a bit in her underbed boxes and managed to locate the Emily File. She flipped through the sheets briefly: she hadn't looked at them for several years, and the drawings were not quite as wonderful as she remembered them. Monsters, horses, aliens, buildings on fire, motorcycles, amateurishly drawn. It might still be possible to find something to use, but she lacked the energy to sort through it all just at the moment, so she closed it up and set it aside.

Andromeda decided she should try to do at least *some* homework, seeing as she was stuck at home and everything, so she opened the journal and tried to write a description of the magical landscape she had experienced earlier that day, but she found she had no words to describe it. You would have to be a poet or a great artist to capture it, it was so beyond the ordinary, which made her think of William Blake, who consciously experienced multiple planes at once and who had been a pioneer in the production of personal magic-talismanic books. The library had a beautifully printed copy of the *Book of Urizen,* and she was positive that Sylvester Mouse and the "Friends" of the Library had designs on it. She sighed. She didn't see how she could function without the IHOB's occult collection, and it was being relentlessly gutted. Thank gods she had her own copy of Agrippa's *Three Books of Occult Philosophy,* at least. Theoretically, the whole of Western occultism, were it ever to be forgotten, could be reconstructed from Agrippa, *True and Faithful,* the tarot, and *Sepher Yetzirah.* That was how the Golden Dawn had done it, adding Egyptian trappings. But Andromeda would really rather have the whole library even so.

In her journal, she wrote a little description of the method by which Agrippa had constructed mathematical magic squares and derived planetary sigils by tracing the numbers within them.

Her trigonometry problem set was trivially easy—she always dashed math homework off quickly during Nutrition or secretively during Sustained Silent Reading, so she had no need to worry about that.

The only remaining schoolwork she had was a brief autobiographical sketch for her project group for Contemporary Social Sciences. That would have to be done on the family computer, which would have to wait till the mom was safely in bed and unconscious. She would have to be really quiet, though, because if the mom happened to hear any typing in the night, she would almost certainly creep down the hall to investigate what was being typed, and by whom. But why not write the rough draft in her Language Arts journal and type it up later to turn in to Contemporary Social Sciences, killing two assignments with one shot? To ask the question was to answer it, so she dipped her pen in a pot of green ink and began to write:

> *In the great holy city of Sacramento, California, North America, in 1990 era vulgaris, as Neptune the Seventh Wanderer entered the lonely constellation of Capricorn, in the mystic Twelfth House, it awakened in the prison of earth and flesh and fluid. Fact! Its terrestrial father used to be a famous sound engineer from New York. Fact! Its mother doesn't know the difference between Austria and Australia, and claims to be an Indian princess. It spent three early years at a Gnome School, where it was baked in the sun and fed potatoes to cure it of its slow, irritating walk, but it found it could never smile at rainbows. It aspires to be the girl Agrippa and to keep up the Great Work. It has written the grimoire of losing its virtue to an idiot. Its emblem is the Two of Swords, kneeling, and The Lovers. Let he who hath understanding add it up, for it is the number of a girl, which is an M, ten times ten times ten. What is it?*

And she signed it *Andromeda Krystal Klein*, adding an *M* with crossed swords forming the *M*'s *V* and an Eye of Horus for good measure; and, taking a page from Mr. Crowley, titled it "Autohagiography." Of course, she couldn't use it for the Contemporary Social Sciences get-to-know-you-better paper, but it was fine for the Language Arts journal. She was pretty sure Baby Talk Barnes never read the entries that carefully anyway.

Sacramento. The mom and the dad had met there, and Andromeda had indeed been born there, though they had moved to Hillmont when she was very small. Could the King of Sacramento have something to do with that?

"Gods, Dave," she said. "He couldn't be my dad, some-how, could he?"

Dave shuddered and stretched, which seemed rather like a no. He was in a rare needy, insecure mood, which was how she liked him best. She stroked his *M* and kissed his head and felt like she had at least one non-insane ally in the world. But even though she mentally arranged herself in the most secure box her imagination could construct, she didn't feel safe in the slightest and ended up getting hardly any sleep at all. How was this King of Sacramento supposed to find her if she never managed to sleep properly?

viii.

Andromeda managed to avoid running into Lacey for the entire next day, leaving only one more day in the week before the weekend.

Yet another apartment building had caught fire in the neighborhood overnight. Andromeda hadn't heard any sirens, but the sour, wet charcoal smell was unmistakable, and she had taken a slight detour on her way to school to follow it to the scene. It looked a lot like the other one, a gaping, blackened mouth in an upper-floor, corner unit of a small apartment building on Redwood Avenue five blocks west of Casa Klein. Though there were no books in the trees this time, Daisy's scent was certainly there. The building's garage door had a large X on it, which felt like a synch, even though it was certainly possible that one straight line could cross another without necessarily referring to the Two of Swords.

Andromeda had learned her lesson about the bike rack. In fact, she thought it best to avoid the racks completely, so she found a spot just beyond the far edge of the school fields. Fairly hidden from view, between ranks of eucalyptus trees, there was a metal thing, a pump or generator or meter of some kind, entirely enclosed in a metal cyclone-fence cube. There was a sign saying DANGER with a silhouette of a man being struck by lightning, but the fence itself didn't seem dangerous and she was able to loop her new U-shaped lock around one of the metal posts and the bar of her bike. The walk to the school building was long but pleasant: damp, gray-dark, wet from the previous night's rain. The smell of rained-on grass and trees was one of her favorite things. She could have sat there smelling everything for the entire day, and she was sure she'd have gotten more out of it than she would get in a whole day of sitting around at school.

Empress stopped by their spot at lunch as usual.

"Don't you worry about that Lacey, KK," she said before she moved on to the next table. "I'll take care of her. I've got your back." Then she patted Andromeda on the head.

"Yeah, Cheska, what happened between you and Lacey Garcia?" asked Rosalie van Genuchten. *Cheska* was . . . well, it was short for Francesca, and people sometimes called

Andromeda by that name because Flat Chest-a was a common nickname for it.

"I heard," said Mercedes Jackson, one of Rosalie's outer-order hangers-on, "that you went psycho on her and she kicked your ass and you ran home crying. Then you weren't at lunch, so . . ." Mercedes was Bryce's sister, and wasn't too fond of Andromeda.

"No," said Andromeda. She didn't really want to talk about what Lacey had done to her or her bike, but she had to say something. "She thinks I'm a toe-ass butter-sucking fish, though."

"Toe-ass–" Rosalie almost snorted her contraband cola through her nose.

Mercedes said: "I think that must have been "no-ass mother–"

"Fish!" Rosalie interrupted. "Fish. Oh, man. Fish."

Amy the Wicker Girl was there as well. Andromeda had gotten her number, all right: she was wearing a couple of rings with eyeballs in them, pentagram earrings, and a T-shirt from some "dark"-looking rock band called Twisted Moon that looked a bit too big for her; probably a boyfriend's shirt, Andromeda surmised. "I bet her other car is a broom," said Altiverse AK, and Andromeda couldn't help inwardly cracking up at that. Amy the Wicker Girl saw and smiled back at her. Apparently she had forgiven Andromeda for being a weak freak the other day.

"You should really stay away from that Lacey Garcia," Amy said. "She is one mean, nasty girl."

"She's more like two mean, nasty girls," said Rosalie, and the rest of them, even Mercedes, demonstrated the degree to which they wanted to seem like they were on Andromeda's team by spending the rest of the lunch period making fat jokes, though they threw in some flat jokes as well to balance things out. This struck Andromeda as pretty distasteful and she didn't find much comfort in it.

"That's what friends are for," said Altiverse AK.

Rosalie had repeated her offer to give Andromeda a ride to Afternoon Tea, but Andromeda declined and said she'd meet them there. Rosalie had the Volvo at school this week, and Andromeda's bike would have easily fit in the back. But even though it was mostly uphill and the house was quite far from McKinley Intermediate School, she couldn't think of a good way to explain to Rosalie why she had to make a stop to deliver a dirty magazine to Daisy Wasserstrom's twelve-year-old brother. She had the bagel worm agony in her bag, in an envelope, along with *S.S.O.T.B.M.E.* and *Shadows of Life and Thought*.

The dad had moved his sad little box of dirty magazines from its previous location under the parental bed out to the carport, but it hadn't been too hard to find, hidden amongst the sound equipment and nonfunctional appliances. She hadn't riffled through it in some time, and neither had he or anybody else, by the looks of it. She was surprised at how tame it was. If such tepid material really "did it" for the dad, she actually felt a little sorry for him. Perhaps he had some better stuff on the computer at the studio or something. She hoped so, in a way. She chose a Scandinavian magazine that was more or less like a sports magazine swimsuit issue where the girls seemed to have forgotten to bring along their swim-suits. Den wouldn't even be able to read the text unless he studied Swedish for several years, and anyway, it looked like the articles were mostly about motorcycles. It would do little if any damage, she reasoned.

"Ninety-three," he said, beaming, after he had punched his fellow bear cubs goodbye and run over to her. He was carrying a big paper grocery bag.

"Ninety-three ninety-three/ninety-three," she said indulgently.

"What does it mean, ninety-three?" he asked. It was a wonder he'd never asked about it before. But how to explain to a kid?

"There are two Greek words," she said after thinking for a moment. "*Thelema* and *agape*. *Thelema* means 'will.' And *agape* means 'love.' So in magic, letters are numbers, and if you add all the letters up, words are numbers too. And *thelema* and *agape* are connected because they both add up to ninety-three. They're important magic words, so it's an important magic number."

That was the simplest she could make it, without getting into St. Augustine and Rabelais and Mr. Crowley and Aiwass and *AL*. Den was nodding, but his thoughts seemed to be elsewhere already.

He was clutching the grocery bag closely, shielding its contents from view with his oversized jacket.

"Okay," he said. "Ninety-three!"

"Yes, yes, ninety-threes all around. I have something for you."

She pulled out the envelope and he snatched it and tore

it open. He seemed quite pleased with the bagel worm agony, making her think, briefly, of the dad as a chubby twelve-year-old.

Den's pawing through the magazine had a frantic quality.

"Don't hurt yourself," she said, and then felt weird when she realized that was one of the frequent phrases the dad used anytime anyone attempted to do anything; the mom had a similar approach, except that she shortened it to "Don't."

The reason for the frantic quality, she soon realized, was that Den hadn't been able to find Daisy's tarot deck as arranged and was trying to absorb as much Scandinavian skin as he could just in case she decided to take the magazine back. He hadn't shown up empty-handed, though, and what he had in the bag seemed like a fair trade, because it was filled with a jumble of Daisy artifacts. He rummaged through the bag, pushing aside a tangle of old, traumatized Barbies, a blond wig, and a big, floppy sun hat, digging for something.

He explained that Mizmac had begun seeing a new boyfriend and had spent the last few days in a kind of cleaning frenzy, going through the house top to bottom and throwing practically everything away. Andromeda's mother went through phases like that as well, but she never followed through very far and everything only ended up in the carport, or, on rare occasions, at the Goodwill or Savers parking lot, where it could be retrieved if you got there soon enough. According to Den, though, Mizmac was actually destroying things. Lots of things. A truckload of plastic garbage bags full of Wasserstrom junk had already been taken to the dump;

what had remained of Daisy's father's papers and files had been put in the recycling; and Den even thought she had been burning some stuff as well—it had smelled that way.

"Synch," said Altiverse AK.

"This?" he said. "The Eye of Horse bag, right?" He was holding what had clearly once been the Eye of Horus bag. It was the purple top half of it, anyway, the drawstring intact, but the rest cut to shreds. The yellow Eye itself had been cut out, missing along with, apparently, the black box and the cards themselves. "I think maybe my mom did it. She could have wanted to use the Eye of Horse for a quilt."

Eye of Horse—Andromeda liked it. He had rescued it, along with the rest of the contents of the shopping bag, from the trash before it had been taken away.

Miz MacKenzie did indeed sew quilts out of a wide variety of materials—she was in a quilting club at the Community Bible Center Church, which she had flirted with during her divorce and had fully joined after Daisy's death. The idea that Mizmac would want to put an Eye of Horus on one of her Jesus quilts and would stoop to pillaging Daisy's room for quilting material seemed farfetched. It was more likely to have been the result of one of her senseless, destructive rages. She had a reputation for slicing things up. What would she have done with the cards, if so? Cut them to shreds, or burned them, just like the dream. As had Agrippa and Giordano Bruno and persecuted sorcerers and witches through the ages, Daisy had had good reason to hide her Book of Thoth. No Hierophant or Priestess was safe. The mob had destroyed Dr. Dee's library at Mortlake, and Mizmac was just the sort of person who would have joined in.

"She even went through my room," said Den, with an air of tragedy. "She says she wants to remodel. She wants to knock down walls. It's going to be a snowy moon."

"What?" said Andromeda. "Oh." A sewing room. Disaster strikes yet again. Like the 133s of the International House of Bookcakes, the Forbidden Temple of Twice Holy Soror Daisy Wasserstrom's Lingering Nephesh had seemed eternal. *They are burning down my room.* That certainly seemed to explain the IM dream. No wonder Daisy, whatever state she currently was in, was agitated. Her little world, the temple that had trapped and magnified whatever was left of her presence, had been desecrated. And Andromeda had failed to rescue the tarot deck as directed. The Page and his fish and the Hierophant and everybody else had been destroyed after all.

It was hard to believe that this grocery bag was all that remained of Daisy.

Den could tell what Andromeda was thinking.

"I can't get you in," he said. "She is scary right now. I swear to you this is all that's left." An exaggeration, maybe, but also maybe not. Mizmac could be relentless and, Andromeda had no doubt, thorough when she was manic. Den didn't know where the dump was. Where were the dumps in this area? Maybe there was more stuff to rescue, somewhere. There was bound to be more in the house, perhaps even the tarot deck or its remains, if only she could search for it herself.

"What about her camera . . . or her phone?"

He said that Mizmac had the digital camera. "She uses it to take pictures of her quilts."

He said he would look for the phone. It might be small enough to have been overlooked, though his mom was clearing out junk drawers like crazy. After a bit of haggling, she offered him two more bagel agonies for it and any other items he might find.

"Can I see your–"

She looked at him warningly. No conversation with a twelve-year-old should ever start with those words.

"–tattoo!" he said. "Your tattoo, I meant your tattoo. That's all I meant."

The only one of her tattoos he knew about was the unicursal hexagram on her hip. She looked around to make sure no one else could see and dipped her skirt and tights down just a little to give him a quick look. She had done a pretty good job on it. It looked almost professional.

He asked if she'd show him how to do it sometime. She was about to say "You're a little young," but stopped herself just in time. He'd have hated that.

"Maybe one day," she said, and she asked what he was thinking of getting.

"Maybe ninety-three," he said, which was kind of cute. "Or one of those ninety-three words." He made her tell him the words again, and she wrote out *thelema* in Greek letters for him on a page from her Moleskine. Actually, she had to admit, that was kind of a great idea for a tattoo.

"Aren't you worried about your mom with that?" she asked as he was about to go, pointing to the Scandinavian agony in his hand. "You want me to hang on to it for you for safekeeping?"

Den zipped it up in his coat protectively.

"I have a hiding place," he said, scampering off, as though worried that she might change her mind.

"Good." Of course, he would have to, wouldn't he?

One of the Barbies was missing a head. The two others were randomly and severely mangled. In happier days, Daisy and Andromeda had operated a Barbie hospital in Daisy's closet that gradually transformed itself into a torture dungeon Dream House. Later on, they had attempted, on the model of the magic described in the *Asclepius,* to draw down powers to animate the Barbies so they could speak secrets. These attempts had been weedgie and rewarding, though unsuccessful.

The Gnome School had banned all plastic toys, and even after Daisy had finally left and begun to go to public middle school with Andromeda, her house remained a Barbie-free home. By that time, they had moved on, but the Barbie-hiding skills they had developed were useful when they had other things to hide. It was certainly possible that Den had missed a hiding place. They were all over in that house, and all over town, too, when she came to think of it. Maybe, she thought, she should check some of their old "secure locations" as well, like the space behind the loose brick at the old, boarded-up Hillmont High tower, or the ceiling-lamp cover at the rec center girls' vacuum, which could be reached if you stood on the sink and were light enough not to break it and carefully leaned toward the fixture.... She hadn't been to those places in ages, and certainly not since Daisy had died. It was unlikely that the tarot deck would be in any of them, but they had used both locations as temples for performing magic. Perhaps something, material or not, still lingered.

The blond wig had been Daisy's. Andromeda didn't want to get it dirty by putting it on the muddy ground under the tree, so she put it on her head instead. She doubted the sun hat had been Daisy's, but she put it on too. She seated herself against an elm with the bag between her knees. She pulled out Daisy's vinyl coat and her studded leather belt–she put those on too, like a little girl playing dress-up. The belt was loose at its tightest and she had to bump out her hip, even while sitting, so that it didn't slide too far down. It would have been a different story with jeans or if her skirt had had loops.

Andromeda herself had knitted the long, fingerless gauntlets, using small circular needles, as a birthday gift for Daisy several years earlier. Daisy had always worn long sleeves, pretty much exclusively, since Andromeda could remember, no matter how hot it was outside. Initially copycatting her, then as a way to allow more space for secret tattoos, Andromeda had followed suit. Long sleeves and tights, almost always. No one in public, and neither of her parents, had seen Andromeda's arms, or her legs above her knees, since she was ten. People assumed from this, and from Andromeda's demeanor, that she was a cutter, but they had that very wrong. Daisy had been the cutter, and that was why she'd loved the gauntlets so much.

Andromeda put on the knitted gloves and tied them at the elbows. She had done a great job on them. Andromeda had learned the basics of crocheting and knitting at the Gnome School, where they called it handwork. It was the only useful skill she had ever learned in any school, though she rarely used it anymore. She was good at sewing, knitting, sigils, and other tasks requiring precision and attention to detail. Daisy hadn't had the patience or precision to excel at such things.

What else was in the bag? A pair of Daisy's shoes, China flats. She didn't put those on, because they were a little too big, and she was wearing her boots and wouldn't have anywhere to put them. Some CDs. An old plastic horse that Andromeda recognized, named Jenny. One of Daisy's empty birth control pill cards. Some crumpled receipts and other scraps of paper. Some funny glasses or goggles of some kind. (She was going to put them on, but they had a cord attached and were a bit awkward and you couldn't see through them anyway.) A small notebook, with a bit of scribbling in it: flipping through it quickly, Andromeda noted that there were a couple of spells copied, in the grand tradition of the grimoires, from what were probably library books. "The Hand of Glory," said one entry in Daisy's round handwriting: "Step one–get a hand . . ." Oh, Daisy. Also an account of the barbaric Toad Bone Ritual. Andromeda wrinkled her nose in distaste. Daisy's tolerance for wicker and the lowest forms of folk magic had always ruffled Andromeda's refined high-magic Renaissance feathers.

There really was a lot of stuff in that bag, much more than she had time to inventory just then. It was a gold mine of random items, the sort of thing Daisy would have just loved if it were someone else's bag that she had found somewhere.

She dug further, and pulled out some *ouijanesse:* Daisy's old Little One from the Gnome School, the one that had originally belonged to Andromeda, looking very much as it had when she had last seen it twelve years ago–that is, the day before yesterday. Megasynch. And at the bottom of the bag, beneath a ragged book of sudoku puzzles, were two other books, a small coverless paperback *Liber AL* and *The Book of the Sacred Magic of Abramelin the Mage*.

"My goodness," she said aloud. She supposed she must have left the book at Daisy's house while she'd had it staff-checked, and had forgotten about it. The other reason she said "my goodness" was that when she pulled the book out of the bag she was suddenly aware of Daisy's scent, quite strong, almost overpowering, that slightly sour, lemony smell with just a hint of cinnamon. It was no big surprise: it was all Daisy's stuff, after all. Still, it felt weedgie, as it almost always did.

Andromeda put the Little One, the books, and the paper items in her book bag, which was more or less waterproof, and rolled over the paper shopping bag and bundled it into her bike's front basket, the wig and sun hat still on her head, while the elms and poplars stood by, silently disapproving, it seemed to her, of the notion of a lesser mortal assuming the raiment of Twice Holy Soror Daisy Wasserstrom. She had barely left them behind when she felt the first large raindrop on her nose. Then another. The paper bag wouldn't last long if it kept up. She stopped under the overhang by the water fountains and took off the sun hat and arranged it over her basket, tying it down with the hat's green ribbon. That would afford some protection, at least.

By the time she reached Rosalie's house, the rain was coming down hard. She was soaking wet on the outside and sweaty underneath the vinyl coat, but the paper Daisy bag was more or less intact. She parked her bike under the patio roof in the back. She was torn about whether or not to bring in the Daisy bag. She doubted anyone would be around to steal it if she left it out, yet it was a risk. In the end, though, she decided to leave it in the basket with the sun hat tied around it, because the Thing with Two Heads was likely to be there and Mizmac went to the same church, and Andromeda didn't want it getting back to Mizmac that Andromeda Klein was carrying around a bag of her deceased daughter's stuff, especially with all that *ouijanesse* kicking around in there.

The van Genuchten house was huge. The far end of the basement was set up like a second living room, with couches, chairs, and an entertainment center. Rosalie's mother left it pretty much exclusively to the kids; that is, Rosalie and her little sister and the brother who still lived at home. Rosalie's mother would even knock on the door before entering, and the door had a lock that worked. The basement room had its own entrance at the back of the house, through a sliding glass door, looking out on the patio and pool.

The pool had been left uncovered. Andromeda paused to admire the beautiful sight, the needles of rain and speckles of reflected light on the water's surface, seeing quite clearly in her mind how Pixie might have painted it as a backdrop for one of her Swords cards. Then she shouldered her book bag and walked over to the glass and knocked.

She might as well not have bothered with trying to be discreet about the Daisy bag, because as she was knocking she caught sight of her reflection in the sliding glass door and was reminded of what she was wearing. She had meant to remove at least the wig. The door slid open. The Thing with Two Heads was right in front of her, the rest of the company stretching for what seemed like several layers behind it.

"Is that Daisy's kibble wig?" said one of the Thing's two heads, the female one, Siiri Fuentes. "Chemo wig," she meant. It wasn't really. Daisy had liked to wear wigs even before being diagnosed with leukemia; this one probably predated her chemotherapy by at least a year.

In the confusion, Andromeda forgot to keep her hip cocked to the side to keep the belt up, and it snaked past her hips and down her legs like an inexpertly managed hula hoop. Someone took a cell-phone picture. "Not good," said Altiverse AK in a Groucho accent, mimicking the dad.

The Thing stepped aside and Andromeda pulled up the belt and walked in, taking off the dripping wig and hanging it on the corner coatrack as she went by, as though it were a hat. No one thought this was as funny as it actually was. There were way too many people in that room, and she instantly regretted having come, but at least Jesus Truck wasn't one of them.

"You really know how to make an entrance, Man-drom-eda," said Rosalie, holding an enormous jug. "I made a pitcher of martinis. You can have one if you behave yourself. What is up with your hair?"

"Seriously," said Amy the Wicker Girl.

Rosalie poured her a drink in a large coffee mug with Winnie-the-Pooh and Piglet on it.

"I want you in me," said Rosalie van Genuchten, addressing her martini glass, holding it up before taking a quick gulp.

Andromeda Klein was still cringing inwardly at "Man-dromeda"–a new one that Rosalie had probably been preparing all day, waiting to spring on her; that could indeed have been the sole reason Andromeda had been invited to this session of Afternoon Tea. Or perhaps *Man-dromeda* was just a comment on the way Daisy's studded skull belt had dramatically highlighted the accursed narrowness of her hips.

Two boys were on the couch in front of the TV playing a zombie video game. One was Rosalie's brother, Theo, and the other was one of the monkey boys who had helped with her bike the other day. The Thing with Two Heads ambled over to sit down next to them, Siiri on Robbie What's-his-face's lap: her hands were on his knees, and his hands were on her hands, making them look even more like a single creature. Amy the Wicker Girl and two girls Andromeda didn't know were standing by, waiting to be introduced.

"Bethany and Stace, meet Andromeda," Rosalie van Genuchten said. "She can't drive, she dances like a boy, she's got no ass, and she's a teenage witch."

"Oh, brother," said Altiverse AK.

"I'm just kidding," Rosalie added. "And you all know Elisabeth," she continued, slapping her stomach. The summer before last, they had all named their stomachs, though Rosalie seemed to be the only one who still kept it up. (Daisy had, in fact, mischievously named hers Rosalie.) Rosalie was always talking about how she needed to "get rid of"

Elisabeth, or at least get her under control, but in fact Rosalie looked great and Andromeda would have traded anything for a body even remotely like hers. No one would ever call Rosalie Flat Chest-a.

"And Charles is here too," Rosalie finally said, blowing a kiss at her laptop, which was open on the table. She turned it around, and Andromeda saw Charles Iskiw's face looking out of a video chat window. Charles was Rosalie's dime soda boyfriend. He was away at college in Southern California and was now touring with his rock band back east, but evidently they still kept in touch through video chat.

"He's having martinis too," she added. "A small and sensual get-together, coast to coast. We are Afternoon Tea, and we are awesome."

Rosalie pressed some keys and Charles's face grew to full-screen size. His pixelly hand raised a paper cup, and the crackly, metallic voice coming out of the laptop speaker said something Andromeda couldn't quite make out over the sound of the video game, the scattered conversation, and the throbbing machinelike music coming from the stereo speakers. As she always did when entering a new room, Andromeda identified the exits. Even a slight increase in chaos could quite well push her over the edge into an anxiety attack, and she paused to make certain she knew the quickest way out, just in case—it would have to be the sliding doors, rather than the door to the stairs up to the main house, because she would need to get her bike before she could escape. The rain was really coming down hard now. The strip of sky just visible through the glass door above the curtain was extremely dark for the time of day, late afternoon.

The girl named Bethany said, "Andromeda, that's such an unusual name."

"What?"

In Greek mythology, Andromeda is an Ethiopian princess whose parents chained her to a rock to be eaten by a sea monster sent by Poseidon to punish her mother for insulting some sea nymphs. She is rescued by Perseus, who takes possession of her after turning her fiancé to stone with the Gorgon's head he is carrying in a bag. Or it's also a constellation and galaxy M31, or a science fiction book about a space disease . . .

Andromeda was so caught up in her own train of thought that she couldn't choose what to try to say.

"It means sea-monster bait," she finally said, on Altiverse AK's prompting. "The Chained Maiden."

Bethany responded with a nod and a quick though not unkind "whatever" expression.

"Our Andromeda is just a bit weird," said Rosalie. "I'm just kidding."

"It's good to be weird," said Bethany. Oh, if only the people who went around saying things like that really meant them.

Bethany reminded Andromeda of somebody, but she couldn't quite place it. A familiar-looking face. Kind of soothing to look at.

"You're hopeless," said Altiverse AK, and there was no denying it.

"Come on, everybody," said Rosalie without looking up from the laptop monitor. "Drink more!"

ix.

You could stab yourself in the heart with the pointy top of the floor lamp. You could unscrew the lightbulb and stick your fingers in the socket, sucking on them first to get them wet. If you were strong enough, you could attach a couple of long extension cords to the television and carry it out through the sliding doors to the pool, turn it on, and jump in with it, or you could simply fill your pockets with stones. You could expose the wires of the electrical outlet and hold on, or simply poke something thin and metal into the socket. You could pull the weatherstripping off the windows and door, tie the pieces together, and hang yourself from a door or window frame. You could take all the heavy objects in the room, load them on the couch, prop it up with a yardstick, position yourself underneath one of the legs, and knock the yardstick down. . . .

Taking an inventory of the room and imagining all the possible ways in which these objects could be used to commit suicide was a reliable method of distracting and quieting the mind in stressful social situations. Andromeda had once counted twenty-nine in this room, though at this moment she was stuck on eighteen.

It didn't take many swallows for Andromeda to feel the martini. She quickly lost track of time. The space between her and the others in the room seemed to expand. This was partly because of the drink and partly because she never understood much of what they were talking about anyway—the TV shows she'd never seen, the celebrities she'd never heard of, and all the bands, bands, bands. She couldn't begin to keep track of them, and she failed whenever she tried to educate herself about them because they all sounded the same to her, and when it came down to it she wasn't that interested. Absolutely everyone seemed to be in a band, and all the people in their bands were in other bands too, plus there were other bands, real ones, from other cities, who had CDs and so forth, who were exactly like the ones who weren't famous. She couldn't tell the real ones from the fake ones by the way they sounded or looked. The thumping machine music had been replaced by one of these bands: baseball caps, sneakers, sunglasses, growling voices saying "hey" and "whoa" all the time, and "I'm in love with" this or that.

She had regretted coming almost as soon as she'd entered the room. That said, she had to admit, the martini was helping.

Andromeda leaned against the wall sipping, more or less enjoying the faint sensation of the center of consciousness in her head falling backward and righting itself, then beginning to flip again. Mixed drinks did that much better than wine, which was what she always drank at home, when she refilled the Daisy scrying bottle with Carlo Rossi from the parents' jug in the pantry.

Christmas trees, she thought, sipping her drink in silence. It wasn't the best martini in the world. Everyone at the Old Folks Home knew that Andromeda Klein's drink was a Bombay martini, up with olive. This had come about because it was the only drink whose name she could think of at the time, a choice that charted the course of the rest of her short drinking life up to the current moment. While the others occupied themselves killing zombies on video, and nodding to the monotonous music, and chattering about things she couldn't really hear anyway, Andromeda stared at her cup and thought. The thought chain could be traced, quite far back if you stretched it, all the way to the gods and goddesses of the Egyptians and even perhaps to the formation of the earth and heavens out of limitless nothing, but at least as far back as the Water Tower Temple Working that had predicted St. Steve's arrival. The backward sequence went: cup, Ned Ned, the Old Folks Home, the hedge behind John Street, the Gold Duster, the DMV, the IRS, the library, the copy machine, St. Steve, A. E. Waite, Daisy, the Water Tower Temple . . .

It had once been a functioning water tower or storage tank, but now it was simply a great cylindrical shell of deep-rusted, flaking iron on the hill overlooking, yet far, far above, McKinley Intermediate School. From a distance it looked like a tiny reddish earthen jar or a pot missing its lid. It had been damaged by fire. The roof was long gone. There was a bit of illegible graffiti on the outside, up to a height of about ten feet or so, but there wasn't as much as there might have been because it was actually rather hard to reach. It sat on a narrow shelf of rock, with a sharp drop on either side, created by a series of disastrous mudslides in the seventies that had destroyed several houses–the kind they built propped up against the hill on stilts–and even killed some people below, including some children at McKinley, which had been a high school at the time. (This account was in the Hillmont-Clearview land survey publication documenting the event in the IHOB's reference collection, and it had been discussed in the news again because of the recent heavy rains and the fear of more mudslides in the softer areas of upper Hillmont.)

To get to the abandoned tank, you had to climb a steep, crumbly hill in the front, or take the long way around the back and climb down, and this way involved traversing a gulley. There were more conveniently located spots for clandestine drinking and drug-taking and making out and whatnot. Every time Andromeda noticed evidence of people having made the effort, beer cans or cigarette butts or the like, she was surprised. It was quite rare.

The only way to enter the tower cylinder itself was through a small hole in the side, where a pipeline had once been. Andromeda could make it through easily, as could Daisy with a bit more effort. Rosalie and Elisabeth would have had a tough time, had they ever been in a position to try. It was the perfect temple. They used spray paint to decorate it with the proper symbols, modifying them for this or that working, hanging silks and banners when necessary. Never did they find anything disturbed when they returned. The floor didn't drain very well, so during the rainy stretches it would get boggy and clogged with fallen eucalyptus leaves. They had used large rocks and other objects to build a causeway through the mud, leading from the opening to the center altar and from there to all four compass points. It was even possible to circumambulate the altar, with large steps, though there were gaps in the circle of stones because it was a work in progress and it wasn't all that easy to find stones of the right size in the vicinity.

This was the scene of their best and most effective magical workings. On a clear night with a good moon, there was just enough silver light coming through the open roof, filtered through the eucalyptus, to read by; and when it had rained heavily enough to flood it, the light reflected from the pools of water was beautiful and weedgie; the interior was sheltered from wind, so candles and lamps tended to stay lit.

One of these workings had, in Andromeda's view, directly conjured St. Steve, who appeared exactly three days after the elaborate love spell (which had incidentally conjured a boyfriend for Daisy as well, a boy named Lawrence, who had been found parked outside Daisy's house when they got back home). St. Steve she had first noticed trying to use the library's ancient copy machine, which wasn't working at the time. Andromeda had added toner, but it still didn't work, so she offered to make copies for him on the machine in the back. It was a flyer advertising a car for sale and some tax forms from the tax form binders in Reference. She noted the name, Andrew Elliot, though she was later to regret not thinking to look for other information, like the address or birth date. She never did learn his exact age or where he lived.

"Sorry they didn't come out that well," she said when she emerged from the staff area. "This isn't the best place to make copies." She was nervous talking to him, but she was nervous talking to most people. She wondered if people in the library, Marlyne, Gordon, or any of the patrons, were watching her. Her face felt red and her heart pounded. There was nothing very special about him, and he seemed completely uninterested in her. There was no reason for her to react that way. It was as though her body could tell the future and was getting a head start, as though it knew she would soon be all twisted up mentally on his account, for his sake. There might have been a bit of the trademark Andromeda reverse magic going on, because the thought did occur to her and she might well have articulated it, as a kind of joke: What would happen if I flipped out and got totally obsessed with this guy just because of the stupid Water Tower Working? It seemed so unlikely, but it was what happened.

She was sweating, like she did all too often, and it must

have been obvious to him because he asked her if she was all right.

"Yeah," she said. "No. It's always too hot in here."

"It is, yeah," he said. "Well, thanks anyway, Monique? Maryanne? Madeleine?" If he hadn't tried out those names and pointed to her *M* pendant, she might never have thought to check his name against Agrippa's Latin gematria tables. But he had asked and she had begun to tell him, "Mille," meaning "one thousand." And then he said, "Thanks, Millie," and turned to walk away.

For some reason she'd never been able to figure out, she had blurted out: "Hey, I might be interested in that—what you're, what you're selling."

"The Duster?" he said kind of doubtfully. Well, why not? Other than that she didn't have a license or any money. "It's kind of a handful, to be honest, but it's still a nice car. 'Seventy-four. Slam sex." He had added that she didn't seem the muscle-car type. Later, researching everything she could find in the library and on the Web about "muscle cars," she learned he had meant to say "slant six," which was apparently some wonderful type of engine. It was certainly true that if there was a muscle-car type, she was not it, but it offended her nonetheless to be excluded. Why couldn't she be a muscle-car girl if she wanted, except for the small matter of not knowing how to drive? As Marlyne always said, maybe she could find a boyfriend to drive her around in it. She could just pick one out and hand him the keys.

Andrew Gold Duster Elliot told her his number, squinting and jokingly reading it off his own flyer as though he couldn't remember it.

"You gonna write it down?" he said.

"No, I'll remember."

She was reciting it in her head, singing it to herself like Gordon, but as soon as he was gone and she was out of sight in the vacuum she lifted her shirt and wrote it on her stomach. It was an unfamiliar area code. She looked at herself in the mirror, and tried to be objective in considering whether it was possible to see her as attractive from some angle, and was relieved that she didn't look *too* too bad. He was just like any other patron, besides not being elderly or smelling like milk. Why had he made her so nervous? she asked her reflection, and Altiverse AK had answered: "Because he looks like A. E. Waite." And it had a point, he did. The mustache, the sad eyes. Plus a smell that she realized later was sweat and oil (because the Gold Duster still burned oil a bit and you always smelled a little oily after riding in it).

After that, back at her post at the desk in the Children's Annex, she calculated the Agrippa Latin gematria value of his name–1234–and thought about his resemblance to A. E. Waite and his Roman numeral I baseball cap. A discreet consultation of the cards in a space cleared out of the center desk drawer revealed the Magician, the King of Pentacles, the Devil, and the Lovers, a card that not only suggested lust but also was "her" card, according to Daisy and the Golden Dawn. She found nothing about him on the Internet. Reverse lookup of his number showed no listing, but the area code was a mobile number from Hammerfield, Illinois. She pictured a field with rows of neatly ranked hammerheads. Just visiting, then? She felt a little disappointed at that possibility, though also slightly relieved, perhaps, because the obsessive maelstrom she was anticipating and half planning for the sake of argument would obviously lead to tears in one way or another.

Illinois—a little research revealed that that was where the *I* on his cap most likely came from: the University of Illinois, the Fighting Illini. Illini was the name of an Indian tribe. She was already planning a way to try to work this knowledge into a conversation. "Ah, the Fighting Illini. Part of the Big Ten Conference, of course." Whatever the Big Ten Conference could be. She'd have to ask the dad about it.

Maybe Mr. Fighting Illini was selling his car because he was moving back to Illinois, where he most likely attended college. Champaign-Urbana, Illinois. Approximately 140 miles from Lake Michigan. By the time she had finished this research, she had already started, she now believed, looking back, to develop a crush on him. But almost more than that, she was loving the research, the calculations, the coming together of elements, and her own slightly strange interest. If she had had anything else to do with her time, if she had not been in the desolate Children's Annex, the whole thing might not have even happened. But it all made sense when you realized it had been foretold and ordained by the Water Tower Working, and by her own instinctive, uncontrollable reaction to his physical presence. Daisy had gone through a precocious boy-crazy phase at an early age, and Andromeda had faked it well enough to keep up with her, but now, six years later, she was finally getting a sense of what it was not to fake it, and it actually felt kind of wonderful and awful because she hated the idea of being a late bloomer like that.

Right up till the time she picked up the desk phone,

pulled up her shirt to read the number, and dialed, she had been telling herself she wouldn't really call. Then she just abruptly did it. He answered "Yellow" instead of "Hello," just like the dad did sometimes. There was a lot of commotion in the background on his end, a TV and other clanking and clattering, so she had a little trouble hearing him. She had to remind him who she was, the girl from the library, and she told him her real name was Andi, not Millie.

"Me too," he said. Right, his name was Andrew. He didn't seem like an Andy. He seemed like an A.E. He didn't act like he thought she was crazy when she explained the *M* was because her name added up to a thousand and told him that his name added up to 1234, and in fact he acted as though it were entirely plausible that she really would be in the market for a restored muscle car with a slam sex. "What time do you get off?" He said he could make it back to the library by nine-forty-five to let her try driving it. A test drive. She hadn't thought of that, that she might really have to drive it. "If you're really interested," he added.

She said yes, but started to regret saying so immediately after hanging up. She was terrified of driving. She almost called back to cancel, but Altiverse AK stayed her hand on the phone, saying something like "Just play it as it lays," meaning just let it happen, because AAK had no intention of listening to her agonizing over it for the rest of the night, and plus, he did look an awful lot like A. E. Waite.

So Andromeda was waiting on the steps in front of the dark library, lit only by the path footlights, when he pulled up around ten minutes late. He opened the driver's door and scooted over, giving her a "come on in" look. It was a clear night, and everything from the shiny hood of the car up to the highest heavens was shimmering and sparkling. As if in a trance, feeling slightly numbed and robotic, she got in and shut the door.

The engine was running and the car was shuddering. She sat there with her hands on the wheel, nearly paralyzed: what a crazy idea. And what was her plan supposed to be, anyway? She blamed the Water Tower and Thoth Hermes Trismegistus.

" 'Seventy-four with a rebuilt slam sex," he was saying. "It needs a little work but runs fine and doesn't burn much oil. You sure you know how to drive?" She had hardly realized they were moving. She didn't know where she was going. It was a lot more jumpy and powerful than anything she had ever tried to drive. A hypercormorant automobile; "high performance," that meant. For a long, slow-motion moment she was going along almost smoothly. She managed to get out of the narrow library parking lot just fine. Then the streetlights dazzled her and she panicked and ended the driving session in the traditional manner; that is, by running into a hedge.

"Christ on a bike," he said.

Andromeda let her head hit the steering wheel and began crying silently, and he was actually very nice about comforting her. He was a genuinely kind person. She had expected him to call her a crazy bitch or something, and she wouldn't have blamed him. Yes. Yes, I am. A crazy, crazy bitch. How was it possible, she thought then, as she was to think quite often as time went on, that he could be so nice to her? The dad would have yelled at her and the mom would have hit her on the head with her keys or something. But he was more interested in her than in the car. He didn't even investigate to see if there was any damage till they had reached the Old Folks Home parking lot and she noticed him looking discreetly down at the front bumper.

His arm felt great against her shoulder. She often found herself missing that feeling, wishing she could go back just so she could experience that arm again, despite the circumstances. A strong, comforting arm.

He said he knew just what she needed, which caused her to giggle in spite of herself and Altiverse AK to say "Oh, do you, now?" But what he had in mind was a surprise to both of them:

"A visit to the Old Folks Home. I'll drive."

It took quite some time to get there, mostly because he was avoiding the highway for some reason. Or perhaps the highway didn't go there directly from Clearview Park. He didn't seem to know the area terribly well, but once he got on the main road he drove faster and more purposefully.

Right up to the point where they pulled into the gravel parking area, she had thought they were really going to some kind of charity home for the elderly, though of course it made more sense that he would be taking her to a bar. It was small, almost like a little shack, the only lit-up building in a deserted area of warehouses and empty lots, and there was no sign outside that she could see. If she had been alone she would have been frightened to be there: it looked exactly like the sort of place where you get kidnapped and tortured and raped.

Lots of bars had that kind of name, it turned out, and

when he told her about it she thought it was a very cute idea, really. The Office. My Brother's Place. The Civic Center. The Hospital. The joke was, when people ask you where you are or where you're going or where you're going to be you say, "I have to stop by the Office," or "I'm at My Brother's Place." Thus, the Old Folks Home.

"Get it?" he said. And she had gotten it.

"I don't have an ID," she said uncertainly as he let her out of the car, but he waved it away. She kept expecting him to ask her how old she was, but he never did. It was hard to tell how old he was. She had assumed that, like the dad, he was wearing the baseball cap to cover a bald spot or thin patch of his hair, and she hadn't expected him to take it off. The dad hardly ever took his off, even to sleep. St. Steve did, though, as they entered, and he turned out to have thick, dark hair. In fact, he looked a lot younger with the hat off, rather than the other way around.

There weren't very many people inside besides the man at the bar. She would get to know most of them by name, or at least by nickname, over the next few weeks. How many times had she been there in total, by the end? No more than six or seven, if she added it up, though her experience felt so much more extensive. She had only seen St. Steve in person a few more times than that. "Old Folks" was actually not a bad description of the staff and clientele—all were ancient except for St. Steve and a trio of younger people who looked to be in their twenties, who were there sometimes, though not on that first night. Frederick, Sam, and a girl named Amanda, who was either Sam's or Frederick's girlfriend. The guys were that kind of hip, offbeat, rock-and-roll-looking guys, the slightly more adult version of the Charles Iskiw type of guy—geek chic, with heavy glasses and just-got-out-of-bed hair and clothes that looked too small—and the girl was always dressed pretty slutty. She usually got so drunk she had to be carried out by the end of the night. They were the only people there who ever played music on the jukebox, which was always loud and obnoxious, and very annoying to Andromeda because she had a hard enough time hearing to begin with.

No one looked up when they walked in, but people seemed to know St. Steve. The bartender, whom St. Steve called Ned Ned and who looked like a guy who works in a paint store, poured him a beer without asking and handed it to him.

"And for your daughter?" he said, kind of twinkling.

Andromeda didn't know what to ask for. She was completely shocked that she hadn't been asked for ID. It was a lot easier to drink in a bar than she had expected. The only drink whose name she could think of was a martini, so that was what she said. The first sip of it made her head shudder and caused an electric tingle in her jaw, but it was fine once she got used to that.

"It tastes like Christmas trees," she said, when she tasted it, still standing at the bar.

From then on, Christmas trees was her drink. "And Christmas trees for the young lady," Ned Ned would say. St. Steve placed a couple of dollars on the bar after he got the change, and Ned Ned tapped them twice with his knuckles before scooping them up and saluting.

They sat in a booth. They discovered the mishearing

game. He listened to her speak, and for some reason, a great deal came pouring out of her, almost as though he had unlocked some combination in her mind. "That'll be the Christmas trees," he said when she mentioned it, and maybe that was true. But it was also because he listened to her, neither interrupting constantly like the mom and Daisy and Rosalie, nor paying no real attention like the dad and Bryce. This is the closest I will ever come, she kept saying to herself, to having a conversation with A. E. Waite. By the end of the night, she was floating. She wanted to kiss him, wanted him to touch her; she kept expecting him at least to try, though he never did, not in the bar and not on the drive home, and once again she cursed her aerodynamic figure and her bad hair and skin and irregular features. But just before he dropped her off down the street from her house, she managed to say she wanted to do it again, and he slammed her door and said "Okay" before driving off.

From her cup of Christmas trees to the copy machine at the International House of Bookcakes, to the tip-knocking at the Old Folks Home, to the Plymouth Gold Duster, and back to the cup again. Oh, you could break the window and crush the glass, shatter it into tiny slivers and put it into your food or drink. That would really do some damage, maybe enough to finish you off, right? That was nineteen....

"Hey, we're almost out of ice," the little mouth in the middle of Bethany's nice, familiar face was saying.

"I'll get it," said Rosalie. Then, without missing a beat, she held up the ice bucket and shook it. "Andromeda?"

Andromeda had seen that one coming. But, rude as it was, she welcomed a chance to take a break from the chaos of chatter and music and video-game sound effects.

Andromeda Klein poured more martini into her Winnie-the-Pooh cup and picked up the ice bucket, with an ironic curtsey that no one noticed. She was heading for the stairs when it struck her: if each of these people was to check out the limit of fifteen books from the library, that would be well over a hundred books that could be removed from the list and saved from the "Friends" of the Library's Sylvester Mouse Book Purge.

She paused and turned around and asked: "Do any of you have library cards?"

They, the ones who heard her, looked at Andromeda like she was insane. Even Charles on the video chat screen could be heard to chuckle through the tinny laptop speakers.

No, of course none of them had library cards. Why would they? Anyway, organizing this crew into a Save the Library movement would be beyond her motivational skills.

"My mom's going to be back in a couple of hours," said Rosalie in response, by which she meant "Get a move on, you nondriving no-ass butter-sucking fish," or something along those lines. "Don't die."

Andromeda half smiled sarcastically back at her and got a move on, heading through the door at the far end of the basement room and stomping, though with little sincere anger, up the stairs. She heard some scuffling and giggling, but it was only when she walked into the kitchen that she realized they had locked the door behind her. It was just how it had happened before, the last time Rosalie had so insistently invited her to Afternoon Tea. That time, she had locked her out of the house, and there was Jesus Truck, leaning against the side of his namesake–that is, the truck– waiting for her to arrive so that he could sweep her off her feet and drive her to some love nest of the Lord.

"Andromeda, right?" Jesus Truck had said.

It wasn't Jesus Truck this time, but there was a guy in the kitchen leaning against the counter, a slightly rock-and-roll-looking guy kind of like Sam and Frederick from the Old Folks Home and the ones in Rosalie's (and, seemingly, everyone's) boyfriend's band. There were different categories of this kind of guy, but she didn't know enough to differentiate. It was like they took a bunch of awful-looking elements and put them together, declared it to be cool, and somehow, it ended up being cool according to whoever decided these things. In one way she liked the ragamuffin Oliver Twist look of it and in another she did not, and the like and dislike were just about evenly matched, depending slightly, perhaps, on how tall the guy was. The categories eluded her. There were hipster and punk and hesher and math rock and noise and various other things ending in *core*. There was emo, and she knew emo was bad, she was sure of that. No one ever said "emo" and meant something positive by it, though she was not at all clear on whatever else it might mean, except that they wore girls' jeans, maybe.

Emo or not, this one had the girls' jeans, all right. Also heavy black glasses, longish scruffy hair artfully arranged and product-ed to look like it had just been slept on, smallish earlobe plugs, sneakers, a jacket with a racing stripe that was two sizes too small for him, and an actual necktie with a T-shirt underneath. He also had a skateboard and a huge number of keys hanging from a chain. He really seemed to have patterned himself after the Frederick and Sam type of guy, or they were all patterned after the same original, but Sam and Frederick had seemed more natural, more genuine. This guy, whom she had already nicknamed in her mind Girls' Jeans, looked like he was wearing a costume. "You're all wearing costumes," said Alt AK, which was true, but it didn't make Girls' Jeans's costume look any less costumelike.

He was almost as skinny as Andromeda, which appealed to her no more than her own appearance seemed to appeal to anyone else; in fact, being small and wispy seemed a greater handicap for a boy. No mandals, at least, though the girls' jeans were nearly as bad as that. But what made it clear that the scenario was another clumsy matchmaking attempt was that he was extremely short, shorter than Andromeda, and maybe even as short as Amy the Wicker girl. He was small and spidery. Nothing they would consider for themselves, in other words.

"Andromeda, right?" he said, just as Jesus Truck had said before him. He lit a cigarette, but he held it in a kind of girly way, which might have been part of the style too, for all she knew. He said his name was Byron, and then seemed to wait expectantly, as though the revelation were worthy of comment.

But Andromeda Klein couldn't think of anything to say.

She was staring at his T-shirt, because beneath the tie it looked like it said CHORONZON. The raving, terrifying Dweller in the Abyss known as 333, denizen of the Tenth

Aethyr referred to as ZAX? "Yes," Altiverse AK's thought waves vibrated back to Andromeda, "that's the one." Dr. Dee associated him with the serpent in the Garden of Eden; Crowley had evoked, wrestled, and finally vanquished him in the desert. "Meaningless but malignant," in Crowley's words, "first and deadliest of all the powers of Evil." The scene was almost a perfect mirrored reversal of the Jesus Truck drama, with the Big Ch standing in for the Big J.

"Choronzon," she said, aspirating the "ch."

"Johnson," he said, though what he clearly meant to say was an inaccurate correction of her own pronunciation. "Do you know them?"

Them?

"They kind of rule."

"It's the name of one of those rock bands," said Altiverse AK, but Andromeda had already figured it out. So the shirt was from a rock band that had named themselves Choronzon, which was either kind of interesting or rather stupid, depending on how you chose to look at it.

"They're coyotes," he continued. "You know? I hear you're interested in my geek."

"What?" She pulled her hair back from her ear. "No. Wait, did you just say 'mageek'?" Magic?

He said that yes, that is how "mageekians" say *magic*-with-a-*k,* to distinguish it from what is done in stage magic tricks. Either that or "*may*-jick."

Of course, she was very familiar with Crowley's reasons for adopting the archaic spelling of *magic,* but those pronunciations were asinine. "Coyotes" must have been Chaotes, though in fairness, it had to be admitted she had no idea how this word, which Chaos Magick people sometimes used to describe themselves, was actually pronounced. As a Hermeticist and as an Agrippan and as an A.E.-ian–that is, as a traditionalist–she tended to be skeptical about the coyotes' shortcuts, though she had adopted some of their texts and practices, particularly the sigilization techniques, though there was, of course, solid ground in Agrippa for sigil reduction.

But: mageekians! Please. He went on to mention Chaos "mageek," Cthulhu, the *Necronomicon*, wicca, Crowley, and even Thelema, demonstrating a familiarity with the terms but a lack of real understanding of the subjects. Andromeda could not remember the last time she had heard so many wrongly pronounced words in a single sentence.

She reached three conclusions in that moment: one, she could not possibly date this idiot, if there had ever been any doubt, not even in theory; two, she was from that point forward never, ever, going to spell *magic* with a *k* again.

Altiverse AK articulated the third, and it was totally right: the Chaos current was dead.

✳ ✳ ✳

Self-professed experts and loudmouths claiming to have cornered the market on the truth are plentiful in every science. But as the occult sciences deal primarily in secrets and hidden truths concerning realms beyond the senses, and in meanings within meanings, often protected by multiple layers of blinds, it can be difficult to know whether a given occultist, whatever his credentials, really has any idea what he's talking about. Yet for what it's worth, it is a pretty safe assumption that anyone who mispronounces Crowley's name probably does not. Andromeda, whose knowledge of most everything proceeded entirely from silent reading and whose defective hearing had made her acutely aware of the importance of correct pronunciation and of the implications of getting it wrong, was grateful that the mage himself had provided a clear, definitive answer in a bit of wry verse: the name rhymes with *holy* rather than *foully*. Opinions on the Master Therion might well vary widely, but anyone who did not know this had clearly not bothered to read very far into the material, and had never spoken to anyone who had.

Girls' Jeans, the emo mageekian in Rosalie van Genuchten's kitchen, in fact rhymed the first name with *keester* and the surname with *Rand McNally*. He was clearly trying to impress her with his knowledge and familiarity with this and other random bits of *ouijanesse*, but practically everything he said was mistaken in some respect. Apparently, a man named Jamie, the singer of a rock group who knew his dad, had lived in Aleester Crally's mansion in Ireland, where Crally's coven, the Golden Dawn, used to do Satanic rituals and record rock-and-roll albums. . . . It was as though he had studied for a quiz and somehow managed to hit the main points but get all the answers just a bit wrong. She awarded it a generous D-minus with a *See me after class*.

Andromeda didn't know anything about rock music, and couldn't tell a black sabbath from a green day or a red hot chili pepper, but she was of course reasonably well informed when it came to the vagaries of occultism and she did know this: that the Golden Dawn was not a "coven"; that Crowley certainly was not a Satanist; and that the name of the singer who had briefly owned Boleskine House in Scotland, not Ireland, was Led Zeppelin. And it was a pretty safe bet that Girls' Jeans's dad didn't really know him.

"Amy said you were bacon. You are bacon, at least, right?"

"What?" It sounded sexy, maybe a bit rude. But no, he meant to say "pagan," another perfectly good term muddied up and drained of meaning by all the wicker people. In truth, she was not. She was, rather, anything that she judged to be useful at any given time for the required task. She was a scientist. She was an Agrippan. She was, like her father, Nothing. Or she could even strobe between Jewish and Spinach U-turn. She was a teenage occultist, rather than a "teenage witch," as Rosalie had sarcastically described her. And she was, above all, a girl in need of another swallow of Christmas trees. Or maybe she was bacon after all.

"Mr. Crowley," sang Byron the emogeekian in an unearthly, unpleasant voice, wiggling his fingers in front of his face, immortalizing the mispronunciation in song.

"*Die Goldene Dämmerung . . . ,*" she began, taking a swallow. Then, giving up, she said: "It's Crowley. Crowley. Rhymes with *holy*."

If Andromeda had ever wondered whether it was possible for a short person to look down on a taller person, she had her answer. The emo Chaos mageekian's look was pure condescension.

"Okay, Crowley, I got it," he said, exaggerating the "oh" sound and raising his eyebrows, as though she had said something ridiculously petty and he didn't want to set her off so it was better just to humor her. She got that from the mom constantly, and it was one of her four most hated mom things. She felt that he might have patted her on the head, had he been able to reach it from his slouching, inferior position.

He touched her shoulder. She jumped back like she had been shocked. It was only maybe the fourth or fifth time ever that anyone had touched her in some form of the "Come on, baby" spirit, and that was something you were generally supposed to like. She looked at him with the face you make after you drop a piece of expensive glassware that belongs to somebody else.

"Don't be that way," said the mageekian. "Come on, I've never met a chick who knew anything about Shub-Niggurath."

This was because earlier in the conversation, they had been discussing H. P. Lovecraft and the *Necronomicon* and the Cthulhu mythos and the Deep Old Ones. The band on the T-shirt, Choronzon, had a song about Shub-Niggurath, he claimed, and they conjured Cthulhu at their performances. Well, she very much doubted that. Waking Cthulhu was something you could pretty much do only once, and afterward those in attendance wouldn't be in any condition to stand around in kitchens clumsily hitting on ectomorphs.

"The Goat with a Thousand Young," she said. That was Shub-Niggurath's well-known epithet.

"Yeah, that's right, that's the song." He sang "The Goat with a Thousand Young" a couple of times, looking at her like he expected her to join in. It was, as far she could tell, a single note, and she didn't find it too pleasant.

Andromeda Klein had never, that she knew of, been called a "chick" by anyone ever in her life. Under other circumstances she might have enjoyed it. She had been known to fantasize, idly, about an alternate world where anyone, anywhere, would put her in such a category. If St. Steve had ever allowed his choice of words to communicate this level of appreciation of her attractiveness or broad acceptability as a female, her spirit would have quickly risen to a point just shy of over the moon.

But as for Byron the Emo Mageekian: he was too short, wore girls' pants, and couldn't pronounce Crowley. In addition, he seemed to have acquired most of his esoteric knowledge from rock bands, comic books, computer games, and the Internet, and yet somehow he was still very full of himself. Maybe it was wrong, but she doubted she could ever be attracted to someone dumber than her.

Never ever would I ever, she said to herself. He had his arm around her shoulder now, which had to be a bit uncomfortable for him, as he had to stretch up as if he were holding on to the upper bar of a bus. Okay, maybe not quite that much.

He was babbling about how his band was going to get a manager and perhaps do some recording in a studio.

"My dad works in a recording–" She blurted it out, realizing at around the word *works* that she shouldn't say anything about the dad's being a sound engineer if she ever wanted to get rid of this guy, and managed to stop herself three words later. But the emogeekian was only pretending to listen to her anyway, and it didn't register. He was describing his band's "sound" and "influences," not a one of which was at all familiar to her.

She noticed he had a pretty unappealing smell. He also had a scraggly, wispy growth of adolescent near-beard on the underside of his chin. Yet another thing he had was a surprisingly Shub-Niggurath-focused worldview, considering the fact—nearly as nauseating as the "beard"—that he appeared to be completely unfamiliar with the actual text of Lovecraft's "The Dunwich Horror" and "The Whisperer in Darkness."

Rosalie van Genuchten strikes again. At least Jesus Truck read the real Bible.

"The thing you should say," said Altiverse AK, popping in suddenly, eager to help out, "is: 'I'm sorry, but I am in love with someone who you could never possibly measure up to. It is a long and tragic story that I'd rather not get into.'" But she couldn't say that, true as it was. She twisted away and sat down in one of the kitchen chairs and he looked hurt.

"I have a question for you," she said.

He said he was all ears. That? AAK pointed out, was more or less true—those ugly stretched lobes, right? To be honest, though, they weren't all *that* bad.

She looked at him intently.

"Do you have a library card?"

"That wasn't what I expected you to say," said the emogeekian. "Oh, right, because you're Library Girl. You're carding me! Library police . . ." But he pulled out his wallet and dug out a Santa Carla County library card. "All correct and legal, see? I am a solid citizen. The joys of bleeding." Reading, he had meant to say.

"If you come by the Clearview Park library tomorrow after four," she said, "I can show you some books you might like to check out. On Shub-Niggurath, and, uh, *mageek* and such." There was a nice copy of Lovecraft's *"The Dunwich Horror" and Others* still on the shelves waiting to be stolen by the "Friends" of the Library that would be just perfect for him. And maybe even something about Mr. Zeppelin—she could maybe look that up too.

Ask him if he can read, said AAK in a stage whisper, but Andromeda mentally shushed it.

The emogeekian smiled broadly, though, and made his finger into a gun and shot her with it.

"It's a date," he said, putting on what looked like a little painter's cap and flipping his skateboard up from the floor into his hand.

Oh, gods. But it was the perfect opportunity for a less-than-totally awkward exit.

She was on her way back downstairs, and she could just barely hear the wheels of a skateboard clattering on the walkway, and then she heard a car start up—he skateboarded to his car?

Then she remembered the ice and returned to the kitchen for it before heading back down to the basement. She realized that, with the exception of "bacon" and "bleeding," she hadn't misheard much in the conversation, which was quite unusual. In part, AAK pointed out, it was because most of what he had to say was completely predictable. But also, he took up the slack by mispronouncing things to begin with, eliminating the middleman, in effect, skipping the disorganized collagen entirely. It saved quite a bit of time, and she didn't have to say "What?" nearly as often as she usually did. In other words, he had his good point.

The lexicon now included *mageek* and *emogeekian* as well as *bacon*, that was certain.

WHEEL of FORTUNE

X.

Rosalie van Genuchten pressed Pause on the remote when Andromeda walked in, ignoring a couple of overlapping groans from the basketball boy and one of the Thing's heads.

The door had been unlocked for her as they'd heard her coming down the stairs. The zombie-killing video-game tournament had come to an end. The lights were all out, and it was nearly dark in the room. They had moved the coffee table out of the way of the television. The Thing with Two Heads, Amy the Wicker Girl, and the basketball boy were squeezed onto the couch, and everyone else was sitting on the floor, watching a movie on the TV, passing around Rosalie's bong. Rosalie herself was seated on the floor with her back against the Thing's legs, her open laptop on her lap facing outward toward the TV screen.

Rosalie swiveled to face her. Charles Iskiw's face was still in the video chat window of the laptop; his voice, coming from the laptop's tinny speakers, said "Yo," and he winked. It was the first time Andromeda had ever seen anyone watch a movie from a computer. It was like two machines watching each other. This *was* the future.

"Where's Brian?" said Rosalie.

"It's Byron," said Andromeda.

"Yeah, Rosalie, it's Byron!" said Amy the Wicker Girl. Charles Iskiw snickered from the screen.

"Brian, Byron," said Rosalie. "Okay, Byron, then. Cute– she's defending his honor."

"You be good to my boy Byron," said Charles's voice, crackling through the laptop speakers. "He's good people."

"Mkay . . . ," said Andromeda tentatively. Man, it was weird talking to a flat-screen head in someone else's lap facing out; far weirder, for some reason, than talking to someone's flat-screen head in your own lap facing inward. "He had to go."

Charles, Rosalie, and Amy the Wicker Girl were the ones who groaned, indicating, possibly, that they, and only they, had been the coconspirators.

"Scared another one away," said Rosalie, shaking her head and making a sad, lower-lip pout face, but motioning Andromeda over to sit next to her in front of the couch. "I'm just kidding." She pushed Play and turned back to the movie.

"It's *Chisel Two*," she whispered to Andromeda. "Are you excited?"

Andromeda was, perhaps, just a bit excited. *Chisel II* had just come out on DVD.

Charles's whispered voice buzzed from the laptop, and Rosalie pulled Andromeda's head down near the speakers so she could hear what he was saying, and she caught quite a bit of it because it was all treble tones.

"Tommy just closed the store," whispered Charles's buzzy voice, explaining the plot of the film so far, "and he's following this kid's family to the zoo. . . ."

Chisel II was one of a series of horror movies Rosalie's crowd had been following for years, about a slow-witted psycho killer named Tommy Frederic who works in a hardware store and kills the customers with their own tools when they buy them from the store. Before *Chisel II* there had been *Hammer* and *Screwdriver*, and *Wrench I, Wrench II, and Wrench III*, though the entire Wrench trilogy had all gone straight to DVD and wasn't up to the standard of the others. *Chisel*, the first in the series, was generally regarded as the best one.

Andromeda waved the bong away each time it reached her. Weed gave her headaches.

"Pussy," whispered Rosalie, the consummate hostess, through the bubbles. "You're breathing my exhaust anyway." And it was true. Andromeda was starting to feel some pain in the approximate location of her pineal gland. The Thing's two heads were loudly making out with each other. Thank Horus Andromeda still had her ice-watered mug of Christmas trees resting between her feet, there if she needed it.

Chisel had been Daisy's favorite movie, which made it a little sad that she wasn't around to see *Chisel II*. Or maybe, she was? Andromeda could smell Daisy, all right, despite the weed and the gin and all the other people in the room, but that could be explained, possibly, by all of Daisy's old things she had brought in with her. She could smell the damp wig all the way from the corner, and the vinyl coat was also hanging where she'd left it. Andromeda thought about Daisy's old Gnome School Little One in her book bag, imagined it being inhabited by the gathering Daisy spirit and scrambling up over all the books and other things in the bag, pulling open the zipper from the inside just enough to pop its head through, and watching the movie that way. Why not, if Charles could watch the movie through the computer's camera eye?

Andromeda looked over and saw that her book bag wasn't against the wall where she had left it. The others must have moved it when they'd rearranged the furniture for the home theater setup, she thought. She couldn't very well paw around for it in the dark, and she felt stupid asking about it, but there were important things in there, not even counting Daisy's Little One. She worried about her bag all through the movie, to the degree that she wasn't able to enjoy it all that much, even though there was a clever twist near the end where one of Tommy Frederic's victims used copper wire from the hardware store to fashion a crude chisel-deflecting suit of armor under her clothes. You could tell, though, that it wasn't going to work. The girl had too many curves and too much surface area, and Tommy Frederic was very handy with a chisel. If she had been slight and aerodynamic like

Andromeda, complete copper wire coverage would have been much less of a problem.

✳ ✳ ✳

"Wow, you are quite remarkably drunken," said Altiverse AK.

It was true. The floor was rising and pitching just a bit, producing a very slight antigravity roller-coaster effect, and Andromeda's face felt lopsided. The power of Christmas trees. She felt great. She could be wound all around with wire, underneath the silk ribbon, before being put in her box, and she could drink martinis through a tube and she could practice training her mind to expand and encompass the Universe while she remained compact and stationary and secure, protected by animated swords lying crossed on top of her. . . . She must have fallen asleep for a minute there, because she jolted awake and realized she had missed the end of the movie. The basketball boy and Rosalie's brother, Theo, had left. Someone had put on some annoying, grating music that was making her inner ears buzz unpleasantly.

The laptop was back on the table now, facing them, and Charles Iskiw was still up there, grinning. Rosalie had lit a couple of strong vanilla candles to mask the weed smell. The candles were on either side of the computer, giving the table the look of an altar erected to Charles's glory.

Rosalie was poking Andromeda and shaking her.

"Okay, back to work, kiddo," she said. "Come on back. Come back, come back. Don't go into the light."

"Rise and shine," Charles said.

Andromeda blinked.

"So, now, what happened with Byron?" said Amy the Wicker Girl.

"What she means is," Rosalie said, "what did you do to make Byron run from the room screaming?"

"I thought," said Amy the Wicker Girl, "that the two of you would have a lot in common. He likes evil. All-star Growlie. And books."

"Oh God," said Rosalie. "Don't say 'Crally.' She'll bite your head off. It's *Crow*-ley. *Crow*-ley. Like Stoli."

Byron was in Amy's boyfriend's band, it turned out. And you wouldn't know it to look at him, but he was good at quite a lot of sports.

"You've got it all wrong. We made passionate love all over the kitchen table. I was a voracious animal and he barely got out of there alive. You might not want to go up there for a while. It's pretty messy." That was Altiverse AK, of course. What could Andromeda say in the plain Universe? That she wanted someone smarter than her and taller than her, someone she chose herself from amongst her thousands of ardent suitors? Picky, picky, they would say. St. Steve had ruined her for anyone else, maybe, or at least for anyone else with a scraggly goatee.

"How about," she finally said, "he was even worse than Jesus Truck?"

"Seriously," said Bethany from across the room, in a tone that seemed to suggest that Rosalie might have tried him out on her as well.

How about, no more pathetic matchmaking designed only to demonstrate how much more datable everyone other than me is—but she didn't say that because she couldn't figure out how to phrase it.

"Now, what is he?" she asked instead. "Is he emo? He's emo, isn't he?"

Laughter all around. Charles said "Oh, man" and Rosalie said "Gah" and Amy the Wicker Girl choked on her drink all at the same time. She knew it. Had to be emo. But they were shaking their heads, so it was hard to tell.

"I don't see how you know what people are." All the nonstandard types of guys, the music ones, anyway, looked pretty similar. "What is emo, again?"

"Nobody knows!" said Charles. "Nobody!"

"Seriously," said Rosalie. "He's more like skate rat? Maybe skate rat crossed with art fag?"

"He's mostly into that Cthulhu rock, you know," said Charles.

"No," Rosalie said. "She doesn't know. Andromeda hates rock-and-roll music. It all sounds the same and it hurts her dear little ears."

Cthulhu rock. Was there really such a thing? About half the things these people said were true. The trick was to spot which half. Rosalie and Amy were nodding, though. Choronzon, the Goat with a Thousand Young—that made sense. The idea that there might be a whole genre of music dedicated to Cthulhu with an official name known even to Charles and Rosalie and Amy the Wicker Girl was faintly disturbing. On the other hand, Crowley's work had survived the dabbling of dozens of dumb rock musicians, so there was no reason the Deep Old Ones couldn't as well. Andromeda imagined herself and Dave and Mr. Crowley and A.E. and a *Necronomicon* with eyes, sitting in a row on a ledge, waiting patiently till Cthulhu rock, whatever it was, ran its course and they were once again free to do their work unobstructed.

"Now, what's that weird, creepy music you always listen to in your headphones, again, what's it called?" asked Rosalie. "You know. It sounds like nails on a chalkboard strangling a cat?"

"It's *ars nova*," said Andromeda. "Or *ars subtilior.*" She added that it meant "a subtler art" and it was from the fourteenth century.

"Yeah," said Charles's voice from the laptop speakers in a mock British accent, one of his most annoying affectations. "And arses don't come much subtler than our Androms's."

Rosalie scowled at him but conceded, "Well, you do have a very subtle ass, it's true. Did you at least show Bri-bri your tantoons?" Rosalie was asking. "Tattoos," she meant.

"Yes, I did," said Andromeda, with the tone of voice and facial expression that instructs the listener to understand the opposite of the literal meaning of the words. "Of course. He was blown away."

"I wanna see," said Charles, but Rosalie gave him a look and hit Pause on the laptop so he couldn't see or hear. "Don't even think about it, Man-dromeda. Flaunting yourself like a harlot." Then, brightly, to the others in the room: "She does them herself, just like they do in prison.

"You know," she continued, turning to Andromeda again, "Brian's the only living example of a male with a tramp stamp. Maybe he'll show you his if you show him yours."

Now, she had to be kidding on that one, surely.

"I'll ask him," Andromeda said. "He's coming to the library to check out some books for me."

"Is that what they're calling it these days?" said Rosalie as she unpaused the laptop and blew Charles a kiss, then said to the screen, "You missed it, Andromeda got naked and her tattoos put a curse on everybody but you. You can thank me later."

Andromeda spotted her bag, halfway hidden by the open closet door next to the computer table, and she crawled over to inspect it. It was all intact, though it was a bit jumbled, like someone had kicked it or dragged it. Inconsiderate of them, but there was no damage that she could see, and she set it down gently.

When she got back to the couch, the conversation had moved from her "tantoons" to a discussion of Byron the Emogeekian's scraggly wisp of chin beard, and, to Andromeda's surprise, there seemed to be general approval of it. Maybe they were kidding about that, too. It was grotesque.

Amy the Wicker Girl said that the whole band was thinking of dyeing their facial hair blue. "You should do that with your goatee," she added, turning to Charles, who made a sour face.

"People," said Charles's laptop face. "I'm getting really sick and tired of nobody ever knowing the difference between a goatee and a Vandyke. This," he said, drawing a circle in the air around his mouth, "is a Vandyke. . . ."

Rosalie rolled her eyes and abruptly closed the laptop.

"Don't die," she said.

"Oh my God, you hung up on him!" said Amy.

"I can't take the Vandyke speech again, I just can't."

"Seriously," said Bethany.

"Won't he be mad?" said Amy.

"No, no, he's whipped. Not allowed to be mad. I'm just kidding."

But the real reason she closed the laptop on Charles's

Vandyky face was that the garage door was opening, which meant Rosalie's mother was finally home from Debtors Anonymous. Rosalie wasn't, technically, allowed to talk to Charles Iskiw, even over the Internet. Everyone scrambled to hide the stuff that needed to be hidden.

There was a polite knock on the door, a respectful pause, and then the door opened partway and Mrs. van Genuchten's face appeared.

"Everything all right down here?" it asked, sounding almost as wasted as everyone else.

"Rough session?" said Rosalie. Debtors Anonymous could get pretty ugly sometimes.

Andromeda Klein was in the vacuum, shivering a little, not feeling too good, though not quite all the way sick. It was always the last drink that did it. Up till then it was great. She remembered overhearing one of the rock-and-roll boys from the Old Folks Home–it was either Frederick or Sam, she didn't know which was which–sardonically describe the process after Amanda had, once again, snarled at him incoherently before losing consciousness with her head on the booth table: "It's like, I go to a licensed professional," he had said, pointing to Ned Ned the bartender, "and hand him forty bucks, and in return for this payment he solemnly promises to guarantee that my girlfriend will, by the end of the night, be belligerent and hostile and violently ill all night and for most of the next day." Why do people do it? Because it's fun, all the way up till when it's not, plus some people can't help it. She was pretty sure that Frederick and Sam and

Amanda were too old to be emo, though she had no idea what they were.

How wonderful, though, to be in a vacuum on the other side of a door that locks and has no spy holes. What luxury. The mom would be getting home from the DA meeting any time now, and would soon be calling to harass her, but at least she couldn't barge in physically.

As if on cue, Andromeda's phone vibrated. It was not, of course, the red mom-phone, which was still in her makeup bag in the playroom, but rather her regular blue phone, which she had retrieved from her book bag before heading to the vacuum. The display was flashing "R&E," which was how Rosalie's number was labeled in her address book. It stood for "Rosalie and Elisabeth."

"You having some trouble in there?" said Rosalie after Andromeda had pressed Accept.

"Just enjoying the view," Andromeda replied, and that got a laugh, because the downstairs guest bathroom in the van Genuchten house was known for the garish, vibrantly clashing colors of the tiles and wallpaper, expensive and in great, vintage, restored condition but obviously conceived in the fifties by a schizophrenic designer. There was a picture of a sailboat on the wall in front of the toilet, and if you stared at it, the colors around it would start to vibrate and swim in your peripheral vision and eventually make the pastel background of the painting flash with blotches of random colors. Or maybe it was just that she rarely visited that particular vacuum stone cold sober. This was because Rosalie van Genuchten was such a determined and efficient hostess. "Come on, everybody, drink"–that was the tantoon Rosalie should get, really.

Rosalie was calling to suggest that Andromeda stay the night. Rosalie was in no condition to drive Andromeda home, and Andromeda would certainly have a bit of trouble biking all the way, especially in this weather. Rosalie had already had her mother call the mom to clear it.

"She told her we had to work on our altruism projects tonight," she said. This was a Social Studies assignment that Rosalie and the Thing had been complaining about for some time. The students were supposed to do something kind or helpful for someone and submit documentation and analysis. Andromeda wasn't in Rosalie's class and didn't really understand what it was supposed to involve, but there was no way the mom would know that.

"Just say the word," continued Rosalie, "and I'll call Byron and have him come over. You guys can have the downstairs all to yourself if you want."

"Now, that *would* be an altruism project," said Andromeda, which clearly meant "No thanks," but just to be sure she added: "No thanks."

It was then that something rather amazing happened, and then, following that, that a rather unfortunate thing happened; and then, following that, that an extremely unfortunate thing resulted. Calls to Andromeda's cell phone displayed the phone number through caller ID when it was available, unless they were labeled in her phone's address book, in which case the name, rather than the number, would flash on the screen. If caller ID was blocked, the phone would indicate it by flashing "UNKNOWN," or "WITHHELD," or sometimes "NO NUMBER." When she could be bothered, she labeled the numbers of her few associates and friends with whimsical names in her address book, like "R&E," for Rosalie and her stomach, Elisabeth, or "THE MOM" for the mom, or "TEH GHEY" for Bryce, or "BIG-BOOBS" for Marlyne. How to identify St. Steve in her address book had been a difficult question. He was a secret. She was worried not only that her phone might fall into the wrong hands, but also that someone might see the name flash on her phone when he texted or called. The way she handled it was, she thought, rather clever, though it had also had a cost. St. Steve's "name," in her address book, was UN-AVAILABLE. The idea was that anyone who saw it pop up on her phone would think it was a display like "WITH-HELD" or "UNKNOWN." Her heart would leap when she saw it flashing when he called or texted her, though the fact that the label was so literally, painfully *true* was not lost on her.

So when she was folding up her phone after talking to Rosalie and her stomach, Elisabeth, she noticed the little picture of an envelope in the phone's viewing screen indicating that she had a message. And when she opened the phone back up to check it, the screen said "new text message." And when she pressed the key for "read message" the screen said "new message from UNAVAILABLE."

That was the amazing thing.

The unfortunate thing was that just as she was pressing, with trembling fingers, "read message," she fumbled and the phone slipped from her hand, bounced once on the toilet seat, and landed in the water. She shrieked and fished it out, and dried it as best she could with one of the big pink fluffy towels that said GUESTS. Then she had a better idea and snapped it apart and dried each piece separately before putting it back together. "Thoth Hermes, Three Times Great, Thoth Hermes, Three Times Great, I beseech thee," she was saying over and over again quickly in a whisper. But–and this was the extremely unfortunate thing that resulted–after she had reassembled all the pieces, she couldn't even get it to switch on.

PAGE of CUPS.

xi.

The question Andromeda was turning over in her mind was whether one of her series of "It is my will that St. Steve return to me" sigils had finally worked or the message from UNAVAILABLE had happened on its own. Often, it is said, a sigil that has been successfully embedded in the deep mind will briefly flash and fade in the mind when it has worked. Andromeda had seen a flash of something before the message arrived. But it was very possible that this flash had been Christmas-tree-generated.

Sigil-spawned or not, if it really had been a message from UNAVAILABLE, it would still be there, still marked unread, on the SIM card, Altiverse AK was saying as Andromeda Klein headed down the stairs back to the playroom, still pressing the On button over and over, telling herself that AAK was right, that the SIM card was still okay, that it wouldn't be too water-damaged to function. If, that is, the phone had been set to save texts on the card rather than in the phone, AAK added. Andromeda said "Motherfucker" under her breath, because she had no idea, to which AAK did the Alternative Universe equivalent of what used to be written out as "tut-tut." Andromeda had never meant the exploding head sound quite this much.

No one was in the playroom when she got there. The mom phone in her makeup bag was vibrating, though, and she had to endure an intolerable interrogation and the usual list of complaints and helpful hints before she could get her bearings. She just wasn't in the mood at the moment. She barely heard them, in fact: she was still woozy, and what was left of her mind was otherwise engaged, thinking about UNAVAILABLE and his lost text.

"I love you," the mom was saying in a badgering tone. "Hey, did you hear me? I love you. I love you. . . ."

"Love you, too, Mom," Andromeda finally said, with a great deal of resignation, hanging up just as the door swung open and Rosalie, Bethany, Amy the Wicker Girl, Stacey, and the Thing's female half came in.

All five girls were staring at her with five strange, hard-to-classify expressions. "When you are too wasted," said

AAK, "to manage even the basic minimal level of sarcasm required by the situation, it is time to say when."

"Wait," said Rosalie. "What phone is that? Your phone is blue."

"Blue," said Amy the Wicker Girl, "yes it was," and the other girls nodded, as though the color of Andromeda's phone were the most fascinating, and intellectually taxing, subject in the world.

Andromeda did her best to explain the color-coded mom-phone system, not the easiest thing to do in her current state. Eventually they got it.

"Your mom tracks your calls?" said Amy the Wicker Girl incredulously, as though doing such a thing weren't utterly typical mom behavior. "That is . . ." She searched for the word: "fucked."

"No, that's *genius*," said Bethany. "I can't believe I never thought of two phones."

Andromeda smiled in spite of herself, feeling weirdly proud, though St. Steve was the genius, not her. It looked like they were all going to be getting mom-phones now, anyway.

Amy the Wicker Girl asked how she kept them straight in her head, and how she kept the mom from seeing the red phone. "I don't think I could manage it," she added.

"I keep them separate," said Andromeda. "The red phone is always hidden in my makeup bag and I only take it out when I have to. The blue phone is usually in my book bag or in my pocket." She didn't explain about dropping the blue phone–the explanation was confusing enough as it was.

Andromeda stared at the red phone in her hand, then

turned so they couldn't see and discreetly lifted her shirt. St. Steve's upside-down number was on her stomach, where she had written it in pen the first day she met him at the library and re-inked it as a nightly ritual till she had finally decided to save time by tattooing it. She was marked as his, or as whoever else's who got the number if it was ever reassigned. Texting that number from the red phone would really be a bad idea, though. Avoiding that was the whole purpose of the two-phone system in the first place.

"I need to use your laptop," she said to Rosalie, who said, "Okay, as long as you drink this, and hurry up." She handed Andromeda the Winnie-the-Pooh cup. "Hot chocolate!" she said loudly, then whisper-sang, *Hot damn! Peppermint schnapps! Everybody everybody call call the cops. . . ."* This was the chorus of a song by one of the sneakers-and-baseball-cap "whoa oh" bands they always listened to. It actually wasn't as bad as it sounded. Rosalie was pretty good at making drinks.

Andromeda sat down with the laptop and entered St. Steve's phone number from her stomach tattoo in the phone company's text message Web page for her blue phone account, and checking her dead phone's keypad for likely text typos, quickly typed the following and pressed Send before she could second-guess herself:

"Gooey! Sax wot texted cut can mot seaf bc me phone problems. Nipp you po muah. Docil of?"

(Gooey = honey; sax = saw; wot = you; cut = but; mot = not; seaf = read; me = of; nipp = miss; po = so; muah = much; docil = e-mail; of = me.)

It was hard to know what to write without having seen

what his message was, so she was trying to keep it noncommittal yet positive; this required suppressing some bitterness and avoiding the text version of whining, which was something she knew would put him off. She had always said that if she could do it over she would be, or would at least act, more easygoing and indifferent, and now was a chance to prove she could do it. St. Steve had stopped e-mailing her long before he broke off the texting, and the address she had for him had bounced back an error message for some time, but the phone must still work because she had just received the message from it.

Andromeda closed the laptop, picked up her book bag, and said she wasn't feeling so good and had to go to the bathroom again. Rosalie rolled her eyes and said, "Don't fall in." Then she said Andromeda should hurry back because it was time for "phase two." From the looks of things, the plan for "phase two" seemed to be Irish coffees and more zombie video games. Andromeda trotted up the stairs as quietly as she could, one phone in each of her sweatshirt pockets.

There was a blow-dryer under the sink in the guest vacuum. Andromeda disassembled the blue phone and spread its pieces on a towel and dried them as thoroughly as she could. The blow-dried, reassembled phone would not start up. Plugging the red phone's battery into the blue phone resulted in a lit screen, but it was blank blue and the keys didn't do anything at all when pressed. "Trismegistus motherfucker," she whispered, then said, "Sorry sorry," because blasphemy in such situations was probably ill-advised. But when she replaced the red phone's SIM chip with the chip from the blue phone and turned the red phone on, it chimed and started up.

"Trismegistus!" she whispered. "Oh thank you thank you, Thoth Hermes Mercurius Nebo Odin, twice greatest, thrice great, ibis-headed god, scribe of heaven."

She was reading St. Steve's text message when there was a pounding on the vacuum door, and Amy the Wicker Girl's voice was saying "You okay in there?"

"I'm okay," she called out. "Just a minute." And it was true. She felt like throwing up, but she was very, very okay.

✳ ✳ ✳

"What was the name of your mom's first pet?" said Rosalie van Genuchten when Andromeda came in.

"What?" said Andromeda. "I have no idea." She was holding, or rather caressing, the red phone with the blue phone chip in her sweatshirt pocket in a silent, gloating kind of way. The last thing she wanted to think about was the mom.

Rosalie was sitting against the wall with her laptop on her knees while Amy the Wicker Girl and Bethany played Zombie Nation II. The boys always hogged the games whenever they were around.

"Okay. What was the name of her first-grade teacher? Or wait, what city was she born in?"

"That's complicated," Andromeda replied. "You're hacking into my mom's e-mail?" These were clearly "secret questions" you have to answer to get your password if you forget it.

"Nope, I already got the e-mail. Favorite color: blue. That's some intense security system, right there. Got it on the second guess. No, she changed her account on Virtual-verse."

Virtualverse was one of the mom's role-playing-network alternate-world games. Manipulating Andromeda's mother on the network was one of Rosalie's hobbies. She had set up several fake profiles for flirting purposes and had managed to seduce Andromeda's mother's character a couple of times after luring her to Sex Island, and had even gotten her to agree to a virtual marriage with Super_Doug at one stage. Rosalie's own mother played as well, if not as often or as diligently, and when the Doug character had started showing interest in Mrs. van Genuchten's character and invited both virtual moms to the Sex Island Halloween Fetish Party the past year, the jealousy and confusion and broken-engagement fireworks between the two moms had really been something to behold. Neither of the moms appeared to have figured out the other's identity, which added greatly to the enjoyment of the spectacle. The grand prize of this game, as originally conceived, would be to get one of the moms to agree to a personal meeting in real life, or the both of them at the same time if possible, but Rosalie hadn't been able to manage that yet. Her latest twist was to log on as Tigress_67, the mom's user name, and make mischief that way.

"Come on, hurry up, Dromedary, I want to make Tigress trash Wildman's Harley before she tries to log back on." The mom—that is, Tigress_67—was currently flirting with a guy calling himself Wildman_B.

"You could try *airplane* for the city question," said Andromeda.

"What, like Airplane, Massachusetts?"

The story Andromeda had heard from the mom ever since she could remember was that she had been born in an airplane over international waters between the United States and Australia. Her father had worked for the Austrian FBI and her mother was an Amerian stewardess he had met in his undercover travels, which was why the mom was an American citizen. They made her choose her nationality when she was five, before they allowed her into her foster home after her parents' deaths. She really missed Austria, and the surf, and wallabies, and especially the delicious schnitzel, but she could never go back now.

"Just try it."

Rosalie tried it, and said, "Dude, no way, that's totally it. Unreal. Was she really born on an airplane?"

"No," said Andromeda. "Not really. She just isn't smart enough to realize that that isn't a very convincing lie."

"Why would she have to lie about that?" asked Rosalie. It was a good question, and Andromeda had no answer. Perhaps the mom just wanted to make her life sound more exotic. But Rosalie was not interested in that topic and waved it away.

"Doesn't matter," she said. "Back to the e-mail," she uptalk-narrated to herself while stabbing the keyboard. "Ha. Place of birth: airplane. Password: airplane airplane. You couldn't make this up, you really couldn't."

"The top-secret security methods of the Australian or Austrian FBI," said Altiverse AK. But the primary Andromeda was not really paying attention to the master hacking, or to the swift and efficient motorcycle vandalism Rosalie was track-padding out. She was thinking of St. Steve and his message: "hey hey hot thing you ok? still love me a little? <3."

He had never ever texted her a heart before, and "hot thing" was a new one, too. It was amazing how quickly a message could take you back in time. She was vibrating and anxious just like she had been before, the more sensible, detached, jaded Andromeda Klein suddenly a thing of the past. She had texted back a "toy away" and asked "where are you?" but he hadn't responded. Which was normal: sometimes it took him a while to get away long enough to respond, and often the response wouldn't be till the next day, which was agonizing. But she couldn't help checking her phone approximately every thirty seconds, turning it in her hand inside her pocket, pressing Unlock and discreetly glancing at it when it felt like no one was looking.

"I did it with an ax," said Rosalie, when she had finished with the virtual motorcycle, adding that she left a note that said: "Dear Wildman. Fuck you. I chopped up your chopper! /hugs/Tigress."

"Now," she said, closing the computer. "Time for phase two." Then she whispered the "Come on, everybody, drink" that she would have shouted if her mother hadn't been just upstairs.

✳ ✳ ✳

Phase two of Rosalie van Genuchten's small and sensual gathering was a bit of a surprise. She wanted Andromeda to do drunken tarot readings for everybody.

"Come on, Drom-drom. You want to. You've always wanted to. It is the skill that makes you you," Rosalie said, quoting from a motivational sign that hung above the main entry to the school quad. "And now's your chance. Make yourself useful for once. I'm just kidding." Amy the Wicker Girl and Bethany were looking on expectantly, and the

Thing's four eyes were also looking at her from across the room, as Robbie What's-his-face had returned to assume his place as the Thing with Two Heads's masculine half. They clung to each other like each was the other's home base, as though if they lost physical contact they would shrivel and crumble to dust in the harsh alien atmosphere. It was disgusting. But the two heads were arguing into each other's ears about something and Siiri seemed extremely agitated.

Back in her corner, Andromeda was shaking her head. She didn't do readings for other people, especially not for people who made her nervous, and especially not when drunken.

"I only do them for myself," she said, "and I don't really know how to use them that way anyways."

Daisy used to say, and Andromeda had no idea where she'd gotten this, but she had said it with authority: every time you tell your own fortune you lose a day of your life in compensation. She had obviously said this to Rosalie as well at some point, because Rosalie said:

"It's like smoking cigarettes, though, right? Every time you do one it takes a day off your life?"

"So then," said Amy the Wicker Girl, "depending on how long you were going to live, you could kill yourself by doing it over and over till you use up all your days?"

"And the last reading would say: and then she died." This was from Bethany, who was crowding a little too close for Andromeda's liking.

"It doesn't work that way," said Andromeda, but she was thinking, Damn, there's suicide method number twenty that hadn't been listed yet. But if that counted, you could also count smoking or drinking or just waiting around for natural causes, so really the rules ought to be revised to specify that the death has to take place quickly, or at least in a single sitting.

"Well then, just do it however it works. We need guidance." Rosalie's face assumed a dramatic, serious expression and she raised her clasped hands in a pleading gesture. Then she added, "Daisy would have done it," which was probably true. Daisy was game for anything. And she would have done it well, too. She had been intuitive, sensitive, able to see things without understanding why. Andromeda's mind was just not like that, however much she might have wished it were otherwise.

Rosalie relit the vanilla candles on the table and started turning off the lights in the room and drawing the curtains. "She would do it in the dark, with candles like this, probably, right?"

Bethany asked if Daisy was the girl who had died of cancer, and it somehow wasn't enough just to say yes, that's the one. Rosalie and Siiri began to talk about Daisy, as though they intended to tell her whole life story. It was very strange to hear them describe Daisy to strangers, to Bethany and the Wicker Girl and Stacey, who hadn't known her at all. Had they really held her in such high regard while she had been alive? Could they have? And they all kept glancing over at the still-damp wig hanging on the coatrack while they were talking. Andromeda was trying not to think about the fact that Rosalie and Siiri had been invited to the funeral while she hadn't, but trying not to think of something never works, so she started thinking about how these were the sorts of things people might say at a funeral for someone and soon there were tears in the corners of her eyes that she would really rather not have had there. Somehow, Afternoon Tea had turned into a kind of impromptu memorial service for Daisy Wasserstrom.

"Daisy and Andromeda were super close," said Rosalie. "She was a teenage witch too. They had a coven and wands."

Occultist, thought Andromeda, teenage *occultist*. She could certainly have used an arch comment from Altiverse AK, not to say aloud, but merely to bring her back to earth and settle her emotions, but AAK had completely deserted her, as it usually did when she found herself in groups of more than two people; AAK was even shyer than primary Andromeda.

Rosalie grabbed Andromeda's right wrist and held it up. "And *that's* Daisy's ring, and *that's* her wig." The thought foremost in Andromeda's mind was that she really had never understood Daisy very well at all, hadn't really known her while she was alive and sure couldn't understand whatever part of her was still lingering.

The living Daisy had spent more time with Rosalie and Siiri, doing things Andromeda was shut out of: skiing, dancing, the boys with their endless rock groups, even the church youth group with Siiri and Daisy's mother toward the end. All Daisy had shared with Andromeda was the *ouijanesse*. And now that she was dead, maybe that was all that was left?

"We weren't that close," Andromeda said, "really."

"You were," said Siiri. Then, turning to Bethany: "They were unseparatable. Everybody always thought they were gay together with each other."

This was partially true. At least, Mizmac had thought so,

and had blamed Andromeda, going all the way back to the time she had come home early from work and had found them drawing on each other's legs with marking pens (for vampire tantoons that never happened because they outgrew the idea by the time they got real ink and enough unsupervised time). That was when she had started calling Andromeda an abomination.

"Oh no," said Rosalie. "No, Andromeda likes penis. Whether or not it returns the favor. I'm just kidding."

You could bang your head against the floor till you bled to death. That was number twenty, not counting the tarot method. Then they seemed to notice that Andromeda was borderline crying, and since Bethany was starting to look like she was liable to zoom in for an unsolicited backrub or something, Rosalie added quickly, "No, don't, she doesn't like to be touched," which was usually quite true, but which also made her sound like kind of a dick, so she started to lose it just a bit more. Fortunately, her tears remained silent, subtle, and dignified, little more than a mist, like those of Niobe the Lydian princess mourning the slain Niobids.

Bethany focused a series of what seemed like increasingly reproachful "knock it off" looks on Rosalie and Siiri.

"Well, she's totally skinny and her parents are still together," said Siiri. "What could she possibly have to be upset about?" This was something Andromeda had heard hundreds of times, and she doubted either Siiri or Rosalie had ever experienced anyone expressing disagreement or disapproval of it, even if they did know Andromeda's parents. But Bethany obviously found it shockingly insensitive in the context and fixed Siiri with a clear, solid "what the fuck" look.

The only person in the room who grasped anything of the powerful effect the casual "memorial service" had had on Andromeda was the one she had just met. Bethany leaned slightly against Andromeda, a clear "I'm joining your team now" gesture, and Andromeda let her. Once she gave in, it felt nice. She was telling herself to suck it up buttercup and pull herself together when she noticed that, as though evoked by the conversation about her, Daisy's scent was flooding into the room, citrus and cinnamon and something sour and unidentifiable, first coming underneath and soon overwhelming the vanilla candle scent. Was there any way to ask if the others could smell it too, without seeming like a total freak? No, there was not.

She felt Daisy in the room, as though she had just walked in, almost as though she had been conjured. Deeper shadows amongst the shadows in the corners of the room in the flickering light seemed to move if she squinted, but she couldn't make out their lines. The tears dried up. She was tense, wary now. Bracing herself, feeling a deepening chill.

"Okay," said Andromeda. Something weedgie this way comes. It wouldn't do to waste it, in case it was something instead of nothing, even though it was an unlikely venue for consulting the Book of Thoth. "We can look at the cards a little." You take your *ouijanesse* where you find it.

✳ ✳ ✳

The actual reading was a bit of a dud to begin with, but it ended with a kind of bang. First, Andromeda had to go back up to the bathroom once again, because she suddenly remembered that the mom chip was no longer in the red phone and she wasn't sure what would happen if the mom were to try to call or check her stats while it was still rattling around in her pocket, so she wanted to switch it back just to quiet her anxiety and to be on the safe side. It was unlikely that St. Steve would reply to the "toy away" message till the next day, anyway: he almost never texted in the evenings as a rule, but rather in the day or afternoon, from work.

But when she looked at her phone there was a message, and it was puzzling and a little disheartening. "toy away?" it said. How could he have forgotten *toy away*? Slightly disoriented, she replied, with no cute typos in order to make it crystal clear, "thinking of you and wild about you!!!" surrounded by several asterisks. Gods. What was wrong with him? But she didn't text anything more than that because he didn't like drama and she was trying to start over and behave herself properly this time around. When she replaced the mom phone chip in the red phone, she noted three "good night honey don't forget to . . ." texts from the mom and another one that said "fucking griefers," which meant that Wildman_B's smashed-up virtual Harley-Davidson had had its intended impact.

She could hear the other girls laughing and whispering and scuffling around as she went down the steps. When she entered the candlelit playroom, however, they were seated in the middle of the floor, looking up at her expectantly. They had pushed the table out of the way to clear a space. The room was still dark and shadow-flickered, and the Daisy scent remained faintly. The *ouijanesse* had abated considerably by the time she sat down, but Andromeda's feet and fingertips were still cold from before and her skin was tingling. Daisy had often talked about being "frozen out" by spirits and entities, a phenomenon Andromeda had never experienced with anything like the same intensity. How strange to think that Daisy might well be the one doing the freezing.

"Siiri and What's-his-face and their dear little Jesus friend What's-her-name had to go," said Rosalie. "All this devil worship is against their religion."

Hermetic divination was hardly devil worship; quite the contrary. The exploration of the Universe was a holy thing. Even if there was a dark reality on the nightside of the bright tree, how could anyone object to seeking to understand these balanced processes? That was why Siiri had been so cranky and agitated, and it figured. Mizmac and the other steak antlers in the Community Bible Center Church had been the same way about tarot cards and Ouija boards, one reason Daisy had had to hide her tools and materials so carefully. Unlike the dad, Andromeda did not despise the steak antlers. There are certainly worse and less understandable things in this world than to be dazzled by Tiphareth.

Andromeda's usual method of interpreting tarot spreads involved several books scattered around the room and a notebook and sometimes even a calculator with which to make sketches and diagrams and to test the astrology and the gematria and other correspondences. She would bound from book to book and page wildly through them. It could take hours. In Rosalie's playroom she had none of her reference books with her, no Agrippa, no Master Therion, no A. E. or Frater Achad or Mrs. John King van Rensselaer. This would be more like a game, more like a performance, or a stunt, a test of how well she could fake it, unless the *ouijanesse* returned and took over. She would have to make do, all alone, with the rudimentary little white booklet from her Pixie deck, whatever she could remember of the Tree of Life and the Hebrew alphabet, and the broad structures and analysis of the as-yet-unwritten *Liber K,* the concentrated, unexpanded raw material of which rested somewhere in her deep mind, like a dense unhatched egg.

Andromeda got out her cards and, sitting cross-legged and keeping her elbows at her sides, conducted a quick, discreet library-style LBRP with slight movements of her index fingers, inclining her head to the compass points, and wordlessly speed-incanting in her head. Just in case.

"She's having a fit," said Bethany.

Rosalie assured her that Andromeda was "always like that" and told her to come on and to get with the new age. AAK resurfaced in order to say a single syllable before dissolving again. "Ugh," it said.

"Now, what is your question?" said Andromeda, handing Rosalie the cards. Rosalie had been unaware that she needed to have a question. Can't you just tell my future, she wanted to know.

"A question is traditional. The idea is, you think of your question while you shuffle the cards."

"And what, the cards absorb my vibes? Is that how it works? Okay, then," said Rosalie. "Um. Will I be rich?"

"You're already rich," Andromeda said, and the Wicker Girl was nodding. The van Genuchten household was loaded, even after the divorce. No need to consult Thoth Hermes Mega x 3 on that one.

"Okay," Rosalie said, and paused. "Oh, how about this: is Charles cheating on me?"

"Yes," said Andromeda, and so did Bethany and Amy, in

unison. "Yes," came Theo's voice from over in the other room. This was easy.

"Gah, you guys."

"Ro," said Bethany, "he's in a band. He's on tour. He's the *singer*. You only ever see him on video chat, and when you do all you do is yell at him. He goes to *Cal State Long Beach*. Plus, all guys cheat, and plus, *you're* kind of cheating on *him*, right? You do the math, babe."

"Ow, harsh," said Amy.

It was true, common knowledge, that Rosalie had messed around with quite a few guys since Charles had moved away to go to college in the last year. She didn't even seem to like him very much, but evidently still wanted to keep him in her orbit, somehow. She was a genius at keeping people in orbit around her.

"She just feels," said Bethany, turning to Amy and repeating a line they'd all heard Rosalie say umpteen times, "that if he is going to accuse her of things all the time, she might as well just go ahead and do it, since she's going to be blamed whatever she does. I'm just kidding."

Gods, where did this girl come from? Andromeda thought. She's kind of my hero.

"Oh, ha ha," said Rosalie, stretching out the "ha's." It was a good imitation, however, especially the swift delivery of "I'm just kidding" at the end, and even Rosalie herself was kind of ruefully smiling. But then she said, "Don't wanna play no more."

This Bethany creature was like Rosalie's own Rosalie, and that was wondrous to behold, just to show that it could be done, that somebody could Rosalie Rosalie. Something about the way Bethany was sitting and looking at her gave Andromeda the impression that the barbs at Rosalie were at least partially meant to encourage Andromeda. This is how you do it, was the message. Just say "I'm just kidding" afterward and with the right attitude you could get away with saying anything, even to the world's bossiest person. If Andromeda knew she could never pull that off, it was good to know someone could.

But as much fun as it was to see Rosalie van Genuchten with windless sails, Andromeda still felt bad for her, and knew that if Rosalie did in fact have a soul that could cry, it might be having a rough time right around now. If she were Rosalie at this moment, put on the spot, the focus of attention, she would have been strongly tempted to curl herself tightly into a little ball and roll right into her box. But Rosalie wasn't like that. She got mad all the time but never seemed to get sad at all. Like she was inhuman. Or superhuman, rather.

Which would make Bethany beyond superhuman. She was actually beautiful when you stopped to look at her, the most beautiful thing in the room next to the candle flames. Not even hot or sexy or pretty, but distantly beautiful, like the sky at night, like the dark body of Nut stretched over the earth, spangled with uncountable gems. Andromeda felt herself blush in the dark, she felt it in her ears, embarrassed by the excess, by the degeneracy, of her own thoughts. Thank gods no one can hear them, she thought. I'm just kidding, she said to herself, trying it out.

In the candlelight Bethany's hair looked fire-red and a neat golden flame was reflected in each of her wide, glossy,

dark pupils. A person could scry in those eyes, thought
Andromeda.

✳ ✳ ✳

The wonders continued as Bethany actually sent Rosalie
to the kitchen to get more drinks for everybody, like she was
nothing but a more voluptuous Andromeda. How did she
do it?

"Do me," she said, "while we're waiting for Her Majesty."
She shuffled the cards and handed them over, smiling pret-
tily. "I'm not going to tell you my question."

Andromeda drew Bethany's significator at random
rather than choosing it and it was a synch: Key 20, called
Judgement in A.E.'s deck. (Crowley had renamed this card
for the Thelemic Aeon, and Lady Frieda Harris's painting
had the starry-bellied Nut arching across the top, with flip-
per hands and feet.) And even within the rudimentary Celtic
Cross spread, Bethany's cards seemed almost too perfect.
Andromeda didn't even have to thumb through the little
white booklet to know that it was the most favorably composed Celtic Cross she had ever seen. There was a hint of
strife and possible treachery in the recent past with the reversed Ten of Wands. Otherwise the spread was so incredibly balanced elementally and drenched with promise and
good fortune that there wasn't much to say about it. "The
outcome" was the Ace of Cups, for gods' sake. After everything Andromeda said about each card, Bethany said, "Oh, I
know what that is."

"Well, basically," said Andromeda, "your life is completely
perfect and you can do no wrong and everybody loves you

and it's all going to turn out great for you." Then she added: "Fucker." Then she added, deadpan: "I'm just kidding."

"You fucking whore I'm just kidding!" said Bethany.

Amy said one that Andromeda couldn't catch and added, "I'm skidding." It was clear what she meant to say, and of course *skidding* was instantly added to the lexicon.

Maybe it was because they were all still a little wasted, but saying ridiculous insults and immediately following them up with Rosalie's trademark "I'm just kidding" was the most hilarious thing in the world at that particular moment. The three of them were laughing like crazy when Rosalie came back in with another tray of cocktails and said:

"I made old-fashioneds. What the hell?"

"Andromeda was just telling us how Beth is going to be the ruler of the world, and how her outcome is pure, true Love," said Amy.

"Ew. I very much doubt that," said Rosalie sourly. "Skidding."

They tried to hold back, but they lost it after a second. Andromeda couldn't remember the last time she had laughed till her stomach hurt. Even Rosalie laughed a little, not realizing why–at least, Andromeda hoped she didn't.

✳ ✳ ✳

When they finally did get around to doing Rosalie's spread, it was confusing and chaotic and negative and difficult to read and un-Bethany-like, just like Andromeda's own spreads tended to be. The Two of Swords was even there, a synch, to be sure, but it was no easier to interpret than it had been in the girls' vacuum the other day. Andromeda had to draw more and more cards to supplement the spread, to afford some semblance of resolution, but still it didn't make much sense. There were more than the average number of trumps, but other than generally implying action and movement it was hard to interpret. She held one of the candles above, moving it from card to card, as though more flickering light would make the meaning clearer, trying to think of something impressive to say about it all. The Bethany reading had gone so well, and maybe, she had to admit, she felt like showing off a little, even though the cards weren't cooperating.

A drop of wax hit the Two of Swords girl, right on the blindfold, and Andromeda winced slightly in spite of herself. Andromeda's cards had all sorts of wax drippings and stains, so that was nothing to be alarmed about; she often had to use a fingernail to scrape dried wax away in order to read the scribbled notes underneath. The overall thrust of this spread was duplicity, tragedy, confusion, chaos, and false hope, and Rosalie didn't seem to be enjoying hearing about it very much. The little white booklet wasn't of much help, and neither were the distracting questions and comments from Rosalie herself.

"Wait, is that Empress?" Rosalie said, pointing to the Empress card, which had turned up reversed in the crowning position. "No way. That's actually kind of spooky." She explained to Bethany that Empress was the Clearview High candy dealer.

"It's *the* Empress," said Andromeda, trying to explain how sometimes cards can turn up as actual people in the querents' lives, but they are more usually symbols for forces and processes that affect people, or categories and group-ings, sometimes quite abstract rather than literal. "She's the letter *daleth,* which is a door; she goes from Two to Three, from Wisdom to Understanding. If she is a person she's usu-ally a mother or someone very womanly. You know, she's Venus. . . ."

Rosalie was staring at her like she was a crazy person.

"Yes," Andromeda finally said, giving up. "You're right. It's Empress. There she is. Hello, Empress. How are you doing down there?" Andromeda began to point sarcastically from card to card. "She's going to wear a flowing dress cov-ered with flowers and sell some candy to this guy on a horse, and then she's going to use a chisel to do some carvings on a cathedral arch and hang someone from his ankle and give some coins to some poor people, and then she's going to go on *Wheel of Fortune.*" She pointed to the Death card, and added, "And then she's going to die.

"I'm skidding," she added, as deadpan as she could make it.

"But how do you know if a card is a person or a force?" said Bethany, as though she really wanted to know. "Like, is there a card for me? If I were in this, what card would I be?"

Andromeda could have said "I audaciously identified you moments ago with Key Twenty, the Aeon or Judge-ment, because you reflect the terrible beauty of the star-encrusted night." But she didn't.

What she said was: "Actually, you could be on here. The small cards are numbers and the trumps are letters, so some-times they can spell out names or other words. So, here's the Magician, who is the Hebrew letter *bet,* so that could maybe be you, depending." Thoth speaks in riddles and puns and games. "But see how the letter *bet* looks like a house? So it could also refer to a house or an enclosure, maybe, either something small like a person or this room, or something really big like space, everything there is, anything you can put something in." Andromeda thought of her Language Arts notebook and its symbols and added: "And the Five of Cups here could even maybe be Amy, because that card can represent the first decan of Scorpio. That could just mean a date, but half of that decan is ruled by the angel PAHLIAH, whose Goetic counterdemon is called AMY." It was so much easier to look like a hotshot when you had all your notes written on the faces of the cards. And once she had explained that the zodiac, like any circle, is divided into thirty-six ten-degree segments known as decans, three for each sign, they were looking at her like they were almost interested. She felt herself blush again and looked down at her knees. But the way she would write volume X of *Liber K* had become infinitesimally clearer.

"There's actually more to this than I thought," said Bethany, and Andromeda beamed in spite of her best efforts not to. But Rosalie was not impressed.

"So basically, everyone but me is in my reading."

"Maybe this reading is for when you were in the kitchen getting the drinks," said Amy, who really didn't seem to mind at all that she shared a name with a demon who comes first as a flame and next as a man. "Skidding."

"But just say what's going to happen. Give me one thing. And who is Charles cheating with?"

"That was your question? Who's Charles cheating with?" Rosalie nodded, which seemed pathetic enough that

Andromeda started to feel sorry for her again. This was going to be a cheap trick, and not the most elevated or valid interpretation, and she silently said a prayer of apology to Thoth-Hermes and to A.E. for what she was about to do. But Andromeda took a breath and looked at the trump pairs that by position or by relation to the other cards seemed to relate to social interactions in each spread. The Magician (*bet*) and the Empress (*daleth*) in one; and the Hanged Man (*mem*) and the Wheel of Fortune (*kaph*) in the other.

"If that's what you want. Okay, if I had to guess, and I wouldn't necessarily put money on this, but I would say that there are probably at least two. One might be named Deb or some other form of Deborah like Debby. And the name of the other one might be Kim, or something else with a *K* and an *M*. Possibly Mickey or MacKenzie or something, or if it's a guy it could be Mike." She ignored Rosalie's scrunch-face over the "if it's a guy" comment and continued: "I'm not sure about Kim or Mike, but if I had to pick, I would guess that he got together with Deborah on–" She looked at the date on her watch. "Either today, or sometime in the last week or so." This was because of the Seven of Swords, representing the third decan of Aquarius; the following day the first decan of Pisces was to begin.

"I could be wrong, though," she said.

"Holy fuck," said Rosalie. Then she said, "Oh, sorry," because she had knocked her drink over and it splattered and soaked several cards before Andromeda could pick them up and dry them. Wax was okay, but hot chocolate and peppermint schnapps would leave a stain. Her notes were running and a few cards were limp and waterlogged.

"You're kidding, right? That's really in those cards?" said

Amy. They were all staring at her with "No way, dude" expressions on their faces.

Rosalie said, "I'm calling him."

✳ ✳ ✳

Charles was evidently not answering his phone, and Rosalie had left a whispered message that Andromeda couldn't hear. It was hard to see what the point was–it was easily denied.

"Just don't tell him you heard it from me," she said.

Pulling out names from the trumps in what Rosalie had already begun to call Andromeda's Whore Spread, not to mention the guess about the date, would probably not go down as Hermetic-Qabalistic divination's finest hour. Like the god it invoked and to which it was dedicated, the Book of Thoth was fluid, tricksy, as difficult to grasp as the moon, especially when used as an oracle. If Andromeda knew Rosalie, Charles was not going to enjoy his next chat with her. But Andromeda had to admit to herself that she loved the effect the reading had had on the audience. That effect would only last till the prediction failed to come to pass and she was revealed to all the world as a charlatan. Or at least to Amy, Bethany, and Rosalie, three six-billionths of the world.

As they were straightening up the playroom and calling it a night afterward, Rosalie said:

"So basically, Gypsy Woman, what you're telling me is that someone is going to die, and Empress is not involved, and it could be in a house, or somewhere out in space, and it could involve somebody's mom, and my boyfriend is doing it with a guy, and Bethany Stone is superwoman and is going to be the ruler of the universe."

"Pretty much," said Andromeda Klein.

Amy remarked that she had had no idea that tarot cards were so Hebrewcentric and asked how Andromeda knew so much about Hebrew. "Is it because–or are you–I mean, I wasn't even sure if you were–I mean, you don't really look that Jewish." As though having a Jewish parent automatically means you are fluent in Hebrew. If only.

Andromeda squinted at her, not knowing what to say. She didn't like thinking of what she looked like under any circumstances if she could help it. The dad sometimes joked around about how she was lucky she hadn't inherited any Jewish hair genes from him. Not that the Spinach U-turn hair genes would win any awards either.

"Oh, come off it. Dromedary's a total Jew," said Rosalie. "Fifty percent at least. My lovely, lovely half-Jewess. I'm skidding."

"I'm a big old Jew too," said Bethany. "Two hundred proof. We're not religious or anything."

"Neither are we," said Andromeda. "We're Nothing." Couldn't the dad have raised her as non-Nothing for just a little while so she could have at least learned a little Hebrew? Then she could have changed to Nothing after that, no problem. That was what he had gotten to do. It wasn't fair. Andromeda sure loved the way Bethany looked when she smiled her little half-smile. It was just nice. It was then that she realized who it was that Bethany reminded her of: Katherine Mansfield, the New Zealand writer of short stories who once took drugs with Mr. Crowley at a London party. Andromeda had a photocopy of a 1914 cameo photograph of her on her mirror, right under the picture of the young A.E.; she had always dreamed and wished and prayed that by some miracle she herself could be made to look like Katherine Mansfield. As Katherine Mansfield, she wouldn't even have minded being flat, which was supposed to have been quite fashionable in the days of Katherine Mansfield and A.E. But if that wasn't possible, at least it was good to know that someone in this day and age looked like Katherine Mansfield.

Rosalie let Andromeda borrow some of her harem pajamas, which were far too big on her. They would stay up on her hips only if she cinched the drawstring and secured it with the world's largest bow.

"You can sleep in my bed with me," Rosalie said, "as long as you don't slobber on me."

"Don't spoon," said Bethany as she and Amy were leaving.

"Oh, you better believe we're gonna spoon, Bethlehem," said Rosalie. "Full-on spoonathon, right here."

Andromeda was very, very tired. The room began a slow counterclockwise rotation, once it was certain she was safely lying down. She scrunched as far as she could to the edge of the bed, flat on her back, arms folded and eyes closed, determinedly spoon-resistant. She felt cool, reassuring hands draping her with raw silk, wrapping it around her, pulling it tight, and sewing her in. She settled into her box, thinking about St. Steve's texts, and about Bethany's easy smile and deep, dark, enormous pupils ringed with gold-flecked green.

"The drummer in Charles's band is named Mike," she heard Rosalie say as the lid lowered and the chains fell heavily and scraped as they were wound around. By the time the chains were being locked, she was already drifting, tight, compact, secure, the sound of whatever else Rosalie might have been saying the faintest, unintelligible tremor.

Some time thereafter, she was awakened by the sound of someone loosening the screws around her iron face mask. Daisy's scent fell on her like a mist. And when the mask had been removed and her blindfold had been taken off, she saw that the one who attended her was the King of Sacramento.

"You're back," she managed to croak out, with a great deal of difficulty.

xii.

"That is rather an interesting perspective on the matter," said the King of Sacramento's voice, coming from a corner of the room Andromeda couldn't see. All she could see was the patch of misty ceiling directly above her box. The King of Sacramento was fiddling with some metal objects, from the sound of it, and doing it in a rather workmanlike, routine way, as though he were opening a shop for business. Just another day at the office, thought Andromeda. But she immediately took his point: she was the one who was "back." The chamber of purple smoke was his, not hers.

The hands that had unscrewed the iron face covering of the Andromeda Box were bright, nearly dazzling white. When they touched anything that was touching her, the wood of her box or the chains that secured her, she felt an electric tingling throughout her body, but mostly on her lips.

She could only catch glimpses of him when he entered her field of vision as he circled the box, and these were fleeting. But she recognized him immediately as the figure who had identified himself as the King of Sacramento in the Daisy dream by his dusk-colored Tau robe and by the motions of his arms, which had looked like dancing from afar in the Pixiescape but now appeared more like ritual gestures. Though she felt wide awake and lucid, she found it difficult to make her lips form words. The King of Sacramento took the hilt of his sword and knocked it on the top of the box, and after several blows, she found she could just barely manage to utter an audible sound.

"How do I know?" was what she said, and the effort of saying even that took a great deal out of her. What she meant was, in the spirit of Solomon's questioning of his demons, "How do I know what manner of creature thou art, O King of Sacramento?"

She heard the response in her head, like the voice of Altiverse AK, and yet different. It was deep, and if it had been an actual sound rather than pulses of information in her mind, it might have been described as resonant. She wasn't sure if he had understood her.

"You need to improve your lantern anchors" was what it said.

I don't think I have any lantern anchors, she tried to say, and it came out: "Don't think."

"Yes," he said. "*Nein.* Quite so." Again, if a series of pulses of information could be said to have an accent, he sounded a bit British; or perhaps it was merely his withering, detached headmaster attitude that made her think so.

"Who?" she managed to get out, by concentrating very hard and focusing every bit of her attention on projecting her question from inside to out. She felt limp and faint.

Her box began to shake, because the King of Sacramento had sat down on it and seemed to be trembling with laughter.

"Six," said the King of Sacramento. "One naught, one five, seven seven one. In the manner of your two one eight. But the stars, like Henry Cornelius's books, are easier read than carried."

There was a stick in his hand, and he began making notches in it as he recited his numbers once again. Then he drove the stick into the earth at the foot of her box. He fiddled with it, and when he stepped back there was a piece of cloth attached to it like a flag. There was a pack of cards in his hand, and he fanned them out and waved them at the flag, till a wind was raised and it flew out from its staff. There was an image on the flag–it was two crossed swords. Then he blew it the other way, and on the other side was the design of Pixie's Three of Swords card, a heart pierced by three blades.

"Two swords?" she managed to get out. That was what she should have been asking from the beginning. The King of Sacramento held an electric finger to her tingling lips and began tying on her blindfold. He was replacing the screws in her iron mask as he said:

"Any anchoress can play the Popess with the proper hat. Have a nice day."

Then the King of Sacramento, along with everything and most of her recollection of it, was gone. Her box dissolved into the ground, which was strange because she had never managed to see where it went when she woke up.

The next thing Andromeda saw was Rosalie van Genuchten, already dressed for school, holding out a cup of coffee for her and staring down at her saying:

"Why do you sleep like a vampire, Drama-dairy? The world wants to know."

* * *

Clearview High School was not the best place to be when feeling "delicate."

"Never again?" said Rosalie with air quotes, when she saw Andromeda with her head on the table and a faraway look in her eyes during Nutrition. "Someone up there must like you, Klein, because look: no Lacey today. You'd be easy pickin's in present condition. You should see Amy: she looks like a used piñata. My work," she added piously, "is done."

Rosalie too spent the first half of the day with her head down whenever there was any opportunity to put it down, but this was largely to hide her continuous texting. Andromeda saw her surreptitiously checking her phone for replies even when she was leaning into another boy she was playing with. That was when she was caught by Ms. Chang and got her phone taken away for the day. Shortly after that, she went home sick, as much to be able to retrieve her phone,

229

Andromeda suspected, as to recuperate. Rosalie could bounce back from just about anything.

As for Andromeda, she was also secretly riding her phone all day. Having a one-woman Gestapo for a mother had been excellent training for unobtrusive phone checking. She had received four texts all told from UNAVAILABLE since the ones on the previous night. That was far more than the usual per-day average from their original phase of texting, and very satisfying. She couldn't believe how lucky she was all of a sudden. She even forgave him for having a bit of trouble getting into the swing of messaging again.

She hadn't been able to resist calling once, on her way back from locking her bike in the woods, even though she knew that was pushing it. It had always displeased him when she called, especially when not specifically invited to. In fact, he had limited her to one message a day at one point, a very difficult rule indeed. She certainly wished she could unleave the messages she had just left on his voice mail. She had modeled the call after a previous message from long ago, about how she hadn't been expecting him to pick up but had only wanted to hear his voice saying "I'm not available to take your call right now." But since that time, he had changed his outgoing message to the phone company's generic robot voice recording, and it wasn't till she was halfway through her sentence about wanting to hear his voice that she realized how inapt it was. She sputtered a bit and said a couple of frustrated "blahs" and then she was tongue-tied and silent except for sighs long enough that the recording timed out and hung up on her. So she had to call back again (pushing it even more) to say "Okay, I am an idiot. But it is true I would love to hear your voice, and . . ."

She couldn't help asking if he was still in New York, which was where he had been during the text-message-only phase of their relationship, the phase culminating in the "hi there." But it sounded awkward and, though it didn't seem too much to ask, it still felt like prying. Then she was stumped and got cut off again. She didn't dare call back. The last thing she wanted to do was to irritate him this early into their reunion. She had already blown her chance at behaving perfectly and making no mistakes from the beginning this time around. She could only hope she hadn't blown it too badly. He could be very hard to please.

The best she could do in the circumstances was text "poppy," which was "sorry" in the predictionary. Next time she dared to call to leave a message, she would write out a script, which was what she should have done this time.

By the time school let out and her shift rolled around Andromeda was feeling quite a bit better physically. No new messages from St. Steve, but that was normal. Evenings weren't his usual messaging times. As long as she hadn't ruined everything with her awful voice messages. She just had to hope he would find them amusing rather than irritating.

Her cards, when she laid them out in the Children's Thoth Annex before her shift began, were encouraging. Subthemes of magic, technology, and reunion intertwined. The return of St. Steve and the return of the King of Sacramento had synched up beautifully; and the discussion of Daisy in Rosalie's playroom, though difficult at the time, had conjured her presence more strongly than any formal ceremony had succeeded in doing, so that was a reunion of a sort too. And then there was the lovely Bethany, Katherine Mansfield and the night sky rolled into one. It was perhaps the most hopeful, and certainly the least grim, self-reading she could remember.

But what to make of the King of Sacramento? Like an ordinary dream, the memory had dissipated over the course of the day, till it was so diffuse that all she could be certain of was that it had happened. One thing she knew: she would have to get better at asking questions. Perhaps she should write a script ahead of time for him as well as St. Steve.

Rosalie called while Andromeda was on her break, and she was able to take the call in the breezeway.

"Dude," said Rosalie. "You're not going to believe this. I talked to Charles. You totally called it. Debby? Check. And not Kim, like you said, but *Cam*-eron." Ah, yes, that was possible too. She hadn't thought of the name Cam. "You totally fucking called it. And Debby *did* happen the night before, just like you said. Why haven't we been doing this all along?"

Andromeda said she was surprised he had admitted it. "Isn't that your philosophy? Deny, deny, deny? How'd you swing that?"

"I told him I had hacked into his phone. And he believed it. But if I hadn't had the names, I don't think it would have worked."

"Oh." Andromeda paused. "Are you–okay?" Rosalie sounded pretty okay.

"Of course I'm not okay. When has anybody ever been okay? But he has been trying to kiss my ass over the phone for the last four hours. It's a good time. Plus there are other options in play. How's your imaginary boyfriend these days? You've been working your phone a lot today."

Rosalie's real reason for calling was to say she wanted Andromeda to do more readings for her.

"With this power, there will be nothing stopping me. Us, I mean. Nothing stopping us. But especially me. I'm skidding."

Andromeda said that her cards were a little worse for wear. She had tried to dry them with the hair dryer in the guest vacuum, but the affected cards were stained and kind of wavy.

"I can only say I'm sorry so many times, Andromeda," said Rosalie. "Don't worry, though. I have it taken care of. Big surprise for you. Oh—gotta go. That's Charles on the other line and I have to take it so I can hang up on him. Don't die."

xiii.

When Byron the Emogeekian arrived at the hidden Temple of Thoth Hermes Mercurius Termaximus, that is, at the Children's Annex of the International House of Bookcakes, Andromeda had his Sylvester Mouse books ready for him in three neat stacks of five.

"Check these out, please," she said.

It was quite a good list, if she did say so herself.

She had started with Lovecraft's *"The Dunwich Horror"*

and Others, and added, also from the fiction section of the Sylvester Mouse list, *Zanoni* and *The Sorry Tale.* That was for fun. Then there were *True and Faithful, Gems from the Equinox,* and *Nightside of Eden,* to which she had added Euclid's *Elements* in one volume and *Babylonian Liver Omens.* From there she had gone to Crowley's *Book of Thoth,* Westcott's translation of the *Sefer Yetzirah,* and both of Mrs. John King van Rensselaer's books on playing cards. She rounded the whole thing out with *On the Mystical Shape of the Godhead,* a mid-nineteenth-century edition of the *Rituale Romanum,* and, because of his professed interest in chaos, *S.S.O.T.B.M.E.*

Byron picked up *The Sorry Tale,* which was on top.

" 'A story of the time of Christ,' " he read aloud, " 'by Patience Worth. Communicated through Mrs. John H. Curran.' " He turned to the first page and read:

"Panda, panda, tellest thou a truth? Panda, thou whose skin is burned to saffron from desert's blaze . . ."

"Is it a code?" he said.

"Everything's a code," said Altiverse AK, which was true enough. Andromeda was seated in one of the children's chairs at one of the children's tables, and the emogeekian was standing across the table from her, staring at her with an unreadable expression. He wasn't dressed nearly as horribly as he had been the previous day, and actually would have looked relatively okay, other than in the respects in which he resembled a spider monkey, and the irredeemable wispy chin beard.

"It was dictated via Ouija board," she said, "letter by letter, by a spirit named Patience Worth in 1917." A mere curiosity, compared to the others, but worthy of being saved from the clutches of the "Friends" of the Library. She wished she could save them all, of course, but she'd had to prioritize, and to stick to a list that would be halfway coherent and defensible in case her scheme was ever found out. Of course, anyone who checked out *Nightside of Eden* would naturally also check out Lovecraft and *Gems from the Equinox,* she could say, if called to take the stand in her own defense at her trial, and it would take a slick lawyer indeed to poke holes in that argument.

"If anybody asks," she said, "you can tell them you're doing it for a research project."

He was giving her the "Huh?" stare again.

Andromeda tried to explain the relation of *Liber 231* to the *Book of Thoth* and *Nightside of Eden* and why understanding the angel magic of Dee and Kelley required a knowledge of Euclid's *Elements* as well as *Liber Loagaeth,* but she got very confused by the end and wasn't sure even she understood what she was saying. There was an awkward pause, during which he finally sat down in the chair opposite her.

"You and your *libers,*" he said. "So if I read these books, I get to be in your coven?"

That creaky shuddering vibration that could be felt faintly but deeply and all over was the sound of the Universe rolling its eyes.

"You don't have to read them," she told him, adding that all that was required was that he check them out and keep them for at least a few days before returning them. "But you might want to read the Lovecraft, at least. Just to back up that Shub-Niggurath hobby of yours." She had even book-marked the beginning of "The Whisperer in Darkness" for him.

He nodded with a half-frown, pretending he intended to do it. "I'll tell you one thing right now," he said. "I am totally changing the name of my band to *Babylonian Liver Omens*." Andromeda was getting pretty tired of people making fun of *Babylonian Liver Omens* around there, but she managed a weak smile in response. "Sot-bm-ee," he said, pointing to *S.S.O.T.B.M.E.* "What's that mean?"

"Sex secrets of the black magicians exposed," she said. An important text in the Chaos tradition you claim to espouse, she thought, but didn't say.

"Seriously?" he said in an astonished way, and started paging through it. "He's salivating," said Altiverse AK, adding: "Let's see how many times we can make him rename his band."

He had brought two things for her, one of which was rather pointless and the other of which was—well, in a perfect, less Andromeda world, it would have amounted to something like the best pickup line ever, though she sincerely hoped he hadn't meant it that way.

The first thing was on his iPod.

"Choronzon," he said, and he handed her his earbuds, obviously wanting her to listen. "Shub-Niggurath, the song." She inspected the earphones for wax buildup or anything gross, but they were fairly clean. Her ears did not work very well with earbuds, however. The shape of her ears was all wrong, and the buds just would never stay in. And inside, of course, there was only disorganized collagen, so nothing was ever loud enough. She could barely hear the song, though what she could hear of it sounded like chaos, which was appropriate.

"Louder," she said, pushing them in, and closing her eyes tightly to concentrate. "Louder. I can't hear."

"That's as loud as it goes," he said. "Boy, you must really be deaf." She could barely make out what must have been the chorus, which seemed to be: "Shub-Niggurath–the song! Shub-Niggurath–the song! The goat with a thousand young!" So that really was the title; in spite of herself, she found that adorably stupid.

Byron told her he had made a CD of it for her, and he took it out of his bag. It was in a little sleeve that he had decorated with pentagrams and 666s in what was meant to look like dripping blood. The big mass of spiky blobs at the top, she realized after looking at it for a while, was the band's name, Choronzon, the most illegible logo imaginable. She had to admit he could draw well, which she envied.

"There's a special song at the end," he said.

Altiverse AK said, "Oh goody," and it was possible that that influenced that fact that Andromeda herself sounded way more sarcastic than she intended when she said: "I can't wait."

"You don't have to take it," he said, looking hurt, and Andromeda felt bad, and also thought, though she would never say it, You're cute when you're hurt. And he was, sort of almost, actually, even in spite of the near-beard. She said she didn't mean it that way, and thanked him as graciously as she could and said she would listen.

He perked right up, looking a lot like Dave did when he saw you reaching for the treat drawer.

"Yes, let me know what you think," he said. "I mean, if you want. You don't have to. Only if you feel like it."

The next thing he said was the thing she believed would be like the perfect pickup line in a world where pickup lines were ever good and where girls like Andromeda got them from people.

What he said was:

"Hey, want to see my *Necronomicon*?"

Okay, she thought, in the direction of Altiverse AK, which was saying "Oh brother" in a series of what would have been sputters if Alt AK had had physical lips and tongue and saliva with which to sputter. Okay, so he managed to put the emphasis on the wrong syllable (the *cron* rather than the *nom*), something she would have previously thought almost impossible to do. But you have to admit, altithing, that a world where boys pop up and say "Want to see my *Necronomicon*?" every now and again is a better world than the one we previously thought we had.

He pulled it out of his backpack. Altiverse AK burst into derisive laughter, but Andromeda shushed it.

It was, in fact, the *Simonomicon*. The mass-market paperback was familiar, though not part of the IHOB's collection. It had been a craze when it was published in the eighties, and it was everywhere: Savers always seemed to have a few ragged copies in the book section. But Andromeda had never seen one of the original limited, leather-bound editions of it in real life. Black with silver-gilt-edge pages, silver decorations, and a black ribbon bookmark, much like her own planned limited edition of *Liber K*. As she did with all important books, she sniffed it. And she had to admit, in response to a query from Altiverse AK, which had to rely on Primary World Andromeda's reports to assess such things: it smelled amazing. Dusty, and rather darkly sweet, with an acrid bite around the edges. Hoax or not, it smelled like magic.

"Wow," she said. "I've never seen one of these. You know it's a fake, right?"

"Yeah," said Byron. "It for sure is. I tried it out and it didn't work at all."

AAK's laughter began again, nearly drowning out Andromeda's own response; she was aghast.

"You're not supposed to *try it out!*" she whispered when she had found her voice. "Are you insane?"

"Running off the rails on a crazy train," he said enigmatically. "But what does it matter if it's a fake, anyway?"

It was hard to explain why, and Andromeda was lost for words. Maybe because the line between *hoax* and *blind* could be exceedingly thin when it came to ceremonial magic? Maybe because fooling around with a graded system of imaginary initiatory gateways could still attract mischievous entities? Perhaps she would have to let him into her "coven" just so she could keep an eye on him and confiscate the book and prevent him from accidentally awakening something that could eat the world.

"Anyway, it's for you," he said, as though reading her mind. "Now you have to let me be in your coven."

Andromeda was speechless, for a variety of reasons. It was a hoax, but it was a fun hoax, and hoax or not, it was a cool book. And it was worth quite a lot of money. She said "No, I couldn't" a few times, and asked where he got it.

"The Internets," he said. He must have lots of money

floating around, she thought. If she had that kind of money, she would bleed the Internet dry of rare books, of course. Maybe she could get him to buy some of the Sylvester Mouse books when the "Friends" of the Library auctioned them.

As these thoughts were running through her head, the emomageekian picked up the *Rituale Romanum* and asked, "What's this one?"

"The Roman Catholic ritual handbook, circa 1870," she said matter-of-factly. "Now, that one *is* real." She added that, as the weedgie knew quite well, the Catholic Mass and other rituals were extremely powerful and well-developed pieces of ceremonial magic and that it could be very useful to consult them when planning your own ritual practice or studying older writings on high magic.

"Ha," he said. "It's not."

"What's not what?"

"A powerful magic ritual. No way. The Catholic Mass is—" He paused, then said: "The Catholic Mass is like a gay man smiling at you and telling you you're wonderful and that everything is going to be all right. And you sing folk songs. I'm Catholic. Trust me. Why, what are you, again?"

"Half Spinach U-turn, half Jewess," she said. "And bacon. And Nothing."

They argued back and forth about the matter, and he finally said, returning to his habitual question, that he would prove it by taking her to St. Brendan's this Sunday if she would let him into her "coven."

She bowed to the inevitable.

"Okay," she said. "But you have to stop saying 'coven' and 'mageek,' and you have to shave off the lesbian beard."

"Ha," he said. "I shall be reporting *you* to the library police for that remark. Deal. Consider it shaven offen."

So that was how Andromeda Klein ended up with a neophyte disciple, and a date to go to church in the name of magical research. "Wait till the dad gets wind of this," said Altiverse AK, and it had a point. He must not be told, it said warningly. He must not. The only thing the dad hated more than places of worship was the Pentagon, or maybe McDonald's.

Andromeda had been trying to draw a small stylish letter *bet*, to be printed on a piece of transfer paper so she could tattoo it on her inner upper arm, and it wasn't going too well. She was only good at drawing geometric shapes. So she handed Byron the paper and pen and her Hebrew book and asked him. With no questions, he picked up the pen and dashed it off quickly, and it was just about perfect.

"Ergo, draco maledicte et omnis legio diabolica adjuramus te per Deum," Byron mispronounced, reading from where he had randomly opened the *Rituale Romanum.* Andromeda hissed and put a finger to her lips, half librarian, half sign-of-Harpocrates, and she put another finger to his lips as well, and then pulled it back quickly because it almost looked like he was going to try to kiss it or something.

"That's the Ritual of Exorcism," she whispered. Best not to recite ancient banishing incantations in a temple consecrated to gods and planetary demons, thank you very much. The last thing she needed was to chase off the King of Sacramento just when he was beginning to show himself. Her disciple had a lot to learn.

"No way," said Byron. "Spooky. Someone bookmarked it."

It was true: someone had bookmarked the exorcism section long ago with a tiny scrap of paper, now quite yellowed.

"Why does the library even have that?" said Byron.

It was a terrific question, in fact, and Andromeda Klein was rather shocked to realize that this was the first time it had occurred to her.

Just then the overhead lights in the Children's Annex flickered twice, seemed about to go out, then came back on. Such flickers happened on occasion, but the timing made this an extremely weedgie synch.

"Daisy?" said Andromeda, sniffing. She could detect no Daisy scent whatsoever. Then she tried: "King of Sacramento?" The lights stayed on, but Andromeda felt, between her shoulder blades, two distinct shivers in quick succession, which certainly seemed like a yes.

"King of Sacramento," she said, nodding.

Byron was staring at her with his head cocked to one side and his eyes narrowed, waiting for an explanation.

There was no way to explain, so Andromeda simply shrugged.

"You're scary," he said.

✳ ✳ ✳

"Who's your boyfriend?" Marlyne asked, as soon as Byron the Former Emogeekian had checked out his fifteen books and left. Anyone seen talking to anyone was "your boyfriend" or "your girlfriend," or potentially even "your Latin Loe-ver," in Marlyne's vocabulary. "He's cute," she added, revealing, for perhaps the first time in recorded history, that there was a way to say that phrase that implied "He's too short for you."

"I'm helping him with his homework," said Andromeda.

"Yes, I noticed he had all your spooky books that nobody ever checks out. He majoring in Andromeda Studies?"

Andromeda had Den's stack of fifteen books ready for him when he came in, but after the conversation with Marlyne she decided to switch out a few to make it less obvious and more age-appropriate. Some kids' books wouldn't be a bad idea anyway. She removed *A Wicked Pack of Cards* and the *Voynich Manuscript* and replaced them with *Five Children and It* and *Story of the Amulet*–they deserved to be saved too, after all, and they had led quite a few children, including herself, to *ouijanesse*. The *Magical Papyri in Translation* would have to be saved too, certainly, but just to be on the safe side she also replaced it and Wright's *History of Caricature and the Grotesque* with a couple of the more popular kids' books about wizards and dragons. There was little chance that Den was going to read any of them, though. He just wasn't a reader.

Den was extremely disappointed that there was no bagel worm agony for him, as she had promised. Andromeda had gone to school directly from Rosalie's house and had come to the library straight afterward, so there had been no time to visit the dad's sad little magazine box. She tried to interest Den in the illustrations of William Blake's *Book of Urizen*, which were rather sexy to her, but Den didn't have the right kind of imagination for that. He gave her a withering look and accepted with resignation her promise to make it up to him.

Den had brought her some treasures, though: things he had managed to dig up from around the house. There were four Daisy items: (1) a sock with a heavy object inside that turned out to be a small, smoky crystal ball; (2) Daisy's old cell phone, which, sadly, looked like it had been smashed beyond repair and would no longer work; (3) a little radio or music player of some kind, with headphones and cord wrapped around it; and (4) one of Daisy's old, and rather beat-up, teenage vampire books. (Their interest in vampires had been short-lived but intense at its height when Daisy had been diagnosed, sparked by the notion that milky leukemia blood might be rejuvenated by mixing in some regular blood. None of the blood magic they had tried had had any effect, however, and neither, for that matter, had any of the bone magic they had attempted in order to reorganize Andromeda's collagen.)

"What's that? More ninety-three stuff?" he said, noticing the *bet* Byron had drawn for her.

"It's for a tattoo," she said, explaining how you copy a design onto transfer paper and then to your skin to guide your ink-stabbing. "It's going to go here," said added, raising her arm and pointing to the spot. "A nice little *bet*." She pulled out her damaged cards and thumbed through them to show the Magician, who hadn't come out too badly from Rosalie's hot chocolate and schnapps soaking.

Den dutifully checked out the fifteen books, but said he'd never be able to carry them all, so Andromeda said he could put the ten she judged the least crucial right back in the bin. At least she had managed to save the *Turbo Philosophorum* and Giordano Bruno's *Expulsion of the Triumphant Beast,* if nothing else.

"Don't let your mom see," she said as he left with a whispered-over-the-shoulder "Ninety-three."

✳ ✳ ✳

Fifteen books to Byron and fifteen to Den. Thirty books a go wasn't bad at all. She would have new ones ready for them on Tuesday, so that would be thirty more. Until then, Andromeda decided to focus on the least crucial sections in pulling the Sylvester Mouse books, leaving the 133s and other important areas on the shelves till she could arrange to have them checked out, and thus saved. Still, it was sad, whatever books they were. Who knows when you might want to look up something about entomology, biophysics, or even knitting or papier-mâché crafts? *The History and Social Influence of the Potato. Rewinding Small Motors.* What if a small motor ever needed rewinding? How would anybody know what to do?

Andromeda did notice, however, as she was "working the list," as Marlyne liked to put it, that there was something different about weeding these sections. She tried to put her finger on it for some time before she realized what it was: these non-Andromeda sections smelled different than "her" sections, like, say, the 133s or 296s. And the reason they smelled different was that the books in the Andromeda sections tended to be older. Older books smell stronger–better, by Andromeda's lights–and the books in the 133s, along with certain other sections and much of the general fiction section, were older, dustier, and mustier. Andromeda had always known that the International House of Bookcakes had an unusually complete and extensive collection on magic, the occult, and religions, but she had always just counted that her good fortune, that the library happened to match her interests and needs so well. Of course, it had influenced the development of those interests as well, in the long years spent there day after day after school, moving from E. Nesbit to Tolkien, witches, dragons, and vampires, and on up to A.E., Crowley, and Kenneth Grant. But it was only now, confronted with the extremely limited and nonodiferous 700s, that she began to wonder why and how that came to be.

A search of the online catalog, sorted by call number and subsorted by publication date, confirmed this impression. There were an enormous number of 133s in comparison to the other sections, which she had really known already; the bulk of them had been published prior to 1960, and many of them much, much earlier. It was very different from other sections she sorted by, which seemed to have been built up in the eighties and nineties and later. And sorted by acquisition date, it was even more dramatic: other than *True and Faithful,* which she had herself donated to the library quite recently, very few 133s had been purchased or added to the collection since 1977. It was a very clear cutoff. So what had happened in 1977? Elvis had died, that was one thing, according to a quick Internet search. She couldn't think what else, though. She would have to look into it.

There was also a particular notation on many of the individual records that Andromeda didn't recognize: *JE.* There was no indication of what it stood for, and it was in the notes rather than a database field, so it couldn't be sorted for. But she checked several important titles, like *Magick Without Tears* and *Shadows of Life and Thought,* and all had the *JE* notation. *Isis Unveiled* and *On the Mystical Shape of the Godhead* had *EJMJE,* which seemed related. Most nonweedgie titles she tried did not have either notation, though *Rewinding Small Motors* was an exception. Try as she might, Andromeda could not imagine a weedgie reason to want to rewind a small motor, but perhaps there was one.

Marlyne had no idea, nor did Eileen Thigpen, the other LA-2. Even Dorothy Glass, the head librarian, said she had no idea. Gordon suggested that it could be the initials of the person who did the data entry when they made the transition from card catalog to electronic cataloging, but if so it was the only such notation, and the enterer had only remembered to do it for the good, older, and most weedgie books. It, like the presence of the Sylvester Mouse list, was a mark of quality and distinction. She didn't want to probe too obviously on this, because she was in the process of a campaign to sabotage the library's weeding program and it wouldn't do to draw attention to her interest in the matter if she could help it. It was an interesting puzzle, though; all the more interesting because it was the first time she had thought of it. How and why had the IHOB acquired its phenomenal 133 collection, and why had there been such a sudden cutoff? The person to ask would be Darren Hedge, of course, but he was the last person whose suspicions she wished to arouse by showing too much interest in what she was already beginning to call the Eejymjay Collection. He had mentioned, in their conversation in the breezeway, that the building had once belonged to a family that had donated it to the city. Perhaps, then, the books had come with the building, collected by an evidently weedgie family. JE could be somebody's initials; or it could be a shortened form of EJMJE, which sounded more like an organization or something. Jedidiah Easterbrook. Jean Eepertwinkle. The Electric Jesus Maritime Jitterbug Establishment. These were only a few of the possibilities.

The books she had donated, *True and Faithful* and *Nightside of Eden,* didn't have the notation—it would have been rather weedgie if they had had it, because she had data-entered those records herself, but of course she checked just in case.

Andromeda was in the break room eating her plum baby food and paging through Daisy's teen vampire book when she noticed a little folded plastic cardholder inside the book. Inside were Daisy's student-body card, her driver's license, and her library card.

Andromeda paused to consider. The card wasn't expired, and she doubted that canceling a dead person's library card was something anybody ever thought of doing. Would the card work? If it did, fifteen more books could be saved right away, bringing the total to forty-five. At this rate, the "Friends" of the Library's plan would really be in trouble. If Andromeda had been the sort of person to rub her hands together and cackle gleefully, or to punch the air, or to do a little triumphant butt-shaking dance like the mom, that was what she would have done. Instead, she clicked her tongue and said, "A.E."

She had to choose her moment, when Marlyne went on break and she was asked to fill in. But she managed to get all the books scanned in fairly efficiently. It felt a little strange when she saw *Daisy Wasserstrom* pop up on-screen, but it did work. Was that Daisy's scent faintly coming through the heating vent? She sniffed. Yes, very faintly, but maybe it was coming from the card.

She accepted Gordon's offer of a ride, because all those books wouldn't fit in her bag.

"I get off work here, the last thing I want to do is read," he said. "And that," said Altiverse AK, "is the difference between you and him." It's the difference between me and pretty much everybody, replied Andromeda's thought waves.

"Some light bedtime reading?" he said. She looked down and realized he was pointing to LaVey's *Satanic Bible*, which she had checked out on Daisy's card. Not, it must be understood, because she approved of it. She found it shallow and almost completely worthless, a relic and a curiosity from an earlier, misconceived dead-ended strand of the mid-twentieth-century magical revival. However, she wanted to keep the library as intact as possible. And it was certainly conceivable that she would have the occasion to quote it someday in the spirit of irony.

"If you weren't so cute," he said, "you'd be scary."

"You should poke his eyes out one by one with pencils," said Altiverse AK.

"Oh, he's not that bad," replied Andromeda, and she must have said that one aloud, because Gordon heard and seemed to think she was talking about Anton LaVey.

"You know way too much about this shit," he said finally.

Andromeda Klein didn't like the idea of anyone, even someone as inconsequential in actual real life as Weird Gordon, walking around under the impression that she had defended Mr. A. LaVey. But there was nothing to be done. She'd just have to take it. Andromeda Klein, CoS. Ha.

✳ ✳ ✳

Rosalie van Genuchten had wanted Andromeda to do another reading for her that night, and to come with her to the station. (This was a gas station at the top of Ridgemont Way. Rosalie was interested in a guy named Darren who worked there, and she was always trying to persuade people to go there with her to hang out.) Andromeda said she didn't feel good, and managed to get out of it. Was it normal to have to call in sick to your friends?

"Just do me over the phone," Rosalie said, "real quick. Am I going to make out with Darren?"

"Yes," said Andromeda. "If you want."

"Come on, you didn't even check."

"Okay," Andromeda said, pretending to shuffle some cards. "Yes, you will. If you want. And how."

"Seriously?" Well, yeah: it was pretty much up to her, after all. "How much? Can you do bases, maybe?"

Andromeda laughed, but that was actually kind of an interesting idea, so just for fun she laid out three cards. The first two were Cups and the third was the Ace of Pentacles. Why not? Water, the third element, and Earth, the fourth, depending how you count them up. Earth would definitely be a home run, and Water . . .

"Third base," she said abruptly. "Rounding third, but I wouldn't try to go for home."

"Charlatan!" Alt AK was hissing in the center of her brain.

"Okay, but what is third, then? What's the base system we're looking at here?"

"Hold on, I'll look it up in *Liber Baseballius*," Andromeda said.

"Seriously?"

"No. Not seriously."

Rosalie said nothing. Even her silences were bossy, somehow.

"Well, don't quote me on this," said Andromeda, at last, French accented, "but it also looks like there may be quite a bit of uh, how you say, moisture involved." After all, there were all those Cups.

"Okay, Klein, you got me." Rosalie was laughing slightly. "So, curiosity: do you or don't you have the hots for Brian? You had the library date. Your imaginary boyfriend must be getting jealous."

Andromeda didn't even bother to wave away the "date" description, or to say "Byron," but she could not resist mentioning, because she couldn't help feeling slightly, inappropriately proud of such a weird thing, that she was seeing him again on Sunday.

"We're going to church," she said, deadpan. It did get a snicker.

"Is that what they're calling it these days," said Rosalie. "Well, I sure hope your God doesn't smite thee. Remember to use several layers of contraceptive devices, Drama-rama, because the two of you would have ugly, ugly babies."

There was no "I'm skidding" about that one: it was hard to argue with.

"I won't die," said Andromeda. Rosalie had pressed End Call after about two-thirds of an exasperated sigh, which was her other way of saying goodbye.

As Andromeda was setting down her phone, she turned over the next card, the Five of Wands, but she didn't call Rosalie back to tell her she might have some competition at the station because that would have been silly and she was done talking to her anyway.

Just then a text from UNAVAILABLE came in. The sight of it made Andromeda feel like she was full of warm Jell-O. He was still in New York and he missed her. So she smiled real big. For her.

* * *

It was a good time to sneak onto the computer to copy her *bet* onto transfer paper, because the mom and the dad were in the kitchen having the organic argument. With any luck, they wouldn't even notice her doing it at all.

The dad, in a manic phase, was complaining because the mom had purchased corporate onions. Nonorganic produce, on manic days, at least, threw him into an incandescent rage. In the down times, he would just sigh and shake his head and mutter when something disappointed him like that, and Andromeda had to agree with the mom, though she kept it to herself, that she liked him better that way, defeated and manageable.

"It's the same stuff," the mom was saying over and over, and the dad was shaking his head. She: The *organic* sticker is just a gimmick they use to raise the prices for suckers. He: No, it is certified to have been grown with safe, healthful, and environmentally benign methods of production. Andromeda could have mouthed the words.

Andromeda looked down at her right hand. It was a Right Ring Day, which technically meant she was supposed to take the mom's side in disputes, as well as eat meat, enjoy country music and sports, and dislike immigrants. It was extremely rare that she could bring herself to do any of these things, especially agreeing with the mom, which was so extreme it had to count for quite a lot in the

Right Ring reckoning. But she was feeling "full of beans," as the dad might have put it, and exhilarated from the text, so she went for it.

"So," she said, "is this the same government that's spying on you through the TV and tracking you with radioactive money, and staging fake terrorist attacks on its own cities? You think they're trying to kill you, but you trust their little stickers?"

They were staring at her, and the dad looked hurt.

"You got to admit," said the mom, "the girl's got a point."

In the end, it was too much for Andromeda. She couldn't stick with it.

"No," she said, stomping off, "the girl does not have a point." She had betrayed the Right Ring yet again.

Later on she felt bad enough to apologize to the dad, and kind of pet his arm to cheer him up, like you'd do to an animal. He blamed it all on going off the meds.

"The state is not your friend, Dad," she said.

"Ah, my child, I have taught you well," he replied. "Now let's go eat some pesticide falafels that want to kill the planet." That was cute, but Andromeda never ate with them, and had already eaten her lime Jello-O and chickpea salad with a tiny sliver of ham to fulfill the Right Ring carnivore obligation. A different kind of daughter might have done it anyway, but that would have been a different kind of family altogether.

"I hate Israeli food," she said. "It makes me feel awful."

He was never happier than when you copycatted him.

It was comforting to wear Daisy's wig, and she liked the way it looked on her, so she put it on and wore it while she was getting everything ready.

She positioned her straight-backed chair in front of the wall mirror and tied her left wrist to the right post of the chair back. Then she ducked under her arm to sit down so that her forearm was secured behind her head and the underside of her upper arm with the transferred *bet* drawn by Byron the Disciple was secure and in view, and slowly, methodically began the tantooning.

She had banished the room with an LBRP and had consecrated her Makkuro Sumi ink and her thread and her compass point to Thoth, and had lit the room with camels at the four cardinal directions around her and in a semicircle on her side table. Feeling generous of spirit, she had tried putting on Byron's Choronzon CD, but it was just too harsh and distracting, so she wound up, once again, with good old Guillaume de M. Finally, in honor of Daisy, who, it had to be remembered, had been the one to point her in the direction of the King of Sacramento in the first place, she added a few belladonna seeds to the grains of sandalwood incense in her censer, and fanned the smoke a bit with a feather in the traditional manner.

The little *bet* commemorated her appreciation of Bethany, the return of St. Steve, the Magician, and the King of Sacramento, all at once. The very fact that she had had the idea seemed like a kind of magic. She was certainly feeling magic. And just as she realized she had somehow clicked over to magic, she added Disciple Byron to the list of significant items bound to her by coincidence and the indelible mark on her inner upper arm. By the end, she was feeling detached, quiet, drowsy, yet with a sharp, sharp mind. Beyond the shadows, the walls looked slightly liquid and the inside of Andromeda's head felt exceedingly *smooth*. The *bet* was looking very good indeed, even Altiverse AK had to admit.

"One down, twenty-one to go," it had said, referring to the letters remaining. She had room for at least that many, if she kept them small. The question was, would twenty-one further things worth commemorating end up happening to her before 2012?

Andromeda had meant to banish the room and shut the whole thing down as soon as the *bet* was finished, but Daisy's scent began to drift in, discernible underneath and around the edges of the acrid remains of the belladonna and the buttery wax, so she decided to keep it going for a bit longer. She still felt the strong, comfortable low-*ouijanesse* magic. She settled against the door and opened the Daisy bag.

The Daisy scent was overpowering now, far more than what you would expect from the items in the bag. There was a sharp uptick in the *ouijanesse* level, and Andromeda's skin began to prickle. Was she imagining it, or was there a slight intermittent vibration in her chest? It was a similar sensation to the one that had preceded the opening of the Lacey Garcia cone-of-hate gateway, but this time Andromeda felt grounded and calm, in no danger of slipping out of control like before. Daisy was there. She could feel her.

"Daisy, what are you doing?" she said. There was no answer, unless the slight shudder in Andromeda's chest and the weedgie tingles on her arms and ears were a response. She spread the rest of the Daisy bag items, the Barbies, the pill bottles, the plastic horse named Jenny, the books and notebooks, the funny goggles with their strange cord, everything, around her in a large semicircle.

Daisy's round, precise handwriting had been more or less the same for her whole life, and it was impossible to tell when Daisy had copied the Toad Bone Ritual and the Hand of Glory instructions into the notebook, though she might well have been quite young. No one would ever actually try to do the Hand of Glory, and Andromeda couldn't see Daisy doing the cruel, barbaric Toad Bone Ritual either, because she had loved animals and had been squeamish about even the idea of touching a toad's squishy body. But there were indications, in the library copy of *The Book of the Sacred Magic of Abramelin the Mage,* that she had been studying it carefully while she had it in her last year or so of life: the telltale pin marks that Daisy regularly used to mark books unobtrusively. Beginning the elaborate Abramelin Operation with no preparation and very little hope or intention of actually following it through was exactly the sort of thing Daisy would do, in fact; she rarely completed a project. Could Daisy, like Mathers, have accidentally conjured some of the Abramelin demons by playing idle games with the book? In a flash of inspiration, Andromeda paged through the *Abramelin* text, but she found no incantation that mentioned the King of Sacramento. That would have neatly accounted for the King of Sacramento's appearance, but in Andromeda's experience, neat explanations rarely turn out to be the correct ones.

"Well, Dave," she said in the direction of the cat's uninterested, lumpy shape, "we've got Daisy's missing tarot deck, the King of Sacramento, and the Two of Swords." They were connected somehow. The King of Sacramento seemed like the one to ask, but it was not a simple matter. She had forgotten the specifics of what little he had told her. There were numbers carved into a post stuck at the foot of her box. If she could ever return there, she could consult the post and try to hold the numbers in her memory long enough to write them down when she returned. And there was a Two of Swords flag.

There were, no doubt, better and more easily consulted spiritual creatures out there, but the only one Andromeda had a reasonable chance with, whatever his faults, was the King of Sacramento. He was not terribly pleasant. He was actually rather annoying. But you work with the spirits you have. There was no handbook or grimoire for how to summon him. There was only trial and error.

On the other hand, Andromeda had been spending her nights in her box for years and years, since she was very small. Assuming the box was always in the same location, the chamber with the darkly radiant purple walls of liquid and smoke, that certainly seemed like a place where the King of Sacramento spent at least some time. So where was it, this chamber? Based on the colors and the fact that it was most easily reached in a dream state, it seemed like Yesod, the ninth Sephira, associated with the moon and Mercury-Thoth, as it appears in Yetzirah, the Formative World. And if her box and its chamber were indeed in Yesod in Yetzirah, well, it was quite fortunate that she had a map of exactly where *that* was. On the Tree of Life diagram, Yesod was, of course, the sphere or state or world directly above Malkuth on the Middle Pillar. It could be reached through several routes, most directly via *tau,* Key XXI, the World or Universe. The point, then, was, if more regular meetings with the King of Sacramento were desired: to learn how to get there reliably.

Daisy's scent was still heavy in the air. Andromeda felt a remarkable peace, a sense of rightness, a floaty sensation of quiet detachment. She shuffled through her cards, turning up one after another, looking for the World, visualizing where each lay on the Tree of Life diagram. The Moon, Judgement, the Hermit, the Star. Visualizing these dynamic paths, the ten numbers they connected, and the four Worlds that constituted them all at the same time was just beyond her grasp and made her feel slightly dizzy. There was a faint clicking sound in her head and the flat, monochromatic diagram suddenly came alive and seemed to rise out of her. It was a fluid and three-dimensional, many-colored, astonishingly beautiful jewel with uncountable flashing facets, turning itself inside out continuously, hovering above her head.

It was gone a second later. Her head throbbed and ached. The painful rhythmic flapping sensation might have been the sound of her blood pumping in her ears along with her accelerated heartbeat, but it also coincided with the sound of Alternative Universe Andromeda Klein clapping.

And the rushing sound of the cars going by on the highway grew louder in her ears and the static formed itself into words more distinct and prominent than she had ever heard before from AAK. "Finally," it was saying. "Finally. Thoth be praised. Amen. It only took you around a decade and a half to figure it out."

Plain Old Universe Andromeda Klein had no idea what to say.

"Now, there is a relief," said the voice, continuing. "Turn your good ear toward the window and focus on the traffic, otherwise you might lose me again. Have you ever noticed, you are very hard to talk to? Not a great listener. I know, you learned it at your mother's knee. But that Master gave you around a googol-zillion hints and you noticed none of them. Still distracted by your quest for unavailable penis. It is a common problem down there. Unrequited love, they call it, when they wish to be delicate. Tragic."

It was a strange sensation. It was the same inner voice, but with a difference, not louder in her head but more present, each word vibrating with a slight flutter. The most irritating aspect of this peculiar outburst, perhaps, was the fact that her own inner voice seemed to have adopted some of Rosalie van Genuchten's vocabulary as well as the mom's bossiness.

"I can't remember what he said," Andromeda conceded meekly. "You're right. I'm a horrible person."

"You are not bad as people go. Would you like to know what your problem is? I will tell you: you think you know everything. Also, you tailor your behavior so that you appear to be tasteful and humble, and you fool yourself quite easily, so you are not even aware of the fact that you think you know everything. But now you know. I just told you."

"Sorry," said Andromeda, not really sure to whom she was apologizing. Was this what it felt like to go crazy? Was this how it had started with the dad? Had someone slipped her a drug somewhere along the line? Could it be the belladonna? Your own second thoughts weren't supposed to argue with you like that, much less shower you with abuse and boss you around. Most confusing of all, Alt AK's voice seemed suddenly to have some pretty good advice.

"Say sorry to yourself. It is nothing to do with me. So yes, that Master was serving up some pretty hot stuff, but of course you weren't paying attention. Fortunately, I was. He gave you some numbers—no, you don't need to write them down. I'll remember them for you. Ask when you need them. . . ." The voice began to replay the King of Sacramento's words exactly as he had said them, in a mechanical monotone. And it was remarkable: as the recitation continued, the vanished memory of the dream came rushing back as vividly as ever. This could be a useful system.

"So I need to work on my lantern anchors," she said, when the voice got to that part.

"No, dopey," said the voice. "He said you need to work on your Latin, and he called you an anchoress."

"What's an anchoress?" asked Andromeda.

"Look it up" was the reply. "Do I have to do everything around here? Ahem. Oh, and the verses about the anchoress and the Popess and Henry Cornelius just about killed me. A clever, clever Master."

"So," said Andromeda, not sharing the voice's sense of humor. "Now you have a crush on the King of Sacramento. Great."

"Don't be so ridiculous," said the voice. "He seemed well familiar with the one you call Twice Holy, and clearly implied that if you were half the Henry expert you claim to be, you'd have fewer fortune-telling problems."

"The Henry expert," said Andromeda. "Are you going to make me ask?"

"Henry Cornelius Agrippa!" said the voice. "Duh. Try to keep up."

* * *

The question was on the tip of Andromeda's tongue, though she hesitated to say it. Conversing with someone who is in your own head can be confusing, though, since to think it is the same as saying it and the voice proceeded as though she had said it.

"My name? Honey, you could not pronounce it. You have always thought of me as Alternate You, and that suits me. So does 'It,' or 'That.' Carry on as usual."

Carrying on as usual was going to be difficult.

Andromeda thanked it for its help but admitted, as deferentially and politely as she could, that she was still rather confused and didn't know what was going on.

"Going on?" repeated the suddenly loquacious Alt AK. "Lord of the Aeon, you are slow. This is what is known as Knowledge and Conversation. That is what is going on. As in, I'm your Holy fucking Guardian Angel."

And her Holy fucking Guardian Angel chattered relentlessly at her deep into the night.

xiv.

The Holy Guardian Angel would answer no questions about Itself. "And what manner of creature art thou, O Holy Guardian Angel?" met with content-free, rushing silence no matter how Andromeda phrased the query. It was good at math. It was good at remembering things–the name of every doll Andromeda had ever had, for instance, in the order she had had them; the pharaohs of Egypt; the entire list of Sylvester Mouse books, saved and unsaved. And It could be quite funny, even if Its jokes were most often at Andromeda's expense. But It was not a splendid conversationalist: It tended to fade out after short bursts, often, it seemed, as punishment for questions It didn't like. Then, just as Andromeda would settle down and begin to drift off to sleep, the voice would return, buried yet discernible amidst the sound of the cars on the highway or the wind, jabbering on an entirely different subject, keeping her awake.

This was going to take some getting used to.

"Why the Two of Swords?" Silence. "Where do you go when you're not talking to me?" Nothing. "Where is Daisy's tarot deck?" In response to this, Andromeda detected, in the distant buzz of the refrigerator motor down the hall, what sounded like a snort.

If you were a book of unbound leaves, where would you hide? was the response.

"It? It?" she mentally called, and moved her lips in a slight whisper. (The voice would respond to silent thoughts, but she found it easier to articulate thoughts when she spoke or whispered.) "Look," Andromeda finally said, "I can't just keep calling you 'It.' Or 'Alternative Me.' "

Very well, It said, roaring back, irritated. *My number is 1000. So you may call me "One-thy."* It sounded too much like something Baby Talk Barnes might say, and even It could see her point.

"You're the Holy Guardian Angel around here," said Andromeda. "Just tell me. Pick something."

Fair enough. You shall refer to me as Huggy.

"Huggy?" She hesitated. It sounded a little ... stupid. "Oh, I get it: from HGA."

Take it or leave it was all Huggy would say. Then It said: *Farewell,* and Andromeda felt Its presence receding, spiraling into nothingness, or perhaps into a fine mist somewhere inside her, not in her head as she might have supposed but in a spot in her chest.

"Who's the King of Sacramento, Huggy?" Andromeda blurted out, but It was already gone.

✳ ✳ ✳

"Huggy? Huggy?" Andromeda Klein whispered when she woke up on Saturday morning. She tried in the singsong voice she used to call Dave: "Huggy! Huggy!" That brought Dave to the door, scratching. You could say "concrete" or "tomato" in that tone and Dave would come running, treat-mad. He gave her a cold look, however, when she let him in, as though even he couldn't quite believe she was going along with this Huggy business.

"What a *nurse* is going on in there?" said the mom's voice, followed by officious clicking as she clomped down the hall to Andromeda's door. "On earth," she meant, probably. Not "a nurse."

Andromeda managed to slam the door shut with her shoulder just in time to prevent the mom invasion. The mom didn't need to see her bandaged arm or the remains of her tantooning gear or the ropes dangling from the chair back.

"Strength of a tiger, strength of a tiger," Andromeda mumbled, and braced herself against the door. The mom outweighed her by quite a lot and could have easily pushed the door in, Andromeda and all. Whether the simple tiger charm had any effect was impossible to say, but Andromeda won the battle of wills. The mom gave up and clacked off, muttering unintelligible curses along the way.

"Huggy?" Andromeda repeated. In the down-to-earth daylight, Huggy was nowhere to be found.

Andromeda imagined herself shaking her head and saying something like "Wow, what a weird dream" and perhaps recounting it to the dad or to Rosalie van Genuchten, or even to St. Steve if she ever got to talk to him in real time, later on. St. Steve would be the perfect person to tell such a thing. He hardly reacted even to her weirdest disclosures. "I dreamed that the voice I always hear in my head separated itself from me and turned out to be my Holy Guardian Angel, and she, or I guess It, gave me advice on how to enter the realm of the King of Sacramento." Then everybody could laugh, and the story could end. She could finally be a regular girl again. Except it hadn't been a dream. She could never be a regular girl. And she could never tell a soul. While they no longer burn you for such admissions, they do put you in institutions and give you drugs to disconnect your mind from your brain.

Yet while it had been no dream, it had been dreamy. The specifics eluded her when she tried to pin them down, as with dreams. In fact, now that Huggy was no longer there to prompt and goad her, the details about the most recent colloquy with the King of Sacramento were slipping away again as well. There was a string of numbers; there was an order to become better educated, to learn Latin and study Agrippa more carefully. Any anchoress can play the Popess. With the proper hat. The Popess was the name given to the

High Priestess in the earliest tarot packs, a female Pope. And Andromeda Klein was an anchoress, which is a–a female anchor?

"Huggy?" No response. Dave padded up and inclined his little Batman head, as though to say "Yes, mistress?" "Well, Dave," she said, "looks like it's just you and me, kid. And it looks," she added, picking up the library's copy of the *Abramelin* and sliding it into her bag, "like we won't be needing *this* anymore." And it was true: she appeared to have managed to skip some steps, achieving Knowledge and Conversation of the Holy Guardian Angel without even trying to conduct the elaborate Abramelin Operation. If so, it had to be one of the most successful magic operations ever completed by accident, one for the record books. It felt a little like cheating. Perhaps one day, when she had the leisure, she would perform the formal operation anyway, just to make it up and ensure everything was correct and proper. Or maybe, had she done it properly in the first place, she might have wound up with a better, less obnoxious HGA.

"You get what you pay for, Dave," she said, scratching his ears. If it had been that easy for Andromeda to skip ahead, perhaps Daisy's dabbling with the *Abramelin* text hadn't been quite so preposterous. After all, if Mathers had inadvertently conjured some of the *Abramelin* demons merely by translating the text, and Andromeda had actually achieved Knowledge and Conversation with her admittedly substandard Holy Guardian Angel by doing pretty much nothing, who was to say that Daisy couldn't have stumbled upon K & C with her own HGA by sticking pins in a library book? And if so . . .

"Huggy," said Andromeda. "Is the King of Sacramento by any chance Daisy Wasserstrom's HGA?"

"Meow," said Dave.

Daisy, and Mathers, for that matter, might well have done other things as well. What had Andromeda done, prior to Huggy's emergence? Belladonna seeds mingled with the sandalwood incense, the combination used in her and Daisy's most successfully weedgie séances and operations; restraint, an arm stretched behind her head and tied to an object; hundreds of needle pricks, in her arm rather than in a book; the letter *bet* inscribed on her body, or the act of inscribing it; the act of imagining Bethany Stone's deep, enveloping, scryable eyes; energy from St. Steve's reappearance and unusually forthcoming texts; and, possibly, Byron's having submitted himself for discipleship and gifting her with his *Simonomicon*. Perhaps it wouldn't have worked at all without a *Simonomicon* nearby. All this preceded, of course, by a Daisy-sparked disordering of her state of mind and the Eejymjay crisis–involving, it must be remembered, her having laid hands on each important magic book in an organized, systematic way. And finally, a lifelong habit of imagining herself bound and locked in a box and of holding imaginary conversations with a self-critical inner voice.

In a way, it was a kind of ritual, and a rather elaborate one at that. It could be repeated and tested by science, certainly. Though, and this seemed the most important realization of all at the moment, only by her. No one without a box and an Alternative Universe voice, not to mention a St. Steve and a Daisy and the IHOB and Bethany and Byron, would have a hope of re-creating those conditions, even with detailed instructions. How would you even begin to write the grimoire of that?

She spoke the question aloud to Dave: "Is that why the rituals in books never seem to work no matter how careful you are?" But to ask the question was to answer it. Of course it was, or at least, it was one reason why. Deliberate blinds were another. And of course, it was possible that some of them had never worked in the first place.

She paused to allow either Dave or Huggy to confirm this insight, perhaps to congratulate her. Dave blinked at her. What would Huggy say? Something like "Bingo," sarcastically delivered, probably, and she thought she might have heard a distant "Bingo," in fact, though it came from far off and not from within her breast or head, so it might well have been her imagination or merely a slight variation in the faint rushing sound always in her ears owing to her disorganized collagen.

At any rate, if Huggy's mission was to help Andromeda sort out her King of Sacramento and Daisy situation, It was going about it rather strangely. It had certainly helped organize the interaction with the King in a way that could make a kind of sense, though she had a hard time remembering much of it now. But Its incessant chatter all through the night had kept her out of her box and prevented any possibility of another dream session with the King of Sacramento. How are you supposed to float in your box to a shadowed astral chamber with a sarcastic, know-it-all HGA prattling on and on in your ear all night?

"And there's another one, Dave," she said, pulling on her jeans and checking her phones. She meant another possibly important element of what she was now beginning to think of as the Huggy Tantoon Working. Christmas trees and old-fashioneds the night before, horror films, and fortune-telling. With, let's see, six additional possibly unwitting celebrants, two of whom must leave in the midst of the divination, and one of whom must have deep, lovely scryable eyes.

No messages from St. Steve. Three from the mom: "I love you, honey"; "don't forget to eat today"; and "what's the matter don't you love me anymore?" Sad. "I love you just fine," she texted back.

"Want to see my *Necronomicon*?" she said to Dave with a sly, flirtatious wink and a saucy pose, jeans still halfway on. She had pulled the book out of her book bag and held it up like a game-show assistant.

Dave made a sound she had never heard from him, a kind of deep-throated whimper. She dropped to her knees and held the book so he could investigate. He sniffed it carefully, gingerly, then suddenly yowled and ran off to hide deep in the closet. She had never seen him act that way. Had this happened at night, it would have been quite weedgie, in fact, but in the morning it was only curious. For a cheesy hoax, there sure was something about that book.

"The *Simonomicon*," said Huggy, reappearing in a rush. "As powerful as a vacuum cleaner." But it was a shadow of the Huggy of last night, more like the usual Alternative Universe Andromeda Klein, which, despite the sarcasm, was still like a gentle voice, offering a self-questioning thought here and there. The loud, aggressive, assertive Huggy of the previous night was gone. Maybe It had to be conjured. Which was another way of saying, perhaps, that Andromeda had to alter her mind so she could hear It properly.

Andromeda made the mistake of looking at herself in the mirror at that point and realized that if she were to be quite scrupulous she would have to add yet another instruction to the preparation section of the Huggy Tantoon Working ritual: celebrant must have bad hair. Bad hearing, too, though for someone with supremely well-organized collagen, earplugs would probably suffice. A bad mind. And no ass. How a normal adult female celebrant would swing that one, she had no idea. Males and young girls were more likely to meet the requirement, she thought, though this thought made her sad.

"That's where Isaac Newton went wrong," she said, thinking it might be something Huggy would say or at least appreciate. She imagined Huggy's "voice" agreeing, and she imagined what It would probably say, which was "Yes, he should have taken off that wig." But no, that wasn't right: she *had* been wearing a wig, Daisy's wig. So wigs were back in, Isaac Newton's judgment reaffirmed.

Andromeda waited for, then imagined, Huggy's confirming "Bingo." But imagining it and hearing it were very different. She couldn't make it happen. It figured that Andromeda would get assigned such a stubborn, disagreeable HGA. It just did.

"Do you know how to hot-wire a car?"

Rosalie van Genuchten was on the phone, and the mom was pretending to take inventory of the refrigerator's contents while straining to hear every word through the kitchen wall. Andromeda had availed herself of a rare opportunity to use the computer in the dining room to look up *anchoress* on the Internet. Huggy had popped up to tell her the word, which she had forgotten, while she was in the bath, the still-distant voice bubbling up from the sound of the rushing tap. Perhaps this is always what happens when people "remember" things; they're just not sensitive or knowledgeable enough to realize that Some Thing is bringing it forth. Strangely, the voice she had always thought of as her Alternative Universe self had never been so quiet and elusive as it was now, when she had finally experienced it in its full, uncloaked form.

Still, It had also, in passing, told her that she shouldn't wash her hair so much because it deprived the scalp of essential oils, and reminded her that she had left the *Simonomicon* out and recommended putting it back in the bag, just to be on the safe side. Huggy could be positively momlike.

"I don't know anything about cars," Andromeda told Rosalie, which pretty much went without saying. "My dad uses a screwdriver in his van."

"What kind of screwdriver?" asked Rosalie, but Andromeda didn't know, and she said she didn't suppose it mattered what kind. Rosalie had been caught raiding her mother's supply of weed and had been "grounded." Practically, this meant nothing, because her mother was spending the weekend with her boyfriend in Carmichael and anyway Rosalie laughed at such weak-willed attempts at parental discipline, as one does. However, her mother had taken both sets of keys to the Volvo with her.

"Wow, mean," said Andromeda.

"I did get the door open, but now I'm stuck," said Rosalie, adding that they needed to be mobile because there was a party at the station that night. "You have to come. Josh wants to hang out with you, and you have to witness the awesome continuing adventures of Rosalie and Darren, the service-station years."

"Can't Darren just give you a ride up there?" Andromeda asked. Rosalie loved to bore her with rapturous descriptions of Darren's car, which was a something-or-other.

"No, it's a, uh, *surprise* party. But they're going to be there and so are we, so how could that not be worth your while? Isn't there a thing where you can start a car without the key if you roll it down a hill?"

"Probably a bad idea," said Andromeda Klein. "I'm still not feeling–"

"Ask your dad, maybe," said Rosalie, interrupting. "And don't die."

Andromeda had no intention of surprising the gas-station guys with Rosalie in a hot-wired parental Volvo. She had more weedgie things on her agenda.

She shoved her phone in her sweatshirt pocket, narrowly avoiding a disaster as the mom came in saying "Who was that, what did they want?"

The blue phone no longer worked, so Andromeda had had to adopt a new phone strategy till she figured out something better. She kept the red phone's SIM card in her right jeans pocket and the blue phone's SIM card in her left pocket when it wasn't in the phone. That was so she wouldn't get confused when she switched them; obviously the blue phone's card stayed in the still-functioning red phone till it needed to be switched. But if the mom spotted the red phone, there was no telling what might happen, so she had to keep it hidden. This scheme required that she wear jeans and a sweatshirt with big pockets in which to hide the phone suddenly when necessary. Andromeda found that the pockets of Daisy's vinyl coat were good for that purpose. Possibly it might require being seen pretending to talk into the dead blue phone from time to time. In a way, having only one handset to carry around was more convenient, though she would have to find some of those tiny jewelry bags to keep the SIM cards dry on those days when they turned the heat too high and she ended up sweating like a pig. Which was pretty much all the time in Clearview.

"Who's this Darren?" said the mom. Andromeda held up a finger, as though to say "Hang on a second," and deftly slipped out the kitchen door and down the stairs.

The dad was out in his van with the door open and his headphones on.

"Cupcake!" he said with an enormous smile, stopping the tape and cranking down the window when he noticed her standing there watching him. "So you escaped too? Good good good. There's plenty of room if you want to hide out with me. Your mother will have to content herself with yelling at the fridge. Meanwhile, we will tunnel our way to freedom and build a new world on the other side." He had to get out and let Andromeda slide in because the passenger-side door didn't open.

"You're in a good mood," Andromeda said.

"I know! I know!" he said. "Isn't it grand? The new meds are supposed to level me off, but here's the beauty part: they don't work! Not even a little." He gave her an exaggerated crazy-eye look. "Not to worry, though. Soon I'll crash and you will have your customary demoralized parental unit who failed in life back again. But what's the use of having two balls if you can't swing on one of them sometimes?"

"Good one," she said after a brief, faintly disturbed pause during which Huggy whispered that he was making a bipolar disorder joke and had meant to say "poles."

"I got a million of them," he said, "but technically you're only allowed two." There were probably many pretty good pole jokes that could have been made here by someone who wasn't his daughter.

The dad explained that he was "nuts about" this band he was recording later in the week, and that he was listening to their demo. He took out the CD and Andromeda nearly fell over with surprise when she read the label.

"Choronzon?" she said. "You're recording them?"

"Yeah, you know them?" he said incredulously. It was well known that Andromeda had little familiarity with, and still less interest in, rock music of any kind. And it seemed a pretty good bet that it was an obscure outfit anyway.

"I have a friend who does," she said, bracing herself for skepticism on this point. It was true, too. She did have a friend who liked Choronzon the rock group. As ridiculous as it sounded, it was rather neat, like how regular people probably are all the time, having friends who are into all sorts of things, and you know about it. Because they tell you. And on occasion you are called upon to describe these interests, and doing so amounts to a public announcement that you are in their confidence.

"They're Cthulhu rock," she added, trying to sound knowledgeable, but the term didn't seem to register.

Byron had talked about it as though they were a real, legitimate band, but they couldn't be that big if they were recording at the dad's little hole-in-the-wall studio. She waved away the headphones when he held them out to her.

"Can you make me a CD?" she asked, knowing exactly what he was going to say in response, and knowing that he would know that she would know.

"Sure," said the dad. He wiggled his fingers at her. "Poof: you're a CD!"

✳ ✳ ✳

The dad had tried to explain to her how to start a car by pulling down some wires under the dash and connecting them to each other. He seemed a little confused by it himself.

"It's better," he finally said, holding up his screwdriver, "if you have a key."

It didn't matter: Andromeda had no intention of being Rosalie's enabler at car theft and vandalism, especially if all that was in it for her was a trip up to the gas station to watch Rosalie flirt with Darren What's-his-dick. Then she laughed on the way inside, because she realized he and her boss had the same name and had an image of Rosalie kissing and grinding on Darren Hedge at the reference desk.

You should talk, jailbait, came another short burst from Huggy. Did all HGAs talk like that? How on earth had she ended up with such an obnoxious one? She'd have preferred a more weedgie-sounding vocabulary, too.

"What's going on out there?" said the mom suspiciously– the kind of question that did not deserve an answer. Andromeda just stared at her, but Huggy said *Hatching a plan to tunnel to freedom and start anew* and Andromeda snickered.

276

"Yes," said the mom, "yes, that is just so amusing that I would want to know what's going on in my own house. Hardy-har-har. And here's another great big huge joke: that van Genuchten girl was here yesterday."

Rosalie hadn't mentioned that on the phone, but true to form she had left some random items for Andromeda: a half-full packet of Empress's tearjerkers, two paper clips, and a pencil. The mom also handed her a new pack of disposable contacts in her approximate prescription and size that she had swiped for Andromeda from the mall optometrist where she worked, and accused Andromeda of trying to hack into her e-mail, stealing and hiding the TV remote, eating all the baloney, and just being a difficult child who couldn't look anyone in the eye. Andromeda had to acknowledge the last of these, and to thank her for the first, because her last pair of contacts was getting pretty crusty.

"So you're spending the rest of the day in virtuality?" said Andromeda as she headed for her room, but the mom was already on the computer with her headphones on, typing furiously and saying "Goddamn network . . ."

✳ ✳ ✳

Once back in her room, Andromeda got out her notebook and compass and straightedge and drew her own Tree of Life, as carefully as she could. She had never thought of doing this before, nor had she really considered it as an actual map. In a sense, she realized, the Tree of Life diagram itself is a glyph, a kind of sigil, and the very act of trying to envision its workings, how it related to the reality it diagrammed, could cause her state of mind to shift ever so slightly. Perhaps more intensive work with it as a sigil was in order. It was obvious once you thought of it, but she had certainly never considered trying such a simple technique.

Andromeda's many attempts to meditate on tarot cards and use them as gateways to astral realms as taught by the Golden Dawn had never worked, but that was before Huggy and the flashing, spinning, undulating Universe-gem. She retrieved her liquor-damaged deck and sorted through the cards, once again looking for the World. She couldn't find it. It wasn't there. She was usually so careful with her cards, but she had been a little trashed that night. She had probably dropped it. It was still at Rosalie's house, no doubt, under the sofa or somewhere.

Obviously, this was another, perhaps crucial, element of the Huggy Tantoon Working: the tarot deck resting on the tantoon desk–that is, on the altar or Table of Art–must be missing Key XXI, the World. If you took it far enough, you could say that the card would have to be clear across town, at the same location where the previous divinatory operation had been conducted the previous evening, with the six unwitting celebrants. Would the two who left before the divination begins have to be a Christian Thing both of whose heads objected to the *ouijanesse*? Perhaps they could simply be adepts playing that role, maybe even sewn into a single garment with two neck holes. They would probably have to make out, though. When she got a chance she would have to check the star map of those particular days and hours, too. That undoubtedly had had an effect as well.

Perhaps the message of the missing card was that the World was the correct path, or perhaps it was to suggest alternate routes instead, Judgement and the Sun through Hod, or the Moon and the Star through Netzach. At any rate, having an incomplete deck made Andromeda feel a little incomplete herself.

She had done a terrific, precise, even artful job of drawing her Tree of Life glyph, but no amount of staring at it would cause it to come alive and spin into the flashing jewel. Her desire to glimpse it again was something like lust, something she felt with her entire body.

She was about to give up and put the diagram away when the city recycling truck pulled up and idled in front of Casa Klein, and in the midst of the sputtering rumble of its engine and the shouts of the men, Andromeda detected Huggy's voice.

Have you ever noticed, It said, *how much better you were in her presence?*

"Daisy, you mean," said Andromeda after thinking a moment.

No, Eleanor Roosevelt, said Huggy. *Yes, of course I mean the one you call Twice Holy, you ninny. She was a gifted natural medium. Spirits loved her. You, on the other hand: not so much. Some spirits, however, are notorious for their lack of attention to detail. SALLOS once mistook Monsieur for Solomon the Great just because he was gnawing on Henry Cornelius's wand.*

Monsieur was Agrippa's big black dog. Andromeda laughed, because it sounded like it was supposed to be funny. But it was true enough. Traditional magicians sometimes dressed like Solomon, wearing lion-skin belts in hopes of fooling the spiritual creatures into believing they were actually Solomon.

"You're saying I should wear Daisy's, er, cow-skin belt?"

I'm saying, said Huggy, *that any anchoress can portray the Popess. With the proper hat.*

Andromeda reached up to her owl statue, retrieved Daisy's wig, and put it on her head.

The sound of the recycling truck was fading as it headed down the road, and Huggy's *Bingo* was a little hard to catch.

"You know," said Andromeda, "it would save a lot of time if you guys could just, like, say: 'Hey, Andromeda, wear Daisy's wig more.' "

Thanks for the tip, said Huggy dryly. *I'll be as plain as I can. You have in your possession a whole bag of equipment–*

But the truck was gone and so was Huggy.

Just to see what would happen, Andromeda gathered all the Daisy materials–the ones from the original Daisy bag, along with the items added to it from Den's subsequent excavations. She put on everything that could be worn in addition to the wig: belt, knitted gauntlets, China flats, vinyl coat. As before, she put the strange goggles on top of her be-wigged head, and wrapped the cord around it like a headband. She put the Little One in the coat pocket with just its head peeping out. What else? She hesitated at the bottle of antidepressants, but then abruptly popped one in her mouth: one probably wouldn't do much harm, and they had made Daisy's dreams more vivid. She spread the rest of the stuff out, the books, the papers, the headless Barbie and the Barbies with heads, the crystal ball, Jenny the horse. The weird little music-player thing . . .

All of a sudden she knew what to do with that. The cord from the goggles fit perfectly in one of its jacks, and with the metallic locking sound it made she thought she could just hear another *Bingo* from Huggy. She had to get her headphones and plug them in too as the ones that had been attached and wrapped around the unit originally were broken. Then she put the goggles and headphones on and pressed Play, changing no other settings.

It was not music in her ears but pulses and toneless, gentle white noise. Lights pulsed in front of her eyes as well, but soon she felt floaty and detached and distant from her senses. She had slipped into another world. Huggy's voice was crystal clear in the tones in her ears, though all It said was: *Bingo*. Then Andromeda saw the Universe jewel, spinning and turning endlessly inside out, even more vivid and beautiful than before. She couldn't see the King of Sacramento but she felt him there with her somehow, and at one moment she had the distinct impression of his hands on her shoulders.

✳ ✳ ✳

The unit's batteries ran down soon enough and Andromeda slipped back into the mundane. She felt wonderful. So that was Daisy's secret. She was going to have to get more batteries for that thing.

Dave had emerged from the closet and was sitting on top of Byron's *Simonomicon* purring. So much for Simon, thought Andromeda. Even less powerful than a vacuum cleaner, in the end.

"Or maybe it's just not turned on?" she said to Dave, who returned her stare coldly. There was still something faintly weedgie about the book, but it was a bit of a relief that its *ouijanesse* could no longer be regarded as proven by objective animal experiment: there were many, more reputable tomes whose *ouijanesse* was far more legitimate and established. Dave seemed calm, serene, like a Buddha in compact form, like a big furry egg with a Batman head.

A text from UNAVAILABLE vibrated in. She was suddenly tingly and out of breath and nervous. Earlier that morning she had texted him a request for a photo.

It had been a daring request. St. Steve hated the very idea of her having photos of him, and she had dutifully deleted the few reluctant pictures he had sent her way back in the beginning of their—what was the word for what it was? *Relationship* sounded wrong, though accurate in the sense that any two objects had some sort of relationship to each other. *Association,* perhaps, was better. *Affair* sounded grown-up and rather marvelous, and *The St. Steve Affair* would have made a terrific title for a spy novel, but that overstated things. The shadowy picture she had secretly taken of him at the Old Folks Home with her old digital camera had melted down with the camera, and even in that one, he'd had his hand in front of his face. She had loved looking at that hand, however, and she could still see it vividly, if not clearly, in her mind.

She knew there was a good chance he would be mad, and was bracing for a blow. So she held her breath and made a wincing teeth-clenched face when she pressed Yes to view the message.

"You first," it said.

She spent the next two hours trying to take a sexy-enough phone picture to send him that she didn't look too dumb in. It sure wasn't easy. Finally, as the sun began to sink past her window and seep through the blinds, and turned the room slightly reddish, she was able to capture an image in which her skin looked less horrible than in real life, and to frame it so her hair wasn't terribly involved. She would have loved to smile at him in the photo, but her smiles all looked stupid and dorky, so she pursed her lips in a kiss, and tried to make her eyes dreamy. It didn't look too bad, unless she was kidding herself. In fact, it didn't really look much like her at all, thank goddess.

She had imagined, but never dared, doing something like this before, and now she had done it. Instantly she felt like she shouldn't have. But it was too late, and anyway, he had asked, something he had never, ever asked before. Perhaps it was the jewel that made it happen. Or maybe the St. Steve sigils were finally working; he was doing everything she had prayed for, even if he was still a continent away. Perhaps one of the sigils would eventually bring him back to Clearview.

It had been quite an effort, and Andromeda had had practically no real sleep the previous two nights owing to Huggy's chatter. Imagining St. Steve receiving her picture and fantasizing about her—it felt wonderful despite her fear that maybe it wasn't quite the right thing to do. Almost suddenly, she crashed into deep sleep.

XV.

Andromeda's phone was vibrating in her hand, but it didn't say "UNAVAILABLE." It said "R & E."

"First you say hello, then I say hello, and so on and so on," said Rosalie when Andromeda pressed Answer but couldn't manage to say anything. She was still in her photo position with her knees tucked under her and her arms outstretched and her face on the floor.

"What?" she finally managed to say.

"Get it together, Klein. Look, can you be ready in fifteen? I need to pick you up like right now. I'm afraid to turn the engine off now that I got it going." Apparently she had managed to hot-wire the Volvo.

"What?" said Andromeda, still disoriented. "Where are we going?"

"To the *station*, An-dumb-eda. I will pause to let it sink in," Rosalie said. But she didn't pause. "Remember, we agreed ages ago, and I don't have time to go over it again. Party at the station. Big surprise. Dress cute."

"What?" said Andromeda, but Rosalie had already hung up.

Dave, still sitting on the *Simonomicon,* gave her a silent meow, as though he understood it all.

"Stop looking like a person, Dave," she said. "This instant."

Andromeda's arms and legs were all pins and needles, as though they had really been bound with silk and rope. The room was dim, near dark. Eight-thirty. She had been asleep for four hours, and she was still half asleep now.

There was no way she could get ready in fifteen minutes. Her hair was hopeless, matted and flat on one side, curled and wispy on the other, like waving strands of seaweed. So, of course, she put on Daisy's wig. Besides its Huggy-approved weedgie-ness, it was better than her real hair, and actually, if she held her head a certain way and unfocused her eyes a little, she looked okay as a blonde in the mirror. She was emboldened by the wig to try one of Daisy's tight, sheer, long-sleeved shirts; it didn't look as good on her as it had on Daisy, but St. Steve had seemed to like it and it wasn't all that bad on her, really. Though of course, she hid it with her large black hooded sweatshirt zipped up all the way.

"Why am I even doing this?" she said to the Andromeda in the mirror, and the mirror Andromeda rolled her eyes.

The mom was still on the computer, communing with Wildman_B in the persona of Tigress_67. It would be the "real" Wildman_B rather than Rosalie impersonating him now, since Rosalie was not at the computer but in the car; though, who knew, there could have been other Wildman_B impersonators out there. Andromeda left a note on the kitchen table saying she was going to Rosalie's and wouldn't be home late. Tigress_67 had her earbuds in and couldn't hear Andromeda as she crept out the door. The dad's van was gone—so he had escaped into the night too. Good for him. Or maybe he was recording Choronzon, inadvertently summoning Cthulhu and dooming the world.

"Like I said, good for him," she said, more for Huggy's benefit than anything, though there was no answer. The world was annoying and if not already doomed, in desperate need of dooming.

"Twenty twelve," she said. "That's all I ask."

The usual pickup spot (for St. Steve as well as Rosalie) was the corner of Cedar and Hacienda Terrace, half a block away from Casa Klein. Rosalie wasn't there yet. The rain had cleared up, but it was windy, making Andromeda wish she'd thought to bring Daisy's vinyl coat. She hugged herself inside her sweatshirt, her hood pulled tight and drawstrung around her face and wig, counting the minutes as they ticked by, each one making it ever more clear how unlikely it was that St. Steve would actually send a photo in response to hers.

"This is your idea of cute?" said Rosalie, cranking down her window. "Grim Reaper couture? Sorry I'm a few minutes late."

"You're fifty-three minutes late," said Andromeda, sliding in, checking her phone again. "No, fifty-four."

"Yeah, sorry, I had to make another pickup first." Bethany Stone was in the back, leaning over. Her smile was a wonder of nature, like the aurora borealis or Yosemite. Despite the complaints about Andromeda's outfit, Rosalie was wearing her usual getup of sneakers, pegged jeans, and leather jacket; it was the costume of the rock bands she and the rest of them were into, the boys and the girls alike. Somehow it looked feminine and pretty on Rosalie, though also rather theatrical, as though she were playing a juvenile delinquent in a high school play. Bethany looked dazzling in a retro dress with little ties on the sleeves. Andromeda was distinctly unsurprised to note that she had perfect upper arms.

Andromeda hadn't recognized the car at first as it had backed slowly down the hill toward her. It wasn't the Volvo. It was the old Impala that had been in the van Genuchten garage for years.

"I thought this car didn't work," said Andromeda.

"Oh, it works," said Rosalie, rolling back down the hill. "To a certain extent." Andromeda expected Rosalie to go into a three-point turn, but when she reached the corner she rolled to a stop, then continued backing through the intersection.

"Slight transmission problem," said Rosalie in answer to Andromeda's stare. "I managed to move the Volvo out of the way and back the Impala out of the garage, but it doesn't seem to want to get out of reverse. The Gimpala! Poor little thing. It takes some getting used to, but I think I'm getting the hang of it. Tell me if I'm going to hit anything," she added to Bethany as she accelerated in reverse down Redwood Grove Boulevard, her neck craned and her arm across the seat back.

"You're going to back up all the way there," said Andromeda.

"The girl catches on fast. Great at math," Rosalie said, to Bethany.

"On the freeway."

"Yes, it's not too far," Rosalie responded, as though driving in reverse on the freeway were something people did all the time when their transmissions acted up. "We'll be fine."

Bethany was nodding. Funny, she had seemed so sane. Maybe people did do it all the time. Andromeda tried once more:

"You're not worried about dying in a horrifying, bloody car crash? At all?"

"Dying in a horrifying, bloody car crash can suck my dick," said Rosalie brightly. "I'm skidding. That's it, Dramarama. Fetal position, just like at home. It'll be over in no time."

Andromeda had lowered herself to the seat and curled up, trying to clear her mind of everything but St. Steve's arms and Bethany's fiery eyes so she would at least have something pleasant and worthwhile in her head when it was sliced off and incinerated in a storm of glass, steel, and fire. At least the explosion would be beautiful, and there was always a chance that her future self would be born with better hair and bones and skin and parents.

∗ ∗ ∗

Rosalie only ran off the road a couple of times on the frontage road leading to the freeway on-ramp, and when she did she got right back on, hardly slowing down.

"Merging could be tricky," she conceded as the car accelerated. Bethany's method of warning Rosalie of impending collisions was to shriek loudly, which Rosalie acknowledged with an "Oh my God," or an "Aye, aye, Captain," depending, apparently, on the urgency of the situation.

Andromeda's eyes were closed tightly, her fists mashed into them, her knees against her chest. But after a few jerky lurches and stops and starts, the ride became, unbelievably, rather smooth. Mortal terror and panic gave way to an odd sense of detachment, a numbness. So this is how it ends, she said to herself dispassionately. How very interesting. The numbness enveloped her. She could no longer feel the wheels on the road. It was like she was floating away. She saw flashing shapes against the dark purple of her closed lids, crying faces, coils of twisting light like tubes or tunnels, hollow tentacles with dark veins branching all through their interior. They were tunnels to somewhere, or they were structures of her brain that she was floating through, and she felt the sensation of the legs of dozens of tiny spiders swarming along them through the tunnels, through tubes in her eyes and brain.

She was close to wherever it was, as she had been during the Lacey cone-of-hate incident, which had looked rather similar; she felt that with the least effort she could slip right past the here and now, though she wasn't sure she wanted to. These gates presented themselves at such inconvenient times. Gods, we had better hope, she said to herself and whoever or whatever else was there, that riding backwards on the freeway in a car driven by a maniac is not what is required to open that gate. That would be some ceremony, very difficult to replicate, let alone survive.

What was the formula, the escape incantation? *Hekas hekas este bebeloi!*

The car lurched to a stop, the flashing tubes and spiders evaporated, and she opened her eyes to Rosalie and Bethany staring down at her with alarm and something else that was perhaps on the border between slight disgust and amusement.

"You are one weird chick," said Rosalie. "Come on, sit up. We're there." Both Bethany and Rosalie were rubbing her shoulders encouragingly, and she felt the life coming back into her numbed body.

"What did you just say?" asked Bethany, in a confused but not unkind voice. "Some kind of 'Otchie-kotchie Liberace' rhyme thing?" So Andromeda had said the banishing formula out loud.

"Nothing," said Andromeda, still feeling like she was waking up. "No, nothing, really. Just the Cry of the Watcher Within . . ."

"Yes, Beth," Rosalie said. "Get with it. It was merely the Cry of the Washing Machine. Don't you know anything?"

Smooth, said the Altiverse AK voice that might or might not have been Huggy. It's getting confusing in there, Andromeda thought, referring to her head. *No kidding,* said whatever it was.

Rosalie had parked down the road from the station so they could get themselves together. For Rosalie, this meant a fairly elaborate routine of reapplying her makeup. Bethany was one of those girls who always looked wonderful with very little effort. That was like some superpower. Andromeda, for her part, didn't see the point of any heroic efforts of beauty, especially for the sake of impressing these gas-station guys, who were not her project. This was Rosalie's deal. They would not be interested in Andromeda, obviously, and, just as obviously, she did not want them to be. It was clear that Rosalie's objective in bringing her and Bethany along was to give the other guys something to occupy themselves with while she focused on this Darren. Andromeda had played the role of nonthreatening distraction many times, for Rosalie and for Daisy as well, and it was too uninteresting even to waste much effort being irritated by it. Bethany Stone, on the other hand: now, there was some competition, whether or not Rosalie realized it.

As if sensing Andromeda's train of thought, Rosalie said: "They really want to meet you, I swear. I've told them all about you." Then she added, "Oh, and you, too, Andromeda: you and your witchy ways." Bethany's attitude seemed to be benign, amused, self-confident indulgence. How great it must have been to be her.

They saw the wig when Andromeda took her hood off to look at herself in the sun-visor mirror, and after gasping and making a big deal out of confirming that it was Daisy's old wig and shaking her head in a "what am I going to do with you?" way, Rosalie pronounced her verdict that it actually looked pretty good on Andromeda. "Way better than your own flat, mousy hair" was what she undoubtedly meant, but Bethany too was nodding.

"Wig circle," she said, meaning "Wigs are cool." "I don't

know if I'd want a used one, though." She said it with a smile, though with perhaps a hint, Andromeda suspected, of being weirded out by the fact that it had belonged to a dead person.

Like the person who owned that vintage dress with the sleeve ties isn't long dead, said Huggy's faint voice, bubbling up from under the sound of the traffic. *I promise you, she's dead.* The question of how, precisely, Huggy could make that kind of promise was intriguing, but would have to wait for another time.

"Let me try something," said Rosalie. What she wanted to try was to adjust Andromeda's makeup. Andromeda felt like an idiot but let her do it, mainly because Bethany was egging her on and even put encouraging fingers on Andromeda's palm, so it was almost like they were holding hands, almost, and she felt an ever-so-slight electric tingle from it. She even let Rosalie apply the thick, dark lipstick that never, ever worked on her.

"There," said Rosalie to Bethany, turning Andromeda's face toward her. "Now, that's what Daisy looked like. Except less frightened and emaciated. Or is that emancipated? What is it, mance or mace?"

"I think it's mace," said Andromeda dryly.

It was true: she was wearing Daisy's wig, and now she was also wearing a kind of Daisy mask. She didn't really look like Daisy, but Rosalie had captured something of Daisy's style, and it did look pretty good with the blond wig. Andromeda felt like a piece of art.

"I think I lost one of my cards at your house the other night," said Andromeda abruptly, remembering the missing World. "Did you maybe see it?"

"Oh, I almost forgot," said Rosalie, waving away the question. She was repacking her purse and shifting around preparing to open the door and get out of the car. She reached behind the seat and handed Andromeda a book. It was a big, heavy hardcover book, but it was too dark to read the title. Andromeda didn't realize she was sniffing it till Rosalie said: "How's it smell?" It actually smelled very nice, with a slightly different type of mustiness than the older IHOB books. *Dave's head,* said Huggy. *It smells like the back of Dave's head,* and It was right. Andromeda had always loved Dave's head's dusty smell, but this was the first time she had realized that Dave smelled like a book. Suddenly, and somehow, in a tiny, tiny way, just a sliver, her world made a little more sense. Perhaps that was all this night was meant to teach her. If so, she was ready to go home right now.

Rosalie was already out of the car and on her way down the sidewalk to the station with Bethany close behind and didn't even hear Andromeda's "What is it?" There was enough light when Andromeda opened her door to see the title: *Sexual Behavior in the Human Female.* Another classic Rosalie joke: off-the-wall, vaguely insulting in some indefinable way. Perhaps the joke was, Andromeda needed a reference book to know about that topic? She would open the book and it would be inscribed something like: *So you'll know what to do if the time ever comes.*

That seemed to be the thrust of it, because Rosalie called out to her without looking back, using Andromeda's least favorite of all her names: "Come on, Man-dromeda, step it up!" But then she added, "I mean, Androma-Daisy!"

***

"Josh," said Rosalie to the boy in the booth as she set down her shopping bag of supplies. "Where's Darren?"

"Who are you?" said the boy apparently named Josh, looking puzzled and a little sleepy. "And who's Darren?"

Rosalie pulled her hair back and put her face right up to his: "Remember me, from last night? I had my hair up?"

"Oh, right," he said. "The crazy Derek groupie from the high school who claims she goes to the College Behind Mervyn's. Fifi, right? I didn't recognize you with all those clothes on and being able to stand up without falling down and stuff." So he was just teasing her after all. Andromeda really had to marvel at people like Bethany and now this Josh, who could handle Rosalie so easily. Nuit knew, Andromeda couldn't do it, but those who could manage the right dismissive, faintly amused manner could render Rosalie eager to please, almost deferential.

"It's Felicity," said Rosalie. "And these are the girls I was telling you about, Stella and Georgie. So where's Darr–uh, *ek*? Really? It was *ren*, I thought. No, I'm sure it's *ren*. But never mind. We have brought refreshments. We made cupcakes." The last bit was said in a kind of pleading manner. She was craning her neck, as though the elusive Darren-ek might be hiding coyly behind the Coke machine. "He said how much he liked cupcakes."

You've got to be kidding, said the distant Huggy voice, and Andromeda shared Its skepticism about the proposition that Darren-ek had said anything at all about liking "cupcakes" while the two of them had been doing whatever it was they had been doing while "Felicity" had been, apparently, not overly dressed and falling off her shoes last night. But there were the cupcakes in a Tupperware tub in Rosalie's hands. Andromeda was trying to work out whether she was supposed to be Stella or Georgie in this scenario. If you're going to do alternate identities, as Rosalie often liked to do, it's a good idea to tell your accomplices beforehand, isn't it? *Stella* meant "star," so it would have been more apt for Bethany; *Georgie* was boyish, the one who kissed the girls and made them cry, so that was about right; it just figured. Not that it made much of a difference. Andromeda was planning to remain completely silent, whatever her name was supposed to be, and to wait it out. The prospects for a surprise beer-and-baked-goods party seemed fairly grim, and as the actual target of the scheme was nowhere to be found, it didn't seem like it would last too long. She looked at her phone (no messages) and imagined getting home early enough to take another picture for St. Steve or even attempt another tantoon ritual. In the meantime, perhaps she could find a quiet corner where she could read *Sexual Behavior in the Human Female*. Possibly there was a chapter on cupcakes that would explain everything.

Andromeda liked how this Josh referred to the target as Darren-ek dryly and without missing a beat or making a big deal of it, exactly as Andromeda herself had been doing in her head since Rosalie had said it. Other than that, he was not particularly impressive, a generic, uninteresting guy. Darren-ek wasn't working tonight, he said. There was a chance he might stop by later, but probably not. When Rosalie suggested that Josh call him to let him know they were there, Josh said: "Why don't you call him yourself? Oh, that's right, he didn't give you his number!" The secret was in the easygoing, confident, joking tone. Andromeda couldn't have pulled that off if her life depended on it. He was probably a Sagittarius, like Rosalie herself, born with a quiver of arrows and a license to be an asshole.

He said he would text Darren-ek, and he made a big deal out of poking his fingers at his phone, but it looked like pretend-texting to Andromeda. Everybody was smiling good-naturedly, though. Bethany looked nowhere near miserable or annoyed at being dragged there, as Andromeda felt she had a right to be, and even Rosalie's crestfallen look was comparably mild. *Darren-ek doesn't want to be reached,* said a vague, buzzy Huggy vibration from somewhere behind Andromeda's upper jaw. *He's protecting him. That's what friends are for.* Protection from unwanted Rosalie action—everybody could use a Josh, really.

It was decided that they might as well drink the beers and eat the cupcakes while waiting for Darren-ek to arrive.

"Stella can tell our fortunes," said Rosalie, sitting back against the tiny office's partition wall. "She has a gift. Stained flowers." "Strange powers," she probably meant to say. "She did readings the other night and they all came true. She predicted that my fuck-head ex-boyfriend would cheat on me and even could tell the names of the whores he did it with." She continued with a rather inflated list of other aspects of Andromeda's readings that had proven to be accurate, including Rosalie's own activities with Darren-ek ("I'm sure he told you about it, the full play-by-play—and that one she did *over the phone.* That's what I'm talking about.") and her mother's being "called away" on "important business" for the weekend and taking the car keys with her, and being on the verge of a nervous breakdown. There were other ones Andromeda hadn't even known about, such as Bethany's father getting a new job, and Bethany coming into money of her own (she apparently had gotten news of having won a scholarship of some kind) and Empress falling ill and maybe having to go to the hospital.

These interpretations were all iffy, exaggerated reports of Andromeda's own charlatanism, and some were flat-out wrong: the Empress card in a spread suggesting illness or infirmity did not really indicate that someone who happened to be named Empress would get sick. Some of the readings, like the fact that Amy the Wicker Girl had lost four pounds, she didn't even remember having done all that clearly. But the way Rosalie told it, and with Bethany nodding confirmation, it did sound impressive. That's not the way it works, was what she had said at the time, and she also said it now, looking sheepishly at her shoes and wishing herself far away. The Book of Thoth pointed to deep secrets of the Universe, of the complex interplay of forces on the inner planes, not trivial details about what base you get to with a guy whose name you don't quite know, or who has the keys to the family Volvo. Yet on the other hand, it did seem to work that way. Rosalie seemed convinced at least. Perhaps the Universe speaking through the Book of Thoth revealed trivial details to trivial people? There was, maybe, something in that.

In spite of herself, Andromeda felt an ever-so-slight weedgie tingle on the skin of her neck and ears, sparked, perhaps, by the feeling that such an insight about the attitude of the Universe to trivial people was just the sort of thought a nontrivial person might have. Or perhaps it had arisen through the simple act of imagining, for the sake of argument, that she really did have Stained Flowers. It was dark and rather misty as well, and the gas-station office's fluorescent light was flickering in the way that in the movies often heralds the approach of a serial killer or psychotic child. That could have been part of it too.

"So do the lottery numbers," said Josh, holding out his hand facetiously, as though he really believed she could read the lotto numbers in his palm. It was like he'd single-handedly rolled back most of the weedgieness, like he'd done a particularly strong banishing spell. "First thing I do when I win is quit this job, and quit school, and then I will buy you all drugs and guns, all the drugs and guns you want."

Rosalie and Bethany seemed to think that was a terrific idea. Rosalie was already getting that buzzed, distant look, like her eyes weren't quite seeing what they were looking at. After the obligatory "It doesn't work like that," Andromeda explained that she didn't have her cards with her.

"Duh," said Rosalie, kicking *Sexual Behavior in the Human Female* toward Andromeda with her toe. "In there. You are so dense. You can thank me later, in Barbados, after we win big. Just so long as you don't shoot me with all your guns." A drunken Rosalie was a centered Rosalie. She had started teasing Josh in return, and was definitely more at ease now that they were seated and drinking and had more or less acknowledged that Darren-ek was probably not going to be stopping by. She was looking at Josh with the flirty half-smile. If things progressed down the usual avenue she would soon start leaning against him, then touching his arm, and eventually would wind up pretending to be drunker than she actually was, with her head on his shoulder or knee or something. *Better her than us,* said the Huggy voice, *better her than us.* Us?

Andromeda shook away that confusion and opened the book. Inside, beginning at page fifty or so, the pages had been neatly cut away in a tarot-sized rectangle. Inside the rectangle was a Pixie deck. The card at the top was the Three of Swords, very nearly a fairly major synch. She turned it over and let the cards fall into her hand and recognized the diamond pattern on the backs. They were a vintage deck, a pre–U.S. Games edition of the Rider-Waite deck, and she would have recognized it anywhere. Daisy's Pixie deck. Not the one Den couldn't find–that was a Thoth deck, which Andromeda had given to Daisy to replace this one, which had been, supposedly, lost. This was the lost deck, the deck from the dream. The "they are burning down my room" deck. The King of Sacramento deck.

The cards were heavier than hers. Weighty. And whatever the cause, they seemed to bear some type of "spirit" heft as well. Andromeda imagined she could feel them vibrate slightly in her hand, as though all the little figures, the kings and pages and artisans and above all the blindfolded, bound girls, were almost but not quite imperceptibly trundling and squirming inside the deck. Her ears rang and her skin tingled and her eyes felt hot. Now, this, this was *ouijanesse.*

"Daisy's cards," she said, dazed. How on earth had Rosalie acquired them? The deck was supposed to have disappeared ("dematerialized" was how they used to say it).

Somehow, evidently, it had since rematerialized in Rosalie's possession, carefully hidden inside *Sexual Behavior in the Human Female*.

This was not the time to ask such questions, as Rosalie made plain by directing Andromeda to stop "Alzheimering" and get on with the lottery numbers, but first get two more beers from the office cooler and one more for herself if she wanted.

"I'll get them," said Bethany, getting up and squeezing Andromeda's shoulder as she did. She was giving Rosalie a funny look, a look of distaste. It was either because of Rosalie's bossing Andromeda around like that during such a momentous, emotional moment, or it was to register disapproval of her behavior toward this Josh character. True to form, Rosalie was slumping toward him slightly and had positioned her hand so it was grasping her own leg but also barely touching his with the palm's edge; a slight shift would sandwich the hand, the back of it against his thigh. It was so utterly predictable. The fact that he seemed oblivious and profoundly uninterested merely meant that she would persist with even more determination.

Andromeda's concern was different. She knew she wouldn't be able to avoid laying out some cards and faking a lottery-numbers reading. Yet she was determined not to disarrange the order of the cards till she had had a chance to document and study them. For it was likely that Daisy had been the one who had constructed the hiding space in *Sexual Behavior in the Human Female* and had placed the cards in it; and it was possible that she had done this without shuffling them (because there's no reason to shuffle at the end of a reading). Thus, it was just conceivable that Daisy's last spread before placing the cards in the book, whenever that had been, was possibly preserved and might be reconstructed.

Huggy, if you really can help me remember things, now would be the time, Andromeda thought pointedly, imagining a future Huggy-summoning operation in which the HGA would dictate the cards to her as It had done with the King of Sacramento's numbers.

The response came almost instantly, all of a sudden, a powerful, vibrating voice discerned in the hum of the fluorescent lights, not distant but very present, so present that it was astonishing that no one else could hear it: *Don't shuffle,* It said. *Cut the deck in half and deal from the top, and don't use more than twenty-nine cards. Also, don't get back in that car.*

The voice was gone.

Later on, she realized, of course, that that was exactly the way to ensure that the top and bottom ten cards of a seventy-eight-card deck would remain in their original order. And she was glad she trusted the voice. After a cursory lottery-number-generating operation she invented on the spot (reducing the number value of pairs of minor arcana cards, leaving out the court cards, and counting major arcana as single numbers), the top and bottom ten remained in the middle of the deck, separated by the Three of Swords.

The numbers for Saturday had already been drawn, so they played them for Wednesday on the lotto machine at the counter. If their numbers won the jackpot, and no one else did, they would split it four ways, and it was easy to calculate even without Huggy's help: the cash value award would be around $2.8 million apiece.

"One more thing," said Andromeda, feeling shameless, but also rather clever. "I have a bad feeling about the, uh, the Gimpala. Some of those cards were, mm, ominous. Severe numbers like threes and fives, and lots of wands, which are fire. You don't want to mess with that kind of elemental imbalance. I don't think we should drive it home. I mean, you can. But, you know, don't die." It probably wouldn't have persuaded the highest tarot court in the land, but she said it quickly and with as much confidence as she could.

Whatever Rosalie would have said next was interrupted by the sudden piercing sound of sirens in the distance. There was no need to point out how weedgie that was.

"It's like there's a fire every night around here these days," said Josh.

"Elemental imbalance," said Andromeda.

"No kidding," he said.

Josh laughed long and hard when Bethany explained how the Gimpala was stuck permanently in reverse, and said he'd drive them home and would take a look at the transmission in the morning. But he made Rosalie demonstrate her backing-up technique in getting the car to the garage, just because he wanted to see it. Even half drunk, Rosalie managed it expertly and at great speed. After that, Josh seemed a little more interested in her.

Although her house was closest, Rosalie arranged to be dropped off last. Bethany rolled her eyes at Rosalie as she got out of the car but smiled at Andromeda and lightly kissed the top of her head before trotting off. They left Andromeda by the corner, clutching her still-vibrating *Sexual Behavior in the Human Female* and feeling a warm feeling on top of her head and silently thanking, giving praise to, Huggy for making it all happen and enabling them all not to die.

"Wednesday," said Josh as he rolled up his window. "Drugs and guns as far as the eye can see. And for me: hookers."

Even if Rosalie ended up doing something she regretted, Andromeda felt, not dying before having the chance to consult Daisy's Pixie deck was surely worth it.

THE STAR .

xvi.

The first thing to do, Andromeda Klein was thinking, while waiting at the St. Steve spot down the hill for Byron the Emogeekian to pick her up to take her to church, was to set aside half a million dollars for each of the parents. She would have to have a lawyer draw up a contract so the mom couldn't touch the dad's share, because the mom would immediately take it all and spend it if she could. It would be satisfying to cut the mom out completely, but giving her five hundred thousand to squander might give the dad time to make a getaway with his. Den would get something too, in some kind of account that Mizmac could never touch. What was left would be used to buy back all the Sylvester Mouse books and to fund a private library that she would design herself, along the same lines as the International House of Bookcakes but far, far away from Clearview, near Mount Shasta or New York or somewhere like that. Scholars and magicians could visit it by appointment only after having proved their worthiness, via online questionnaire and personal interview. And she, the Mistress of the Library, would live in a tiny cylindrical room atop a tower that would rise behind the main structure, a room that would also serve as a temple and astronomical observatory and house her magical and scientific equipment.

The top ten and the bottom ten cards in the Daisy deck hadn't, when spread out in the Celtic Cross pattern, been particularly illuminating. It was impossible to know for certain what order they had been in, or even if they had been readings at all. As at the station, however, there had been a surfeit of Wands—rather remarkable, in fact, since the lottery oracle had included three Wands cards, and the remaining seven had all managed to turn up in one or the other of Daisy's possible readings. But laying out the cards in the peace of her banished, consecrated room had been satisfyingly weedgie nonetheless. Daisy's scent had filled the space as soon as Andromeda had opened *Sexual Response in the Human Female,* and she had felt an unmistakable tingly chill, particularly on the back of her hand, when she had touched the High Priestess, a card she had always associated with

Daisy, rightly or wrongly. "Who's here?" she had asked. And, as though in response, a rushing sound of the wind in the curtains had seemed to announce Dave, who approached her carrying Daisy's old Little One in his mouth and dropped it in front of her. That was all the more impressive because Andromeda had left it in the Daisy bag and he had had to dig it out.

But it was much harder to read cards without notes scribbled on them. Redoing them would take a great deal of work, and she hated to sully the pristine Daisy deck at any rate. The lottery-funded library-temple in New York or Shasta would have an annotated tarot deck at each table, ready in case any patrons needed to use it to look something up, she decided. And perhaps she could have a limited number of annotated decks printed up for sale in the gift shop.

You're not going to win that lottery, said Huggy. It was hard to know where to direct the glare in response: somewhere inside her head, or her heart, or in another, unseen dimension occupying the same space, or perhaps floating above her. She was trying anyway when Byron arrived, leaning her shoulder in and looking down, and she must have looked weird.

"Why yummy muggy me?" he said, rolling down the window and leaning up to it as he opened the door. "The look of death," he added. (*Mean-mugging,* stage-whispered Huggy in her head. *He's referring to your impertinent countenance.*)

"Shut up," she said, and that went for both Huggy and Byron, though only he seemed hurt by it. Huggy was a help but made things difficult, too. Well, "the look of death" wasn't the nicest thing to say. Andromeda had felt she looked un-usually cute that morning in her own mirror, but that was with the lighting arranged to her advantage, and holding her head just right. No telling what havoc the cool morning light would bring . . . *"countenance."* Now, that was what the dad would call a fifty-cent word (because when he was learning words fifty cents was this huge amount of money), and she chalked one up for Huggy and made a mental note of it for future use.

Andromeda only put effort into figuring out what people really meant to say when there was a chance she'd be inter-ested in their opinions. Otherwise, she'd have spent nearly one hundred percent of her time in a guessing game. She doubted Byron would have much of interest to say on any subject. But pulling her hair and hood back from her ear and tilting her head was an unavoidable reflex.

"What? Oh, I was thinking about the lottery."

Byron waited respectfully, as he always did, as though expecting some significant clarification or words of wisdom to follow. He waited till she was in the car and they were on the road before he said:

"So did you listen to it?"

It took Andromeda a moment and a little prod from Huggy to realize he was talking about the Choronzon CD he had given her. In fact, she had forgotten all about it. The idea of Cthulhu rock was a lot more interesting than the re-ality, which was horrible and hurt her ears and had little value that she could see. Just a growling man with a loud clatter in the background. She hadn't made it through the first twenty seconds. It was funny, though, to imagine the dad in his studio recording stuff like that, saying "Okay, boys, 'The Boundless Daemon Azothoth,' from the top" in his Groucho voice.

"Oh yes," she said. "Thanks. It was awful, but I liked it."

He was silent, as though waiting for her to say more. "Oh, good," he finally said, but he was acting mad. The mom did this all the time, so Andromeda knew what was expected and she followed up with some extravagant words of praise and thanks that would have sounded sarcastic to anyone other than the person they were directed at. Like the mom, Byron ate it up, and was all, or mostly, smiles again.

"I'm so glad you liked it," he said, not letting the subject go.

Ye Gods, said Huggy, *you've hooked up with a moron boy,* not realizing, perhaps, that hooking up and going to church were, in the twenty-first century, often two rather different things. But Andromeda said, "Especially that one song," which finally seemed to put the subject away and seemed to make him smile way too hard.

She caught her reflection in a gutter puddle on the way up to the church steps, and wished she hadn't. It was a bad angle. She curled her hair under a little with her hand and pulled her hood a little farther around her face.

"Okay, Blessed Mary Ever Virgin," said Byron, trying to be funny.

The emogeekian had made an effort and had cleaned up pretty nice. Leather shoes, a kind of suit jacket (no tie, though), and he had shaved off the scraggly little beard. He was still too short, though the shoes made him a little taller at least. Was this how Catholic boys always dressed to go to church when they were trying to impress weedgie girls and persuade them to teach them magic? Maybe so, but he had also pretty closely adhered to her instructions, if taking note of her complaints about his appearance and correcting them as best he could counted as following instructions. *Of course it does,* said Huggy. *That's what* instructions *means.* Andromeda had to admit, it was nice to be listened to.

"I like your cat collar," he said.

"It's a choker," she corrected, but found herself liking that he noticed it and also liked the word *choker,* which she didn't often have occasion to say aloud. Could he possibly really have a male tramp stamp like Rosalie had said?

St. Brendan's was tiny, far smaller than Andromeda had expected it to be, smaller even than the main churchlike building of the International House of Bookcakes. In spite of herself, and to her surprise, she realized she was rather frightened at the prospect of actually attending a service, but the church building was far less scary and Transylvanian than she had pictured it. It looked like a school from the outside.

"Where would the anchoress go?" she wondered aloud to herself, but Byron heard, because he said: "Where would the what what?"

An anchoress, she explained patiently, as though it were common knowledge, even though she had only just looked it up herself, was a woman who lived in a small, sealed room inside of or attached to a medieval church. There was one window through which she could observe the church services, and another on the outside so that villagers could converse with and pass gifts and food to her. Her job was to meditate and pray, a very important role in the Middle Ages. The boy version was called an anchorite, but anchoresses were more common.

"I don't think we have those anymore," said Byron dryly.

Of course, Andromeda had known there wouldn't be an actual anchoress at the suburban church in twenty-first-century California. She had just been trying to picture where the anchoress's cell would have been and what it would have looked like, had this been a medieval church. Because she could see why the King of Sacramento had referred to her as an anchoress: the description on the Internet reminded her very much of her box. She often felt rather anchoress-esque, when she thought about it, shy and self-contained and voluntarily confined in a small space, exploring inner worlds while remaining in a stationary trance. I'd have made a good one, she thought as they headed up the steps and slipped through the main doors.

The vestibule was deserted. Miniature statues of saints, mostly ladies, one bearded non-Jesus man, and a little child in a crown and a dress stood against the walls surrounded by what appeared at first glance to be tiny, flickering candles but turned out on closer inspection to be tiny electric lights. Byron had a point: all the female saints did look like they were wearing hoodies in a way, and they were all thin and frail-looking, too. Maybe their hair underneath was just as awful as Andromeda's. In fact, that was pretty much guaranteed, pre-blow-dryer era.

"These all used to be bacon gods," she whispered, trying to explain how the early Christian church had replaced local deities with its own saints in popular worship. *They're still pagan gods!* stage-whispered Huggy. And of course It was right: changing their names changed little; that was just something humans did on account of their own vanity. A good magician, of course, would know to learn all their names if he wanted to make proper use of them.

Andromeda had expected these incidental shrines, and had been prepared to give this mini-lecture on their origins. She had researched it and even practiced it in the bath that day. Half-whispered, half-thought, it had sounded impressive and weedgie. But as usual, out in the air, the words—from the yet-to-be-written volume XX of *Liber K*—came out garbled and nonsensical, and Byron just stared at her.

"No, I'm pretty sure this has always been the mother-o-saurus," said Byron, pointing to the sign that said MOTHER OF SORROWS.

She couldn't tell which he had meant to say, so Andromeda half smiled in case it was a joke, then added: "Well, the mother-o-saurus looks a lot like Isis." She pulled *Sexual Response in the Human Female* from her bag, found the High Priestess, and held it up against the picture of the mother-o-saurus, whose halo and rays looked, maybe, a *little* like the High Priestess's headdress (though not quite as much as Andromeda had expected it to). "So this crown is the crown of Hathor, the sun with cow horns around it. And Isis was a virgin and the mother of Horus. She's also the Statue of Liberty, too." And Wonder Woman. The crowns weren't looking similar enough to make her point the way she thought they would, but she knew she was right. It was in lots of books. "She was called the Popess in the Middle Ages," she added lamely. An anchoress with a special hat, she thought, remembering the King of Sacramento.

Byron said "Holy shit" to indicate that he was impressed,

but it didn't seem like his heart was in it. She would have to consult Mrs. John King van Rensselaer so she could describe it better, how the emblems of ancient cults got updated and passed down to future civilizations over and over, how gods and goddesses got recycled.

The mother-o-saurus in the picture had a heart stabbed with swords floating above her chest, just like the King of Sacramento.

Not just like, said Huggy, surging in. *Do I have to count them for you?* There were seven little swords puncturing the mother-o-saurus's heart, rather than the three in Pixie's Three of Swords card that the King of Sacramento had had on his chest beneath his robe. The Seven of Swords is . . . Andromeda couldn't remember the Golden Dawn motto. *Futility,* said Huggy. *You of all people should know: it's futility.*

"Futility, of course," said Andromeda, loudly enough that Byron shot her an "Are you feeling all right?" look.

✳ ✳ ✳

To make an offering, you had to put a coin in a slot, and then you could flip a switch, turning on the little flame-shaped Christmas-tree light on top of one of the fake candles. This Andromeda did. The sound of the switch echoed throughout the room as the light came on, and there was also a little buzz sound, like a mosquito being zapped by a bug light. Huggy said: *Well, now you've done it,* and laughed, if that faint rushing sound was indeed intended as laughter.

"How come they don't use real candles?" Andromeda asked, thinking that at least they had a good echo in there.

"It would cost more to insure with real ones," said Byron, "according to my dad."

That makes a pathetic kind of sense, said Huggy, but Andromeda shushed her.

Real candles were used in the actual service, at least, but Byron had had a point: there was nothing even remotely weedgie about anything to do with what went on in St. Brendan's Church that day, outside of a slight echo and the mother-o-saurus's swords. The church itself was brightly lit, rather than shadowy and dazzling and smoky and terrifying, as she had imagined it would be. The main thing it reminded her of was a school assembly, if you had happened to go to a school with only a couple of dozen elderly students; a lot of them looked like International House of Bookcakes patrons as well. It certainly had not been what she had expected.

There was even one point in the proceedings where everybody shook hands with each other. Byron shook her hand solemnly, with a "What did I tell you?" look on his face.

"You win, sir," she whispered. Even her own cobbled-together Daisy-less ceremonies in makeshift temples blew this one out of the water.

Just as they had finished their handshake, Andromeda's phone vibrated in with a new message from St. Steve. "Do u want me?" it said.

Now, *there* was magic. No matter how many times it happened it was always a shock, the effect a few texted words could have on her when they came from the right person. Her skin tingled; she felt almost unable to breathe. It was a worried, scared, but totally wonderful feeling of anxiety and uncertainty. "Of course," she texted back, and stared at the phone in her hand as though trying to will it to receive another message, rechecking as fast as the display would clear. "How much?" came the eventual response.

Despite the obvious proof of her body's physical reaction, and the fact that there was no other possible answer to that question, she had to wonder as she was entering the text whether it was even really true anymore. But she sent it regardless: "more than anything else in the world" with a "<3." Even if it wasn't quite the same as it was before, she was making a case, now that she had a chance, and she wanted to make the strongest possible argument. Also, to seem positive and surprisingly low-maintenance. No matter how many times she checked, however, no response to this message arrived.

Andromeda had forgotten where she was, and looked up to see Byron staring at her. Texting in church was probably some horrible faux pas, if not a sin, especially if you did it with the intensity of a madwoman.

"You were squeaking," he said, after they were back in the car.

"I was not," Andromeda snapped, but Huggy said, *You most totally were.*

✳ ✳ ✳

The Choronzon on the dad's CD wasn't the same Choronzon as the one on Byron's CD. Byron's Choronzon was from Sweden and had broken up in 1989. Byron's verdict on the Clearview Choronzon was: "Hecka lame." He had quite a few supporting arguments for this, most of which involved different types of "rock" that it was or wasn't similar to. Andromeda couldn't tell the difference between them, and also couldn't understand why, if there was such a thing as Cthulhu rock, both groups weren't both it. In fact, the hecka lame Clearview Choronzon appeared to be the more knowledgeable about the Cthulhu mythos, and they seemed to know a bit about real magic as well, to judge from the song titles "Io Pan" and "I Will Endure." Byron seemed to deem it a real possibility that the defunct Swedish Choronzon might come over to the United States and sue the Clearview Choronzon's asses for being name-stealers. That seemed highly unlikely to Andromeda.

"But I don't know anything about music," she admitted. "Is there such a thing as Igneous rock?"

Byron ejected the CD and passed it to her on one finger. "I wouldn't be surprised," he said. "Hey, are you okay?"

He said this because Andromeda was staring at the track listing written in Sharpie on the CD. She had never looked at it before, and hadn't realized that it contained a major, major synch.

"Play number five," she said, removing the CD from his finger and shoving it back into the slot. Byron winced, but pressed a button till the number five appeared on the display.

The song title was "Toad Bone Ritual." Now, what were the odds of that? A rock band with the same name as the favorite band of her disciple, recording, at her own dad's studio, a song on the subject of, and with the same title as, a spell found copied out in the notebook of her dead weedgie friend, which had surfaced in a random posthumous sweep of her effects.

"I wouldn't say they're my *favorite* band," said Byron, after she had explained.

"Not the point," said Andromeda, waving him to be quiet and listen.

The lyrics of the song, spoken rather than sung in a reverberating computer-sounding voice, turned out, even more remarkably, to consist solely of instructions on how to conduct the ritual, and they tracked Daisy's notes, as Andromeda remembered them, very closely.

Same source, said Huggy. *Guaranteed. Too close to be accidental.* That was what Andromeda had been thinking too.

Byron was listening to the lyrics, an expression of distaste on his face that was so clearly heartfelt that it almost made Andromeda love him just a little.

"Really?" he said. "They put the toad in a box with holes and let it get eaten alive by ants? That's psycho."

Andromeda nodded. "And then they would dig up the box and float the bones down the river, and use the one that floated upstream as a talisman to tame horses. They used to call the operation 'going down to the river,' and the people who did it were referred to as Toadmen. Weird, old folk magic."

"We're not going to be, um, going to any rivers, are we?"

"We most certainly are not," said Andromeda. "I don't doubt it can be powerful, but it's also a very negative kind of magic, and that can really backfire on you."

Byron smiled wanly and gave her a relieved "The animals are our friends" look.

"God, this song is bad," he said.

✳ ✳ ✳

"So when does the actual Satan worship begin?" said Byron, after a pause to regain his composure.

Andromeda rolled her eyes. At least he had said it in a jokey way.

316

"Just do your reading," she said. He had a stack of new books from the Sylvester Mouse list on the backseat, alongside the previous batch to be returned, including a translation of the Greek Magical Papyri and *The Golden Bough*.

"Yes, ma'am," he said, saluting. "How about Lucifer?"

"See, magic is not like that," she said, in a "You have so much to learn, my child" tone, refusing to elaborate. "Anyway, *Lucifer* just means 'the morning light,' so if you want to worship that, be my guest."

A truer name for that spiritual creature, according to Dr. Dee's angels, was in fact Coronzon. It was hard to explain to someone with no education how that was both wrong and right at the same time. She retrieved the rescued *True and Faithful* from Byron's backseat and flipped to the primary Coronzon passage to try to show him.

"Wow, it's right before page ninety-three," he said. At least he had retained that much. And of course, it was indeed quite a synch that four hundred years before Crowley such a significant page numbering would occur, and it was fairly gratifying to Andromeda as a teacher that Byron had appreciated the fact without prompting.

"See now, they're all misspelling it," she said. "Crowley replaced the *C* with a *Ch* so it would add up to three-three-three in his system, but the *C* is more correct." What it really added up to was a complicated question she couldn't really begin to explain, so she continued: "But they're talking about the same Coronzon, the Dweller in the Tenth Aethyr called ZAX." She pulled out *The Vision and the Voice* and read aloud Crowley's description of the babbling, meaningless, malignant, formless entity against whom the only weapon is silence; a thing to be endured and vanquished, certainly not worshipped. Finally she pulled out her Moleskine notebook and drew a diagram of the Tree of Life, pointing to the area below the supernal triad, the area that symbolized the Abyss.

"That's where he is. He's there to destroy your ego, if you ever get far enough for your ego to need destroying. It has to happen if you want to become adept, but it's something you work with and operate, not something you worship."

She must have sounded uncharacteristically confident, because Byron said: "So nobody's destroyed your ego, then."

"Not yet," Andromeda replied. "Anyway, we're not going to be Coronzonists, either. We're not going to worship anybody. Worship is very old aeon."

"So what are we going to do?"

The incorporeal equivalent of an elbow in the ribs from Huggy drew attention to the *we* in both of their sentences. *You're going to have to make some sacrifices if you want this* we *to work for you,* It said, and though Andromeda pretended not to know what It was talking about she knew she was promising something by choosing to participate in the *we. There are things you can't do properly alone.*

Andromeda imagined things she would like to have said and done to her had she herself ever been lucky enough to find an instructor in magic. She felt a little lost, but Huggy came to the rescue and fed her the words, and they were pretty good. They were the sorts of things Daisy would say and had said, and Andromeda said them now.

"If you really want to learn about magic," she said slowly, following word by word the pattern Huggy laid out for her, "you have to do everything I say. You can ask questions if you don't understand something–it's good to ask questions–but you still have to follow your instructions, even when you don't understand them." Rather amazingly, he was nodding. She had never spoken this well or impressively in her life, but she was a little uncomfortable. It would have felt far better if someone had been saying it to her, but someone had to be in charge and it sure wasn't going to be him. When she started thinking of it as Huggy directing both of them, but without Byron's being aware of that fact, it started to feel a little easier, so that was what she did. Huggy was leading them both. Andromeda was just the mouthpiece, the oracle, the sybil.

"We'll have to get you a ring," she said, thinking maybe she could even design a little ceremony to go along with it, once he had acquired it. Andromeda hadn't had the opportunity to design a ritual that would be observed by anyone other than Dave in quite some time. She liked to think she had a bit of a talent for it–and she knew Byron would probably be impressed with the least little thing. She explained the dual-identity ring system. "When my ring is on my right hand, I am a vegetarian, and a socialist, and a Giants fan, and I like jazz, and I dislike my mom. When it is on the other hand, like now, I'm the exact opposite. And if I make a mistake and act the wrong way according to the Ring Day, I have to punish myself."

"There's no way you'd ever like your mom," said Byron, "no matter what finger your ring's on." He had picked up that much.

"You're right," said Andromeda. She took the kitten pin from her bag strap and quickly poked herself in the knee with it, through her tights. A tiny dark bead of blood formed where she pulled the pin out.

"Holy fuck!" said Byron, staring.

"I punish myself," she said, simply, enjoying the look of bewilderment on his face. But he was still clearly on board. He wasn't kicking her out of the car, anyway. *This guy will love you forever now,* said Huggy, *so watch out.*

"And this is magic?" he said, turning the volume knob all the way down.

"It will be," she said. Huggy said, *Pinch him,* so she did, not quite knowing why, hard, just above his knee.

"Ow."

"You were questioning," she said, following Huggy's lead, and as she said it she realized it was probably true. "Weren't you?"

Byron admitted he had been.

"First lesson," she said. "Don't." Wow. She had never been so . . . *effective.* "Now," she said, getting a little caught up in the feeling and remembering an old story about Mr. Crowley. "Shall I give you the serpent's kiss?" Then, when Byron looked puzzled: "Say yes."

"Yes."

Andromeda grasped Byron's wrist and bit it as hard as she could.

"Ow! Jesus. Magic hurts!"

It most certainly does, she thought.

✳ ✳ ✳

What in the Universe, said Huggy, when Andromeda was in the bathroom at the Burger King afterward, *was that*

*"serpent's kiss" nonsense? You really almost lost him there. You
need to stay well to one side of freakishness.*

"Something I learned from Uncle Al," replied Andromeda defensively.

The Beast, said Huggy with a kind of sniff, *has his place,
but he is not one to emulate in social situations. Stick to the plan.*

"And what is this plan?"

But Huggy was silent once again.

"I don't know nothing about no plan," Andromeda said
to her reflection, and instantly regretted looking in the mirror at all–she had deteriorated since the morning, and the
harsh Burger King vacuum lights were no help.

"So I have to be a vegetarian every other day," said
Byron, when she returned, "and I have to dislike my dad, and
then like him, and I'm either a Democrat or a Republican."
He sounded dubious, as one might if one were forced to be
the disciple of someone with such flyaway curly-outy hair.
Andromeda felt so much less confident now that she realized exactly what she looked like. *Calm down,* said Huggy,
popping up. *You're not trying to seduce him. You just want him
for his library card and assorted services.* Assorted services.
Gods.

But then Byron said: "Okay. What else?" So they were
still in business, curly-outy hair notwithstanding. "Shall I give
you the turban skins?"

Andromeda shook her head. He had meant to say "serpent's kiss."

"Come on, I want to give you the turban skins," he said,
in a forced-playful manner. He was reaching for her wrist.
Huggy's voice came to the rescue.

"We're not doing the turban skins anymore," It said, using Andromeda's voice, more emphatically and harshly than the real Andromeda would probably have said it. Then It had her reach for her kitten pin warningly.

Byron got the message and backed away. He was sulking, however, with obviously hurt feelings.

Now just don't say anything, said Huggy. That was really challenging, and ran counter to her own inclination, which would have been to try to appease him. She really wanted to say "Sorry." But, Daisy-like, she forced herself not to.

It took a while, but before their meal was over, Byron was the one who was apologizing, and criticizing himself, and promising to follow the rules, and asking if she was mad at him, and trying to persuade her to come around and be nice to him again.

Boy, he sounds like me, thought Andromeda.

Yes, see how that works? said Huggy, and she did see, even though she really had to wonder what was the point if all you wound up with was a short, slow-witted, eager-to-please, male Andromeda Klein on your hands.

※ ※ ※

She hadn't really wanted to do his tarot particularly, but that is the drawback to having disciples, she was already learning: they expect you to provide them with activities and to keep them entertained, and even if you are the one theoretically in charge you really have to hop to it. With the thought, though, that perhaps the pictorial wisdom of Thoth Hermes Trismegistus might reveal something of the contours of Huggy's alleged plan, she did a brief invocation and banishment, and removed Daisy's cards from *Sexual Response in the Human Female*. Then she had Byron shuffle them, and began to lay them out on the Burger King booth table.

Andromeda decided, as she had been doing ever since the Two of Swords had popped up in her world with such impact, to allow the deck to "choose" and to use the top card of the shuffled pack as the significator.

"This is you," she said, drawing it out. The Five of Pentacles. Perhaps the worst, least fortunate minor card of them all. Worry was its traditional title, which Crowley likened to the image of a dog strangling a sheep.

"Is that good?" said Byron.

"Oh yes," she said. "Very good."

Just then, a text came in from UNAVAILABLE. Finally! She got just a hint of that heart-stopping feeling, as she always did when St. Steve popped up, but she was also feeling rather in control of things, and easy. It was Byron whose cards were a little off, not her.

"RU being a knotty girl" said the text. *Knotty!* Cute. And encouraging. St. Steve was only rarely playful like that. Holding up her finger to say "Hang on" to Byron, she one-thumb-texted back with her other hand: "knot I, said the Millie," and added a "<3."

She put the phone down and continued. "This crosses you." Another five, the Five of Cups—gods and goddesses, this guy is cursed! "We are looking at a stable situation being disrupted, set in motion," she was beginning to say, thinking she should probably consult A.E. and Mr. Crowley's book, when St. Steve's response arrived.

"Take off your bra," it said.

Andromeda got that can't-breathe feeling and dropped the pack of cards, scattering them all over the table, bench, and floor. Byron gave her a weird look and scrambled to pick them up. "Whisky tango foxtrot," she texted back, feeling her face turn bright red.

"Bad news?" Byron said, with that familiar "Maybe this girl is crazy" look in his eyes. She waved him and his question away and excused herself to go to the vacuum.

Why am I doing this? she thought as she unhooked it and threaded it through her sleeves, holding her hooded sweatshirt between her knees.

Because you want to be good and you don't want to blow it this time, came Huggy's, perhaps sarcastic, reply. *See, look at you: you're all excited.*

"ok zebra she eez off," she texted back, on her way to the table, feeling funny.

Two hours later she texted a "now what?" But there was no response. Not then, and not for a long, long time.

xvii.

Andromeda had the Three of Swords out on the Burger King table and was trying to explain synchs to Byron and he wasn't getting it.

"So it's a coincidence," he said. "Like, I put three gallons of gas in my car, and then I eat three Whopper Juniors, and then you show me this picture of three swords stabbing a heart. And then what: I get to third base with you?"

"No," she said, reaching for her kitten pin, and feeling

Huggy do a little fluttery twirl of approval somewhere around the region of the left side of her chest as Byron cringed back toward the wall. Sometimes she felt she could almost "see" Huggy, somewhere in there or out there, just beyond reach, shiny, silvery, and fluttery.

If St. Steve had said that, of course, she'd have melted into a puddle in an instant.

"No, a synch would be like: we're discussing Coronzon, who in Mr. Crowley's system has the number three-three-three, and then maybe you look at your watch and the time is three-thirty-three; and then you remember you had a dream last night where three men are hitting you with sticks, and then you see a three-legged dog running over the hills. So, you know, the Universe is nudging you a little there. There's a kind of three-ness about things as they stand at your current point in time and space. Maybe it's telling you something that's going to happen, or maybe it's showing you something about what is happening. Or maybe it just wants to wake you up a little."

He was staring at her.

"You have dreams like that? People hitting you with sticks?"

"Yes," she said. "Don't you?"

Byron said that his dreams were all about not being able to find his shoes or losing his keys. But he was poking her and pointing, because a homeless man had just walked in out of the rain with a soaking wet black plastic garbage bag over his head with a hole cut out for his face, and he had a dog on a leash trailing behind him, and the dog had three legs.

"You must have seen him outside earlier," said Byron. And maybe, just maybe she had, though she didn't think so.

"That's a synch," she said. Goddesses, that example had worked out great.

"Weedgie," he said. And she mentally gave him a gold star for proper use of authorized vocabulary. "So what's going to happen, then?" She silently took back the gold star.

"It doesn't work like that," she said, but she had to admit she was wondering what was going to happen herself. Two to Three can be a rough transition, two opposites joining to produce a third via a pregnant Empress, a line becoming a plane. No reason to think Swords, except for her Two of Swords Daisy situation, and the fact that things were very swordsy lately.

Just then her phone vibrated, and if it had been from St. Steve that would really have been something, both synch-wise and just hotness-wise. But it was from Rosalie. "look up," it said.

Andromeda looked up. Rosalie and Bethany were sitting in the Gimpala in the parking lot just outside their window and Rosalie was smiling big and waving her over. Byron said he had to go anyway, but that he would do his reading and would write in his journal and would try to obey the ring. He slinked off to his car through the rain, as though embarrassed to be seen with her, as Andromeda climbed in behind Rosalie and Bethany.

"So Gas Station Boy managed to fix the Gimpala after all?" Andromeda said.

"Not yet," said Rosalie. She explained that her mother had extended her trip for a few more days and she wasn't ready to give up her transportation while she still had it. "Anyway, Joshua has been a little too busy to return anyone's phone calls lately, so he can suck my dick. The car is fine."

She began to back out of the parking lot. "Scream if I'm going to hit anything. Bethlehem, you take the right side, Dromedary, the left. I'm really getting the hang of this," she added. And it was true, she was doing remarkably well at reverse driving. When Bethany yelled "Cop!" she managed to pull into a parking space deftly while they all ducked their heads down until the police car had passed. "Close one," she said. "It's trickier in the rain."

"What kind of violation would that be?" asked Bethany as Rosalie backed the car back back onto El Camino. "Driving backwards?"

"Not too bad, probably," said Rosalie. "Unless I kill somebody. But I'm not going to." She paused. "Or . . . am I? Klein! Cards! Now! Eenie meenie miney moe, will the fabulously glamorous Rosalie accidentally kill someone with her retardo-mobile?"

Andromeda checked. Ace of Cups.

"No," she said. "Actually, you won't kill anybody, and maybe that person who you don't kill will hand you like a big box of money or something." Some people just really were that lucky.

"Excellent! That's what I like to hear." She and Bethany play high-fived. "But it won't be that lottery because fuckhead still has our ticket."

Ah, lovely Bethany, looking over her shoulder and still resembling the hell out of Katherine Mansfield, holding hands with Andromeda over the front seat in the solidarity of mutual terror.

"Hey!" said Rosalie. "We can go anywhere we like. Let's go to Reno!"

"You're gonna back up all the way to Reno," said

Andromeda, not meaning it as a question. Bethany nodded at her to say "Yes she really would maybe probably do it."

Rosalie waved the topic away, and commanded Andromeda to "dish," by which she meant to tell her everything that had happened on the Church-State. "Church date," she meant. Did they hold hands in the pew, did he feel her up when they were kneeling, did they do a kiss of peace and make out when the nun wasn't looking? The nun!

"It's not that kind of a church," said Andromeda dryly. "And he's too . . . short for any of that stuff. I'm seriously just teaching him about magic."

"I'm sure you are, honey lamb," said Rosalie. "I'm sure you are. I'm sure you're way nastier than he could ever dream, down deep in your corrugated soul." Corrugated? "Go ahead: show Bethany your whore face."

Andromeda rolled her eyes. Not that again. Rosalie slammed on the brakes and said, as their three backs slapped against the seats: "See? Driving backwards is going to catch on. Simple law of thermometer dynamics: no seat belts needed." She switched on the ceiling light. "Now, Andromeda: whore face. Quickly." Andromeda sighed and pulled her hair over her eyes and struck the lip-pursing kissy pose she had sent to St. Steve. "Okay, not bad," Rosalie said. "Here's mine." She pulled her lower lip down with her index finger and winked, twisting her shoulders to the side. "See, I don't know how he could possibly resist. Don't let him see me or you'll lose him forever. I'm just kidding. And don't show me yours, Beth. You're so sweet and innocent it would probably just make me cry."

Andromeda checked her phone as discreetly as she could: nothing from UNAVAILABLE, which sucked quite badly, but she had to admit that Rosalie was cheering her up at least a little.

"Message from lover boy?" said Rosalie; then, noticing the red phone, she added: "Okay, talk me through this. That's the mom phone? And your regular phone is the blue one? Or wait . . ."

Andromeda had to explain that she had broken the blue phone and had to use the red one and switch the SIM cards depending on what she was using it for.

"You live in a dark coagulated world, Dromedary," Rosalie said. "I *thought* it was weird that you were feeling up the mom phone. Seriously, you hold that phone like a hand pants on fire." "Hand pacifier," she meant. "But what happens if your mom sees it?"

"I just have to be really careful," said Andromeda, demonstrating her shielding method, her slender fingers cupped around the colored areas on the phone.

"You could always paint that blue one," said Bethany brightly.

Andromeda declined the offer to back up, up and down the road with them for the next few hours and Rosalie agreed to drop her home.

"By the way," said Rosalie, en route. "I thought you might want to know that another one of your breathtaking predictions came true. My brother said he heard that Empress fell down the stairs after PE and broke her leg on Friday. And she's blaming Lacy Garcia for it and is gonna kick her ass or sit on her or something as soon as she gets her cast off." She whispered to Bethany that Lacey was Andromeda's sworn enemy because she put her bike in a tree.

"I predicted that? When did I predict that?"

330

"You said that Empress was going to get into something involving *betrayal*? And I think you even maybe said the person's name would begin with an *L*? And that she was going to maybe get *pregnant*? And that she was going to *fall*? And that she was going to *die*?"

Andromeda hadn't said any of those things. But she focused on the weakest link.

"But she didn't die. None of that stuff is even close to true."

"Details, details," said Rosalie in an attempt at some unplaceable accent. "She fell down the stairs, and even if she's not pregnant she's a big girl, like four Elisabeths' worth. And she *could* die. You know what hospitalization is like. Anyway, you said there were different kinds of death. This was the tragic death of a leg. You predicted the names of Charles's on-tour sluts, too. You're on a roll. I hope you use that power wisely, Klein-o."

"Speaking of which," said Andromeda. "I've been meaning to ask: How did you manage to get hold of Daisy's deck anyway?"

"Oh, she just left it with me for safekeeping," said Rosalie, an intriguing notion to be sure, as Rosalie was perhaps the last person on earth you'd select for that purpose. What else had Daisy left with her?

But Rosalie waved the topic away with a fly-swatting motion. She pressed some buttons on her phone and pointed it toward Andromeda, and said: "Recording. So Andromeda, how does it feel to be an all-knowing and all-powerful fortune-telling genius? Would you say it has had a positive affectation on your self-esteem and well-being and that you feel more confident and in control of your own destiny?"

Andromeda just stared at Rosalie, who began whispering,

"Say yes, say yes," moving her head and eyes as though to say "Come on, get on with it."

"Um," said Andromeda. "Um. Yes?"

"Rosalie pressed another button and lowered her phone. "Atta girl," she said. "That's what I like to hear."

Sorry, A.E., Andromeda thought as she climbed the stairs to Casa Klein. I'm just so sorry.

✳ ✳ ✳

The dad and the mom were arguing as she went in. The dad was red and sweating, an indication that he was being crazy and that the domestic yelling would be unlikely to die down for some time. The mom was completely incapable of handling these situations. The thing to do was to agree with him about at least some of what he was saying, to say something like "Well, what are you gonna do?" and throw up your hands, and to laugh at one of his jokes; even better, to tell him a joke of your own. The way not to handle it was to say:

"That has got to be the stupidest thing I've ever heard in my life."

And that was exactly what the mom was saying as Andromeda ran to her room to put her bra back on. St. Steve had left her hanging too long.

"Your father," said the mom when Andromeda had returned to the kitchen, "thinks that the CIA has been sneaking into the carport to confiscate his old girlie magazines."

"There is some literature missing, yes," he said, looking at Andromeda meaningfully. "There's no full inventory of my papers, so I don't know the extent of the issue."

Uh-oh, thought Andromeda. She had the second bagel

worm agony in her backpack to give to Den when he stopped by the library the following day.

"I borrowed one," said Andromeda, deciding to take a calculated risk. "It wasn't the CIA. Sorry." They were both looking at her strangely. "For a, um, school project. On, the, uh, role of women in you know, society." Then she added: "Your little girl is growing up" in a slight Groucho voice.

The dad stared for a moment and finally laughed and the redness began to drain from his face. "Our little girl is growing up," he repeated, sounding way more normal.

"Oh, for fuck's sake," said the mom, stomping off.

"Hey, Papa Klein," Andromeda added just to make sure, on her way back to her room. "A woman walks into a bar and asks for a double entendre. And the bartender gives her one." She had been saving that one for a special occasion and it totally did the trick now. He was smiling, proud of her, and she was relieved. She intended to try to conjure the King of Sacramento tonight and she couldn't afford a lot of disruption.

"You're a good kid, baby Klein," he said on his way out the door. "Hey, what did your friend think of that Choronzon?" He'd pronounced it correctly for that spelling, with an aspirated *ch*–he probably got the pronunciation from the band, so maybe they were Crowleyites after all. "I think I may try to produce those guys."

"It was awful," she said. "He loved it."

Andromeda had decided, and Huggy agreed, that she had to change her approach with the King of Sacramento if she wanted better results. Heretofore he had been the one to instigate contact, by visiting her in her box or in the small chamber in some remote corner of Yesod while she was dreaming, but he had also been indirectly invoked by sigil magic, so it seemed at least possible that he could be conjured directly and deliberately.

She had to relax first, though, so she put on her Guillaume de Machaut CD, lay down on the floor, and tried the deep yoga breathing that she could never quite seem to get to work for her. The door swung open suddenly, striking her leg, and there was the mom, sighing with exasperation, and wrinkling her nose at the music as well as the incense.

"Thank you very, very much," the mom said. "You had to go poking around in his stuff like that. Now you've set him off. You know what he's doing? He's collecting all his 'papers' so he can *burn* them and destroy the evidence before the 'crackdown'! He just went out to get lighter fluid. He'll end up setting the whole neighborhood on fire." She sniffed. "And what are *you* burning in here?"

"I'm sure he'll just use the barbecue, Mom," said Andromeda, pushing the door closed and slamming it. So the joke hadn't worked as well as she'd hoped. He had burned "documents" before, and had managed never to burn down the neighborhood so far. The worst that could happen, really, was that the world would contain fewer vintage copies of *Penthouse* and Den's supply of Scandinavian nature and sports magazines might dry up.

Andromeda was more annoyed at the mom than usual, for some reason, perhaps because she had shattered her peace of mind so thoroughly just at the moment when invoking the King of Sacramento had really seemed like it could pay off. How do normal kids express annoyance at their parents? Answer: loud obnoxious music. And Andromeda had access to the most obnoxious music known to man: Byron's god-awful Swedish Choronzon CD. Of course, she would have to suffer through it too, that was the price. More as a stunt to see what it would be like to play the role than anything else, she put in the CD and turned it as loud as it would go. Then, to put the icing on the cake, she started jumping around in the kind of dance she imagined you might do to Cthulhu rock, something wild and irregular and voodoo-y, the grotesque contortions of an ancient race conducting unmentionable rites. And she sang along at the top of her lungs, too. The words were very easy to pick up. "Shub-Niggurath–the song! Shub-Niggurath–the song! The goat with a thousand young!"

Andromeda kept it up till the Champlains downstairs started pounding on the ceiling with a broom. Another first. Part of her wanted to keep going to see what it would be like if they called the police on her, but she wasn't that much of a rebel. She turned down the volume and sank to the floor, rather joyously exhausted, to her considerable surprise. This must have been why people did this sort of thing. Endorphins, like she got from tantooning, except from the inside and all over her body. She didn't think she'd broken any bones.

The horrible cacophony of Choronzon was finally fading and she was just about to remove the CD when she heard a quiet strumming that was very un-Choronzon-like and turned it louder to make sure she'd heard correctly.

It was Byron's voice, singing over a quiet guitar, and it was a song about her.

Andromeda Klein, Andromeda Klein,
Born under a lonely sign . . .

She turned bright red, all over her face, well past her hairline and all down her chest. It was goofy. It was corny. He was an idiot. It was not too good. But it was also kind of great. She listened to it twenty times in a row. It made her laugh and cry at the same time.

Whether it was the endorphins from all the jumping around to the Cthulhu rock, the crying-laughing state of mind brought on by Byron's silly, silly Andromeda Klein song, or the fact that Andromeda had thrown a few dragon's-teeth seeds on the brazier in preparation for the abortive invocation before everything had happened, Andromeda passed easily from semiconsciousness to her box that night. She was lifted directly out of her body on tiny clouds that felt like hands, and she floated into the dark sphere with the purplish yellowish light, then was propelled very quickly down a series of viscous, pulsing tunnels, one of which opened up to the familiar box room with the purple smoke walls, and finally dropped, almost slammed, into her box. She felt the impact on her back, and it felt rather nice: a small, satisfying thud.

She had a pretty strong feeling she was going to see the King of Sacramento, and soon she felt his presence and felt his strong arms taking hold of her and beginning to wrap her in her silk ribbon bindings.

"I do not have a great deal of time for you," he said

brusquely, but not unpleasantly or without kindness. "Just enough to dress you and secure you. You may ask any questions you like, until you are fully secured."

Andromeda found she could not move her jaw, or cause any sound at all to issue from her throat. And she couldn't think of any questions, either.

"No?" he said, lifting the back of her head so he could tie on her blindfold, then setting it down again. She felt the lid drop down on her box, and heard the sound of the iron clasps being fastened and locked in place. She was crying with the effort of trying to form words, even as she sank gratefully into the comfort and safety of being tightly bound in the strong, secure box.

"Very well," said the King of Sacramento. "I must be on my way. I will leave you with a thought or two. A man named MacGregor once endured a lifetime of ruin and pain, hounded by spiritual creatures summoned by a mere senseless act of plagiarism. Monks in scriptoria have not always understood the mischief that their uncomprehending quill scratches might do, especially those scratches which happened to find themselves scratched at auspicious times. Once summoned, such creatures can be hard to control indeed. You could do much worse than consulting Solomon's books, even allowing that much nonsense has made its way into them. Discerning the necessary from the superfluous is the work of a lifetime, but I will tell you that were I intending to confront an infernal duke and his retinue of an evening, I would be quite grateful indeed to have in hand, at the very least, a serviceable blade of iron. Strip away what you like in the name of modernity and the fashionable theories of

Vienna, by all means, but take care you are not thereby stripped to nothing, and armed only with pretense and vanity."

The King of Sacramento then did something strange and marvelous. He leaned over and softly, gently, and, it seemed, rather intently, kissed her on her silk-covered lips before settling her iron face plate in its groove in the lid and tightening its bolts and screws and clicking in its locks. She was seeing waves and stars against her blindfolded eyelids. The King of Sacramento's voice was muffled and distant now that the face plate was in place.

"And as you well know, the Lord of Peace, Restored, can produce the Lord of Sorrow through a process, or bridge, of Empress. But everything is not always so grandiose." He rapped the lid of her box with his stick as though to signal "Job well done," and he was gone.

It was the tightest, most secure she had ever been in her box, in a lifetime of having been there, and it was the deepest, most satisfying sleep she had ever had. She couldn't wait to do it again. Had she been able, she would have thrown on some more dragons' teeth and gone right back to sleep immediately, but it was a school day.

✳ ✳ ✳

Had that been an invocation that she had managed inadvertently in her sleep through exhaustion and strong emotion and dangerously intoxicating perfumes? And perhaps even aided by the ill-conceived (yet undeniably barbarous) "barbarous names" growled by the Choronzon singer? She was still buzzing from the dream kiss, and from St. Steve's text, which had arrived late last night but which she had only seen that morning: "u look good wet." She hadn't even ordered that one.

Listening for Huggy often worked best in the bath; the rushing water and the rushing sound in her ears and head seeming to cancel each other out somehow, allowing the tiny, insistent, often quite cranky voice to become intelligible.

Let me guess, said Huggy. *You're walking on air?*

"Never mind about that," said Andromeda to the swirling silvery Huggy wisp she could barely see, somewhere in there. "Just replay what he said."

Huggy had Its annoying aspects, but It was a terrific memory aid, and It dutifully replayed the King of Sacramento's words with perfect clarity and detail. *I will leave the disgusting final act for you to replay all by yourself, if you don't mind.* It was talking about the kiss. That was the one bit Andromeda had no trouble remembering. Words were hard, kisses were not.

"You're going to be a great help on the SAT when the time comes," said Andromeda, and it was so true that Huggy didn't even recognize it as an attempt at humor.

You will get the score I believe you deserve, It said with complete seriousness.

"So," said Andromeda, getting back to business. "Basically, I need to get a sword."

Bingo, said Huggy. *A serviceable blade of iron.* And then It was gone. Of course.

"Who are you talking to in there?" came the mom's accusing voice from beyond the wall, but Andromeda's head was underwater by then, only her eyes, nose, and mouth above the surface, and she was thinking about being locked in a box and kissed by a man in a hood with a sword and a wand.

✳ ✳ ✳

The dad's paranoid barbecue of documents and other printed matter hadn't gotten too far off the ground, to judge from the scattered half-charred bits of paper and magazine remnants lying in and around the bulbous black barbecue unit's grill. He had even tried to burn some of his records, including some of the stock of the Light Bulb Bomb single he had put out on his own label before getting kicked out of the collective. Poor Dad, she thought. It was really rather sad. He hadn't succeeded in burning down the neighborhood or even much of the actual "evidence." The rain would have made that pretty difficult anyway, but most likely he had just lost interest in the project in its early stages and moved on to something else. That was what usually happened.

The stuff in the carport, however, had been quite jumbled up and disarranged. It looked like a cyclone had hit it. The mom wasn't going to like this at all. Papers, circuit boards, tools, wires, magazines, boxes, were all upended and scattered.

She was unlocking her bike, looking around for any stray magazines that might be of interest to Den, when she noticed a small, crumpled and damp pile of papers that had the unmistakable look of Emily's drawings. They must have been tucked somewhere and dislodged and accidentally excavated by the dad's search for his own incriminating documents amidst all the remains of all the previous inhabitants this house had ever known. She picked it up and got a jolt from the mother of all synchs, because on the top sheet it said, in clear though faded and also slightly running blue ink, *KING OF SAC.* Closer inspection revealed that the full text was actually *THINKING OF SAC,* above a map of the state of California. It looked a lot like someone's school assignment, and perhaps it had been, but then someone had scribbled little skulls and crossbones all over it, as though to mark the cities. She ran inside to spread the five sheets out to dry over her bed, noticing some of the tarot-y themes from her other Emily drawings: the flying eagle motorcycle, the crowned pentagram boy, the burning towers, the demon-alien child clawing its way out of a stick figure's belly, though these seemed a bit less carefully drawn, yet somehow more mature. She sealed her door with a quick "Curse be on all who enter" hexagram ritual, and also said a little prayer to Isis that the mom be prevented from intruding. Now she was going to be late for sure.

There was a smashed-up old portable tape player in the mud by one of the carport posts. Andromeda would have thought nothing of it, except that the partially exposed, grubby, and peeling label of the cassette sticking out of it had some strange writing on it, and when she picked it up it was another huge-ass synch, because though it was very hard to make out what it said, it began with a *ZOS* (clearly a reference to Austin Osman Spare's *Anathema of ZOS*) and it ended with a *666.* Now, that was weedgie.

What could be on the tape? It was her understanding that Cthulhu rock was a fairly recent phenomenon, and this cassette was clearly very old. She removed the tape and pocketed it. She was sorely tempted to blow off school entirely and sift through the newly uncovered carport layers, but she was already near her missed-days limit for the year and she had no intention of repeating the whole asinine junior year if she could help it. Once was far, far more than enough. The total content of her eleven and a half years of formal education, including the years at the Gnome School, could easily have been covered, minus bullying and training in awkward social interaction, in a mildly paced two-week seminar.

"Why don't they at least give you that option?" she asked Dave, who was sitting in the middle of the driveway eyeing her coldly, clearly having no answer for that one.

* * *

She regretted sending her "when can I see you?" reply text to UNAVAILABLE the second she pressed Send. Too much, too much. That was how she'd lost him the first time. And of course, there was no response, though to be fair, he often failed to respond even when there was no possible reason for him to be exasperated with her.

She was giving herself the "You are such an idiot" lecture under her breath as she pedaled to school, while speed-dialing Byron's number, and the timing was such that he picked up just as she was saying it.

"That's the nicest thing anyone has ever said to me," said Byron.

"No, not you," she said. "Some stupid girl." She cleared her throat, thinking about how it was no wonder he had been hurt by her offhand dismissal of the song earlier, and how he might well be hurt by her admitting to not actually having listened to it till now. "So, I listened to the song. I'm sorry, really sorry I didn't notice it before, and..." She braked to let a bus go by. "It was, well, just thanks. It was super nice of you to do." She felt like she was going to start crying again, so she hung up.

That went well, said Huggy.

Was it her imagination, or were people at school looking at her with even greater puzzlement and revulsion than they usually did? Did she look weirder than usual? She was buzzing from the electricity of the successful dream invocation of the King of Sacramento, and vibrating inside from the memory of his gentle, loving, commanding silk kiss–if she had been a cat it would have come out as a gentle purring. She worried about St. Steve. She was inexplicably emotional about the emogeekian's dorky song, though maybe, *possibly,* that could just be period hormone emotions run amok. She was worried about the dad. She was thinking about Daisy. She was listening for Huggy. She was just the same as she always was, except maybe more so.

She was also arrayed in Daisy gear: the vinyl coat, the studded belt with the skull buckle, with new holes punched in it to fit, and the knitted fingerless gauntlets. But not the wig. Rather, a plastic headband that looked kind of mod and hurt her scalp satisfyingly. Few would remember Daisy, or even know about her, but maybe they sensed the weedginess. Andromeda liked the clothes. They made her feel closer to Daisy. And maybe they would help attract Daisy and induce her to reveal more of whatever the hell she was up to out there. Daisy's scent hovered everywhere around her as she rode, then walked, like she was in a little Daisy cloud.

Even Baby Talk Barnes seemed to be eyeing her strangely. When he handed back her Language Arts journal, it was another fairly major synch, because the score he had given her on it was a 93. There had been lots of weedgie items in this one, the GAAP and AMY sigils, the little story about A. E. Waite learning to ride a bicycle and getting his mustache caught in a tree, and the spooky cannibalized Emily drawing of the burning church that looked quite a lot like the Tower. Maybe he was secretly a weedgie person, and this score was a coded greeting. She stared at him, expecting a wink or something.

"Ninety-three," she said tentatively, going up to him after class.

"Ninety-what?" he said. She couldn't tell whether he was teasing her, or really clueless.

"Just, you know, ninety-three," she said.

"Oh, wight," said Baby Talk Barnes, catching on. "Good jou-ah-nal sco-ah." He always pronounced *R*s as "ah" when they were at the end of syllables.

So it was not a message after all; just a synch.

Then came the wink. A.E., she oathed, how would she ever know?

"I weally loved the dwawing," he said. "Gweat stuff. I had no idea you had such talent. Mo-wa like that, please."

Rosalie caught up with her on her way to Nutrition.

"Okay, Androma-Daisy," she said. "Ran out of your own clothes or something? Anyhow, it's an improvement over

344

the Grim Reaper look. Leg warmers for your arms. That's hip. So: good news. The Samoans and the Mexicans all think you put a curse on Lacey Garcia that backfired on to Empress and made her fall and break her leg. So they all want to kick *your* ass now. Well, more than they did before."

"Good news?"

"Oh, yes," said Rosalie, "actually, now that you mention it, that's not really instinctively good news, is it? In fact, it's a little bit bad. But on the bright side, they're all scared of you now, and you can easily outrun the big ones on those sweet little legs of yours. No, the good news is Charles has come crawling back to me and is begging for my forgiveness. He's coming home this week and my plan is to torment him. And I owe it all to you and your gift of prophesary. So, quickly, you have to help: I need you to give me some hickeys for the big night."

"What? No, that would be too weird. What about Gas Station Boy?"

"Joshua's hickeys are no longer welcome in this jurisdiction," she said. "Besides, I'd like a friend to do it. You'd do it for Beth, no fucking doubt. Skidding."

Andromeda turned bright red. Her headband itched.

"I'll think about it," Andromeda finally said. The whole thing could be a big joke, or it could be real. Either way, it was nearly impossible to say no to Rosalie van Genuchten. "Not here, though. I'm sure that would be an expellable offense."

"Fucking pshaw," said Rosalie. "Those socks are just not staying up on you, are they?" And she was right. Andromeda's legs were too skinny for her over-the-knee stripey socks. She had put on two pairs of black tights underneath to add thigh girth, but it just hadn't been enough.

In the vacuum, while Andromeda was sadly taking off the socks, Rosalie explained what she really had meant by good news before she got sidetracked by Empress and revenge hickeys and socks. Word had gotten out about Andromeda's special powers of "prophesary" and pretty much everyone wanted her to do their cards now.

"You trust me," said Rosalie, "there's going to be a line around the block at lunch today. Try to keep it positive, string bean. And don't say I never did anything for you. Remember to have them cross your palm with silver. Make enough money, maybe you can afford to finally put your mom in a home like you've always dreamed of."

✳ ✳ ✳

It was in Trigonometry that Andromeda Klein looked over her Language Arts journal, and thought about MacGregor Mathers and his plagiarized conjuring missteps and the monk copyists with their senseless quills, and it clicked. The GAAP and AMY sigils in the journal. The King was hinting, wasn't he, that simply drawing their sigils might have managed to evoke them by accident, and that now they were bedeviling her, complicating her world and causing mischief?

Then Andromeda said, out loud, it looked like, because everybody turned around and stared at her: "You know, it isn't actually as cool as you seem to think it is to say that all the time."

This was because Huggy had said *Bingo. Okay,* It added, *how about: You are correct, Miss I Think I'm So Much Cooler Than My Own Holy Guardian Angel.*

Andromeda didn't even wait for Ms. Kendall-Hauptmann to kick her out formally. She just wordlessly gathered her stuff, left the classroom, and headed for the café, grateful for the unexpected free period. She saw a couple of Empress's friends in the distance and waited around a corner, just in case Rosalie was right, or not joking, that they were actively seeking her destruction rather than just passively approving of the idea in general as usual. The last thing she needed was to hear them coming up behind her telling her she dropped something or asking if they could ask her a question. That never, ever ended well.

In the café, with her latte and her Daisy deck and Language Arts journal spread out before her, she reviewed the GAAP and AMY situation. For all her ridicule of MacGregor Mathers and Daisy and Byron with his foolhardy *Simonomicon* gate-walking, she had done the same thing herself, and for nothing more than a tiny portion of a grade in a class where no one ever got lower than a B anyway. It had only been a little over a week ago, but the Andromeda of today would never have simply drawn those sigils in such a casual, playful manner. Huggy and the King of Sacramento had changed things quite a lot, without her even quite realizing it. So, GAAP and AMY, if they were around and causing mischief, would have to be banished, and not just casually play banished. Really and truly banished, like Solomon would do it.

She texted Byron: "I need a sword."

✳ ✳ ✳

Rosalie's estimate of a "line around the block" of people wanting tarot readings had proved to be a bit of an exaggeration, but there were plenty of people interested. The commotion at the lunch table attracted the attention of staff monitors and prompted them to call the school cop, worried about drugs or candy or forbidden electronic items, but as there wasn't any specific rule against fortune-telling during lunchtime they did not attempt to break it up.

Andromeda, especially as this was a Right Ring Day, was a bit disappointed when the district cop allowed the proceedings to continue.

She did the best she could with the sincere querents, humored the joke questions, and couldn't resist dazzling a little here and there with arcane-sounding technical knowledge and specific predictions that included possible parts of names and dates (which people universally found to be the most impressive predictions, probably because any who had ever had any experience with divination were used to cover-your-bets vagueness). She sent Huggy on a mission to apologize sincerely on her behalf to the memory of A. E. Waite and to Thoth Hermes Trismegistus for her flagrant charlatanism. But Huggy was quite a help in such readings, producing and feeding her correspondences and variant readings that would have previously taken her days to look up in the library.

By far the most common question was "Is my boyfriend or girlfriend cheating on me?" And she didn't even have to consult the cards on that one. The answer was yes, now or in the future. It was something no one wanted to hear, but they were always interested in the names and dates, that was certain. She had to admit to *slightly* enjoying the attention and feeling like a big shot. And a lot of them did give her money, once Rosalie got the ball rolling by saying: "Cross her palm with silver or curses will be upon your children's children!"

But it was exhausting, and once Andromeda realized that Rosalie was video-capturing much of the scene with her digital camera, anxiety about her appearance set in as well. Halfway through the lunch period Andromeda couldn't take it anymore and excused herself to go to the bathroom as an escape.

To Andromeda's amazement, the impromptu fortune-telling event had even sparked a protest. On her way to the vacuum she passed the Thing with Two Heads and other assorted Christian students standing outside looking on dolefully and disapprovingly, refusing to enter the tainted cafeteria.

"You should come to our church sometime," said one of the Thing's heads. "We have DDR."

Dance Dance Revolution was, however, no enticement whatsoever to one who had tasted the delights of the King of Sacramento's shadowed chamber.

✳ ✳ ✳

It always felt safer, more comfortable, less crazy at the International House of Bookcakes than anywhere else. Marlyne touching up her makeup in the reflective chrome parts of the checkout machine. Darren Hedge rolling his squeaky chair from spot to spot behind the reference desk that no one ever visited. Elderly patrons sleepwalking toward death, outnumbered by paid and volunteer staff by a factor of nearly three to one. Even Weird Gordon leering at her spindly legs and singing his little song about "wheeling the cart to the bin, and then wheeling it back again" had a comforting, familiar charm. And, of course, the satisfyingly diminishing Sylvester Mouse list—all the books saved by the tireless efforts of the Endangered Books Project, which was to say the pooled library cards of Den, Byron, and Daisy. Fifteen books at a time, times three, could really add up to quite a lot once there was a system in place. The "Friends" of the Library weren't going to know what hit them.

The IHOB had five decrepit check-out-able cassette players for books on tape, pretty much the only place outside of a car where anyone ever saw those machines. She selected the most functional-looking one and settled in the back of the Children's Annex with her headphones to listen to the ZOS cassette, not knowing what to expect.

It was music. And it was weird. She had pressed Play without rewinding, as rewinding can be hard on old tapes (she knew this from years of cassette surgery on the library's books on tape collection). It was hard to tell where the beat began, or to know how you'd dance to it if you were to try. On top of that, there was a woman screaming—no, more like screeching—about how she was looking for a bridge. Well, that was interesting, anyway; maybe a synch, because the King of Sacramento had mentioned the Empress being a bridge between Chokmah and Binah, hadn't he? And then right at the end, another voice, a man's English-accented voice, sounding exactly like she had always imagined A. E. Waite would sound, said: "Where's that confounded bridge?"

"It's the Empress, A.E.," she said, nearly aloud, "and you'll find it linking Chokmah and Binah, between the Veil and the Abyss!"

The next song sounded like snakes swimming in thick, hot liquid. Then the tape got eaten and the machine stopped. And just when she was almost enjoying it. She stood up to get her tape surgery box from the back room, but on her way Den came in, so she went back to the Annex to give him his stack of fifteen new titles.

"Do I have to pay this?" he said peevishly. He was holding an overdue notice postcard, addressed to Daisy Wasserstrom, for *The Magical Battle of Britain.*

"Fuck," said Andromeda, instinctively covering her mouth, because somehow it seemed wrong to say "fuck" in the library. That must have been one she had checked out on Daisy's card and forgot to scan back in. "Did your mom see this?"

Den said she hadn't seen it. He always tried to get to the mail before her, he said, because you never know what might set her off and it was better safe than very, very, very sorry. Andromeda didn't *think* any others had slipped by, and she would have to look into her records, but she made Den promise to be especially on the lookout in the coming week. A wake-up call. Mizmac mischief could potentially really destroy the entire Endangered Books Project.

"This may be the last one for a while," said Andromeda, discreetly passing him the bagel worm agony wrapped in an old *Chronicle,* and Den looked very, very sad.

She was about to try to comfort him when into the Children's Annex walked Byron, carrying in his hands an enormous sword.

"Sword delivery," he said.

She could have kissed him.

THE FOOL.

xviii.

His grandpa had been in the Knights of Columbus, he said as Den looked on, wide-eyed. It was a great, great sword, over half Byron's height when he stood it up.

"They let you walk in with that?" she said, impressed.

"They did. I think the lady at the front desk might have been asleep. Sorry. I know it has Christianity all over it," he said apologetically, pointing to the crosses on the pommel and the Latin motto containing the word *Christus*.

"There is nothing wrong with a little Christianity," she said. Huggy then fed her the following lines: "Some of the best magicians in the history of the world worked in the Christian tradition. A lot of them were monks. A good magician uses whatever works, not what accords with his vanity." Huggy was going to be a big help not only on the SATs, but also in the composition of *Liber K,* when the time came.

Once again, it was easier for her to think of them both following Huggy's lead, rather than to have the full responsibility of figuring out a way to explain every single thing to Byron. On the other hand, it was rather nice to be listened to so intently. She couldn't remember anyone paying nearly as much attention to what she said as Byron did, not even St. Steve.

She handed Byron his ring (which she had got from the parrot vending machine at Savers on the way over), a new Moleskine book, and her kitten pin.

"Come on, you're not going to pin me for that!" he protested. "Okay, Christianity rules. I was just trying to help."

"No, the pin is so you can pin yourself; the book is so you can keep track of when you need to be pinned; and the ring is so you know who you are. It goes on your index finger, by the way," she added. And his fingers were tiny enough that the little toy ring actually did fit.

"So," said Byron, lifting the sword and raising his eyebrows at Den. "Who are we going to stab?" Den looked like he was about to run from the room.

"Shh," she said. "His mom is a scary knife lady."

"That's okay, chief," said Byron to Den. "Mine is too."

When Den had (reluctantly) gathered his books so he

could be out of there and back home before the mail arrived, Andromeda turned to Byron and said:

"But the answer to your question about who we are going to stab is, the Goetic demons GAAP and AMY."

✳ ✳ ✳

"Well, of course we have to hope it won't come to that," she said. She tried to explain: "See, basically, it looks like I may have *accidentally* summoned these two relatively high-level demons with my homework, and last night when the King of Sacramento was locking me in my box he suggested that they may still be hanging around making mischief for me and that they really should be banished and dealt with properly. We need the sword because demons are afraid of iron, and it has to be a big long one so you can stick it outside the circle to threaten them, if necessary." She paused. "Oh, and Huggy just told me, we should probably try to do it tonight. I think It did the planetary calculations already." Then she added: "Huggy is my Holy Guardian Angel."

That was, perhaps, the longest single sustained uninterrupted speech she had ever delivered in her whole life. Byron was staring at her.

"Is this LARP?" Then, in answer to her quizzical look, he said: "Live Action Role Playing?" She shook her head.

If you run from the room screaming, she said quietly to herself in the form of a prayer, please leave the sword.

The time had come to explain what was going on. It had only been a little over a week since the Daisy dream, but telling him about it, in a hurried whisper, took ages, all the way up to the beginning of her shift at six. She was going to leave the most embarrassing stuff out, and not mention St. Steve, but in the end she couldn't figure out how to explain her sigil activities, tantoons, and current worries properly without spilling it all. And once she started telling him, she started to feel like she really wanted him to know. Of course, it wasn't only the past nine days she was telling him about. It stretched back to the beginning of her life, to Daisy's witch club, the mom, the dad, and, because he knew nothing about history and philosophy, all the way back to ancient Egypt and Sumeria, to the Sea and Star Cults of primordial man. She even told him about Bethany and Katherine Mansfield, the full story of Huggy, her osteogenesis imperfecta, Bryce and his lack of interest in her aerodynamic body, and how when she had broken up with him he had tried to kill himself by swallowing a bottle of aspirin. And how she spent every day hating herself for not being able to be a better sport about having lost the genetic lottery so spectacularly.

And somehow, it seemed, at the bottom of everything, was Daisy, and the Two of Swords reversed.

No one person had ever known all that stuff about her, and some of it was not known to anyone else. Once again, she almost felt like kissing Byron, kind of; not romantically, she assured herself, more like how she would kiss Dave on the top of the head. *Don't kid yourself, sister,* said Huggy.

She was completely drained. Finally Byron said: "So, Goetic demons tonight. Your place or mine?" And something about that made her smile.

"Oh, I think we'll do it here," she said. "In the basement temple." They agreed to meet in the parking lot at ten-thirty, a safe hour and a half after the library closed, and she gave him a list of things to collect and purchase, everything she could think of.

"After hours? Is that . . . allowed?"

"It is completely one hundred percent the opposite of allowed," replied Andromeda. She had keys and the alarm codes, because she opened up on weekends. "You'll be living on the edge."

"I've never felt so alive," said Byron.

Just before six, as Andromeda was getting ready to clock in and Byron to leave, a text vibrated in from St. Steve. Her own reaction to it, and her reaction to Byron's reaction to it, were curious. For the first time ever in her life, she had no reason to hide or cover up or divert attention, because Byron already knew everything. He picked up the phone and read it first and she found she didn't care that much. And that felt amazing, just to decide not to worry, to let things be and not even try to cover anything. His expression told her it was a weird message, and when he held it up it was: "take off your panties."

"So that's Mr. Sensitive," he said. Then, matter-of-factly, "You're going to do it, aren't you?"

Andromeda nodded and didn't even blush. Byron made a "be my guest" motion.

"It's a kind of a game," she said, rather too casually. But she loved Byron's response more than she loved even getting a message from St. Steve, because it meant she could really be herself. He was going to let her get away with it, and she wouldn't have to lie about St. Steve or her box or

Bethany or anything if she didn't feel like it. This time she really did kiss him, quickly, on the side of the head as she tripped off to the bathroom. She was actually sorry to see that he had already left when she returned, because even with two pairs of tights on, library shift commando felt pretty dangerous.

The euphoric feeling of total freedom lasted about twenty minutes before panic began to set in. Of course. That feeling of freedom wasn't her being herself. This was. Terror, remorse, self-loathing, embarrassment. What the hell had she been thinking?

"Help me, Huggy," she said, trying to pick up Its voice in the whirring of the ceiling fan. But Huggy was silent. It would probably be better if Byron were to die, taking himself and all her secrets with him, or just move away and never return. Was there a ceremonial operation for that? There probably was, in Agrippa. Or she could go away. Or die. Agrippa probably had that covered as well.

It was the song that had invited her candor, she theorized ruefully to herself, sleepwalking through her shift. A song, even if it wasn't the best of songs, was an unfair move. It still made her feel like weeping, just the thought of it. She didn't even like the song very much. It was more what it represented, the first time anyone had done anything just for her without her having had to work and work and work for their conditional approval. When someone listens to you seriously and doesn't shun you as soon as you mention your box, it can be like a drug, addictive, and maybe a little scary.

"operation commando: roger that!" she texted back to UNAVAILABLE, the exclamation point making it look just a little more enthusiastic than she felt. Now, that was a joke she probably shouldn't tell the dad. After two hours and no response, she realized she was definitely not having fun with this like she supposed she was supposed to, so she texted: "wtf are you doing?" though she couldn't, just couldn't in the end, resist adding "<3" to mitigate things in case the "wtf" made him mad.

✳ ✳ ✳

A lot of the tape had been eaten in the machine, but she managed to fix the ZOS cassette without losing too much of the tape that remained by fitting the spools into a new, white, noncorroded State of California–issued institutional cassette casing. The corroded *ZOS something something 666* label came off easily in two pieces, and she glued it to the new case. You're good, Klein, she told herself. Sadly, most of the bridge song and the A. E. Waite ending was now missing. There was only one other bit where the A.E. voice appeared, chanting a count-in. The screamy lady was all over it, though. It took Andromeda two listens to decide she liked it. It put images in her head like Guillaume de Machaut and *ars subtilior* but like no other rock music–certainly not Rosalie's crowd's "oh oh oh" Burger King music or Byron's Cthulhu rock–ever had. Not even close. It placed mathematical, angular images in her head, some delicate and twirly, and some hot and bright, and some dim and obscure. By the fourth time through she had decided it was maybe the best thing she'd ever heard in her life. Even Huggy seemed to like it, because she could sometimes see Its silvery shape twirling and vibrating and spinning around on the edge of her field of vision, especially with the "four already" one that painted triangular sigils and maybe even an I Ching hexagram image in her head.

She named the screamy woman Pamela. The A.E. figure was A.E., dressed in robes like the King of Sacramento, seated at a large draftsman's table off to the side of the stage, with a compass and a straightedge, working out the mathematical calculations and the sigilish architecture of the pieces. There was a drummer named Reg, and it sounded like around seven or eight guitarists: their leader was Jeffy, and his minions had kitten heads and were named Red, Blue, Purple, etc., after the color of their instruments and eyes.

Yes, said Huggy. *That is exactly correct.*

The other side of the tape was not nearly as good–it could well have been a different group with a different screamy lady singing. But it was a kind of synch anyway because one of the songs went "Six six six the number of the beast." It was what she would call association *ouijanesse*–nothing on the tape itself was weedgie to any degree, but it referred to other weedgie things, and by that measure–by sheer volume, anyway–it was certainly among the most weedgie accidentally found things she'd ever happened on. Guillaume de Machaut could actually be legitimately frightening, especially in the quiet parts alone in the dark. The 666 song was fun but silly, though.

St. Steve's response to her "wtf <3" text came in just as she was flashing the lights to warn the nonexistent patrons that closing time was fifteen minutes away. It ran: "jj8kk!" That wasn't in the predictionary. Andromeda could imagine no possible meaning. What was he doing, just pressing keys at random to mock her?

Andromeda was already irritated with him, so she saw red and texted back: "you sir are an asshole," the least friendly thing she had ever sent to him by far in their entire association; and she sent it before she realized that "jj8kk!" looked a lot like a password. He must have been entering a password by mistake. But for what? Voice mail? Her heart jolted with the possibilities of *that* before realizing that the voice mailbox probably had to be linked to a particular phone. (She knew that from the mom's bitter disappointment upon learning she couldn't just tap into Andromeda's voice mail anytime she felt like it without having the physical phone. For once, she understood something of how the mom must feel.) How could she use it? She probably couldn't at all, but of course she saved the message on her phone and also wrote it on her upper bicep as neatly as she could in case it seemed like a good idea to tantoon it someday.

She accepted a ride home from Weird Gordon so she could retrieve her robe and other materials and equipment. Sneaking in and out of the house without the mom noticing was by far the trickiest part of the entire operation. She attempted a simple, quick Egyptian invisibility charm and recited a hastily written stealth incantation; whether or not they worked, the mom was, luckily, nowhere to be seen. Dave saw Andromeda, but thankfully his meow was silent.

Waiting for Byron in the shadows near the library's magnolia tree, she risked calling UNAVAILABLE and left a message saying she was sorry for the text and if he by chance hadn't read it yet to please delete it without reading it; it had been a mistake. Like *that* ever worked on anyone. She would have been shocked had there been a response, and there was none.

Byron disappointed her slightly by showing up on time—she had been half hoping he wouldn't show up, or would be late enough that she could pretend to have given up waiting. But any doubts she had about facing him after realizing what an idiot she had been about telling him about her box and St. Steve and Huggy fell away in the face of his friendly and businesslike bearing as he unloaded bag after bag full of the improbable items she had specified, and picked them all up, balancing the sword on top and shaking his head nonchalantly when she offered to help. If he had been repulsed by anything she had told him, he gave no indication. Maybe he just didn't care.

✳ ✳ ✳

They couldn't risk any lights till they got to the basement, and Andromeda had to feel her way to the alarm to enter the code by touch, then push Byron in the right direction toward the door to the storage-basement stairs.

Once safely down there, she lit a long, handheld church taper and by that light set up the seven "lamps"—that is, seven other candles of varying heights to represent each of the seven traditional planets. She used stacks of books from the discard bins to get the right height for each, and a compass to orient them correctly. Byron simply stared, fascinated.

She didn't have a very good text of the Goetia. A.E.

had trusted no one, and the paraphrases in his *Ceremonial Magic* were so heavily blinded and trapped as to be nearly worthless. But A.E. was all she had, and he would have to do. Andromeda knew she was pretty good at writing and conducting rituals on the fly, improvising when need be.

"Pretty much all that stuff is online," said Byron. "Why don't you just download it?"

"We're not going to be downloading Goetic grimoires off the Internet," said Andromeda impatiently. There was no telling what manner of Things might be summoned inadvertently by the decrepit IHOB printer if it were allowed to spray ink on pages in sigil shapes. Besides, a printout would just look wrong and would kill the weedgie mood. There was no substitute for a real book.

She had Byron stand on the end of a rope in the center of the room as she drew a series of concentric circles with a large stick of chalk tied to the other end, and then filled in the necessary names and seals, as Byron looked on, wide-eyed.

When everything was as ready as it was ever going to be, she told Byron to strip naked and put on his robe, deliberately averting her eyes from his spidery, rather surprisingly hairy body, but noting that, no, he did not in fact have a male tramp stamp. That was a relief; it would have been even worse than mandals.

She had told him to get a silk robe of some kind, and the best he had been able to come up with was one of his mother's dressing gowns. He only hesitated a moment. She pinned it up where it was too big and tied it around the middle with some rope. The none-too-weedgie pastel floral pattern was still visible when it was turned inside out, but it was the best he had. "I'll make you a real one soon," she said. She put the goggles and headphones on him and tied them tightly to his head with ribbons. Then she undressed and slipped into her white ceremonial Tau robe and Daisy's coat, gauntlets, shoes, and wig.

"Why do we have to wear the blond wigs?" he asked. He looked rather ridiculous.

The real answer, of course: they're special hats to turn anchoresses into Popesses.

But to Byron, Andromeda put it this way: "We want the spirits to mistake us for Solomon the King."

"Solomon the King wore a discount platinum wig from Walgreens?"

"Yes," she said, "he sure did. So it is written."

✳ ✳ ✳

The ceremony began well enough. Because Byron was essentially blinded by the goggles, she tied his leg to the table they were using as an altar so he wouldn't leave the circle in error. He was especially sensitive to the "perfumes," and several times said he was feeling dizzy. He described the vivid color effects he saw, and they did sound rather spectacular. The goggles created a dark mirror much more reliably and efficiently than a wine bottle or crystal ever had in Andromeda's experience, that was for sure.

AMY departed easily and with a kind of courtly flourish, upon merely being asked, with no physical manifestation other than a light breeze. GAAP proved to be a bit more difficult. The room grew icy, Andromeda's skin crawled with invisible spiders, and the babbling metallic ripping sound was tearing her ears apart. Byron later said he felt sick to his stomach the entire time, and claimed to have actually lost consciousness at a couple of points. He reported seeing eyes and claws. Andromeda's own vision became patchy as well. She was, as the King of Sacramento had predicted, extremely relieved to have had a nice big sword in hand. If she was unable to command and bind like Solomon, with threats and will, she was certainly able to outlast the spirit's patience. In the end she had to resort to smacking the spirit's sigil with the flat of the blade till the babbling and spiders began to subside.

AMY had flitted away cheerfully, GAAP had departed in disgust, but there was little doubt that they had both gone.

Finally, she unblinded Byron and taught him how to pentagram-banish the temple. And this banishment felt unusually wonderful.

"I feel bathed in inner light," she said.

"So do I," said Byron, clearly astonished. "And I don't even know what that is!" Ah, he was kind of funny, this guy. "I can't believe that ice-cold air thing really happens." He was still shivering.

"It really does. Almost every time anyone is there. GAAP really froze me out. I can barely feel my feet."

"Now what do we do?"

"Clean up and go home."

"Aw."

✳ ✳ ✳

"That is the weirdest, scariest thing I have ever done in my life," he said on the way to dropping her home. She searched his eyes to see if he was joking or exaggerating, or trying to humor her, but he looked sincere.

"Thank you," she replied.

Byron looked a bit of a wreck, actually. Andromeda advised him to take a long bath when he got home and to drink a lot of water. And she warned him that he might feel a bit depressed for the next few days.

"I'm always depressed," he said. Now, that was something new. She'd never have guessed that. "And I hate water."

"Don't be ridiculous," she said, "nobody hates water. But suit yourself. It'll hurt."

She bounded out of the car at the spot at the bottom of the hill, as she had done so many times before after seeing St. Steve. If Byron had wanted to kiss her or touch her or anything he gave no indication. He was already looking sad and distant.

"Trust me," she said. "Water."

Walking up the hill carrying a sword felt quite a bit better than walking up the hill not carrying a sword. And standing in the alcove being yelled at from the bedroom by the mom while carrying a sword felt absolutely, unbelievably great compared to standing in the alcove being yelled at by the mom from the bedroom with no sword. Even looking forlornly at a cell phone that displayed zero messages while holding a sword was a bit better than the same thing without one.

There really was nothing like a sword.

Magic with a partner kicked ass over solitary magic, that was for sure. Never had Andromeda felt more confident about a practical working, not even with Daisy, even though it had achieved nothing but to correct a previous idiotic error.

Her own post-ceremony bath had the dual purpose of cleansing and giving Huggy an opportunity to reappear and congratulate her through the medium of the running taps. It had been strangely silent during the ritual, and indeed throughout the whole night.

The voice of Huggy emerged from the rushing water soon enough, sounding rather cranky.

Honestly? It said. *The new medium works right out of the box and has lots of potential. Good choice, maybe even better than the last one. But I can't say I care much for your sloppy, postmodern conjuring.*

"The new medium. The new medium? Byron?"

Yes, the overeager hairy little man you have somehow managed to ensnare in your web of feminine wiles. You should try scrying the aethyrs with that one sometime. He's a sponge. AMY was all over him like catnip. Some of the Shemhamphorashers were actually jealous.

"What's the matter with my conjuring?" It had been completely successful, and with such dramatic effects.

I hate to break it to you, said Huggy, *but you're not really up there to be everybody's friend and dazzle everyone with your "creativity" and enthusiasm. Believe me, these guys have seen it all, and I guarantee you they're not going to be impressed with a cutesy pseudo-Solomon act. Yes, the sword is very nice, but sword or no sword, GAAP could have easily torn you up and worn you as a glove. You're lucky he's so easily bored.*

Andromeda meekly pointed out that the "magic sponge"

they were all so excited about had seemed pretty impressed with her technique.

He would have been impressed with a paper towel. You really wish to impress him, wear heels and a miniskirt. There just isn't any other way to do Goetia than strict traditionalism.

Huggy had more to say, but Andromeda switched off the tap and cut her off.

"Why does my Holy Guardian Angel have to be such a jerk?" she said to the wall, but she knew It had had a point, plus she was impressed with herself for figuring out how to switch It on and off.

She slept that night with the sword in one hand and Daisy's Little One in the other. There was no encounter with the King of Sacramento, that she could recall, but she was granted, just as she was drifting into her box, another brief glimpse of the dazzling, undulating Tree of Life Universe-jewel. Each time she saw it, it was more beautiful than the last. She had no trouble whatever waking up the next morning: even sleeping was better when you were holding a sword, it turned out.

xix.

The dad was sitting in his van with the door open, talking to a couple of people, when Andromeda rounded the corner on her way back from school the following day. She realized, to her horror, when it was too late to turn around and escape, that they were two of the youngish rock-and-roll people she remembered from the Old Folks Home: Amanda and either Frederick or Sam. Why on earth? she thought as the dad was waving her over.

"This is my daughter, Andi," he said as she approached,

hood pulled as far down her face as it would go. "She's a big fan. Big fan. Cupcake: meet Choronzon. Sam and Amanda. They're here to pick up their rough mixes."

Andromeda mumbled a hi, trying her best to avoid eye contact.

Amanda seemed, as usual, too out of it to notice much of anything, but Sam recognized her, she could tell that. He smiled coolly at her, and winked. When it became clear that he wasn't going to rat on her about being underage and hanging out in bars with older men, she relaxed a bit.

"I like the Toad Bone Ritual song," she said.

"Do you?" said Sam, nodding quietly as though he knew something she didn't.

Creepy, creepy guy.

✷ ✷ ✷

"I'm trying to save the books for use by my future self," said Andromeda Klein to Byron the Precious Little Sponge. "But your future self can use them too, of course."

They were in her room, discussing the Greek Magical Papyri and the IHOB Endangered Books Program. Andromeda was trying to paraphrase *Liber K*'s treatment of the papyri–it would be so much easier when she had finally written it down and could just hand it to someone anytime they needed to know something.

"So," she said, "it was a library of magical texts buried in the Egyptian desert in ancient times by an unknown conjuror."

"He buried a whole library all by himself?" said Byron. "What, with all the librarians inside?"

"No," Andromeda said. "Not a library *building*. A library

369

is a collection of books. A bunch of *libri*. I meant that he hid the papyrus scrolls, not an entire building with fluorescent lights and bathrooms. They were actually buried in clay pots, I think."

"There you go again," said Byron. "You and your *libers*. Do you want me to get out the kitten pin?" But Andromeda waved that away.

And that was, in fact, exactly how Andromeda Klein saw the IHOB's collection of Eejymjays. Someone had built it up, and for whatever reason, Andromeda was now the only person in a position to preserve it. True magical training could take several lifetimes, and it was only prudent to lay the groundwork so the next self to come along wouldn't have to start from scratch. She added that she wished she knew who had built up the impressive IHOB Eejymjay Collection, and why.

"You know," said Byron, after pausing to look at her incredulously and getting out his notebook, "for such a hardcore librarian, you really do suck at knowing about looking things up on the Internets. I've been trying to tell you for the last twenty minutes, but you keep interrupting me. The library was donated to the city by a man named"–he checked his notes–"Ernest James Madison Jessup. The *EJMJE* in your catalog stands for the Ernest James Madison Jessup Estate, I would bet you any money. He was one of the people who established Clearview as a town in 1912. He wrote two books on aliens. One of his wives was a spiritualist and faith healer who went insane and was convicted of trying to murder him. People were so much more interesting in the olden days." Eejymjay had, Byron said, lived and stored his private collection of esoteric materials in the building that was now the central churchlike structure of the IHOB, and had willed the library to the city on the condition that it be preserved intact and remain open to the public.

Preserved intact: that was the same phrase Darren Hedge had used to refer to this arrangement.

"So how," said Andromeda, "can they be selling the books off, then, if it has to be 'preserved intact'?"

"Maybe," said Byron, "it's like you were saying just now, about libraries not being buildings. Maybe they think it means the building has to be preserved and not necessarily the books."

"Yeah, maybe they're *pretending* to think that." The "Friends" knew what they were doing, of that Andromeda had no doubt. It was tricky. Nefarious, even. "But that's not fair. They can't do it then, technically."

"They're doing it, though. And what are you gonna do?" said Byron. "Storm City Hall? Bust in on the city council session waving a charter and say 'Stop the meeting'?" And then the judge will say 'It's highly irregular, miss, but you've got five minutes'?"

"Yes," said Andromeda. "That's exactly what I'm going to do." But she remained in position slouched against the bed. She was not about to go busting in on anything. Saving books from the "Friends" by using their own rules and procedures against them was more her style. And at least they had managed to save some of the books that way.

"Anyhow," said Byron, shrugging and turning back to his notes. Ernest J. M. Jessup had, he continued, died in 1977 at the age of ninety-eight, buried by an earthquake mudslide. "You can see the spot in Hillmont. It's right next to the junior high. They built a Dairy Queen on it."

Andromeda was feeling slightly dazed. It was true: she really should have been able to look this stuff up for herself. Why had it taken the Precious Sponge to connect those dots for her? In spite of herself, she began to feel a little irritated at him for showing off, like some kind of teacher's pet.

Don't forget, said Huggy, bubbling up, *you're the teacher in this scenario. Just sit back and enjoy it and let him do the work.* Andromeda sat back, but found herself failing to enjoy it quite as much as she was apparently supposed to.

"Plus," Byron continued, "he was a Rotarian and a Thirty-second-Degree Mason and one of the founders of the Steiner Day School in Clearview Park."

"I went there!" said Andromeda. "Oh my gods! We used to call it the Gnome School."

Byron said he knew people who had gone there, too. "It's a weird hippie school," he said. "With, like, rainbows and rap sessions and crafts. But I guess the founder was a little bit weedgie. Maybe some of that hung around and rubbed off on you. Started you on your journey." He air-quoted the word *journey*.

"Maybe," said Andromeda, finding the idea a little appalling. She was still "processing" the information, as the mom would have put it. There was amazing symmetry in the fact that the same person had been ultimately responsible for both the Gnome School and the IHOB's collection of 133s, each of which had had such a powerful impact on her life. Excitement about the symmetry was battling her customary distaste for all things Gnome School. But Andromeda had to admit, symmetry had a slight edge and would probably come out on top in the end.

"Anyhow," said Byron, "this Jessup character was obviously one spooky, creepy guy." He added that he suspected they hadn't been the first people to perform ceremonial magic in that basement. Andromeda remembered the bookmark in the *Rituale Romanum* and felt a weedgie tingle between her shoulder blades.

"Okay," concluded the Precious Sponge. "I've got one more. The guy they named the school after? He was a totally weedgie guy too. He was in with all those Crowley people and in secret societies and everything. Clearview was a really, really spooky place a hundred years ago, seems like. You were born too late."

"Tell me about it," said Andromeda Klein.

"So why did you call it the Gnome School?"

Andromeda described some of their gnome activities and got out the Little One from the Daisy bag to show him. "Ah," said the Precious Sponge, as though it suddenly all made sense. "That's your little voodoo doll from the library ritual." The Daisy smell filled the room when she opened the bag. Byron noticed and wrinkled his nose, saying it smelled like old ladies.

"Crowley," she said, ignoring this borderline-insulting observation, "had a different approach to storing up knowledge for his future self. He wrote hundreds of books, and made sure to publish each of them in limited rare, expensive editions, so that they would be valuable enough that at least someone would want to collect them and preserve them. Most of his books are in print now, but if they go out of print, some fancy collector will be sure to have saved at least one."

"So," said Byron, "if anyone starts buying up all those books all of a sudden, we'll know who it is."

"Actually, they say he's already reincarnated as a girl in India."

"Man, I hope I don't come back as a girl."

"It's not really your choice," said Andromeda. But secretly, she almost hoped she didn't either. Being a girl took a lot out of a person, and she had never felt very good at it.

Byron knew a lot of things. He had recognized the ZOS chicken scratches on the rejuvenated cassette from the description even before she showed it to him, and he couldn't believe she was unfamiliar with the music on it.

"What planet are you from?" he said, and he sang a bit of a song in a little screechy female voice that went "Hey hey mama" something something and asked: "Is it like that?"

"No," said Andromeda. "It's more like . . ." She asked in the same screechy voice if he had seen a bridge.

"It's the wrong album," he said, "but that, my little alien life-form, is Led Zeppelin."

"No, no, it's not a man, it's a girl," she said. "Pamela."

"No, it's a group, and the singer is a guy named Plant. And of all people, I would have thought you would know that. That was our first conversation. Jimmy Page, remember? Aleister *Crow*ley," he said, exaggerating the pronunciation.

"Oh, I thought you said Jamie," she said, a little lamely. "Really, his name is Plant?" It seemed unlikely.

He hooked his iPod to her stereo and dialed it up. And there it was, filling her room, even better now that it was loud and out in the air. The snakey song. It was just too good.

"You know," he said, when the next song came on, "a lot

of people say this song is about Jamaica, but it's really pronounced 'dyer-maker.' " He turned it up even louder.

There was a sudden, insistent pounding on the door. They were sitting with their backs against it, because that was just what you did at Casa Klein, but both of them combined didn't weigh enough to prevent the mom from pushing it open, sliding them across the floor. Byron stood up, blinking.

The mom stared back at them silently, looking them up and down, from one to the other and back again, several times over, with a mystified expression.

"Well," she finally said, "all I can say is, if you get pregnant I'm not raising the baby."

✳ ✳ ✳

"Nice lady," said Byron.

Explaining the mom to a civilian was just not possible, so Andromeda opted to say nothing at all in response.

Three texts from St. Steve came in all at once, at that moment, reading, respectively: "baby don't be that way," "jj8kk!" and "baby don't be that way." What the hell was his problem? She just stood there looking at her phone.

"Are you going to take your underwear off now?" said Byron.

Andromeda looked at the floor for a long moment.

"Do you want to see my tantoons?" she said. "My tattoos, I mean? You want to see them? No one but me has seen them all." And he was nodding.

In case of another mom invasion, they pushed the bed against the door and sat on it.

"Don't try to touch me, now," she said. "I only want to show you."

It was just past dusk, dark enough for candles, so she lit the green beaded one and reached over to restart the *Houses of the Holy*. And then with the stop-start, sky-opening sound of track number one filling the room, she began to give him a tour of her do-it-yourself body, beginning with the unicursal hexagram on her hip, proceeding chronologically through the Daisy years, to the tiny *B* above her knee for Bryce, to the *Guillaume de Machaut* made to look like a rock band logo that Daisy had partially completed on her back, to St. Steve's upside-down phone number on her stomach. Twice there were knocks on the door, yelling, and attempts to push the door in, but she just ignored them till they went away, and then she resumed. She raised or lowered her skirt or shirt as necessary to reveal each one. And one by one she pointed to each of the seventeen St. Steve sigils that formed a coiled downward-scrolling ring around her left thigh.

"This is my wish to be with St. Steve. It is my will the return of Saint Steve. My will: A.E." She couldn't remember all of the sigil formulae, but they were all the same, basically, and she traced them around and down with her index finger as the guitar line in "The Ocean" began to paint an angular sigil of liquid fire in her mind.

"And this one you know," she said, pointing to the *bet* on her inner upper arm. "It is for a beautiful girl named Bethany. And also, actually, for you. A *bet*, a *B*."

Byron stared at her, and waited till the song was over to say:

"I can't believe you have a guy's phone number on your body."

"Mm-hm," she said. "I can't believe it either." Then she pulled up her sleeve and showed him the newly re-inked string of characters from the mistaken St. Steve text and asked him if he would tattoo it on her.

"What is it?"

"It's a password."

"To what?"

"I don't know," she replied, but somehow she realized that this would be her final St. Steve tattoo. And somewhere in the rushing static hum coming from the overloaded signal-less stereo speakers, she heard Huggy say: *Well, hallelujah.*

"You need to tie my arm to the chair now," she said, and very soon she was floating.

The best synch of a week laden with synchs was finding an old, faded Led Zeppelin T-shirt small enough to fit her at Savers. Byron had made her CDs of all the albums. She just could not believe the vividness of the pictures they painted in her head, unlike any music she had ever heard. No one commented on or praised her for the shirt, but she wasn't wearing it for them, she was wearing it for her, and perhaps for Pamela Plant, and it made her feel just wonderful.

Byron had done a pretty good job on the password tan-toon, though as with magic, he had had no idea how to do it and every step had had to be explained to him. That had been a mood killer, but only a slight one. She had enjoyed how intently he listened when she explained what she wanted, exactly like he did when she was explaining magic to him.

Andromeda had gotten quite good at controlling Huggy's appearances, using continuous sounds like running water to provide a background against which its voice could be discerned and dismissing it by suddenly switching off the source of the sound. She tried it with every appliance and noisemaking item in the house, one by one. The vacuum cleaner and washing machine were particularly good. The only problem was that after doing a lot of this, the distracting rushing sound in her ears seemed even louder and more distracting. *I know what you're doing,* said Huggy in the blow-dryer, *and–* Andromeda switched it off. Oh, this was too much fun. Finding the on-off switch made having a Holy Guardian Angel much, much easier.

"Sorry," she said, switching the blow-dryer back on. "I just had to test."

Yes, aren't you clever, said Huggy. *Okay. Okay. Actually, you know, I've got nothing right now. Switch me back off.* So Andromeda did.

She was sitting in the living room before school with her Agrippa open on her knee, in her T-shirt, singing quietly to herself without quite realizing it the sigil-ish guitar line of "The Ocean," when she looked up to see the just-got-up dad staring at her.

"Jebus," he finally said. "My own flesh and blood. Don't you know the family motto? *Death before Zeppelin?*"

There was no accounting for taste, it was true, but that was maybe the stupidest thing she had ever heard him say.

"As the rope said to the piece of string," Andromeda replied: "I'm a frayed knot. Anyway, I thought it was: *Remember, if the world didn't suck, we'd all fall off.*"

"There are two family mottoes, actually," said the dad, still shaking his head.

Rosalie said it too when she picked Andromeda up in the Gimpala and saw her in the shirt. "Really?" she said. "Really? Death before Zeppelin." How in Malkuth did that ever get said by enough people to become an expression?

"I'm just kidding," said Rosalie. "But you need some bell-bottoms with grass stains on the butt and like a wide leather belt and a gauzy fairy top, or maybe a halter. And a huge silk headband. And war paint."

There had been yet another explosion overnight, this one in the mock campanile of the old, long-closed-down, boarded-up Hillmont High School. A meth lab at a school? Well, they even put them in other people's parked cars sometimes. But Rosalie said no, they were actually saying on the news it might have been a bomb. She backed up the ramp and into a fairly tight space.

"You know, I think this is actually easier than driving forwards. You have more control. I don't know why everybody doesn't do it."

"Well, I don't know why they don't just admit they're meth labs," said Andromeda, gathering her stuff and scanning for any hostile Lacey or Empress minions.

"I know you very, very much *want* them to be meth labs," said Rosalie, "for reasons known only to you and the Hammer of the Gods. The world's gone mad, Andromeda. People are driving backwards and bombing empty bell towers and wearing heavy-metal T-shirts out of the blue all over the place. By the way, is your phone working? I've been trying to get through."

Andromeda checked and told Rosalie she had no missed calls. There were, however, four texts from UNAVAILABLE.

She hesitated with her thumb on the Select button. She thought about the "jj8kk!" tantoon healing on her upper arm, and about the Precious Sponge's song and his eyes fixed on her in rapt concentration; she thought about always dancing backwards and having to do all the work and being everyone's third choice. A smooth, mechanical cadence, the clicks of a delicate lock's oiled tumblers, sounded somewhere in her head. And Andromeda quickly deleted the texts unread.

Now, that was freedom, right there.

✳ ✳ ✳

"I don't know why I never thought of this before," she told Byron back in her room later that afternoon. And by "this" she meant pushing the bed up against the door and sitting on it every time she was in the room. The only drawback was having to pull it back to let Dave in and out, but that was a small price to pay for mom-less-ness. Not only that, but ever since the mom had all but accused her of trying as hard as she could to become pregnant by the Precious Sponge, she had stopped talking to Andromeda for pretty much the first time in recorded history.

"Oh, blessed Silent Treatment, how I have yearned for thee," she said. "Everybody wins, Precious Sponge. Everybody."

"Why am I the Precious Sponge, again?" asked Byron.

"Huggy just called you that once. I don't know why."

"So Huggy is always there talking to you?"

"Not since I learned how to turn It off," she said.

"Is Huggy talking to you now?" She had to hand it to

him. He was as unfazed by any of this as anyone not her could possibly have been.

"No," she said. But she had forgotten about the rushing sound of the highway in the distance. *I am too,* said Huggy. But the voice was faint.

"You don't think your mom would call the cops on you, do you?" Byron said, pointing out the window at a sheriff's car that had just parked in front of the duplex. A uniformed cop was striding up the sidewalk. Byron had said it as a joke, but then they heard the doorbell ring. Andromeda made a "shh" motion for him to be quiet. No way was she going down there to answer it. Gods, the dad must be freaking out, hiding in the closet or something. Where was the mom?

She'd been teaching Byron to read cards, using Daisy's deck, having him practice on her, explaining about significators.

"It's the card that represents the querent," she said, "so in this case, me." Traditionally Andromeda's significator would be the Page of Cups or Swords because of her age and coloring; and of course, since the Daisy dream she had been thinking of the Two of Swords as her significator; and, she added, back when she and Daisy had been learning tarot, they would use the Lovers to represent Andromeda. "But for now just use anything you like."

"Oh, by the way," he said, shuffling through the cards, "I think I figured out your Two of Swords thing."

She doubted he had figured out *the* thing, but she was sure he had *a* thing. Huggy was right. He could be deceptively clever.

He shuffled through Daisy's tarot deck and drew out the Two of Swords and laid it out on the bed.

"See, I think it might be a date." And of course that was possible, since, as she had explained as part of the *Liber K* lecture series on the small cards, each of the minor arcana cards can refer to one of the decans of the zodiac, one thirty-sixth of the circle, a portion of the calendar year. Byron's idea, though, was more specific than that.

"Remember how you thought the girl was kneeling, when on the actual card she's just sitting on the box? And how you thought the background was shallow pools, when actually the card has a deep sea?" He had been taking notes—they were scribbled all over his Moleskine. "Well, look at the moon. Look at the water. The moon is gibbulating, the tide has gone out, and the girl, who is Libra really, right? She has gotten off the box and is kneeling. So you're looking at a point in time just a bit after the moment and lunar phase shown on the card. Closer to when it turns to the next decan, but probably not into the next one, because then it would be a different card."

"Yes, the Three of Swords." Andromeda thought of the two-sided flag in the King of Sacramento's chamber, the Two turning into the Three.

He flipped through the calendar function of his phone, noting that according to the almanac the lunar phases affect-ing tides in that fashion matched up to the Two of Swords portion of the zodiac the previous year and identified the ap-proximate date in late September. That would have been shortly before Daisy's death. Around the time Andromeda and her family had been in Shasta, when she and Daisy had

had a falling-out, and St. Steve had sent his "hi there" and her whole life had started to go wrong.

"That was very clever," Andromeda said, though she was disappointed, "and you get a kiss for how clever it was." She kissed him on the ear. "So it's all about Daisy's death. I'm afraid, Precious Sponge, that I already knew that Daisy died. Well aware of it. It's never far from my mind." She allowed her eyes to roll slightly.

"It's all from your mind, though, isn't it?" he said.

Andromeda's rolling eyes narrowed. This was yet more of the "all in your head" argument that had begun to pop up between them. Byron had been venturing outside the approved reading list, and had somehow picked up the unfortunate modernist notion that occult phenomena were best explained as reflections of the individual's psychology, rather than the effects of "outside" Universal forces or entities. In reality, of course, the distinction between "inside" and "outside" was far more complicated than that when it came to minds and universes.

Stick him with the kitten pin, said Huggy, bubbling up from under the sound of the suddenly heavy rain on the roof. But Andromeda found she didn't feel like it.

"All I mean," continued Byron, unaware of how narrow his escape from the pin had been, "is that if there is something to be figured out, it's all in there, somewhere. Otherwise there would be no point in even trying to figure it out, it would just be random. But I'm not even talking about that right now. What I'm saying is, if the kneeling Two of Swords with the what's it called, the gibbulous moon and the low tide is a date, it's *before* Daisy's death. September twenty-ninth or thirtieth." He consulted his notes. "She died on October third. So that would be the Three of Swords, not the Two. Right?"

But Andromeda was shaking her head. "I don't think tarot is ever *that* precise."

"I'm not talking about the damn tarot," said Byron, "I'm talking about your weird, weedgie head. I just think that somewhere in there you must know something about that date without knowing you know it. Like your own mind is trying to tell you something."

"Okay, fine," said Andromeda. "It's something to do with Daisy. Great."

The Precious Sponge shrugged. "At least I got something out of the deal," he said. It took Andromeda a moment to realize he was talking about the ear kiss.

"Yes, that makes the whole thing totally worth it," she said. "Now focus. Significator."

The Precious Sponge shuffled through the cards.

"Okay, so it's not here," he said. "The Lovers. Not in the deck."

Andromeda didn't believe him, but it was true. She counted only seventy-one cards, and the Lovers was not among them. The Daisy deck that had been hidden in *Sexual Behavior in the Human Female* was missing a card. Had this screwed up all the readings she had done with this deck? But it was even worse than that: it had screwed up only some of those readings.

✳ ✳ ✳

As Andromeda had guessed, the police, who might well have only been selling raffle tickets or something, had spooked the dad, who had fled in his van and was probably camping out in the woods, preparing for the apocalypse or lying low till the "heat" was off.

"Happy now?" said the mom.

Yes, Mother, that was in fact my plan all along, Andromeda silently responded. The mom was the one who should be accused of being happy, if anyone should. She was the one who disliked him most.

"Why didn't you answer the door and take care of it?" asked Andromeda.

"Why didn't *you*?"

"Because, parental figure, I'm the daughter. You're the supposed adult. It's your house. I just live here."

"You know how uncomfortable I am around police, Andromeda," said the mom. "Would it kill you to think of someone other than yourself every once in a while?"

Uncomfortable around police? The alleged daughter of the supposed head of the Australian FBI? It was yet another one Andromeda had not heard before.

THE MAGICIAN.

XX.

Turning Byron loose in the International House of Book-cakes while she did her shift was one of the best ideas Andromeda had ever had. It was like having a roving secretary or research assistant.

"Just find out some stuff," she said, handing him the Sylvester Mouse list. And off he went, eager to please. He would bob in and out of the stacks, paging through indexes and bibliographies and augmenting his searches with queries on his ever-present Internet phone.

Within the first hour he found two interesting things.

The first was the source of Daisy's Toad Bone Ritual, a book on rural folklore of the British Isles shelved in the 900s, so it had not been on Andromeda's radar. The only person who had ever checked it out since it was added to the collection in 1967 e.v. was named Sam Hellerman. That would have been Sam from the Old Folks Home, no doubt, this text being the basis for the awkward Choronzon song about the Toad Bone Ritual. So that was his last name, Andromeda thought. Sam HELL-erman. Strangely fitting. But Daisy's notes, like Sam Hellerman's song, included several phrases from the book verbatim, and the pages in question had the telltale pinpricks in the margin.

"She must have taken her notes in the library," said Andromeda, trying to remember if she had ever noticed Daisy hanging around the 900s.

"Either that," Byron said, "or she was a secret Chronzon groupie or something." He paused. "So, did Twice Holy Daisy Wasserstrom have any horses that needed taming?"

"It had lots of other uses besides that, I'm sure," said Andromeda. "Like I said, it's powerful but negative magic. Crowley did a variation of it as his initiation to the grade of Magus."

"This Crowley was kind of psycho, wasn't he?"

"He was a hell of a holy guru," replied Andromeda, matter-of-factly, "but yes, he had his unsavory aspects. Anyhow, I can't see Daisy going down to the river."

"She copied it down," said Byron.

"Well, so did you," Andromeda replied, pointing to his notes. If people were held responsible for everything they copied down, magic and homework would be in big trouble.

"Okay, but now check this one out," said Byron. "Prepare to be amazed. Did you know that in the Golden Dawn, every initiated magician got a secret code name in Latin?"

"Not a 'code name,' really," Andromeda replied. "They used Latin mottoes for their magic names. I have one too: *Soror Imperfecta*."

"What's my magic name, then?"

How do you say "Precious Sponge" in Latin? Andromeda thought. Huggy? But out loud she said: "I'm still working on it."

Byron opened a large book on the Rosicrucians and pointed to a sentence in it. "You really should work on your Latin," he said.

Under the Precious Sponge's finger it said: *Sacramentum Regis*.

"Not 'the King of Sacramento.' That's fucked-up, totally backassward Latin. It's actually 'the Sacrament of the King.' "

"Sacrament of the King," said Andromeda. "What does that even mean?"

"No idea. But stop hassling me about that. Just look at who it is," said Byron.

Andromeda read the name, A. E. Waite, and shrieked.

✳ ✳ ✳

"Easy, girl," said Byron. "It's okay, she just found out she won the lottery," he said to an elderly patron who appeared to be engaged in a struggle to remember how to turn on his phone so he could call the proper authorities.

Well, said Huggy, drifting in on a wave of heating-duct noise, *you have been invoking him several times a day ever since you were twelve.*

388

"A.E.," said Andromeda.

Exactly.

"So you mean to tell me," said Andromeda Klein, "that A. E. Waite hangs around the astral plane just waiting to give tricksy hints about tarot readings to anyone who happens to come by?"

"Not anyone," said Byron. "Just you."

Andromeda made an exasperated noise. "No, not you. I was talking to Huggy." Byron rolled his eyes.

No, said Huggy, *I don't mean to tell you anything of the kind. I just said you invoke him a lot, and you do have a bit of a fortune-telling problem.*

"So the King of Sacramento is A.E."

No, how could he possibly be?

Andromeda made a noise that is often written as "Arrrgh!"

"Can I talk now?" said Byron. "Thanks. Maybe he could be *Waite's* HGA."

Did that make sense? Andromeda couldn't even tell anymore.

✳ ✳ ✳

I got kissed by A. E. Waite, Andromeda Klein said to herself. I got kissed by A. E. Waite. What did it matter whether it was strictly true or not? She just liked saying it.

The Precious Sponge's little monkey hand was waving in front of her face. Gematria, he was saying. We should check the gematria. Like he knew what he was doing. "What were the King of Sacramento's numbers?"

Andromeda was staring into space.

"Tell Huggy to give you the dream numbers," said Byron.

Wow, a medium and a scholar, said Huggy. *You better step it up, Klein. Soon he'll have no use for you.*

For what it was worth, Byron was able to find variations on A.E.'s name that added up to two of the King of Sacramento's four numbers, using Agrippa's values for Latin gematria.

"Wow, that's semi-impressive," he said, but he was clearly hooked on gematria all the same. "Obviously, you had read about A.E.'s Golden Dawn name and had it somewhere in your mind all along, so that must have been why you dreamt of it, even though you heard it wrong. And then . . . and then your psycho math mind added it up. . . ." He opened Agrippa again and began more trial-and-error scribbling, clearly looking for ways to confirm the remaining numbers.

It's close enough for astral work, said Huggy.

✳ ✳ ✳

That night Andromeda managed through sheer will to force herself into what she used to term the King of Sacramento's chamber, but it was the most unsatisfying box sleep she had ever had. The King never arrived. Her bonds and fittings were creaky and unsatisfyingly loose. And there was an old-fashioned telephone jangling and vibrating on top of her box that her annoyingly unbound hand still couldn't manage to reach.

She woke up and realized she had overslept and that Rosalie was calling her cell.

"Whatever you do," Rosalie said, "do *not* come to school today. Do *not*." Andromeda heard the beep of the Gimpala's horn through the phone's speaker and from the street outside, and waved to Rosalie through the window to come on up.

Andromeda hadn't realized she still had the sword in her hand and the goggles on top of her head till she noticed Rosalie's wide-eyed look of astonishment after she had opened the door.

"My sleeping sword," Andromeda said matter-of-factly.

"Where's Mom?" said Rosalie as she sat at the kitchen table, coffee mug in hand, phone out, as though ready to scan for updates.

Andromeda explained that the mom was probably looking for the dad, who had been in hiding ever since the police had come calling the previous day.

"Just as well," said Rosalie. But they were probably looking for *you*, actually. See, here's the deal. . . ." Rosalie paused. "Could you, like, put that down or something? It's a little distracting."

Andromeda laid the sword across the table and leaned forward, cupping her ears, ready to listen.

According to Rosalie, Mizmac had in fact received an overdue notice for a book checked out on Daisy's library card. The title of that particular book, *The Satanic Bible*, struck terror into her newly reconverted Community Bible Center heart. (*Why in Malkuth would you try to save* that*?* said Huggy, bleeding through the sound of the coffeemaker. Andromeda had no answer besides: completeness.)

A further check of library records had revealed that more than forty books with similarly terrifying titles had been checked out on the same card, and it hadn't been difficult to guess that Andromeda Klein, Daisy's old strange, perverted sidekick who worked at the library, might have had something to do with it. That was, arguably, a kind of fraud, but more importantly, Mizmac had considered it to be harassment and religious persecution. A search of Den's room revealed pornographic materials, which Den had confessed had been furnished by one Andromeda Klein. *Hereafter to be known as the Defendant,* said Huggy.

"Pornographic materials," said Andromeda. "They've got to be kidding. They were snowboarding and motorcycle magazines. More or less."

"Community standards, Drama Llama," said Rosalie. "And don't let the DDR fool you. They're very into the whole 'right versus wrong' thing these days." Andromeda thought of the Thing with Two Heads and shuddered.

In any case, *pornographic materials* was what it apparently said on the complaint section of the petition for a restraining order that Mizmac had filed against Andromeda Klein. The sheriff's department was trying to locate her to serve her the restraining order papers. Meanwhile, the school's policy was to investigate every "sex offense" accusation in cooperation with local police. It was in the course of this incipient investigation that the Defendant's English teacher, one Mr. Daniel Barnes, submitted to authorities a notebook containing bizarre materials, the products of a disturbed mind, that had been turned in as assignments. They included Satanic symbols and several unsettling drawings of burning buildings and towers, calling to mind the horrible series of fires and explosions throughout the city, said by some to have been the result of methamphetamine laboratory mishaps but considered, in at least one case, to be the work of arsonists or even terrorists.

392

"Not to mention," Rosalie continued, with an enthusiasm almost akin to enjoyment, "some of your twisted poetry. Did you really write a poem about shooting teachers in the head and flushing their bodies down the toilet?"

"It's a children's song from when my dad was little! He taught it to me."

"I'm on your team, Andromeda, don't get me wrong. I'm sure there's a perfectly legitimable explanation. But they take threats against teachers very seriously around here. Well, the teachers do, for sure. Did your dad really put out a record with detailed instructions on how to build a bomb out of a lightbulb? Well, I hear they want to talk to him about that, too. You can tell me the truth, Andromeda. Did you set those fires? Or are you a meth dealer?"

Other witnesses, according to Rosalie's account, had described mass hysteria and bizarre rituals in the school cafeteria and even accusations of conspiracy to commit assault on the person of one Empress Katoa, who suffered a broken leg from a fall allegedly precipitated by a person or persons unknown.

"So basically, what you've got is a perfect storm of juvenile delinquency," concluded Rosalie. "You've got your fraud, your harassment, vice, arson, drugs, terrorism, conspiracy, assault, predatorism, contribution to the delinquency of a minor. Everybody's looking for you. You'll be famous."

Rosalie's phone rang and she held up a finger and went into the hallway to take the call. It was, to judge from Rosalie's side of the conversation, Rosalie's mother, who had finally arrived home and wanted to know where the Gimpala was. This was going to take a while.

The thing to do, of course, Andromeda decided, was turn herself in. That was the only option. It would soon become clear to any sane observer that she was an innocent, if eccentric, victim of circumstance and coincidence. *Come on*, said Huggy, bubbling through the sound of the refrigerator fan, *your father taught you better than that*. But the risk of reform school or community service seemed preferable to a life of hiding out in a van, to Andromeda Klein's mind.

Andromeda's eye lighted on Rosalie's half-open bag and noticed a newish, unfamiliar-looking cell phone. So, Rosalie's using the mom-phone system, thought Andromeda. Except of course she wasn't, because she was at that moment talking to her mother on her regular phone. Andromeda picked up the phone and pressed the side button to light up the display, but there was a lock on it; it was password protected.

You've got to be kidding, Andromeda was saying to herself as she lifted her sleeve to read the St. Steve password tantoon and enter it into the phone. The display cleared and the phone made a wind-chime sound. The last three messages: "take off your bra," "take off your bra," and "jj8kk!"

Motherfucker. She dropped the phone and it bounced once, then slid under the stove.

✳ ✳ ✳

"I don't know why I'm even bothering to ask," Andromeda said, after she had snatched Rosalie's phone out of her hand and pressed End Call. "But can you possibly explain this?"

She raised her right arm, pulled back her sleeve, ripped off the bandage, and pointed to the healing tantooned PIN. Rosalie stared at it for quite a while, her face moving in seeming slow motion through a series of expressions of puzzlement before her eyes widened and she said:

"Oh, okay. Yes, okay. Right, you're right. That was bad. That was a really bad one. Should not have done it. At *all*. My bad. I take full responsibility. Won't happen again, sir." And she saluted.

"Your *bad*?" Andromeda was at a loss.

"Okay. You're right. Worse than bad. Really really really not nice. Totally stupid. My fault. It was a joke that went . . . Wait a minute: why do you have my PIN number tattooed on your arm?"

Andromeda walked wordlessly back to the kitchen and reemerged with the sword in hand. At least Rosalie had the decency to look frightened, raising her hands in the air as though someone had said "Stick 'em up."

Andromeda was pushing her toward the door with her free hand. It was maybe kind of funny, maybe kind of. It would have been very funny if it had happened to someone else. Maybe they'd laugh about it later, twenty years on, when Andromeda finally got out of prison.

Rosalie was talking at lightning speed as the door was swinging closed: "It was only for my Social Studies altruism project and it wasn't like the first time–it was only meant to help you with your self-esteem and shyness issues then it got too interesting and fun and hey–"

Rosalie blocked the door with her shoulder. "Question: do I still have any money in my bank account?"

Andromeda slammed the door.

xxi.

The number programmed for UNAVAILABLE didn't match the number tantooned upside down on Andromeda's stomach. They (and she had to assume that "they" included Amy the Wicker Girl, at least, and maybe even the lovely Bethany) had clearly reprogrammed it when she was upstairs in the kitchen meeting the boy who was to become the Precious Sponge. Hence the giggling, the locked door.

But how had they even known about St. Steve and UNAVAILABLE? The only possible answer to that was:

Daisy. Daisy was the only person other than herself and St. Steve who had known about the UNAVAILABLE trick. They had to have learned about it from her.

Oh, Daisy. Had Byron been in on it too? Andromeda didn't think he possibly could have been. He'd have to be a phenomenal performer to act that dumb.

Just how many people *had* been laughing at her carefully composed encouraging texts, her desperate texts, her pathetic phone messages? It seemed like it had involved people other than Rosalie, as the PIN number texts almost certainly had resulted from accidental entry of the password on the part of someone who wasn't used to entering it, and Rosalie herself would presumably have been able to do this with no difficulty.

She tried to listen for Huggy in the refrigerator fan and the sighing freeway sound. She ran the water in the kitchen tap. No words of comfort or abuse bubbled out.

Calls to Bethany and Byron reached voice mail: of course, they would be in switched-off school mode by then.

Oh my gods, she thought all of a sudden. The photos.

✳ ✳ ✳

Andromeda had decided to turn herself in to the school rather than the library or the police. But as soon as she walked into the office of Mr. Venn, the counselor, she regretted it. Rosalie's summary of the charges against her were by and large accurate, and neither Mr. Venn, nor the assorted principals, nor even Baby Talk Barnes, was interested in hearing about the "Friends" of the Library and their scheme to destroy the International House of Bookcakes for personal gain. They certainly weren't interested in her own personal journey of spiritual discovery.

Here's what they were interested in:

" 'Joy to the world,' " said Mr. Venn, clearing his throat. " 'The teacher's dead. We cut off his head . . .' Did you write that?"

"No," said Andromeda.

"So you deny it?"

"No. I quoted it," she said, realizing as she did so that this could well add plagiarism, or citing without attribution, to the list of charges against her.

Mr. Venn said he'd come back to that, and fiddled with his computer's mouse. Up popped a dark, grainy, blown-up picture of Andromeda making a kissy face in candlelight.

"We take these matters very seriously, Andromeda."

"May I go to the bathroom?"

One of the few benefits of being seen as a mousy, shy, nonthreatening girl is that no one imagines you will try to make a run for it when you ask to go to the vacuum. Andromeda slipped out and dashed for her bike. She could ride very fast when she had a mind to.

That accursed Rosalie. Only the thought that the dissemination of that photo might have been unintentional and Andromeda's own good heart prevented her from uttering a formal, exceedingly harsh curse directed at Rosalie. There would be time enough for curses by and by.

Andromeda was halfway home when a call from the Precious Sponge vibrated in.

"Do you have your Agrippa with you? You've got to help me check something. This gematria can really wreck a person's mind. I was up all night but I think I found something, I mean I found a lot of things, I think–"

Andromeda brought her bike to a stop in front of the Safeway.

"Just tell me if you knew about the phone," she said.

"Oh, is this the Rosalie thing?"

Fuck. She hung up.

* * *

Byron was in his car waiting for her outside Casa Klein when she got there, and he did look like he had been up all night. It took a full half hour of back-and-forth between them before Andromeda satisfied herself that the Precious Sponge hadn't known about Rosalie's prank impersonation of St. Steve. By "the Rosalie thing" he had meant that Rosalie had called him earlier that morning to ask if he knew where Andromeda was because, Rosalie said, she had taken Rosalie's phone and had hidden it somewhere.

When Andromeda told him the story he said: "So all those texts from the mystery Waite man really came from Rosalie van G.? Wow, that's twisted."

"We should go inside," said Andromeda. "The cops are looking for me."

"What, because of the phone?" He was to remain confused for some time thereafter.

* * *

"I went a little gematria happy," said a slightly sheepish Precious Sponge. His legal pad had pages and pages full of scribbled numbers and calculations. "But check this out."

He flipped a few pages. "I tried it different ways—"

"Boy, I'll say," said Andromeda. Byron had listed and

calculated the values of hundreds of names and terms related to their recent activities and discussions in various forms and combinations, including *Two of Swords* (2320), *Houses of the Holy* (1090), *GAAP* (69), *International House of Bookcakes* (1125), and even *the Gimpala* (241) and *Rosalie M. van Genuchten* (1434).

"*Detroit Tigers?*" she said quizzically.

"My dad's favorite team," said the Precious Sponge. "Six-three-nine. But check it out," he continued. "*E. James Madison Jessup,* two thousand. *Twice Holy Daisy,* One-nine-nine-nine. Same number."

"That's not the same—"

"It is according to the Rule of Colel," said Byron. "You can add or subtract an *aleph,* a one." He gave her a "Come on, get with it" look.

Andromeda had momentarily forgotten all about the Rule of Colel.

He's good, said Huggy, rustling under the windblown curtains.

The crazed eyes of the Precious Sponge smiled at her triumphantly.

"Okay," said Andromeda, "so?" and his face fell.

"So," said the Precious Sponge, adopting Andromeda's own phrasing, "according to Agrippa and the Rule of Colel, both your friend Daisy and E.J.M. Jessup are forms of the number two thousand."

"Yeah, I got that," said Andromeda. "But what are we saying, then?"

"Well, just that maybe Twice Holy Soror *Daisy* was E.J.M. Jessup's future self, the one he had been preparing his library to inherit, only she died. And the message of the dream was not about her tarot deck but was instead: save the Eejymjays. Come on, you're the one who's supposed to believe in this stuff."

"That is pretty good," said Andromeda, with faint reluctance. Her mind wasn't really on Agrippa's system for Latin gematria at the moment. She was thinking about St. Steve and Rosalie and Bethany. And Daisy. So the final message from St. Steve had been that "hi there" after all. Rosalie had done it because, well, because she was Rosalie. As for the others . . . Andromeda sighed.

"Okay, so what about the Two of Swords, then?" she said wearily, because Byron had retrieved it from *Sexual Response in the Human Female* and seemed to want to say something about it.

The Precious Sponge said he still thought it was a date late in the decan, just before the transition to the Three of Swords. He consulted his notes again. "That would be right near the end of the first decan of Libra, September twenty-ninth or thirtieth of last year. With a gibbulous moon and a low tide, right? So what was going on at that time? What were you doing?"

Andromeda sighed heavily.

"Just the usual stuff," she said. Crying, being yelled at, reading Agrippa, stroking Dave's M, doing St. Steve sigils. Etc. "Okay," she said after a lengthy pause, humoring him. "I was at Lake Shasta with my crazy family. There were Lemurians. There was a burning truck on the roadside. St. Steve broke up with me."

"You mean, he said 'hi there.'"

Andromeda nodded and felt herself blushing. "Yes, he said 'hi there.' And Daisy was mad and not speaking to me."

"And why was she mad at you, exactly?"

Andromeda hesitated. "Because of St. Steve, because I wouldn't tell her about him. And because I went away to Shasta on a weekend when she wanted to do some magic. But it would have blown over if she hadn't died. She was always getting mad and she always got over it."

"I want to check something, if that's okay," said the Precious Sponge.

Andromeda was having trouble giving the Precious Sponge her full attention, which was occupied with replaying in her mind each fake St. Steve message she had received over the past week.

Byron rummaged in the Daisy bag and retrieved the smashed-up cell phone.

"I'm not sure it'll work, but–"

The Precious Sponge pried out the SIM card from Daisy's phone.

"Okay, this won't work with mine," he said, "let me see yours." Apparently Andromeda's phone wasn't the right sort to work with Daisy's phone chip either, because he added: "Got any other phones around here?"

Andromeda nodded and motioned for Byron to follow her downstairs to the kitchen. She used the sword to sweep under the stove and slide out Rosalie's St. Steve phone, along with a great deal of dust and a couple of Dave's fuzzy mouse toys.

Back in her room, when the Precious Sponge replaced the chip in Rosalie's handset with Daisy's chip and switched it on, there was a chime.

"We're in," he said, tapping his phone's scroll wheel. "No call data. Ten saved texts. Last message received on October fifth."

That would have been two days after Daisy died. Andromeda took the phone. Four of the messages were between Daisy and Rosalie van Genuchten, rather poignant in a way, because the two of them were discussing plans for an Afternoon Tea gathering that Daisy would not attend, because she would have died the day before, on October 3. A fifth message appeared to be from Mizmac and was also quite sad when you considered the context: "honey where are you?"

The remaining five were from Andromeda's phone, all identical and unanswered: "Daisy?" Three of them would have been from the time when Andromeda had been with her family at Lake Shasta, and Daisy had been giving her the silent treatment and refusing to answer. The remaining two had not been answered because Daisy would have been dead when they were sent.

Andromeda's eyes misted slightly. Oh, Daisy. She handed the phone back with a rueful smile.

"That was fun."

"Wow, there are pictures on here too," Byron said, resuming his scrolling. "These are weird. They're, like, bushes and rocks, parked cars, a trash can . . ."

Andromeda knew exactly what they were from the description without looking. Daisy had often used her cellphone camera to take photos of landmarks along the way in her rambling walks around Clearview and Hillmont, particularly when she was drunk, so she could follow the trail back if she ever got lost.

"Like visual digital bread crumbs," Andromeda said. "Hansel and Gretel style. I recognize that one." She pointed. "That's the Water Tower Temple. We used to do a lot of magic there."

"So maybe she did the magic you couldn't show up for anyway?" said Byron. "Date: September twenty-ninth. The kneeling Two of Swords, baby. See what I mean?"

"Yes," said Andromeda. She did.

"So," said the Precious Sponge. "Wanna go?"

"I'll get my sword," said Andromeda Klein.

It had never been easy to reach the Water Tower Temple, but the rain made it that much more difficult. It was drizzling when they left the car in the middle school parking lot and continued up the hill on foot, and it had started to rain harder by the time they climbed to the narrow ridge above the gulley that bordered the tower's north edge.

Andromeda couldn't resist pausing to show him the Temple.

"So that's where the magic happens," he said, sticking his head through the hole and pointing to the spray-painted glyph opposite. "Nice heptangle."

Yay, said Huggy's faint voice, somewhere amidst the whipping sound of the wind. *He can count to seven.* Andromeda rolled her eyes, as if to say: Is that all you got? He had really learned quite a lot in the past week, and Andromeda was realizing she was getting weary of pretending she didn't like having him around, just a little.

They held hands the rest of the way. Andromeda had

the sword in her free hand while Byron held the phone in front of them, like a lamp.

The trail of the subsequent photos was not difficult to follow, though it was quite a long hike. It led them past the water tower and farther up the hill and into the little woods beyond it and finally to a relatively clear space near the edge of the woods overlooking the golf course and the Larchmont development, largely shielded from the rain and wind by an outcropping of rock. Someone had used it as a place to dump old leftover construction materials, odd pieces of lumber, concrete blocks, heaps of gravel and debris. The pile of earth and rubbish in the final photo on Daisy's phone hadn't changed too much since the picture had been taken.

It didn't take much digging to find it, not too deeply buried in the debris. A small black box, grimy and dusty, but still easily recognizable as the little box Andromeda had given Daisy to house her tarot deck: the heptangle sigil on top was still visible, though much of the gold leaf had been rubbed off or obscured by grime. The surrounding rubbish and the overhanging rock had protected it from the damp: it was still dry despite the rain. The lid had been nailed shut, and several holes had been drilled in the sides and on the top and bottom.

What sounded like several objects rattled inside when Byron shook it.

"Sounds like some, er, negative magic to me," he said.

"Oh, Daisy," said Andromeda.

Back in the Precious Sponge's car, the windows fogged as the rain poured all around them, they stared at the box silently for several minutes.

"We could just not open it," said Andromeda.

"That would probably be best," said Byron, even as he reached for the screwdriver in the glove compartment and began to pry up the lid.

The Lovers, the missing card from Daisy's tarot deck, was in there, torn in half and attached to the bottom of the box by a nail that had been driven through it, as well as through a small bulbous object covered with an inexpertly sewn little purple velvet covering or hood, clearly made from what had once been the Eye of Horus bag.

Byron pulled off the hood. Underneath this hood was the missing head from Daisy's Barbie. The nail had been driven straight through the top, skewering the head and the two halves of the tarot card and pinning them to the bottom of the box.

"I think that's supposed to be you," said Byron with a kind of fascinated distaste. "Your head." The hair had been colored reddish brown with a marker, and Andromeda's trademark Egyptian eyes had been drawn on in ink.

The other objects in the box were a few animal bones and a desiccated green butterfly or moth.

"Are those really toad bones?" said Byron.

"I have no idea," said Andromeda, not really wanting to look.

"Well, she didn't follow the recipe very well, did she?" said the Precious Sponge, replacing the lid.

"She liked to make things up as she went along."

"Here's how I would choose to look at it," said the Precious Sponge after a lengthy silence. "Daisy's last act before dying was to attempt a final spell directed at you, meant to cure you of your bone disease."

She shook her head.

"Maybe on Right Ring Days," said Andromeda Klein.

One thing led to another. And then that thing led to one more. Andromeda's previous making-out experiences, in cars and out, had been, she had to admit, rather less interesting than this one. It was a floaty feeling, similar to magic. Then, just when it was getting good, there was a sharp, biting pain in her arm where the Precious Sponge had been holding her down by the wrist.

"I think you just broke my arm," she said.

Byron recoiled, aghast, unable to say anything, apparently, beyond "Oh my god."

"No, it's okay," said Andromeda. "This happens. Welcome to the wonderful world of *osteogenesis imperfecta*. You can go ahead and finish up. But then you need to take me to the hospital."

But Byron was already fumbling for his keys. His vocabulary had expanded to include "Oh my god I'm so sorry."

It hurt like a motherfucker, but she also felt pretty badass, with such an extreme make-out injury.

The Precious Sponge picked up on it.

"You're like Clint Eastwood or somebody," he said, driving.

It wasn't a break but rather merely a sprain. The emergency-room doctor put it in a brace and gave her a prescription for pain medicine. But now that she realized it wasn't broken, it didn't hurt nearly as much and didn't feel nearly as cool.

The doctor was Dr. Hu, a fact that would really make this a good anecdote to tell one day.

"Barbados patootie Polaroid pennies," said Dr. Hu.

"What?" said Andromeda, pulling hood and hair back and turning her better ear toward the doctor.

"Heavy jawbone with your earring?"

"What? Oh, trouble with my hearing. Sorry, yes." She explained about her brittle bones and the disorganized collagen in her ears.

Dr. Hu gave her an unreadable, brow-furrowed look.

"Have you ever been told by a doctor you had *osteogenesis imperfecta*?" he said, slowly and loudly, peering into Andromeda's left ear with a lighted instrument.

"Yes," she said. "I mean, they told my mom."

"I see," said Dr. Hu, switching to the other ear. "And how long has it been since you were examined by a medical doctor?"

That was a tough one. Not since she was very small, not since the Gnome School.

"Well, you've got quite a bit of crud in there. I think we can take care of some of that hearing problem right now."

A suddenly action-populated Andromeda struggled for words, at a loss.

"Wait," she finally said. "Are you saying I don't have OI? What are you saying? That I just have plugged-up ears?"

"No, you may well have it," said Dr. Hu, "but at least some of your hearing trouble seems to be caused by massive obstructions in your ears that I'm going to remove in a moment."

Dr. Hu left the room and returned with a plastic tub and a huge syringe.

"I'm going to take a wild guess: you've never had your ears cleaned before."

It was incredibly uncomfortable and gross. Dr. Hu said the wax and other matter had formed a kind of shellac or varnish on her eardrums over the years and would be very difficult to remove. He used a chemical to dissolve it, and a metal instrument to scrape at it, and the syringe to shoot warm water into her ears to wash it out. It was amazing how much gunk there can be in one tiny ear. And it was amazing how your head feels when the obstruction is finally removed.

Most amazing of all, though, was what the world is like with superpower hearing. A deafening ripping, clattering sound behind her turned out to be the sound of the doctor's sleeve rubbing against the side of her coat. The shimmery clappy echo was the sound of her own shoes on the linoleum.

"You'll be hyperaware of sounds for a little while here, but your ears will adjust very shortly," said Dr. Hu. "And you should see a regular doctor about your other issues. It may be time for a re-diagnosis."

On her way back out to the hospital lobby, Andromeda allowed herself to indulge in an absurd thought: that Byron had been right about Daisy's last ritual after all. That it had been an attempt to cure Andromeda of her bone disease and that retrieving the box had finally set the spell in motion, resulting in a sudden, miraculous reorganization of her collagen. But that, of course, is not the way magic works. At least, that's not the way it ever worked when it came to Andromeda Klein. She had, she supposed, merely been mistaken about the cause of her hearing trouble, that's all.

The Left Ring answer was, as usual, more in keeping with Andromeda's temperament. In that view, Daisy's spell had been intended to break up the relationship, such as it had been, between Andromeda and St. Steve; and it had, indeed, resulted in a "hi there."

Either way, the negative magic of Daisy's ill-conceived Toad Bone Ritual had quite possibly backfired on Daisy in the end. Whether the truth was Saturnine or Jovial, at least Andromeda had gotten a Precious Sponge and improved hearing out of the deal.

Bethany Stone was sitting with Byron when Andromeda emerged.

"You only left like thirty messages," she said in response to Andromeda's look. "So what happened to you?"

Andromeda raised her braced arm in a mock-triumphal gesture.

"Run-of-the-mill sex injury," she said. Byron's wince at that was rather cute.

It was clear from the look in Bethany's lovely Katherine Mansfield eyes that she couldn't really have been in cahoots with Rosalie van Genuchten. Could she have? Evidently she and Byron had been talking about it, because she fixed Andromeda with a direct stare and said:

"How about that Rosalie?" Then, after a pause: "I knew about the phone. I mean, I was there when they fiddled with it. But I didn't know they were going to, you know, 'punk' you with it. It was just supposed to be part of that school thing. The 'altruism project.'"

According to Bethany, Rosalie's plan had been, as she had explained it, to help build Andromeda's confidence and self-esteem by having her do tarot readings and then making them "come true." Well, that explained Rosalie's sudden interest in tarot and her simpleminded, overliteral interpretations of the results, if nothing else.

"Remember how she recorded you in the car about self-esteem and videoed you in the cafeteria?" said Bethany. "That was going to be the centerpiece of her project, playing them for her presentation. I actually don't know how reprogramming your phone was supposed to fit into it, now that I think of it. It seemed like it made sense at the time. Sort of. You know that girl. She steamrolls you."

That was for sure.

"Well, her 'project' isn't looking too good," said Andromeda. "I'm Clearview's Most Wanted at the moment."

"Definite Fail," said Bethany.

Byron had been tapping away at his phone. "I've got some bad news for you," he said, holding it up.

It took Andromeda a moment to realize that he was showing her an online auction site, and that the IHOB's *Magick Without Tears* was up, though it had, as of yet, no bids.

"They sure didn't waste any time," said Andromeda bitterly.

"But check it out," said Byron. He grabbed hold of her wrist and raised her arm so he could see the PIN number tantoon, and then one-thumb-entered it into his phone. "Ah," he said. "I had a feeling. See, Rosalie's using that as the password for her PayPal account, so . . ." He pressed a few more buttons and said: "There. Rosalie just bid five hundred dollars for *Magick Without Tears*. I can even change the address to yours so if she doesn't notice it and the charge goes through, they'll deliver it to you."

"What if she does notice, though?"

Byron said that then she'd probably close the account and the auction would be derailed and the "Friends" of the Library would have to re-list it. "And that's probably what will happen," he added. "But it would at least slow them down. Buy us time. And then: bake sale!"

Andromeda paused to reflect: this was clever, but it would add yet another charge against her, probably. She wasn't sure exactly how much trouble she was in, in reality. People did all sorts of way worse stuff and managed to get away with it. She supposed she'd find out soon enough. What's the worst that could happen? she wondered, and then waited, as this was a classic opening for a barbed Huggy comment. But there were no insults to be discerned in the buzz of the fluorescent lights or the crisp sound of the rain hitting the lobby's window and skylight.

"Let's get out of here," said Byron, as though reading her mind. "Before this place is crawling with coppers."

The bin marked BIOHAZARD DISPOSAL on the way out seemed like the perfect place for Daisy's Toad Bone tarot box.

Andromeda hesitated, though.

"We could, you know, 'go down to the river,' with this," she said.

"Oh, you've got some horses you need to tame?" said Byron.

"Maybe it would work on Rosalie," said Andromeda.

Bethany was looking thoroughly confused. The box sounded like a small metallic bomb when it hit the sides of the chute going down.

"Hey," said Bethany. "I was thinking of taking Hebrew at Hillel this summer. Would you like to maybe do it with me?"

Would I like to maybe do it with you, thought Andromeda. She supposed her smile was answer enough.

The sound it made when Byron kissed her on the top of the head sounded like it could have shaken the building. The jangling keys on Byron's belt were shimmery like tiny bells. But she was already getting used to it, just as Dr. Hu said she would.

There were so many buzzing, humming staticky sounds in the hospital and in the parking lot. Andromeda listened carefully to each of them, straining to discern a voice beneath the surface. At times she felt she could almost make something out. She wondered, truly wondered, if she'd ever hear from Huggy again.

But no matter.

At least she had Katherine Mansfield and the Precious Sponge. She'd always probably have that.

LEXICON

action-populated: agitated, distressed, bubbling over with concerns.

Agrippa, Henry Cornelius (1486–1535): a sixteenth-century soldier-magician-physician-scholar whose *Three Books of Occult Philosophy* aspired to encompass the whole of Western occult science.

Aiwass, Aiwaz: a Secret Chief and minister of Hoor-paar-kraat (Harpocrates) who dictated *The Book of the Law* to Aleister Crowley over three days in Cairo in 1904 e.v.

ars nova: "a new art"–weedgie polyphonic music from the fourteenth century.

ars subtilior: "a subtler art"–even weedgier and more complex polyphonic music from the end of the fourteenth century.

the Asclepius: a Hermetic text concerned with the ancient technique of drawing down spirits to animate stone idols.

bacon: pagan.

bagel worm agony: naked girl magazine.

the Beast 666: an allegorical figure in the Book of Revelation, and Aleister Crowley's self-proclaimed office.

belladonna: deadly nightshade.

Blake, William (1757–1827): an artist, poet, mystic, and magician of the late eighteenth and early nineteenth century.

blind: a deliberate inaccuracy in an esoteric text, meant to hide the true meaning from all but the initiated.

Bonewits, P.E.I. (1959–   ): He received a Bachelor of Arts degree in magic from the University of California, Berkeley, in 1970 e.v.

Bruno, Giordano (1548–1600): an Italian Hermetic magician burnt at the stake in 1600 e.v. Also known as the Nolan.

camel: candle; also, the letter *gimel,* Key III, the High Priestess or Popess.

Christmas tree: two jiggers gin, ⅔ pony vermouth, plus one olive.

Coronzon, Choronzon: the Dweller in the Abyss known as 333, denizen of the Tenth Aethyr referred to as ZAX, associated by Dr. John Dee with the serpent in the Garden of Eden.

coyote: a chaote, a proponent of Chaos Magick.

Crowley, Aleister (1875–1947): magician, mountaineer, novelist, poet, mystic, astrologer, artist, libertine, spy.

Cthulhu: ph'nglui mglw'nafh C'thulhu R'lyeh wgah'nagl fhtagn.

the Cry of the Watcher Within: a banishing formula adapted from the Eleusinian Mysteries of ancient Greece for use in Golden Dawn rituals.

de Machaut, Guillaume (c. 1300–1377): a French poet and composer in the fourteenth-century *ars nova* style.

Dee, Dr. John (1527–1608): an Elizabethan mathematician who talked to angels.

dime soda: kindasorta.

Dion Fortune (1890–1946): Also known as Violet Mary Firth. Her magic thwarted the Germans in the Battle of Britain during World War II.

dragon's teeth: Syrian rue, also known as moly or harmal.

ectomorph: a person with a slender body.

eucalyptus: a tree imported to California by Australians during the Gold Rush.

Euclid (c. 300 B.C.): an ancient magician and a holy man from the time before magic and mathematics were thought of as different things.

e.v.: *era vulgaris;* i.e., the common era.

gematria: the method that reveals the numbers symbolized by words.

glyph: a sign or symbol.

godbotherers: non-silent un-atheists.

Goetia: *Ars Goetia,* the "Howling Art." Solomon the Great bound and imprisoned in a brass vessel the seventy-two demons he had employed to help build the Temple and then threw this vessel into a lake. The Babylonians, imagining it to contain treasure, retrieved the vessel and unsealed it, releasing the seventy-two Goetic demons and their legions.

griefer: a computer-game vandal or online mischief-maker.

grimoire: a grammar of magic.

the Hand of Glory: a special candelabrum made from the pickled and dried severed hand of a murderer; said to open locked doors and paralyze all those who look upon it.

Harris, Lady Frieda (1877–1962): the artist who collaborated with Aleister Crowley on his Thoth tarot deck.

headacid: a headache.

the Hermetic Order of the Golden Dawn: a short-lived but extremely influential magical society whose membership included Aleister Crowley, A. E. Waite, Pamela Colman Smith, E. Nesbit, Charles Williams, Algernon Blackwood, Florence Farr, Arthur Machen, Allan Bennett, Bram Stoker, and William Butler Yeats.

Holy Guardian Angel: an otherworldly entity charged with guiding the magician to his or her true will.

hypercormorant: high-performance.

IHOB: the International House of Bookcakes. Also known as the Clearview Park Public Library.

Jessup, Ernest James Madison (1879–1977): Twentieth-century American occultist, folklorist, criminologist.

Jovial: of or like Jove/Jupiter, that is, warm, cheery, optimistic, sanguine, red.

Kelley, Edward (1555–1597): Also known as Edward Talbot. Dr. Dee's medium.

kibble wing: chemo wig.

lantern: Latin.

large bundle of Arthur eggs: undisclosed.

LBRP: Lesser Banishing Ritual of the Pentagram, a banishing ritual used by the Golden Dawn and its descendants.

Led Zeppelin: a rock band from the 1970s e.v.

the Lemegeton: the *Clavicula Salomonis* or *Lesser Key of Solomon,* a seventeenth-century Goetic grimoire.

Liber AL: The Book of the Law: the founding document of Thelema, the text of which forbids its study and recommends destroying it after the first reading.

Lovecraft, H. P. (1890–1937): a holy dreamer of unholy dreams.

magic: practical *ouijanesse.*

magick: an archaic form of the word *magic* adopted by Aleister Crowley to distinguish his magical system from mere prestidigitation; the addition of *K,* the eleventh letter, also has an esoteric significance in Crowley's system.

mandals: man sandals.

Marx, Groucho (1891–1977): an American actor with a mustache and a cigar.

Mathers, Samuel Liddle MacGregor (1854–1918): a founder of the Hermetic Order of the Golden Dawn and translator of *The Book of the Sacred Magic of Abramelin the Mage.*

me: of.

mother-o-saurus: Mother of Sorrows.

muscle car: an automobile with a high-performance engine, usually from the 1970s e.v.

the Necronomicon: Knowledge of this rarest of ancient magical books came to H. P. Lovecraft in a dream. Also known as *Al Azif,* which denotes a howling Goetic sound.

occult: hidden.

occultist: a spiritual scientist or technician.

of: me.

ouijanesse: the state of being weedgie.

pants on fire: pacifier.

predictionary: a list of predictive text-message typos.

prestidigitation: nimble-fingered stage conjuring.

PSDTN: p.s. destroy this note.

Regardie, Dr. Israel (1907–1985): a chiropractor who was Aleister Crowley's onetime secretary, editor, and chronicler of the Golden Dawn.

Rule P: *see* PSDTN.

Saturnine: of or like Saturn, that is, dark, moody, melancholy, introspective, slow, deep, or with a surfeit of black bile.

Sefer Yetzirah: the Book of Creation, an ancient book explaining how the Universe was created by means of numbers and letters.

Shemhamphorash, Shem Ha-Mephorash: Three consecutive verses of the Book of Exodus in the Hebrew Bible have exactly seventy-two letters, which when written out one on top of the other yield seventy-two columns of three letters each. These are the seventy-two names of God.

Adding the proper suffix (*-ih* for mercy, *-al* for judgment) to each yields the name of an angel.

Shub-Niggurath: the Black Goat of the Woods with a Thousand Young.

sigil, sigillum: a seal or seal-like symbol.

the Simonomicon: not the Necronomicon, but an incredible simulation.

skidding: just kidding.

slam sex: slant six (a type of car engine).

Smith, Pamela "Pixie" Colman (1878–1951): the artist who painted the images on the Rider-Waite tarot deck. In later life she ran a retreat for priests at her home in Cornwall, adjacent to a chapel known as Our Lady of the Lizard.

soupy soupy chang chang: Lapsang souchong, a kind of tea with a smoky flavor.

spinach U-turn: Finnish Lutheran.

stained flowers: strange powers.

Star Ruby: an elaborate variation on the Lesser Banishing Ritual of the Pentagram.

steak antlers: snake handlers; i.e., religious people (cf god-botherers).

Sylvester Mouse: some extra hours.

synch: a meaningful coincidence; i.e., a pointer to a window looking out upon eternity.

tarot: the unbound leaves of the Book of Thoth, comprising a symbolic map of the Universe.

Tau robe: a ceremonial robe shaped like the Greek letter *tau,* T.

Teenage Head: a Canadian rock group from the 1970s e.v.

thelema: a Greek word meaning "will"; also the philosophical, magical, and spiritual system revealed to Aleister Crowley by Aiwass in 1904 e.v.

Thoth Hermes Trismegistus: The Egyptian god Thoth was known to the Greeks as Hermes and was venerated as Trismegistus—"three times great"—at his Temple at Hermopolis. A disputed tradition traces the historical origins of tarot symbolism to the beliefs and practices of this temple.

Tiphareth, Beauty: the sixth Sephira on the Tree of Life.

toy away: thinking of you and wild about you.

Uncle Al: an affectionate term for the Beast 666.

unicursal hexagram: Unlike a traditional hexagram, this can be drawn with a pen, finger, or sword in one continuous line rather than as two triangles.

vacuum: bathroom (also mushroom, ashram).

van Rensselaer, Mrs. John King (1848–1925): a lady of New York high society who wrote two books on the history of playing cards and the tarot in the late nineteenth and early twentieth centuries and who later engaged in devastating magical warfare against the Freemasons who controlled the New-York Historical Society.

Waite, A. E. (1857–1942): a mystic and scholar of esoterica, and designer of the Rider-Waite tarot deck illustrated by Pamela Colman Smith.

The Warburg Institute: Aby Warburg's library of sixty thousand volumes was transported from Hamburg, Germany, to London in 1933 and joined with the library of the University of London in 1944.

weedgie: spooky, creepy, magic, spiritual.

Yates, Dame Frances (1899–1981): a twentieth-century scholar of Renaissance culture and Hermetic magic.

Thanks to:

Krista Marino, Steven Malk, Beverly Horowitz, Tamar Schwartz, Colleen Fellingham, Tim Terhune, Angela Carlino, and Tristin Aaron.

PAIGE O'DONOGHUE

FRANK PORTMAN (aka Dr. Frank) is the singer/songwriter/guitarist of the influential East Bay punk band the Mr. T. Experience (MTX). MTX has released about a dozen albums since forming in the mid-eighties. *Andromeda Klein* is Frank Portman's second novel. His first novel, *King Dork*, was an ALA-ALSC Best Book for Young Adults and a finalist for the Quills Award. You can visit him at www.frankportman.com.